Coldharbour:

A Gothic Tale of Love and Death

Laura Clarke Walker

Text copyright © Laura Clarke Walker 2026
Design copyright © Alex Mansfield 2026
All rights reserved.

Laura Clarke Walker has asserted her right under the Copyright, Designs and Patents Act 1988 to be identified as the author of this work.

No part of this book may be reprinted or reproduced or utilised in any form or by electronic, mechanical or any other means, now known or hereafter invented, including photocopying or recording, or in any information storage or retrieval system, without the permission in writing from the Publisher and Author.

This is a work of fiction. Names, characters, businesses, places, events and incidents are either the products of the author's imagination or used in a fictitious manner. Any resemblance to actual persons, living or dead, or actual events is purely coincidental.

This title is intended for the enjoyment of adults, and is not recommended for children due to the mature content it contains.

First published 2026
by Rowanvale Books Ltd
The Gate
Keppoch Street
Roath
Cardiff
CF24 3JW
www.rowanvalebooks.com

A CIP catalogue record for this book is available from the British Library.
ISBN: 978-1-83584-108-2
eBook ISBN: 978-1-83584-109-9

Printed and bound in Great Britain by Bell and Bain Ltd, Glasgow

For Alan

Friday 1 October 1999

1
Stronger Than Real Life

Before Alex knew it, she was staring at the sea.

That chill, churning sea, cloudier than the sky, blacker than the crows pecking at the scraps of crisp packet caught up in the rocks. She had always known those waves, she could name them, not aloud but in her soul, as sure and as certain as the water that clawed its way in to shore and slunk back out like an alley cat on the prowl. She had let that sea embrace her up to her knees as a toddler, her ankles as a teenager, and the very tips of her fingers as a woman.

But there ...

Where slivers of bright, salt-licked foil were trapped in the pebbles ...

There was a glow.

The iridescent glow of Power.

But that wasn't Alex's Power, it was the wrong colour, but Power belonged in blood, which meant ...

No.

Alex dug her broken nails into the beach wall.

No. No, this was how it started before. Seeing things.

With a gulp of stringent sea air that scraped at her throat as much as it scratched her skin, Alex shoved herself away from the beach wall and towards the café, where just one word from the waitress stopped Alex mid-drag of her suitcase through the café door, the bell still tinkling behind her.

Hello," the waitress repeated, standing there patiently. "Good afternoon."

Alex's brain and mouth worked together just enough to manage an "alright", which earned a nod and a half-smile from the waitress that made her stomach lurch. She'd been stuck in the "facility" too long if the slightest bit of attention was all it took.

With a heave of her suitcase towards the nearest table, Alex slid onto the closest seat and fumbled for a menu.

She had told them she was ready to go home.

Just one of the lies she had told them that morning.

She had half-believed it, just like she half-believed what they'd had her chanting like a mantra:

Seeing is not believing if you're seeing things that aren't there.

But there Alex was, a country crossed, having convinced enough people that her grip on reality wasn't as slippery as it had been. Gone were the pot plants and the perfectly neutral bedrooms with no hint of anyone ever having stayed there. Here was the café with its nicotine-stained net curtains, and peeling wax tablecloths getting picked into shards by her broken fingernails. At least this was the same. The café. Same curtains, same tablecloths, same cloying smell of grease ...

Different waitress though.

Alex didn't need to give that many surreptitious glances over her menu to be sure that she would've remembered her. She didn't think she'd ever seen hair that unapologetically ginger outside of the Spice Girls for a start and it didn't look dyed, at least not from where Alex was sitting. Then, which other people probably noticed first, there were the scars that skewed the waitress' mouth into a crooked not-quite smile that revealed canines that were as sharp as they were chipped and slightly yellowed, just like all the mugs stacked precariously on the counter. Alex wondered if she stared at the waitress forever if she would always find something new to fixate on.

The face split into a dark grin and said:

"I promise I didn't get them in the kitchen."

"Sorry," Alex said with a dry swallow, "I wasn't ... I didn't mean ..."

There was a gleam in the waitress' eyes, as if they were sharing a joke that Alex should've been in on, yet she was sure she wasn't. Almost sure. She was finding it hard to be sure of anything anymore.

"I was just daydreaming," Alex continued, trying to look out of the window, but then she remembered about the crisp packet and the rocks and what *couldn't* have been Power. "I ..."

"Holiday?" the waitress asked, nodding at the suitcase propped up against the table.

Alex snorted before she could stop herself.

"No one comes here on holiday."

"Back from, then?" the waitress asked.

"This ain't a tan," Alex replied, "I was born this way."

She smiled despite herself when the waitress let out an awkwardly sincere laugh, pad and pencil loose in her long fingers as the last customers shuffled out. Her nails were painted the kind of fire-engine red that would've shown up any chips, any scratches. There weren't any. A waitress in a café with perfect nails ...

Dodgy teeth and perfect nails ...

Teeth couldn't always be helped though. Alex and Matthew had both had braces for eighteen months, only to get back into the orthodontist's chair, get the metal stripped off, and have their Power kick in instantly, pushing their teeth back into their apparently rightful places, premolars crowding their canines, incisors overlapping and jutting out.

But dodgy teeth didn't mean that the waitress had Power. Ken Dodd and Shane MacGowan probably didn't have Power. Power was rare, Power was ...

Power was on the beach.

"Are you wanting anything?" the waitress asked. "I'm closing up—"

Alex muttered an apology and turned over the menu, the plastic singed and wrinkled.

"No," the waitress said, her smile too curious to be completely kind, "I mean, I'm closing up and everyone else has gone so I could keep you company? If you're planning on daydreaming a wee while longer?"

"I'm probably not the best company at the moment," Alex said, sort of believing herself.

What to believe anymore, what to believe ...

"You don't have to talk about it if you don't want to."

Alex scoffed and glanced at the menu she must've looked at a million times before, as a kid at least. When was the last time she'd actually been in there? How did she even end up there? It wasn't like the promenade was even on the way to the house from the train station. Would she have ...?

No.

She'd just been lost in her own thoughts.

But then the sea was home in a way the rest of Coldharbour just wasn't.

The sea would've been peace.

Not that Alex particularly knew what peace could've been, what peace actually looked like, or if she'd have even recognised peace if it was creeping up behind her in that moment, ready to sink its not-quite-so-peaceful-after-all teeth in her behind.

It was a dreary drizzle of an afternoon, anyway. Completely nondescript, completely without event, completely not the way she liked it.

Just Alexandra Wilde sitting in a greasy spoon on the promenade of a hometown that didn't particularly feel like home, wondering where it had all gone wrong, without the energy to even pretend she didn't know the answer anymore.

You don't have to talk about it if you don't want to.

Made a change.

"How d'you take your tea?" the waitress asked.

"Builder's," Alex said, "if that's alright."

"Of course," the waitress replied, returning to the counter, "I'm here for a reason."

Alex nodded and hid her flushing neck behind her hand as she stared down at the heat-bobbled plastic menu, the edges puckered and peeling away. Perfectly painted nails in a job like that, constantly scrubbing dishes ...

"I'm still having trouble getting everything working," the waitress explained, moving around the counter with the kind of purpose a drunk had when they were trying to convince that they were anything but, "so the best I can do you is a defrosted doughnut or a slightly sad sandwich. If you're hungry, that is."

"Oh, I'm not," Alex said, forcing herself to make eye contact without feeling the need to scramble away from the waitress' gaze, "But thanks."

"Do you mind if I have something?" the waitress asked, pouring out the tea into once-white cups, their veins spindly and brown like the trees that bordered the towns.

Alex tried to shake her head with as much nonchalance as she could muster, which had never been much at the best of times, but now ...

She felt like she was in a job interview. Or about to propose.

Or about to propose to her job interviewer, because she had such a stellar record as both an employee and a fiancée that definitely didn't involve skipped deadlines or running from altars in huge meringues—

"Your caff."

Those were the words Alex's mouth settled on while her mind ran away from her.

"Apparently so," the waitress said, holding a triangle of what was probably a cheese sandwich aloft, like she was handling a dead mouse by its tail.

"I've never seen you here before," Alex said, unable to help herself because of those nails, those bloody perfect nails. "What's your accent? Glasgow?"

The waitress was from Glasgow. Alex just knew it, in the way that Power meant Alex just knew things whether she liked it or not, but the part of her mind that hadn't run away from her was telling her that she was hearing too many distorted vowels, too much of a twang, enough not-quite-right grammar, all those witness marks of a traveller that hadn't been home for a long, long time.

"More or less," the waitress replied, but while her voice seemed as light as ever, her cheek did twitch and her eyes did narrow. "I've never seen you here either."

Alex wasn't quite sure what she saw in that fire-forged face, but it did warn her that the waitress didn't quite mean what Alex had intended.

"That's different," Alex said, giving in to the urge to scrutinise her properly like she really was halfway through an interview veering off the rails, or worse, standing at that altar again, working out where it had all gone so horribly wrong. "I live here."

"I live here too," the waitress said, sliding onto the seat opposite Alex with two cups and a saucer of sandwiches, all limp bread and sweaty cheese. "Sure I can't tempt you?"

Alex winced and shook her head again. It was too late for nonchalance.

"No, I mean, I *live* here," Alex explained, "I've lived in this town my entire life. You don't seem the type to be waitressing. *Here.* In Coldharbour."

Coldharbour was a strange place, really: the name referred to the seaside town, the Victorian part where Alex was being all insistent at that moment, but also the area in general, which included Crossgate, with its Roman ruins under Christianised cobbles, and Northmere, a tiny mediaeval village that was more marshland than civilisation and had more than one story about the Devil himself visiting in the middle of the night and strolling away with a sackful of lost souls. But either way, it wasn't exactly a prime destination for anything anymore; all that New Labour money was passing it by, that much Alex could see.

Coldharbour wasn't getting a Millennium Dome any time soon.

"I'm not waitressing," the – well, the waitress replied.

Alex gazed around the café. When her very pointed stare didn't work, she waved her hand around instead.

"I own it," the waitress – fine, *café owner* – said, flourishing her own hand in an oddly playful imitation of Alex's. "All mine."

"Why would you buy *this*?" Alex laughed, trying not to gawp at such an obviously put-together person with perfectly painted nails, who held herself like ...

Well, like she did actually own the place.

Even if she couldn't make anything in the place work.

The waitress was apparently taking Alex's question as rhetorical, seeing as she just tapped a sandwich against the saucer, the thud suggesting that the bread was a bit beyond fresh in the same way that Princess Margaret was a bit beyond ingénue.

Alex dumped a crusty sugar lump in her tea and gave it a sloppy stir, but it was hard to pay it any attention when the sky was just beginning to darken, drawing her back towards the promenade, towards that Power that couldn't have been there, and to the sea.

That chill, churning sea.

"You've been missing all the fun."

Those waves ...

They had welcomed her so well ...

Alex.

"You've been missing all the fun," the waitress said. "Three bodies in the last month have been found on that beach. Bets are out on how they died."

The waitress raised her teacup to her lips and paused to ask:

"What do you think?"

"It doesn't matter what I think," Alex said, which was as much as she could manage when her chest was tightening and her stomach was stiffening until she felt like her tea had been spiked with cement. "I – I haven't been here."

It was just anxiety making her clench, wasn't it? Not the way the waitress was looking at her, surely? Because

Alex knew she looked an absolute state after the month she'd had (more like the summer she'd had), so there was absolutely no way someone with such obvious elegance, with that crooked smile that *radiated*, would look twice at Alex. Not anymore.

The waitress raised a finger in anticipation and returned to the counter, where she leant over and pulled out a newspaper.

Which of course, Alex groaned to herself, as she made her nausea wash over her disappointment, had to be *that* paper.

Alex gave the stark letters of *The Coldharbour Chronicle* as much of a derisive glance as she had the energy for, before taking in the headline (the usual alliterative rubbish) and the photo that a national wouldn't have printed for fear of being sued by grieving relatives or being eviscerated in Parliament by an old duffer banging on about family values, providing that the family consisted of one man and one woman willing to settle for each other and their equally miserable children forever.

"I really wouldn't put much stock in that," Alex said. "Half the staff are old soaks."

"And the other half?" the waitress asked, utterly unperturbed by what Alex had been hoping was just enough hostility in her voice to make the paper vanish.

Next time, she'd have to use her Power, clearly.

"They're alright, I suppose," Alex muttered, reading the headline again.

Murder Mystery or Sea Suicides? Body No 3 Unnervingly Unidentified.

Looking at the picture, it was easy to see why it was unidentified. And unnerving. Matthew had once told Alex in one of his particularly morbid moments that it was called *grave wax*: that shiny, bloated look that made a corpse look like the skin was so stretched and swollen that taking a scalpel to it would've been like popping a balloon with a pin. Bit more gore than the average children's party, though. Not suitable between rounds of pass the parcel and ice cream and jelly, not even in their house.

"That must've been in the sea for weeks," Alex said, "right?"

"I'd say at least a fortnight," the waitress agreed. "The sea's cold enough at this time of year."

"And the other bodies?" Alex asked, "The same condition or ...?"

"They've identified the first," the waitress said, peering over the paper, close enough for her cool breath to prickle Alex's dry lips. "Fifth paragraph, I think."

Then their eyes met.

Just long enough.

Just until Alex knew that the waitress could see her.

Really see her, like hardly anyone ever—

Alex blinked first and sat back, scanning down the front page with twitching fingers until she found:

The first body, discovered by a dog walker on Sunday 5th September, has now been confirmed as being that of Heather Abbott, a first-year nursing student at Crossgate University who had recently moved to the area. Miss Abbott had last been seen on Friday night by her housemates but had been presumed to have made new friends during the Freshers' Bar Crawl. Acting Detective Chief Inspector Samuel Meyer—

Acting Detective Chief Inspector? Someone had been busy while she was away. Shaz hadn't mentioned that.

Acting Detective Chief Inspector Samuel Meyer insisted that all lines of enquiry were still open, including the possibility that Miss Abbott, 18, became inebriated and had an unfortunate accident on the beach, an idea that her family strongly refutes. Her mother told The Chronicle exclusively that: "Heather didn't drink, did not have 'accidents', and was an exceptionally strong swimmer." In fact, Miss Abbott was not only the Under-16s County Swimming Champion, she was the lone survivor of the infamous pleasure boat tragedy that occurred off Lowestoft in 1994—

Alex looked up at the waitress, who was screwing her nose up at her own sandwich.

"She didn't have an accident," Alex realised.

"I don't think any of them had an accident," the waitress said, slapping the sandwich back on its saucer. "For one, accidents don't happen like clockwork, do they?"

Alex snorted.

"You'd be surprised, round here."

"So what do you think?" the waitress asked.

Alex strained her neck towards the promenade, trying to get the right angle through the blinds. Had she really seen Power? All wrapped up around that crisp packet?

"Whereabouts on the beach?" Alex asked.

"The bodies?"

"Yeah," Alex said, sliding back onto the seat with a squeak. "Sorry, I dunno why I'm asking like you'd—"

"Aye," the waitress said, tapping Alex on the arm as she leapt into action, "c'mon."

"C'mon where?"

"Where—"

The waitress rolled her eyes and grabbed both the paper and Alex's suitcase.

"I'm showing you where."

"And I think I can carry my own suitcase, thanks," Alex said, snatching it back with the kind of force that had probably bruised her hand, but it was rather hard to care in the face of the waitress' dark smirk and the rush of blood through Alex's soul.

"Crown Jewels in there?" the waitress asked.

"Something like that," Alex muttered, deflating at the waitress' frown.

"Something like that" being a load of old clothes that other people had picked out for her, and a single picture. Just one. Just Maddie. Knowing Alex's daughter, she'd probably forced it into Shaz's hands and insisted that it travelled that lonely journey with her mother.

And now it was back, never having even left its home between an old T-shirt that Alex hadn't worn since the Eighties and a jumper that was probably Maddie's.

"Don't you need to lock up or something?" Alex sighed.

"Nothing to steal," the waitress said, rushing down the promenade. "And you've got your crown jewels, so ..."

"Only cos you were kidnapping them," Alex replied, remembering just in time to check the road both ways as she followed the waitress to the beach wall. "So, how comes you know where they all washed up?"

The waitress spun around, walked backwards down the shingle, and pointed up at the café—

No. Above, at the bay window jutting over the canopy.

"Cos that's my flat," she shouted above the roaring waves, "and it's hard not to notice all the flashing lights and sirens when I'm trying to kick back with a book and a brandy."

Alex hauled herself over the wall and let the suitcase clank against a moss-encrusted groyne. The wind bit at the raw flesh around her fingernails as she pointed at the sand that was more mud than gold.

"So right here?" she asked. "Really?"

"Really," the waitress said, tracing her boot through it. "All of them. All washed up right here."

"The chances of that are ..." Alex threw up her hands and shook her head. "And why are you so interested?" she asked. "No offence, but you run a caff."

"Why are *you* interested?" the waitress asked. "No *offence.*"

The waitress stared at Alex for a moment too long and a moment longer still when it must've been bleeding obvious that Alex didn't have an answer.

But Alex didn't care, not when the waves almost drowned out the roar of her heart in her chest. She was fascinated by those eyes, their washed-out blue reminding Alex of the coolest summer days when there was just a wisp of cloud softening the sky. The left eye wasn't just bloodshot, it was blood-soaked: pupil blown, permanently, by the looks of things, like a David Bowie kind of thing, which deepened what was left of the iris into a stormy grey. It had been hard to notice at first, hidden as it was among the jagged scars that fell like burning lightning from the waitress' temple to her cheek and down the side of her neck, tugging and twisting at the skin until freckles were more like paint splashes and the lines around her lips weaved their way across her cheek.

So she let the waitress stare at her.

Because then Alex could stare back all she wanted.

And she wanted.

For the first time in exactly a month, Alex Wilde *really* wanted something, though hopefully this something was a little less lethal.

"Alright," Alex laughed, trying to shake off the heat rising under her skin before it turned into pure Power, "I get your point."

"Nothing wrong with being curious, Alex."

Alex shook her head. Thirty years and someone had finally said that to her. She asked the waitress where exactly the most recent body washed up, letting herself be steered up the rocks, a few feet away from the crow-pecked crisp packet.

The tiniest wisps of gore were trapped in the crevices of the rocks, all mud-pocked and ...

Alex crouched down.

It hadn't been a trick of the light.

It was Power. Pure Power caught up in old blood.

Alex just couldn't help herself. She had to reach out and she did, she reached out and sank the tips of her fingers into the cracks ...

And she's consumed by fire, choking on it as her skin peels away from her soul and the pain ...

She smacked back onto the sand, water soaking through her jeans.

"Alex?" the waitress asked, looming over her. "What did you see?"

Alex stared at her hands, her unburnt hands, and shook away the burgundy rising from her skin.

It was Power. Caught in the cracks was enough Power to bring out her own.

Enough blood.

"What else have the police said?" Alex gasped, slapping the colour off her hands, but it clung, it stuck until she clenched her fists so hard her knuckles ached.

"Well, the paper—"

"The paper's always making something of nothing and nothing of something," Alex rushed out, letting the waitress help her up. "*Why aren't we getting an Eden Project on our bogland? What does Sam Meyer say?*"

"Ach," the waitress said, unfolding the paper anyway and holding it away from herself until she could stop squinting, "what all coppers say when they've nothing else to go on. 'All lines of enquiry are open.' But the paper keeps bringing up their state of mind, you know, if someone had upset the girl and she wasn't thinking straight or that body number two was a homeless alcoholic, blah blah blah."

"Blah blah blah?" Alex asked.

"And there was someone that didn't die," the waitress said, but her glistening skin was flushing and there was something wary in her eyes. "The paper mentions it every time, that a month ago, someone tried to take their own life in the sea, so maybe all these deaths are just some big hysterical reaction. Mass hysteria, like the dancing plague or Salem."

That cement in Alex's stomach churned itself and settled even heavier than before.

"Have they named the wo— the person who nearly died?" Alex asked, wiping her clammy hands against her soaked jeans and trying not to look down at the rocks. Or the waves. Or the waitress.

The cold really was beginning to stick to her bones.

"No," the waitress said, with an unbearable softness that Alex couldn't bring herself to question, "there was just some wee quote from some bystander."

"Some quote?"

"Alex," the waitress sighed, reaching out ...

Alex recoiled, her instincts returning in full force for the first time in a month. A waitress with painted nails and terrible teeth? The picture wasn't just wrong. It was upside down and back to front and was probably a forgery and all.

"I never told you my name," she realised. "Three times. You've said it three times now."

It wasn't a grimace, it wasn't even a flinch, but something in the waitress' eyes sharpened just for an instant.

"And?"

Even her voice was colder.

"And," Alex spluttered, "the point is, I didn't tell you my name."

They were back in the staring game again and Alex wondered why she ever thought her heart beating that fast could have been thrilling. All the emotion had washed off that fascinating face, leaving Alex feeling like she was facing some avenging angel cast down to Earth to mete out unjust judgement for whatever her sins were.

"You didn't need to," the waitress said. "And you know why. Alexandra."

"I need – excuse me," Alex said, clambering up the shingle, suitcase grabbed roughly enough to slice open her hand ...

Which the waitress seized, blood pulsing between their tangled fingers as the sting turned to a throb, which was washed away by the cool, familiar feeling of ...

Power.

More bloody Power.

The waitress did have Power.

What's more, it was making Alex's own Power thrum under her skin, as if ...

"Good as new," the waitress said, turning over Alex's scar-free hand, a hint of silver dust sparkling between their fingers. "How about we—"

"I have places to be," Alex said, snatching her hand back, "I'm expected."

She dragged her suitcase towards the wall with the kind of panic that was sending her Power through her skin.

"The quote was," the waitress bellowed over the wind, "'How do you survive a sea like that?'"

Alex turned back. The expression on the waitress' face was so terrifyingly knowing that it thrilled her to her core.

And she was beautiful.

Standing there, the wind whipping her red hair, those eyes reflecting the sea and the sky ...

Whoever she was, Alex had to muster the last of her courage and throw away the tatters of her instincts by spitting at her:

"Why don't you find out for yourself?"

The promenade was darkening, street lights slicing through shadows as Alex yanked her suitcase up the street, wheels clicking as her sneakers clacked on the cracked tarmac. This was too much already, she thought, as adrenaline, indignation, and something else that she refused to even entertain surged through her, and she was halfway up Hangman's Hill when she discovered that she finally felt alive again.

Alive again with Power in her blood and a name sounding through her soul like that cathedral clock chiming out six in the distance:

Elizabeth.

2
What it Means to be Young

Elizabeth.

Her name was Elizabeth.

Alex didn't want to know, just like she'd never wanted to know those pictures of grave wax Matthew had shoved in her face, but there it was, resounding in her mind and in her soul, just like those waves she could name:

Elizabeth.

And Elizabeth had Power, even though Power was rare, Power was hereditary (and both parents had to have it to pass it down), and as for those perfect nails and those storm-drenched eyes ...

To think Alex had thought it was going to be a completely nondescript afternoon. Then again, she'd also imagined that Coldharbour had just been frozen in time for thirty days, ready to be defrosted like one of *Elizabeth's* doughnuts as soon as she got off the train, but October came quickly to a place like Coldharbour; it always had, and as far as Alex was concerned, it always would. Like the clockwork in the cathedral tower, like those shallows washing up the shingle onto the shore, October came as it always had:

The mist would settle on the marshes, the dew would cling to the crevices in the cobbles, and the clouds choked the moon until there would only be street light and shadow on the promenade.

There'd been an Indian summer, as far as Alex knew, at least from Shaz's sporadic phone calls full of strained small talk and kind questions, but that would've been swept away long before September had surrendered to the strange season that wasn't quite winter but didn't have much right to autumn either.

The witching season, the locals called it, but then, Alex had always thought, they wouldn't have known a witch if she'd kneecapped them with her broom, thrown a black cat in their faces, and put on her very best cackle.

Alex grabbed at the nearest wall and heaved in a breath, sick sticking to the back of her throat.

The sun was setting. She had barely noticed.

She hacked up a phlegmy cough, watching burgundy hang in the air.

But that didn't matter. Not really. Not when Elizabeth's name chimed in her mind like the bells in the cathedral, not when the skin of her shoulders was prickling with the sensation that she was being watched.

Watched by what?

"Y'alright, Miss?"

The voice was so small, so tentative, that Alex thought she was now hearing things as well as seeing them, until she looked down into the gutter at a pile of grubby, frayed blankets that could apparently talk.

The pile then looked up, revealing a young woman's face, her dyed pink hair peeking out of the edges of a felt hat that was far too big for her, paper cup held tightly in her hands.

"Yeah," Alex breathed. "Um ... You? Alright?"

The woman shrugged, holding out the cup to a passer-by who didn't even glance her way. Alex gave up the struggle to get her breath back and waved the white flag at the tightness in her chest. As soon as it showed her mercy and began to loosen, she asked the woman if she did this every day.

"I don't have much choice, Miss."

"Alex. My name's Alex."

"Are you sure you're alright?" the woman asked, watching Alex cling to the wall, "Alex?"

"Just dizzy," Alex said, but there was still some kind of residual fear sliding through her skin so she kept talking as if that could stave away the cold and the dark that knew her much better than that elusive peace did. "Do people give you money? Help you?"

"Some do," the woman said, holding it out again, getting ignored again, frowning again, "and I sometimes sell pictures. There's a girl who stands outside the cathedral and just sings *Perfect Moment* over and over and she gets more cos she even looks a bit like Martine McCutcheon, but every little helps, you know."

With every passer-by, Alex could feel her skin scorch from the inside out. Did nobody see them? Really? Would she have to step out in front of them and manhandle them until they actually looked at a girl sitting on a bit of soggy cardboard?

"I've got some water if you want it," the woman said. "I'm clean, I swear."

"I'm fine, honestly," Alex said. "Doesn't it ..."

She leant back against the wall, not quite caring about the damp soaking into her shoulders, not when it was still clinging so stubbornly to her legs. She probably looked like she'd pissed herself.

"How do you feel when people just walk past you?"

Alex didn't know why she was even asking the question, but then it was coming off the woman in heavy waves of feeling: fear, resignation, an aching gratitude that Alex was even bothering to talk to her.

And then the atmosphere shifted towards disbelief.

Distrust.

"You ask a lot of questions," the woman said. "You a copper?"

"I'm a journalist," Alex said, shoving her Power back down before it made her dizzy. "Well, was. Can't help it, I'm just nosy, really."

"Well, thanks, Miss," the woman said, still civil enough but she was back looking at the crowd, "but I'll be alright."

With a reluctance she couldn't quite place, Alex pushed herself off the wall and gave her a small smile.

"It's Alex," she said, pulling out whatever was in her back pocket: two tenners, a twenty, and a cinema ticket for ...

Never Been Kissed?

She didn't even remember watching whatever that was. Had she gone with Shaz? Or Maddie? Was it for work? Would she have even been paid for that last bit of August? Had she actually even done any work? There'd been the Bank Holiday and all ...

She shook her head and stuffed everything back into her jeans, except a tenner.

"It's not a trick," Alex said, "really."

"Then why?" the woman asked, hand close enough to take the money, but not quite.

"Why not?" Alex sighed.

"Could spend it on drugs or something," the woman said. "Isn't that what people usually think?"

"Yeah, well, I voted for Blair, if that helps. And it's your money now. Spend it how you like."

The woman frowned, but took the note anyway, the very tips of their fingers just making contact.

Enough contact for Alex to feel a spark of Power.

Enough contact for the woman's kohl-lined eyes to widen in confusion.

Enough contact for Alex to be groaning again at how people with Power seemed to be like buses. She hadn't seen one that wasn't Uncle Harry for nine years and now ...

The woman mumbled out an awkward thanks as Alex backed away with a polite nod.

"Take care," Alex said, never having hoped it more in her life.

She continued down the street with her suitcase, dodging bins stuffed in the mouth of an alleyway. Horrible coincidences, that was what Shaz would say. Just a strange, horrible coincidence that she came back to Coldharbour and started bumping into people with Power everywhere and something was haunting the back of her neck, a horrible coincidence that she had to put to the back of her mind because there was only one thing that mattered in that moment and that was finding Maddie, finding her little girl, the one thing that still mattered, and ...

Alex growled into the sunset and dragged herself to a halt, letting the suitcase smack into her calves.

Power on the beach. Power in the waitress. Power in the pink-haired woman.

It wasn't so much one bus after another than some horrible crash with so much gnarled metal no one could see where one bus ended and another began.

And she couldn't stop thinking of Matthew.

Nine years of stuffing down the memories and now she couldn't stop thinking of Matthew.

That had to mean something, didn't it?

She rushed back up the street.

Five more minutes, just five more minutes, just to find out the woman's name and hadn't *Elizabeth* said something about one of those dead people also being homeless—

Vanished.

The woman had vanished.

Alex would've thought she was in the wrong part of the street, but the cardboard and the blankets and the backpack were all still there ...

Along with the cup. And the tenner.

She looked down the street. And up the street.

And down again.

There wasn't even anyone milling about anymore.

The wind snatched up a crumpled Tizer Ice can and chased it straight into the canal.

"Hello?" Alex called, stepping off the pavement.

Even with Power, the woman couldn't have vanished into thin air, especially not without that money. Probably.

And Alex couldn't have been talking to a ghost because she couldn't see ghosts, that was Matthew's job—

Enough.

Enough of bloody Matthew.

But there was something else. Something else Alex's Power was screaming at her to notice ...

The smell of petrichor in the air. The ozone. It tickled her tongue and stung her nose like lashings of salt and vinegar on freshly cooked chips.

Power.

Alex chased the sensation back up the road, but that new crackle of someone's Power against her skin wasn't that woman's. The spark off that woman had been warm, wild but natural. This Power chilled and lurched like the worst squalls in winter and told her that her bus pile-up was the least of it, that actually all those buses had been caught on a train track and now there was this huge thing bearing down on them, on Alex, and it was screaming at her to turn and run, because it was close, whoever it was, whatever it was—

Smack straight into a bin.

Pain punched through her hip.

Starting around the bins, Alex tried to stare down the blind alley, but there was something, some cloud obscuring everything.

It was the Power.

It was dark, *raw* Power.

The woman was down there, shrouded in the fog, Alex was sure, and she was breaking her rules already, letting her own Power gather in her hands, rich and wine-red.

"It's Alex!" she shouted, getting as close to the cloud as she dared. "Can you hear—"

Alex smashed onto her back, slipping down damp-slick steel that scorched her skin, but the woman was screaming inside Alex's own mind so she had no choice, she ignored the clench in her chest, she scrambled to her feet, and she pushed her Power, as much as she could muster, from her hands in burgundy cascades and into the darkness, until—

Someone was standing over the woman.

Tall, hooded—

Alex was thrown back into the wall, hard enough for stars to burst in her eyes, but she lunged again, she grabbed for the man—

Who scurried past her faster than her heartbeat.

More sick to swallow.

Sour this time. Really ...

The woman was sobbing.

"Did he hurt you?" Alex asked.

She wiped blood from her top lip. That'd heal. Probably.

"I'm fine," the woman cried, cradling her arm.

"Don't be stupid," Alex said, ignoring the ache in her own back as she eased the woman up, "that's my trick. Can I ...?"

The woman removed her hand, revealing a burn that criss-crossed her upper arm. It crackled with Power the colour of magpie wings, dark and glowing, the skin around it red raw.

"What happened?" Alex asked, gazing at the burn. If Power had done that, she wouldn't be able to do anything about it ...

"He— he was trying to kill me," the woman sobbed, hiccoughing and heaving. "He said he wanted my Power. Why—"

"What's your name?"

"Why—"

"My name's Alex, remember?" she said, wiping the pink hair off the woman's clammy forehead. "What's yours?"

"Pandora," the woman gasped.

"I'm just gonna try something," Alex said. "I'm not very good at it but ..."

She really had no choice. It really was an emergency.

Alex took a deep breath, reached right down into her soul, and then ...

Her hands glowed.

Just a tickle, dancing around her clammy fingers.

She ignored that snarky voice in her head that reminded her that Matthew was the one who could heal other people and warned Pandora that it could hurt even more, just as she began pressing her hand against the wound—

It scorched Alex, sending her reeling right back into the wall with a sickening crunch to the back of her head, the type that had her blinking grey when there weren't flashes of the beach and Elizabeth and Matthew piercing her retinas.

Alex winced at the steam prickling her cheek, the whir of a vent drilling into her skull.

"Oh my God," Pandora was saying somewhere close to her, "I'm so—"

"It's not you," Alex groaned, peeling her head off the wall with a shudder, waiting until she felt the sting subside into a throb. "It's ..."

She pointed at Pandora's sizzling arm.

"That."

Alex swore under her breath, blinking again as she felt her Power stitch her head back up.

How many times was she going to end up using it?

Some people had good relationships with their Power, apparently. Healthy relationships. For Alex, it had always felt like she was going back, over and over, to an ex who she knew full well would be no good for her.

"I don't understand," Pandora breathed, "I ..."

"Come on," Alex said, hand on Pandora's shaking shoulder, "we'll grab your stuff."

"But—"

Alex held up a finger, just in time to chuck her guts up in the gutter.

That snide voice was back in her head:

Power always took longer with concussions.

3
Lost Long Ago

"Wow!"

"It's just a house," Alex sighed, helping Pandora through the front door.

It was just a house.

An old house, a house Alex hated, a house with ghosts, but as Matthew used to say, sometimes reassuringly, more often sarcastically:

You don't have to be scared of a ghost you haven't wronged.

"Anyone in?" Alex half-heartedly called, as if the absence of a car in the drive didn't give the game away.

She threw the door closed with a twitch of her fingers.

"Wow," Pandora gasped *again*, "your Power does that?"

"Does what?" Alex asked. "Come in, love."

"You don't need keys," Pandora said, whipping her good arm through the air, "you can just ..."

"It's just this house," Alex explained, "Power's in its bones."

She didn't even know why she tried the hallway lights, Bakelite sticking under her fingers, but then she thought that Uncle Harry might've bothered to get someone in.

It had been nine years, after all.

More or less.

There'd been that time, after *that* day, when Uncle Harry had been insistent that she should come home, but Alex just did what she always did: forced Shaz to take sides, which meant letting Alex and Matilda kip on her sofa for a month.

All because Alex wouldn't return to the house.

No.

Not after *that* day.

But there she was, gripping her suitcase far too hard again, staring into the gloam of an old house that had no business existing, a century's murk musting up the corners.

And she was meant to convince Sam to let Maddie move in with her?

Here?

Because Alex had lingered, loitered even, at the train station, where she had sat herself down on the least sticky bench and hung onto her suitcase with both of her chill-cracked hands as she stared at the opposite platform, the "Coldharbour" sign still emblazoned with some faded Fifties illustration of the beach, which, apparently, was all sand and stripy umbrellas and not the fag-ends and the straggly, slimy bits of seaweed that Alex had abandoned a month ago.

And when a bell had chimed five, it galvanised her into action, but with the kind strange automatic force of will that propelled her right past the house and all the way back *there*.

To the sea.

Not to the house.

To the sea and to blood and to Elizabeth.

Alex stuck her head into the living room, which looked the same as it ever did with too many childhood photos and the brown second-hand velveteen settee. It wasn't exactly *Through the Keyhole*, was it?

"Still in pain?" Alex asked, leading Pandora into the kitchen with its avocado fridge and its chipped tiles and cookware that had probably remained as untouched as the vacuum cleaner. No, Loyd Grossman wasn't about to jump out and make some pithy comment about her mother's early Seventies interior design choices.

"I don't know," Pandora said, rendered docile enough from either the pain or the wonder of such a ridiculous house that she landed in the first chair Alex steered her towards. "So what kind of Power does your sister have?"

As soon as Alex and Pandora had got away from the canal, Alex had launched herself into the nearest telephone box and had left a deliberately vague message with Shaz's pager operator:

Alex is at the house. Need help.

She really needed to get one of those mobile phones Sam was always banging on about.

"The power of a medical degree," Alex said, the tap groaning when she tried to fill up a dust-smeared glass. "She's adopted, she doesn't have Power with a capital P."

"I was adopted," Pandora volunteered, her face lighting up for the briefest of moments before it settled into that same solemness that Alex had first encountered.

"I dunno if we can do anything about your arm," Alex tried to explain, "and I don't want you to run it under a cold tap yet till she's here, alright?"

She slid the glass of water across the table and wiped her clammy, brick-grazed hands on the nearest tea towel, just about managing a rictus grin when Pandora blinked up at her with a nod, sticky black tears stuck to her cheeks. Her arm was still crackling away with iridescent sparks.

"This is a great house, by the way," Pandora whispered.

"You'd think," Alex gasped more than laughed, "Will you be alright for a minute?"

"I really can't stay long," Pandora argued, "I go down the prom at seven, to the pub. The Neptune's Arms. Sometimes we have luck, if people are feeling drunk and generous."

"You can't go to a pub looking like that," Alex said. "You're ..."

She shook her head and drifted down the corridor.

There was shock and then there was not accepting that your arm was on fire.

Elizabeth could've helped. Elizabeth would've known what to do.

A woman Alex had spent ten minutes with half an hour ago and it made her want to scream that she *knew*, that she knew Elizabeth's name, let alone that she would *help*.

Bloody Power.

She reached the study, its door firmly shut.

Of course.

As far as Alex knew, it had remained locked since she'd rebuilt it with nothing more than a twitch of her fingers and a touch of that regret already stirring in her veins. Occasionally, in those intervening years, Harry had mentioned the study, lamenting to her about how it still wouldn't open for him but might for her, as if it ever would have obeyed her again after what she'd done.

Alex did try the door handle to the study, but she wouldn't have blamed it for being pissed off at her. She'd brought it down in the first place, after all. Nothing appreciated being crumbled into matchsticks and cinder. The door didn't budge, not even when she let the tiniest amount of burgundy Power slip out of her fingers and into the keyhole. It was cheating. She knew that. Not that it stopped her crouching down, blowing the Power through the keyhole, and peering into the nothing.

Great. Alex had been back in Coldharbour for not much longer than an hour and she was letting all the old ghosts get to her, prod at all the open wounds with freshly sharpened claws. They'd had to wait a month for her, after all. Let the feeding frenzy commence.

There was a knock at the front door.

"I'll get it!" Alex called, rushing towards it with a flick of her fingers.

A blonde blur yanked Alex into a hug that made her bones creak and threatened to choke her with a cloud of whatever upmarket perfume said blur was wearing that season.

"Missed you, sis," the blur formerly known as Shaz mumbled into Alex's hair, her breath warm and moist on Alex's forehead.

"Missed you too," Alex spluttered, "but I really can't breathe."

Shaz apologised and tried to untangle herself, her glasses catching in Alex's curls.

"Hang on," Alex said, "you take them off and I'll get them out of my hair."

She fumbled with Shaz's specs as if it hadn't happened a hundred times before.

"Have you pissed yourself?" Shaz asked.

"I ..."

Alex tutted and wiped her hand against her jeans. How had she completely forgotten ...

Adrenaline had a hell of a lot to answer for.

And that concussion, still ringing through Alex's skull like the cathedral bells, faint but insistent.

"It's just a bit of seawater—"

"What were you doing in the sea?" Shaz spluttered, "And why is there blood on my fingers?"

"It's really not what you think," Alex said, handing her the glasses. "That screw's coming loose again."

"Did your Power heal it?" Shaz asked, squinting.

"Dunno," Alex said. "Probably."

She twisted her head away from her sister and tugged her into the house.

"Sis, head injuries—"

"Thank you, Doctor Evans, I'm well aware."

"A head injury, though? How did you get a head injury? Haven't you been on trains all day? I would've picked you up from the station—"

"Jesus ..."

Shaz took Alex's hands and asked her if she really was alright, though, and if she'd been getting enough sleep, and if they'd given her anything to take, and when therapy would start, and Alex was just about to snap back that she was fine when Shaz went:

"Oh, hello."

Pandora had stepped out of the kitchen with a feeble wave of her steaming arm, the skin crackling like oil spitting in a too-hot pan.

"Hello," she said. "Are you the doctor?"

"Do you mind examining Pandora?" Alex asked with a squeeze of Shaz's hands.

"Examining her for what?" Shaz asked, balking at Pandora's faintly smoking skin. "Is that a *Power* injury? Sis, I'm a doctor, not a witch."

"I'm not a witch either!" Alex said, "but Power can't heal Power—"

"Neither can Savlon and cling film," Shaz said, but she was still staring at the wound with the kind of wonder that made her a Wilde deep down. "Matthew was scarred for life!"

"Oh, that was nothing."

Alex could still do nonchalant after all. Also, Matthew had deserved it after what he'd done to her Barbies. Makings of a serial killer, as far as she was concerned.

"Tell his shoulder," Shaz replied.

"Please, Shaz, I can't do everything at once!" Alex said, rushing down the corridor.

"Who's Matthew?" Pandora asked, and Shaz was saying that he was their brother, before Alex could turn round with "Doesn't matter."

And she hid.

She hid in the toilet, the calendar on the back of the door telling her it was apparently still Christmas 1989.

The lock still stuck. Did Uncle Harry not even buy WD40 anymore?

Alex huffed out a groan and dug her broken nails into her palms.

Twenty-nine days.

Twenty-nine days in that bloody place wishing she were back in Coldharbour and in the space of an hour, Alex had:

Used her Power.

Sensed Power mixed in with blood and God knew what else on the beach.

Met a stranger (albeit an extremely attractive one, not that that mattered) with Power.

Stopped someone else with Power getting killed by yet another person with Power.

And Jesus, stuck in that bloody house again, did Alex want to just slam her head against a wall and scream.

No, she'd already done that once that evening.

But anyway, she thought, as she wiped down the mirror, that would probably provoke her Power, and Power never did anyone any good, as far as she was concerned.

At least Shaz hadn't noticed the gravel stuck in her hair too.

Maybe she should've said she'd pissed herself.

Manic incontinence was probably easier to explain away than her café encounter and that gore on the beach that definitely, might've, *may have* glistened with Power.

No wonder Elizabeth had looked at her funny, though.

Alex was looking gaunt.

Haggard.

She'd thought she'd been sleeping alright, at least better than she usually did, but her eyes were looking sunken and her skin was looking sallow and just as dry as her hair.

Thirty years old?

By whose standards?

She'd seen *The Mummy* at the pictures. She could see the similarities.

So much for a convalescence.

A convalescence throughout which she had thoroughly suppressed her Power, beating it back and down like a bear in a cage, punishing it for misbehaving, for making her cling onto life against her will, for forcing her to hold on just long enough …

She wasn't particularly vain, but …

Still.

If her Power was that insistent.

It wouldn't hurt, would it?

Power wasn't like karma.

There'd be no consequence for scrubbing herself up, just fewer pitying looks.

Alex dragged a hand over her face, letting it glow as it stretched out her skin, took out the worst of the crow's feet, smoothed that bit of latent eczema on her jawline …

"Sod it," she whispered, letting her Power take her over, the whole room rattling as burgundy surged through her, flaring brighter than the light above her.

Well, she looked a bit less like the walking dead, in the sense that she didn't look like she had just crawled out of a coffin anymore, at least not without a good dust-down and fixing the mortician's make-up.

"I don't like you either," she muttered at her—

The door swung open, smacking Alex towards the loo.

"Just a minute, Sharon," Alex hissed, "please!"

Shaz stood in the doorway, conspicuously alone, with a roll of cling film in her hands and the kind of guilty grimace that would sway even the most sympathetic jury towards the prosecution. Her foot was tapping nervously against the flagstones. Christ. Not the foot. Alex didn't have time for the foot.

The front door was ajar, dragging in damp air.

Alex didn't so much as let out the sigh as let it fall out of her headfirst.

"Shazza …"

"She did a runner."

"What d'you mean, she did a runner?"

"She didn't want to talk to me—"

"I didn't need her to talk to you, I'd have done that!"

"I think I just freaked her out by mentioning Sam and you know, the fact that he's a copper."

"Yeah, I saw he's an *Acting* DCI," Alex said, grabbing the doorframe. "You ain't gonna tell him about this, are you?"

"Well, if you really don't want me to," Shaz mumbled. "It's Code Bananarama, innit?"

"Sharon Evans," Alex said, "are you invoking Code Bananarama behind your fiancé's back?"

"We're not kids anymore, sis," Shaz said, turning an extraordinary shade of red. "We're thirty— well, I'm thirty one—"

"You know how it works," Alex said, "how it's always worked. You, me, Matthew. The secret doesn't leave the three of us. That's it."

"There's only two of us now."

"There's only two in Bananarama now," Alex replied. "Clearly, he was Siobhan. Keep up, Sharon."

"Siobhan came back," Shaz argued, "last year. For *Eurotrash*."

Alex didn't want to glare at her sister, but to insinuate that somehow it could ever be possible ...

"But how are you?" Shaz asked. "Really? Are you sure you don't wanna come to ours for dinner? It is Friday Night Dinner, we get takeaways now, I'm sure Sam'll let you choose—"

"And Maddie?"

"She's over at Stacey's—"

"For the night or what?"

"Al, Sam and I both work funny shifts."

"He's still Matilda's father," Alex said, her skin prickling with what she hoped was irritation but knowing her luck, was Power, "and you're her aunt. Slash stepmother. Didn't realise you've been palming her off."

"A whole month of living with a kid's just a bit different to just seeing them on weekends, isn't it?" Shaz sighed, trying to do the placating smile on Alex.

Nice try.

"Twenty-nine days," Alex said.

Shaz's placating smile had gone. Bit difficult to keep it up when her jaw was clenching like that.

"And it's been a difficult twenty-nine days, Al."

"I'm sure that cramming your fridge with Sunny Delight and playing that Vengaboys album over and over has been really challenging," Alex scoffed. "Don't you like to party?"

"You have no idea how much I hate Ibiza," Shaz muttered. "Anyway, she's in Year 9 now."

"And?" Alex said, as if she hadn't been the one who'd had to traipse around Clarks and Woolworths to find a pair of new school shoes her daughter would even put on her feet.

Had she though? This year? Or was that last year?

"And it's a difficult year," Shaz decided to say, "and she's at a difficult age—"

"Can you stop calling my daughter 'difficult', please?"

"I'm just saying." Shaz sighed. "Maybe Sam—"

"I can do without the Spanish Inquisition from Samuel over a lukewarm balti," Alex said, "but thanks."

"Could get a madras," Shaz suggested.

"It'll still be lukewarm," Alex replied, heading towards the kitchen. "You can't tell me they've finally sorted out their deliveries."

"When's Uncle Harry due back?"

"No idea."

"Al, I'm just asking a question—"

"And I'm saying I don't know—"

Shaz was shaking her head.

"What now?" Alex snapped.

"I'm just ... This is how it started last time."

"Last time?" Alex scoffed.

"Shutting down," Shaz explained, "not talking to anyone about what's going on—"

"I just said I don't know when our uncle's in, it doesn't mean I'm ..."

"Ill?" Shaz suggested.

"I'm not ill," Alex said, "just ..."

Exhausted. To the bone. Beyond the bone.

It had slowly slid its claws into her when she wasn't looking, it had crept into her bed, it had caressed its way through her skin, until one day, she woke up and that had just been that.

Just her life.

And she couldn't even remember who'd bought Maddie's new school shoes anymore.

"Tired," she insisted, "and I was tired then but I'm fine, I'm a good mum, I don't need everyone treating me like I can't even keep a Tamagotchi alive."

"Al," Shaz said, "if I'd had any idea how bad things were ..."

"You were busy," Alex replied, not even caring this time if she sounded bitter. "Planning a wedding."

"Even so, if you need me to help—"

"Please can we stop overdramatising what happened?"

"Sis, you almost died."

"Almost," she said, giving her sister a tight smile. "Power does have some benefits, apparently."

Shaz made the mistake of hesitating, so Alex told her, over the sick churning in her throat, that she needed to unpack. The last thing she needed was to vom over her sister, the doctor.

"Weird thinking of this place as home again," Shaz said, gazing around the hallway.

"Yeah, well," Alex said, easing her sister out of the door with a kiss on her cheek, "won't be for long."

But the sun had finally set.

And the shadows were settling.

And the unquiet chilled Alex as she wandered back towards the kitchen, because surely Pandora couldn't have grabbed all of her stuff before—

She paused.

There. Down the hallway, in the corner of her eye and the edge of her perception, Alex could sense that the door to the study was open.

And there he was.

Deep in the dark, in the shadows obscuring the worst side of his face …

A ghost she hadn't seen in years.

"What?" Alex spat. "I'm back. So what?"

So what?

The realisation sunk through her and she didn't know if it was even her own thought, like the instinct that had told her Elizabeth's name, but the three words that chimed in her mind still mattered:

Pandora.

Seven.

Neptune.

4
A Piece of the Night

The Neptune's Arms was one of those old man pubs which by the brink of the Millennium had fallen into the same category of "artefacts of a seaside town well on the decline" as the café. It was the opposite of that new bar in town that played *Genie in a Bottle* on repeat; it was a battle against brown and beige to even get near the bar, where the fag smoke finally subsided enough for Alex to stop batting her hands through thick air that clawed at her pores. Balancing herself on a stool, she scanned the pub for a shock of pink hair among the grey and white and brown and blonde and—

Red.

Elizabeth.

She was sitting in a booth to Alex's right, wafting her own streams of smoke from the shadows like a vampire in a black and white film.

But then vampires in black and white films probably didn't read newspapers and even at that distance, Alex recognised that schlocky font. It was one thing reading it for the latest on horrific crimes, but to read it recreationally over a Scotch was up there with hanging out with Slobodan Milosevic.

Elizabeth was already smiling at her.

Knowingly.

Again.

Alex tried to ignore the odd tightness in her chest and searched the bar for Pandora again, twisting until she almost fell off the stool. No pink hair in sight. Just the colour of fire in the corner of her eye.

It wouldn't hurt.

Would it?

Alex returned her gaze to Elizabeth and offered her a tentative smile, catching her breath when Elizabeth gave her a little wave. Alex gestured at the bar and when Elizabeth nodded and tapped her glass with a sharp fingernail, she asked the barmaid for a vodka and tonic.

"Single or double?"

Her stomach still churning at the thought of Pandora and her arm (or so she told herself), Alex asked for a double and whatever Elizabeth was having.

"Glenlivet," the barmaid replied, her Pat Butcher earrings clinking like rubies in the smoke. "Didn't even realise we had a bottle before she came along."

"Make that a double as well," Alex said, sliding her last tenner across the bar mat.

When the barmaid warned her that it wasn't cheap, she pulled out the twenty from her pocket with a wince, but her reward ...

Well, that was being the lucky recipient of Elizabeth's small smile of approval when Alex finally dared to hover by the booth, condensation and sweat slicking her fingers.

"May I join you?"

"After earlier?" Elizabeth said, but she still slid along the seat.

"I'm waiting for someone," Alex explained, turning back to the bar to confirm once again that Pandora wasn't hiding in some funny little alcove, like a post-punk *Where's Wally* among the geriatrics. "Sort of. She don't know I'm waiting and I only met her earlier."

"You only met me earlier."

"Exactly. And I don't know the first thing about you. Except what I think your name is."

Elizabeth sipped at her whisky, but when Alex just continued to stare at her, she patted the seat and said:

"Aye?"

"I think," Alex said, shuffling onto the seat with sweaty hands, "your name's Elizabeth."

"Surname?" Elizabeth asked, lips still poised over the glass.

Before Alex could even blink, her mind was assaulted by an overwhelmingly silent darkness, which compelled her to say:

"Black," as airily as she could manage when her Power was trembling inside her throat. "Or at least, that's the name you've been using."

Not airily at all then.

Elizabeth smirked and finally deigned to put down her whisky, resting her chin on an elegant hand. What was it with those painted nails?

"And why, Miss Wilde, have you been hiding your Power?"

"Why aren't you hiding yours?" Alex asked.

"Why should I?"

"It's not like it helps anything," Alex said, trying to cling to her defiance as she stared into her glass. "Or anyone."

"It could."

Of all the things Alex expected from Elizabeth, she didn't expect this softness, the way she was one wrong move from cricking her neck as she tried to recapture Alex's attention.

"I don't expect you to tell me everything," Elizabeth continued, "Or anything at all—"

"Good." Alex laughed. "Cos I'm sick of talking about it. I've done nothing but talk about it for the past month."

Now, that wasn't entirely true, was it?

She hadn't spoken at all that first week.

"And having people treat you like a child?" Elizabeth asked.

Alex dug her fingers into a damp paper napkin and let the soft strands of crimson catch in her broken nails.

"I'm jobless and homeless. At thirty. Can hardly blame them."

"Are you needing somewhere to live?"

"My uncle's taken me in."

"Another Wilde?"

"A Sharpe." Alex explained, "Harry's my mum's brother. He never sold the place, even after we all left, so now I'm in my childhood bedroom in a spooky old orphanage."

"The job, then?" Elizabeth said, as if being told her drinking companion was living in a haunted former children's home was perfectly normal.

"I *was* Deputy Features Editor of that," Alex said, prodding *The Chronicle* with a hard finger, "Sounds *Ab Fab* but it was a lot of leisure centre openings and dogs that say 'sausages' so I'm not sure how transferable my skills are."

"Would you work in the café?" Elizabeth asked. "It's a step down, but I can't run that place on my own. As you may have noticed."

She pulled out a black box of cigarettes, the golden lettering glinting under the warm lights.

"Is it true?" Alex asked, "People with Power can smoke without their lungs turning into schnitzel? The same way it's hard for us to get drunk?"

But not impossible. Her own mother and brother had been testament to that.

Elizabeth nodded and offered a cigarette to Alex, who declined as politely as she could when her mind was getting dragged back to Matthew and the way he'd stash the fags he'd nicked off their mum under his bed …

Alex caught herself and returned to her drink, swallowing away her thought. It was just being back in Coldharbour that made her think of him. Just Coldharbour and Power.

"Do you mind if I do?" Elizabeth asked, placing a cigarette between her red lips. Alex hadn't noticed that before. The red lipstick gleaming around those crooked teeth …

"Alex?"

"Go ahead," Alex said, before taking an ambitious gulp of her vodka that scraped its way through her with the burning viciousness and unpleasant suddenness of being glassed in the throat.

Elizabeth lit the cigarette, a thick strand of smoke weaving between them.

"I'd have to work it out around my daughter," Alex continued. "Matilda. She's old enough to walk home on her own and all that, but even so. With people turning up dead all the time."

"Aye, alright," Elizabeth said, impossibly elegant with a fag in one hand and her whisky in the other. "How old is she now?"

"Thirteen. Fourteen in a month."

In exactly a month. What the hell was Alex going to do about her birthday?

"And what about your husband?"

Alex spluttered out a shocked laugh, wiping bubbles of tonic off the back of her hand.

"My what?"

"Your husband," Elizabeth said slowly, colour creeping through her scars. "The father—"

"I never married him," Alex said, pushing down the thought of *that* day that stirred deep in her stomach. "If it's good enough for Madonna ..."

"Apologies," Elizabeth said, but there was something else in her gaze that spurred Alex on.

"It's fine. I'm the local single mother who's had more girlfriends than boyfriends and don't forget: I'm the only face in this pub right now that ain't white."

"Your girlfriend, then," Elizabeth said, shockingly smoothly for someone blushing that beautifully.

"I'm single," Alex replied, and never let it be said flattery didn't work on her because she was letting herself sink back into her seat, old leather squeaking against her jumper. "Very single. Most people round here listen to the rumours."

"Well," Elizabeth said, "I don't. Do you?"

When was the last time anyone had spoken to Alex like that? Like she wasn't one of those flimsy bits of glassware that was teetering on the very edge of the shelf above the barmaid, one loud noise or rogue vibration away from a very dramatic shattering?

Alex sighed and gazed out at the pub too, trying not to frown at the absolute, obvious absence of anyone under fifty, let alone thirty.

Still no Pandora.

And the funny looks.

They never quite looked away quick enough, but Elizabeth appeared utterly unmoved by the idea of anyone gawping at her.

"My mum used to work here, you know," Alex murmured. "She was working here the night ..."

She'd smashed a glass, somebody had said. Alex thought that she'd heard it through Matthew or Shaz, who'd heard it from Sam, who'd heard it from one of his parents, Leo more likely than Marilyn, who'd have heard it from someone else who might've actually been there. But apparently, according to this story made up of half-whispers and the usual rumours:

Carrie Wilde had been pouring a pint.

She had dropped the glass.

She looked like she'd seen a ghost.

She *said* that she'd seen a ghost.

Alex had never believed that part. All the time she'd known her mother, for all those fifteen fraught years, they'd kept their Power tightly under wraps. It had been bad enough Shaz and Sam knew.

So.

So Carrie Wilde had been pouring a pint and she had dropped the glass and she looked like she'd seen a ghost and she said that she'd seen a ghost.

And she ran out.

Didn't say another word.

Didn't even pick up her bag.

Or her coat.

Or her wages.

It was the end of the month, after all.

A long month.

And long months meant having to fill the last week with the bits of bread that were just on the turn, toasting them to buggery and slathering them with acres of marge, long months meant stretching out the pocket money and the little they got from their part-time jobs, long months meant, on a noticeable number of evenings, conveniently being in the vicinity of the Meyers' when it was time for dinner and Marilyn had, just as conveniently, somehow made enough for six kids and not three.

So Carrie would never have left without her wages.

She just ran out and she ran home and that was where Alex could pick up the whole horrible story for herself.

"The night she died," Alex explained, after a long gulp of cheap vodka that scorched her throat, "she was working here the night she died."

Elizabeth peered around the pub again, an uptick of an eyebrow towards someone she must've caught staring.

"Do I need to be on the lookout for an angry ghost?" she asked, turning back to Alex. "Telling me to get away from her daughter?"

Alex gripped her glass and shook her head.

"She didn't die here. Don't worry."

No. If Carrie Wilde had died in the pub, at least she wouldn't have been alone when it happened.

"So," Alex said, dragging herself back from the past, "are you one of those who sees ghosts?"

"Sometimes," Elizabeth replied, "but I have to be really paying attention."

"I don't usually see them," Alex admitted. "I think Harry does, my uncle. Other people in my family did. And now and then, there's something just at the corner of my eye but …"

The one in the study.

Staring at her from the shadows.

She'd always seen that one.

Alex shook off her shudder.

"Or a smell or a sound. I dunno."

"Your Power's probably stronger in different ways," Elizabeth said. "I didn't get to grips with mine until I was twenty-five."

"Why?" Alex asked. "What happened?"

The tumbler hovered under Elizabeth's lips. Her eyes had darkened but her smile was wry in a way that told Alex that she was used to the same innuendo when it came to talking about Power.

"Let's just say," her eyes falling to Alex's hand, "there was an emergency."

Elizabeth's fingernails caught the edge of the scab on Alex's palm. Before Alex could hold onto her hiss, Elizabeth was cradling her hand with a frown, thumb stroking Alex's in a strangely reassuring way, as if it was perfectly natural that she was holding the hand of someone she barely knew.

No. No, that didn't feel right to Alex, the idea that they barely knew each other. It was more that they had just met. Why else would that cool hand and its reassuring thumb feel so familiar?

"I thought I healed this perfectly," Elizabeth said, before leaning around to squint at Alex's head.

Alex hadn't washed that blood from her hair. The blood Shaz had noticed.

"And what happened here?" Elizabeth asked, gently brushing Alex's ponytail over her shoulder. "Has someone hurt you?"

"I'm fine," Alex snapped, flinching away. "I healed it."

"Alex, there's blood *dripping* down your neck," Elizabeth replied, her hand surging silver.

"I said, I'm fine!"

The glow had gone by the time Elizabeth had sat back with a clench of her fist.

Alex downed the rest of her vodka, slid off the seat, and stood with a stare and an "excuse me" that she hoped was as cold as she felt. She battled her way back through the pub, back through that brown and beige and *smog* until she was throwing herself into the bitter darkness of the promenade, where, over the beach wall which clung to her hands the way she was clinging to it, she retched, pure alcohol shooting up her nose.

Five.

Five things she could see.

Her hands. The wall. The light from the lighthouse. From the moon. From the streetlight.

Four.

Four things she could feel.

The wall under her hands, rough and crumbling. The wind clawing at her bare forearms. The sea spray tickling her cheeks. A cold hand on her shoulder.

Three.

Three things she could hear.

The roar of the waves. The squawk of a seagull. Elizabeth whispering her name.

Two things she could smell.

The stench of the seaweed, left to rot. The bergamot in Elizabeth's perfume.

One thing she could taste.

Iron. The blood in her mouth.

"I'd like to apologise," Elizabeth began.

"It's fine," Alex croaked, still shuddering, still clinging onto the wall with her bare hands until what was left of her nails started to bend and crack. "It's not your fault."

"I know I said that you didn't need to tell me anything, but if you're wanting to …"

Alex shook her head and slumped forward, elbows grazing the wall. They'd probably heal. Elizabeth reached across and pulled a curl of hair out of a bit of sick that hadn't quite gone over the side.

"No Power," Elizabeth murmured, pulling a handkerchief through Alex's hair, "promise. But I would like to check your head."

Alex nodded and let cold fingers slip through her hair. She didn't know whether to just focus on the careful scrape of nails against her scalp or try not to think of it at all, but when the hankie caressed her neck, she had to clench to hold back her shudder.

"There," Elizabeth said, presenting Alex with the blood-blotted, sick-smeared hankie. "It's always the smallest cuts that makes the biggest mess. Your own Power must've stitched it up."

"I didn't even feel it," Alex whispered, patting her traitorous head.

She should've known there'd be consequences for her vanity. If her Power would sort out her crow's feet, it would've had something to say about her gouging her head open.

"I'm ..."

Alex sighed and sank her head into her shoulders, her embarrassment creeping up behind her exhaustion.

"I'm sorry," she said.

"Happens to the best of us," Elizabeth said. "The last job I had, well ..."

Alex glanced up at her, just catching the clench of Elizabeth's jaw before she looked down at Alex with an awkward smile, her teeth all crooked and fanged. She tried to imagine Elizabeth with braces, but it was impossible because, Alex found, she couldn't even see her as a teenager, although she must've been as gawky and spotty as the rest of them. Elizabeth Black with growing pains, slamming doors and shouting at her parents?

No, Alex couldn't imagine it and she suspected, with the kind of inexplicable dread that the Grim Reaper would've bottled, that Elizabeth Black had never had growing pains.

"I promise I'm a good boss," Elizabeth said, with an earnestness that sat strange on her. "I know all the latest employment laws, Blair's new minimum wage and so on."

Elizabeth Black as a teenager. Impossible. Alex found herself laughing, actually laughing, until the air was ripping its way out of her chest, and when was the last time—

"I'm being serious," Elizabeth said, but then she should've told her smile that. "Now you don't take me seriously?"

Alex probably should've done the 5-4-3-2-1 again, but she couldn't have looked, heard, felt beyond Elizabeth Black at that moment, haloed as she was against the moonlight, hair ablaze and eyes gleaming like a fallen angel.

Yes.

Fallen angels didn't have braces and growing pains and annoying parents.

Apparently fallen angels had dodgy teeth and red nails and fancy cigarettes.

And apparently Alex liked fallen angels.

"Want another drink?" Alex rushed out. "Discuss terms and conditions."

"Weren't you waiting for someone else?" Elizabeth asked, jumping down off the wall.

Alex groaned.

Pandora.

The girl with pink hair and kind kohl eyes and an arm on fire.

"It probably doesn't matter."

But then a shiver drove through her and it wasn't just the brisk wind.

It was ten past seven.

"Probably?" Elizabeth said, her frown stretching the shining lattice across her left cheek.

"Can I ask how you got your scars? You don't have to answer, it's just ..."

Elizabeth shrugged off her coat.

The scars shot down her arm, thick and gnarled like tree roots at her shoulder, as thin and intricate as a spiderweb by the time they reached her wrist. Every time Alex thought she was close to understanding Elizabeth ...

"Pure Power," Elizabeth said. "It's exceptionally rare, seeing as—"

"It should've killed you?" Alex guessed.

"Aye," Elizabeth replied, something warm in her eyes that was a little bit impressed. "It's very hard to burn someone with pure Power. You'd have to be trying to get at their Power and feeling pretty sadistic about it too."

Alex watched Elizabeth's eyes drop to her arm and she couldn't help but reach out, her hand hanging in the cool night air.

"Did it hurt?"

Elizabeth nodded, with a clench of her throat that Alex couldn't help but mimic.

"Does it still hurt?"

"Not anymore."

With her unscarred hand, Elizabeth took Alex's outstretched one and brought it closer to her arm until just a whisper of wind separated it from Alex's fingertips. Alex stared into that searching gaze and nodded, ghosting her fingers over the scars as they both watched the iridescence dance through Elizabeth's skin.

"Is it cos I also have Power?" Alex whispered, fascinated by how the scars could feel so rough and smooth at the same time.

"No idea." Elizabeth laughed.

"The person I was looking for," Alex said, ripping her hand away before she would surely lose herself in the feel of Elizabeth, "she was being burned. She was being attacked with Power. I stopped it, that's how I ..."

She gestured to her head.

"But her arm was ..."

Like nothing Alex had ever seen before or hoped she would ever again.

"It was a bit gory," she said, "let's put it that way."

"Did she understand what was going on?" Elizabeth asked.

"Well, she said she felt like she was being drained, but I don't know if she realised it was her Power," Alex said. "I knew she'd be here at seven, only ..."

"She never turned up."

"See anyone go in with pink hair?" Alex asked.

Elizabeth frowned at the pub and shook her head.

"Do you think," Alex began, an echo of the panic she'd felt in the alley looming out of the dark. "I mean, there are other pubs. She might've changed her mind."

A cold hand wrapped around hers.

"Come with me."

5
A Shot in the Dark

"Drink?" Elizabeth asked, striding towards the kitchenette.

"Whatever you've got," Alex said, rushing towards the phone. "Have you been here long?"

Alex had definitely had a stereotype in mind when she thought of a poky little flat above a greasy spoon on the promenade: wallpaper even older than the stuff clinging onto dear life back at the house, white goods that hadn't been white for a decade, and as much natural light as the well in the back garden could boast.

Elizabeth Black's flat was not that.

It was clean, Alex couldn't deny that, but it was also bare. Bare-ish, though Alex had just come from that ridiculous house of hers, which wasn't much better than a haunted car boot sale.

But Elizabeth's flat had a record player, old-fashioned, with a stack of records underneath; a small bookcase absolutely crammed with battered, bound volumes, their edges foxed and frayed and fascinating; a red rotary phone that belonged in a Sixties film; a burgundy chaise longue that looked like it had been hauled out of some knacker's yard; a large poster, well, photo, of somewhere possibly on the Amalfi coast or somewhere else in that stretch of the Med; and a kitchenette, all chic sleek lines, that looked just as unlived-in.

That was it.

The whole place looked unlived-in.

Alex started painstakingly dragging the dial to every number, keeping an eye on Elizabeth as she fixed the drinks.

Perfect nails on a waitress' hands and a flat that looked unlived-in.

"A few weeks," Elizabeth replied, pulling a bottle out from somewhere.

She turned to Alex with something curious in her eyes and added:

"I haven't finished unpacking."

It was a lie.

Alex knew it was a lie, just as she knew that Elizabeth knew that she knew.

Shaz answered the phone with a "Doctor Evans" far perkier than a Friday night in Coldharbour deserved.

"It's me," Alex mumbled, clinging to the receiver. "Is Sam there?"

"He's not in the best mood, Al—"

"I think Pandora's in trouble," Alex said, struggling to catch the breath that insisted on escaping her. "Real trouble, Shazza. Can you fill him in? Break the Code, I don't care."

There was a pause, some frantic muttering, and then:

"Here," Sam said.

Alex's breath caught in her throat. A month – well, twenty nine days – of not hearing each other's voices, the longest time since they were four years old, and that was what he said:

Here.

"We think this woman," Alex forced out, "Pandora, is in danger. With Power. Something's going on with Power."

"Who's 'we'?" Sam asked.

Elizabeth was unfolding a gigantic map on the floor with more of a roar than a rustle.

"Can you just ... I don't know," Alex said, "send out cars or something? That's what they do on *The Bill*."

"Al." Sam sighed. "I thought if Power was involved—"

"Power or no Power, she could die," Alex said. "We need to find her."

It sounded dramatic, of course it did, but Alex had a tendency towards the dramatic and when it came to convincing Sam of anything, it was a sort of perverse *boy who cried wolf* situation where Alex had to maintain the level of drama to be taken seriously.

It had been the way through to him in the playground and their bedroom, and now there they were, everything changed except Sam was still agreeing with her.

Even now.

He said that he would see what favours he could pull in, considering that Pandora was easy enough to spot with bright pink hair.

"I'm gonna need an explanation," Sam warned.

"Yeah, I know." Alex sighed. "I'm on the promenade, by the way. She would've – she should've come this way from the house."

She squeezed the phone until the plastic squeaked, and whispered her thanks.

When she put the phone down, Elizabeth passed her a tumbler of brandy.

"It's meant to warm you up," Elizabeth said with a shrug that suggested she held as much stock in that as the local rumours.

"It's a myth," Alex replied. "It's just vasodilation."

"Vaso what?"

"Your blood vessels expanding. Shaz told me. My sister, the doctor."

"Here's to vasodilation," Elizabeth said, clinking their glasses together.

Alex sipped at her brandy as she peered at the map, tracing a shoreline with her eyes ...

"Coldharbour."

The cliffs, the spits, the promenade ...

When Elizabeth nodded and unfurled a crystal from a chain, she realised with a shudder what was happening and what had happened the last time she'd tried it.

And what came after.

"Dowsing," Alex said, her voice sticking to her throat like the brandy.

"In our case," Elizabeth explained, swinging the crystal over the map, "to find Pandora."

"That's as real as when you swing a ring over your stomach to decide what gender your baby's supposed to be. It never works."

Alex and Sam had tried, "discovering" that the baby was a boy. They'd run into the living room and excitedly announced, as excitedly as two still slightly shell-shocked sixteen-year-olds could, that Christopher James Meyer would be joining the family that November.

Matthew had looked up from his magazine, singularly unimpressed at the interruption which had mainly consisted of Alex saying "Mouse" over and over and over again, and with a languid blink, declared that *Christopher* was actually a girl.

Undeterred, Alex and Sam then announced that Claire Rachel Meyer—

Matthew had held up a hand that time, not even bothering to glance up from his magazine, and said that she was clearly called Matilda Catherine Meyer and could he please finish his article in peace?

Matthew, of course, had been right.

Both times.

"Most people don't have Power," Elizabeth said. "We do."

"Even so," Alex said, pushing that whole other world of grief back into the mists of her mind, "I know for a fact it doesn't work."

She had that queasy thought again, before the first pregnancy, of the night ...

"It can't find people," she insisted. "I've tried to find people."

"Dead or Living?" Elizabeth asked.

"Does it matter?"

"Well," Elizabeth said, "I know for a fact it does work. On the Living, at least. Wee bit more complicated with the Dead."

"It's still swinging," Alex said.

"Because I don't know who I'm looking for, besides 'she's called Pandora and she has pink hair'."

"Isn't that enough?"

"Would that be enough if you called up Directory Enquiries?" Elizabeth asked, with the kind of demanding sniff that could really grate if Alex wasn't finding her so violently, relentlessly winning with that bloody smile. "That she's called Pandora and she's got pink hair?"

Alex crossed her arms over her chest and said:

"She has a nose piercing and a fluffy backpack."

Elizabeth, also annoyingly to her credit, did not rise to the Wilde sarcasm and held out her hand.

"What?"

"Gimme your hand."

"Again?"

"You've seen her," Elizabeth explained, the raise of her eyebrow clearly designed to remind Alex who had been reaching out to whom on the promenade, getting all moony over a scarred arm. "Touched her?"

"Only to help her," Alex mumbled, stepping onto the map and covering Elizabeth's hand with her own.

"Think of her," Elizabeth murmured as the pendulum swung, but every time Alex tried to think of pink hair, she saw red; every effort she made to remember heat, she felt cold; and the pendulum reeled around the map, spinning faster and faster ...

Until Elizabeth snatched it away from Alex with a frown.

"Lot of emotions for someone you've just met."

Alex held out her hand, her fingers quivering with every pulse of blood punching through her hand.

"Let me try on my own," she said. "Maybe there was interference."

Elizabeth passed Alex the pendulum and stepped off the map, leaning against the bookcase with her brandy.

"Just to warn you," Elizabeth said, "it was tapping into my Power before. Now it'll be tapping into yours."

Alex nodded, but her chest was tightening. It'd only be for a minute. Moments, seconds, even. As quick as her little vanity project that at least made her look closer to thirty than forty. Closing her eyes, she took as deep a breath as she could manage without swaying and held the pendulum away from her body, feeling the chain against her fingers as it roamed around the map, and before she knew it, she could breathe again, warmth spreading through her body. It was like a song that only she could feel, dancing under her skin, this was how it could be so addictive ...

The pendulum went thunk.

Alex opened her eyes.

The pendulum had indeed thunked, firmly, a few streets behind the promenade.

"Did we find her?" Alex asked, unable, unwilling even, to stop her runaway grin. "Did we do it?"

"No 'we' about it," Elizabeth said, crouching down to examine the pendulum's exact location before looking up at Alex with a wry smile. "*You* did that. With *your* Power."

"Can it really feel that good?" Alex asked, rushing towards her. "Power?"

It should've been impossible to just trip into someone's gaze like that. And then that blood-soaked gaze flickered down to Alex's mouth and—

The pendulum skidded across the map, dragging Alex like a toddler being pulled along by a Dobermann and knocking her onto the coffee table.

"Coming down Hangman's Hill," Elizabeth read, putting on the most incredible milk-bottle glasses Alex had seen since Douglas Hurd. "Is it really called Hangman's Hill?"

"Welcome to Coldharbour," Alex said, trying to untangle herself from the pendulum as it skidded onto the map promenade with a bright, burgundy glow. "Can I have a hand? Please?"

Elizabeth shook her head and squinted at the map.

"Gotta stay connected."

"Oh, great," Alex gasped, clambering over the table before she got her wrist burned off, "I'll just stay connected while you just go and find her or what?"

"If the pendulum's right," Elizabeth said, jumping up and rushing to the window, "she should be under us ..."

Alex barely heard the "now".

"Elizabeth?"

The pendulum was crossing the promenade.

The pendulum stopped.

Right in the middle of the sand.

"Stay here."

"Following the pendulum?" Alex asked, ducking as Elizabeth leapt over the map and ran out of the flat. "Elizabeth ..."

The pendulum still wasn't moving. Alex set it swinging again, but this time it just swung and swung and swung, just like it had when they'd been looking for their father, for David, a man she thought could be Dead, and it was swinging interminably even as the anxiety squeezed ...

Alex's heart battered her ribs as she unfurled the chain from her fingers. Five – five things she could—

Glass burst through the lounge.

Alex skidded into the kitchenette and slammed into the cupboards, her skin stinging as she tried to shake off the shards biting into her legs, her arm, her hands, and once her Power healed the scratches, she wiped the blood on her jeans and clambered up the cupboard.

There was Power in the air.

Power that felt dark and wrong in that horrible, just-about-familiar way, like recognising someone who should be a stranger.

Alex staggered across the glass, cringing at its crunch as she stumbled towards what had been the window.

Elizabeth was glowing moonlight-silver on the beach, but the other person, the attacker, the *enemy*, was absolutely surging with Power, erupting in thick, dark waves that were battering Elizabeth, and there, between them, a flash of pink hair on the sand—

Elizabeth fell.

The figure loomed over her.

He – it – whatever – *burned* with Power.

Alex held her breath.

He froze.

Elizabeth hadn't, she was scrambling back on the shingle, but Alex had done it.

For the first time in *years*, she'd frozen something.

Someone.

But how long would it hold?

Alex leant out the window. Jumping that far, she had no idea if the levitation would kick in, not after so long, so she turned and she lurched her way out of the flat and down the concrete stairs and across the empty promenade, just the rumble of pub noise and the roar of the waves.

"Is she alright?" Alex yelled, stumbling down the rocks towards the women. "Elizabeth, is she alright?"

They couldn't have been too late, it had only been seconds ...

Elizabeth launched herself at Alex, knocking the breath out of her as her leather-clad arms wrapped around her and then ...

The Power scorched them.

Except it didn't.

Burgundy and silver flooded the beach, throwing the dark Power right back at the attacker, catching his arm.

Alex and Elizabeth stared at each other, wide-eyed.

"Was that you or me?" Alex whispered.

Elizabeth just threw Alex in Pandora's direction and ran at the attacker.

Alex smacked against wet sand, struggling towards Pandora as the tide rushed in.

Just unconscious. She must've just been unconscious. Alex reached ...

Power singed the hairs off her arm.

The battle had restarted.

But Alex couldn't care, not when Pandora was being washed into the waves, rolling into the tide, and every time Alex almost captured her hand or her arm, they were being pulled further into the sea, water sloshing around Alex's waist as it yanked her in – down – towards – away – up to her neck and she was screaming Pandora's name, crashing her arms through the waves until a strong arm dragged her up and out of the water.

"She's still in there," Alex spluttered, head hitting the hard sand.

"She's Dead, Alex," Elizabeth groaned. "If she were still alive, he'd have stuck around and finished off the lot of us."

Alex smacked herself onto her front, squinting around the beach.

The attacker had gone. Vanished into the darkness.

With a salty retch, Alex heaved herself onto her elbows and looked at Elizabeth, who was also doing her best impression of a beached catfish. Blood ran through the canals of her scars.

"You're hurt," Alex said, trying to reach out with heavy shoulders.

Elizabeth grimaced, a spark of silver Power on her temple.

"Power's depleted," she said, with a lot less teeth and a lot more blood in her mouth than she had five minutes ago. "I can't. Not yet."

"Come on," Alex said, slipping on the sand as she reached for Pandora's soggy bag, "or we'll get washed away and all."

Elizabeth nodded and took Alex's hand to wobble to something like standing.

"I told you to stay inside."

"Really?" Alex asked, reluctant to release Elizabeth's hand, sand sticky between their fingers, so she simply didn't. "Is that what you're taking from this?"

Elizabeth shook her head, her hair limp around her still-healing face, giving her an odd vulnerability that made something in Alex break.

"What do we do?" Alex sobbed, starting to shiver. "We just—"

Elizabeth tugged her into a tight embrace, fingers clutching skin, pulling at hair as they shuddered together in the cold, their chests heaving against each other, reminding them – reminding Alex – that they were alive. At least they were alive.

"We've got company," Elizabeth murmured into Alex's hair, as a pair of familiar voices grew louder and louder with the shaking of the shingle.

Sam and Shaz slid down the beach hand in hand, and even in the low light, Alex could imagine their faces.

If Shaz had thought she looked a state before ...

"Did you really try again?" Sam yelled, which had Alex flinching into Elizabeth, who tightened her arms around her. "The first – how selfish—"

"Who the hell do you think you are?" Elizabeth asked, her lip curling at Sam with such confusion and disgust that Alex was sure the look had a name.

"Who—"

Sam spluttered, looking more like the boy Alex had left at the altar than the *Acting* DCI he was meant to be now. She'd always thought he was tall, coming from a family of short-arses as she did, but Elizabeth's glare was dead level with his.

"Who are *you*?" he demanded, flipping out his police warrant.

Teeth chattering on every consonant, Alex told Elizabeth to tell Sam the story. At least Elizabeth had half a chance of being believed. When Elizabeth finished, Shaz slapped Sam on the arm with a knowing flash of her eyes.

"See?" Shaz said. "I told you she wouldn't."

One hand on his side and the other in hair that didn't look as dark as Alex remembered, Sam panted for a moment before shrugging at Alex.

Was that it, then? The same coldness that had settled between them after *that* day, when Alex (and Matthew) had proven to be such a disappointment?

"So, how did she die?" Sam asked, kneeling down to inspect the blood-speckled sand like he was in an episode of *Dalziel and Pascoe*.

Yep. There it was. Sammy Meyer could do no wrong, but the moment Alex tried to decide something for herself ...

"I thought coppers could read between the lines?" Elizabeth snapped, clamping her mouth shut when Alex pinched her side.

"Burned again?" Shaz gasped. "Jesus, her arm was bad enough! And I've seen some things in A&E."

"So what do you actually expect me to do?" Sam asked. "With no actual evidence? And no body?"

"There have been other bodies though," Alex said, turning in Elizabeth's embrace. "That girl, Heather. And the others."

"They were just mysterious deaths," Elizabeth said. "I was just making conversation."

"The blood I touched," Alex explained, "it had Power in it, Elizabeth. I thought you knew. At least one of the victims had Power."

"You could see Power in the blood?"

"Couldn't you?"

Elizabeth was frowning at her, like she'd said something wrong, but Alex didn't even know in what way that could possibly be wrong. People with Power could see Power. That was just a fact. Wasn't it?

"Is this a serial killer then?" Shaz asked. "Going after people with Power?"

"But there was nothing in the description of the bodies," Elizabeth argued, glancing away from Alex. "Nothing suggesting Power wounds—"

And then Sam just had to open his big mouth and ask...

"Do Power wounds always look like burns?"

6
Shiver by Shiver

She'd almost got it.

Alex had almost got Pandora's hand.

She had let Elizabeth's shower batter and scorch her skin as she scrubbed away the salt sticking to her neck, her cheeks, her fingers. It was too hot, too hard, but at least she had known under the brilliant white light that it couldn't be the sea, that chill, churning sea.

It had been there, the hand had been there, soft, slippery ...

Lifeless.

And now, in the doldrums of the darkest night, they were back out there at the beach wall, Alex in borrowed pyjamas that swamped her and Elizabeth in swathes of black silk that pooled around her ankles.

Elizabeth lit a white pillar candle with a spark of silver Power.

"Have you done this before?" Alex whispered. "Held a vigil?"

"Once or twice," Elizabeth murmured. "Rumour has it, the person's soul should follow the light of the candle onwards."

Alex turned towards the sea and hissed at the force of the wind scraping sand against her skin. She had tried so hard to grab Pandora's hand ...

She wiped the tears from her eyes, ready to make out it was just the bitter, strident wind and not the utter wretchedness of being so close ...

So close.

Elizabeth said her name.

Alex shook her head, which did nothing to drive away the misery that was resurging through her soul, smashing its way through the shoddy defences that she'd spent a month rebuilding, only to find they were as flaky and fickle as the Victorian groynes overtaken by flotsam and jetsam.

"I'm fine," she ended up saying, not yet able to look Elizabeth in the eye to lie. "Doesn't matter."

"It does to you."

"How many people in Coldharbour d'you reckon have Power?" Alex asked the candle.

"There's a concentration of Power here," Elizabeth explained, "but they estimate one in a thousand people have Power, so ten, plus a few more to account for the concentration."

Well, that explained how Alex had gone so long without meeting someone else with Power.

"It's gonna keep happening, isn't it?" Alex said. "Unless we stop it."

"I suspect so."

Alex glanced at Elizabeth and snorted softly at the little dribble of blood at the corner of her mouth.

"You look like a vampire," Alex said, smiling despite herself. "I think your teeth are growing back in."

Elizabeth cringed and wiped the blood from her mouth.

"It's fine," Alex said, "it's not as bad as you think it is."

"Tell your face."

Alex glanced at her watch. Almost midnight.

"Whatever you're thinking," Elizabeth said, "you agreed to keep out of trouble."

Annoyingly ...

Elizabeth was right.

Sam could only confirm with the barmaid that Pandora had definitely never entered the pub, at which Elizabeth had sneered with a bruised mouth.

Anyway, they all agreed that the killer probably wouldn't be striking again that night, not after getting a bit of kicking from Alex and Elizabeth, and with the total absence of evidence and witnesses they could all probably get some rest and regroup in the morning. Except, although Alex's attempt at cheery accord had somehow worked on both Sam and Shaz, the smirk in Elizabeth's eyes was ...

Well, how it usually was.

"I don't know what you mean," Alex said, looking straight at her with a wan smile.

"You said you wanted to sleep here," Elizabeth replied.

Alex had declared that there was no point going back to the old house because Harry probably wasn't there, nor any point going to Sam and Shaz's without Maddie there either. How could she explain that she just felt safer with a stranger?

"And I will," Alex said, "once we've done this. Anyway, there's more than enough room in your flat. Seeing as you don't really have anything to unpack."

"Excuse me?"

"You said you hadn't finished unpacking," Alex explained, watching Elizabeth's eyes narrow just ever so slightly. "I've got boxes everywhere."

"I travel light."

"Do you travel a lot?"

"Is this an interrogation?" Elizabeth laughed.

"It's called making conversation," Alex said, feeling her neck warm as she realised that she'd clearly lost her touch. "You know, getting to know the person whose sofa you're gonna be sleeping on."

"*Chaise longue.* Or you could sleep in my bed," Elizabeth suggested with such innocence that Alex tried to stop her own brain short-circuiting.

Instead, Alex landed on that moment in the pub, seeing Elizabeth for the first time in that dress, dark and iridescent like magpie wings, and finally mustered the courage to ask:

"Where were you going tonight? You looked ... beautiful."

Alex thought that Elizabeth would've had the good grace to blush, but instead she just looked at Alex as if she had sustained a nasty bang to the head. Well, Alex had sustained a nasty bang to the head, but she had already thought Elizabeth had something of Carolyn Bessette-Kennedy about her when she was just wearing that ratty old apron.

Elizabeth pulled a soggy slip of paper from her dressing gown pocket, flinging it in Alex's direction. Some kind of receipt or ...

Ticket.

Crossgate Theatre.

Tosca.

20.00. *Friday* 1 *October* 1999.

Seat D2.

"I was gonna be late anyway," Elizabeth said, "I knew that when you offered me another drink. And before you ask, I was going alone."

"I'm still sorry, though," Alex said. "We don't tend to get operas down here all that often."

When Elizabeth shrugged yet again, Alex felt a strange, indefinable urge to rectify something.

"You're taking the bed," Elizabeth said, just about smiling again. "I don't need you moaning about your back in the morning, all cos you won't bother healing yourself."

"I really can't make you sleep on that chaise longue," Alex said, "not after ..."

Not after the healing experience that had made Alex feel like she was knee-deep in some trench somewhere, stinking of other people's blood.

Elizabeth had almost tripped on the glass as they'd got her back into the flat. Shaz had slipped into doctor mode and Sam was barking out a new question with every breath until Alex had told him to be quiet, because that was the problem, wasn't it? If she was going to use her Power in that moment, she was going to need to concentrate.

Because Elizabeth's Power was still exhausted.

Because Elizabeth had dragged her sodden dress up her leg to reveal a kneecap that was so far out of place, Alex had to catch the bile in her throat before she could even look away.

Because Shaz had turned to Alex to ask how good her healing was.

What a question that was.

Not as good as it could've been if she hadn't been suppressing her Power for half her life, had been the obvious answer. Either way, Matthew had always been the better healer. He had more patience, even the time Sam fell out of the tree during that stupid dare right before their O levels and Shaz was panicking and Alex blurted out that she was pregnant.

So, instead of replying, Alex had taken a step closer and held back another retch at the sight of a distended, bruised, gleaming *blob* where Elizabeth's ankle should've been. The skin was angry, a queasy swirl of colours where her Power had tried and failed to rectify the snap.

Shaz had been explaining in her matter-of-fact way that the blob, or rather, broken ankle, represented six weeks of healing for a normal person but Elizabeth clearly wasn't listening. She was staring at Alex, increasingly pale, increasingly blotchy, increasingly sweaty.

Even the not-bloodshot eye was bloodshot.

So, because Elizabeth's Power was exhausted, because she had a dislocated knee and a broken ankle and a livid scrape of bruises and grazes up her arm, because of another feeling Alex was nowhere near ready to confront, she climbed onto the chaise longue and took Elizabeth's clammy, tepid hand, warning her to watch her nails.

And as their fingers had entwined, as pure Power had flowed between them, Alex found herself arrested in Elizabeth's gaze, which wasn't as angry as she had thought. More wounded, frustrated, frightened.

Typical doctor.

Shaz had taken the opportunity to reset Elizabeth's knee "while they were so distracted".

But the marvel had come next:

Elizabeth thrumming with Power, at first magenta and then silver.

Alex hadn't been able to help but watch as Elizabeth had breathed in and then out, Power weaving through her body as the bruises melted away, the grazes stitched together, and, with just a touch of concentration on her face, her ankle snapped upright and deflated. Leaning forward, Elizabeth had stretched out an arm and flexed her fingers, the crumbs of glass rising in the air and fusing together as they floated towards the window, where the pane now sat, almost perfect, framing its owner in the darkness.

Elizabeth's voice jolted Alex out of the memory.

"You mistake me for someone who sleeps," she said, tightening the belt of her dressing gown.

"It's only midnight."

"And our arsehole of a murderer'll still be around in the morning."

"And what?" Alex asked. "In the meantime, I'm just meant to pretend that I didn't see an innocent woman get murdered in front of me? And washed away? Like she didn't even exist?"

The spark in Elizabeth's stare slipped away, like stars blinking out of the night sky.

Alex muttered an apology and turned away.

The candle flickered between them as they sank into silence.

Elizabeth took the blanket she'd been holding in her arms and draped it over Alex's shoulders and then her own, searching Alex's eyes until she nodded and let Elizabeth shuffle closer.

"So," Elizabeth said, "Shaz is your sister."

"Yep."

"I'm not wanting to pry …"

"She's as pasty as you," Alex said. "I think you can guess that one of us is adopted."

Elizabeth chuckled to herself, nodding at the candle.

"What's the story, then?" she asked.

"Long story short," Alex sighed, "her real mum, *Belinda*, was what they used to call 'flighty'."

"Abandoned her on your doorstep?"

"More that Shaz was round for a sleepover and she never came to pick her up. Last we heard she'd buggered off to Spain."

"No old man on the scene?" Elizabeth asked, and when Alex shook her head, "And your parents just took her in?"

"It was just Carrie – I mean, Mum," Alex said. "And yeah."

"That was very kind of your mother."

There had never been any question of it, really. Shaz had already been spending so much time at the house and she was the one child guaranteed to actually do everything Carrie said. Teas turned into sleepovers, mornings turned into days, weekends turned into whole half-terms, and so on. It really hadn't been difficult at all for Shaz to complete her assimilation into their crackpot family.

"It was just the right thing to do," Alex said, "I wouldn't call it kindness. Anyway, then Mum died, so Uncle Harry came home."

And luckily, he hadn't made them homeless either.

Where would they have ended up?

In the sea, like Pandora?

Dying alone, thinking no one cared?

Alex managed a shallow sigh and wafted her finger-tips over the flame, letting her Power dance through the fire.

"Any other brothers or sisters?" Elizabeth asked.

No.

That's what Alex had said for nine years, ever since *that* day.

No, Alex just had a sister.

But now, something was changing. If Time and Space were sand, the grains were shifting, washing back in, but not in the same order as before. The world was *happening*.

"I have a brother," Alex confessed, clinging to the wall until shards of stone crumbled under her grip. "Matthew. He's called Matthew."

"And do you know where Matthew is?" Elizabeth asked.

Alex just shook her head, trying to clench away the burning in her chest.

"And then there's Sam," she said. "We've all been friends since primary school and he's Maddie's father—"

"I thought Meyer was engaged to Shaz?" Elizabeth said, her scars crinkling when she screwed up her nose.

"Yep," Alex said, "I did say I didn't marry him."

And with one confession, came another.

"My daughter's been living with them for the past month," Alex whispered into the still night air. "I've been away. I've been ill. Mentally, not physically, though I know I look like I've taken a bit of a battering—"

"You look lovely to me."

Elizabeth's earnestness seemed to take them both by surprise, according to the blush creeping up the scarred throat in front of Alex.

"I'll take it," Alex rushed out before *that* thought could settle and take a hold. "The job, I mean. If it's still going. If you really were offering."

"Really?" Elizabeth asked, "It'll be a lot of mopping—"

"And investigating?" Alex suggested.

"Perhaps a wee, light bit of investigating. Just round the edges."

"Oh yeah," Alex said, letting herself drift closer, "Just round the edges. Cos we've got Pandora's backpack upstairs …"

"Well," Elizabeth sniffed, a smile creeping onto that crooked, kissable mouth, "Inspector Meyer didn't ask after it—"

"Which means it doesn't matter if we have it and maybe have a little look-see—"

"It's mainly soggy paintings and crumbs," Elizabeth said, "but we are technically involved now. The killer has involved us."

"Exactly!" Alex said, "We're involved! It's like an X-files thing. Mulder and Scully."

"Which one of us is which?" Elizabeth asked, scrunching her nose again. It even changed her freckles.

"Well," Alex said, left catching her breath again, "you're the ginger, I'm the loon."

Elizabeth retrieved her hand from inside the blanket and held it aloft, the moonlight casting a skeletal sheen over her pale fingers.

"Deal?" she asked.

"Deal," Alex said, giving the hand a firm shake.

Cold.

Elizabeth's touch was always so cold.

"Miss Wilde," Elizabeth said, her grin revealing what was left of her perfectly imperfect teeth, "I think it's going to be a pleasure doing business with you."

That bloody smile. It kept wrenching something in Alex's soul, like she'd been hooked by a fishing rod.

"Are the teeth coming back in funny?" Elizabeth asked, breaking the spell when she snatched back her hand, "cos that's happened to me before. I've got some Theramed—"

"No! No," Alex blurted out, cringing as Elizabeth started pushing her knuckles against her canines. "They're fine. Normal. They weren't straight to begin with, were they?"

Elizabeth shook her head and gave her tongue an experimental gnaw, but Alex didn't quite have the attention span to be mortified, not when she could feel they were being watched.

From the sea.

That chill, churning sea.

Alex squeezed Elizabeth's arm, knowing that her stare alone would guide her.

"Can you feel that?" she whispered.

Elizabeth gave her the tiniest nod, her hair tickling Alex's throat.

"It's ... It's not ..."

"Pandora," Elizabeth murmured, "no."

"The killer?" Alex asked. "Somehow?"

Another infinitesimal incline of the head.

But there was something, some*one*, far beyond the shallows, watching them. Alex knew and Elizabeth knew too, because even in the darkness that the half-moon couldn't touch and the street light could only dream of reaching, even before the glow from the lighthouse could inch near it, there was someone there.

In the waves.

Watching them.

Watching them specifically with a strength of intent that insinuated its way under Alex's skin.

Like she was being searched.

She could name all those waves, but whatever it was in them ...

Something snuffed out the flame on the candle.

But there was no wind.

Alex thought her stomach would've lurched or her chest would've clenched, but nothing came. She was a fish caught in a net.

"I suggest," Elizabeth said, taking Alex's hand, "we go back into the warm."

The warm. What even was that anymore?

"But who is it?" Alex asked. "Can you tell? Cos I can't."

"It doesn't matter," Elizabeth said, pressing Alex into the road so fast, they nearly tripped over the blanket. "You of all people shouldn't be out here during the witching hour."

"But—"

"Don't look round."

Alex twisted in the blanket.

"Please," Elizabeth said, "don't."

"Why?" Alex asked, as they stopped in front of the café. "Elizabeth, what is it?"

"There are things out there that would love to see your soul," Elizabeth whispered.. "The Flitting, the Undead, vengeful spirits ..."

"And what's in the water?"

"Something that doesn't belong here," Elizabeth said, her stare as urgent as her voice. "Please, Alex."

Alex could've turned to look. She could still feel whatever or whoever it was still looking at her, after all. The temptation was there. Of course it was there, but Elizabeth didn't exactly strike her as the type of person to plead unless it really was necessary, so instead, she took Elizabeth's hand and started towards the stairs.

The witching season had begun.

Saturday 2 October 1999

7
Under a Spell

Alex runs through colour.

The woman runs faster.

A flash of bright hair.

A glimpse of white skin.

A shard of a smile with too many teeth.

No time to wonder who she could be.

Alex chases her from indigo to purple to violet to green to scarlet to gold to blue to silver until she's almost close enough to touch when they lunge into pink—

Black.

But it's a black that Alex can see and understand, as profound as the thought that told her Elizabeth's last name in The Neptune's Arms, and it tastes of petrichor as much as it feels like pins and needles, and even if she doesn't know where she is or even when she is, she knows it's the Ether.

She couldn't explain what the Ether is even with a gun to any part of her body that won't just instantly heal, but it's always been the answer to any question about Power that she's actually bothered to ask anyone.

Where does Power come from?

The Ether.

What's Power made of?

The Ether.

The Ether's as much a part of her blood as all the platelets and cells Shaz tried to explain once, just as it dances in the air between oxygen and nitrogen.

Everything in this room is the Ether.

The enormous ebony grandfather clock, identical to the one in the house hallway, even down to the frozen pendulum.

Ether.

The wonky window – with no wall – staining shadows the colour of blood onto the floor.

Ether.

The table from the study, gushing waves of blood – or is it just the light? – as it transforms and twists its branches into a gleaming slab, it's Ether, it has to be, and Alex can't explain it, but for a heart-stopping moment, she expects to see—

But it's Pandora.

Pandora, pink hair plastered to her grey cheeks, sitting up as the slab collapses into a cascade of shingle.

She opens her mouth as if to speak, but she's choking, rheumy eyes bulging, and she reaches out to Alex like she recognises her, like she does know her, and she's waving her hand towards Alex and then towards her own throat and Alex finally unfreezes and drops to her knees, peering into the darkness of Pandora's mouth, where something's moving ...

No.

It's only moving when Pandora's trying to breathe.

And how can someone Dead breathe?

Alex winces in apology when she brings one hand to Pandora's cheek and hooks her fingers around whatever the hell is in her mouth and pulls, both of them gagging at the jagged, slippery stuff that's catching in the grooves of Alex's fingers.

Seaweed slaps onto the floor.

And of all the things Pandora says ...

"Is this real?"

"I don't know," Alex whispers, staring down at the seaweed, "I have no idea."

She knows Pandora's Dead.

She knows that.

She felt her limp hand slipping away and into the waves.

"I was wrong," Pandora says, holding her arm, "it did hurt. I've never felt pain like it."

"I'm sorry," Alex whispers.

Pandora shakes her head, the flesh of her neck twisting strangely like some sick kind of silly putty, stretching far beyond the realms of reality.

"S'not your fault," she sighs, "you tried."

Real or not, Alex is overtaken by urgency so she asks if Pandora saw him, whoever did this to her. Pandora frowns, but as she takes a moment in the silence, Alex realises what's different.

What's changed.

The clock is ticking.

And a bell is tolling.

"'And Darkness and Decay and the Red Death held illimitable dominion over all,'" a lilting voice announces in the blood-drenched gloom.

The woman steps out from behind? – beside? – *inside?* – the clock, her face cut by shadows, her cascade of blonde hair almost bronze in the strange bloodlight.

Alex drags Pandora into her arms and asks the woman, with all her strange familiarity, who she is.

"How do I look?" the woman asks, tipping her own chin up with the backs of her fingers. "Am I pretty again?"

No, she isn't pretty.

That's not the right word.

Statuesque.

Yes.

Whoever this woman is, she's statuesque in all its forms.

Tall, and not just by Alex's standards, she's all careful moves and cold smiles, with the kind of beatific beauty that wouldn't look out of place on the content face of a Victorian cherub.

But the skin isn't flawless.

It's veined, red, like she's been broken and then pulled back together, but that's not why Alex feels absolutely repulsed by whoever she is.

It's the look in her eyes.

That she's just waiting for Alex to take a step too close so that she can unhinge her jaw and devour her whole.

Whoever this woman is, Alex understands that, despite her smile, she's the opposite of content. No one can possibly be that content with that kind of starvation pulling at every sinew in their body.

And as for beatific ...

Angels don't have fangs.

Alex may have been brought up atheist, but she's pretty sure about that.

"Who are you?" she asks, keeping her hands on Pandora.

"Ask me no questions, I'll tell you no lies." The woman laughs, with a sharp kick of the shingle. "Well ..."

Alex starts.

The woman's so close.

Close enough to breathe on her, if she could breathe on her.

How did she move so quickly?

"What do you see in her?" the woman asks.

"What?"

"Lizzie," the woman says, her plush lips curling into a sneer as she enunciates the name. "What on Earth do you see in her?"

"You mean Elizabeth?" Alex asks. "Elizabeth Black?"

"Elizabeth," the woman says in a deep, grand voice before scoffing, "*Elizabeth Black*. Elizabeth the *Unkillable*. Oh, Lexy. *Can't you see?*"

Silver shines through the room, sending the woman scuttling back into the shadows.

"There she is," the woman says, curling in on herself, but Alex can still see the feral glint in her.

"Alex, get away from her."

Alex looks ...

Looked.

Alex looked down, wondering what the weight was around her legs. Water, dragging at the dressing gown Elizabeth lent her, up to her knees. She stumbled in surprise, her bare feet slipping against the shingle.

She was in the shallows, in the darkness, ice gripping her shins.

She was in the shallows with nothing, no one, in her arms.

Pandora had vanished.

But then Pandora was ...

Pandora was Dead.

Was Alex dreaming?

Elizabeth called her name from the shore, hand outstretched, her face pulled rigid into an expression Alex couldn't work out.

"But—"

"Now, Alex."

"Why don't you come and get her?" the woman asked. "Lizzie?"

Elizabeth wasn't looking at the woman.

She'd look at Alex.

She'd look at the waves.

But she wouldn't look at the woman.

And wherever she looked, it was with that same stiff look, like she couldn't trust her face not to split into a scream.

"Alex," Elizabeth said, both arms out now as her pale, twitching hands beckoned, "come with me."

"Who is she?" Alex asked. "Do you know who—"

"Alex!"

"Lexy!" the woman called with a cackle.

"I don't understand," Alex said, struggling to shake off the sleep that had made her so sluggish.

She had been asleep, hadn't she? Before ...

"Why don't you come and get her, Lizzie?" the woman taunted.

It was a taunt but it was also a good question.

Alex had seen Elizabeth fight off a serial killer.

She had rushed into the water to get Alex out before.

What was she doing staying on the shore?

"I'll tell you anything you want to know," Elizabeth said to Alex, taut with urgency, "just—"

"Will you, though?" the woman asked.

Elizabeth whipped her head up, finally confronting the woman with a snarl that would've chilled Alex if she didn't already feel the cold leeching through her bones.

"You touch her," Elizabeth warned, "you try and *breathe* in her direction—"

"You'll what?"

The woman's voice was right behind Alex.

"Kill me again?"

Alex should never have turned round.

The woman had vanished.

And what was in her place had haunted some of the worst of Alex's nightmares for half her life.

The Shadow.

It roared with pink Power, feasting on the life in the air.

"It's good to see you, Lexy," it said with the woman's voice.

She was the Shadow?

A hand scorched through Alex's chest and she—

Gasps for breath, the sea seizes her, and she tries to scream but there's no air and what's the point when she's so tired and it's easier, much easier to just give up, just like before, because she can't even feel the cold anymore and she can't feel anything anymore, even as the water forces itself down her throat and there's—

Alex.

A voice in the darkness.

"Alex!"

Again.

"Alexandra!"

Alex tries to shout, but her throat is salt-scratched, there's blood in her mouth—

A cold hand seizes hers.

It tugs, yanks, *drags* her from the waves and back into the Land of the Living, where Alex spluttered out a raw breath, her heart stuttering in her chest as she clung to Elizabeth.

"You're with me," Elizabeth whispered, her fingers digging into Alex's shoulders. "Stay with me."

The Shadow had gone.

Darkness had fallen back into its rightful place.

"Where was I?" Alex gasped, sinking into the sand.

"Where did she touch you?" Elizabeth asked, shaking Alex by her arms when she couldn't reply. "Alex, where did she touch you?"

Alex raised a trembling hand to her chest ...

And retched up half the sea over Elizabeth.

Including ribbons of bottle green seaweed, just like ...

"Did she burn you?" Elizabeth demanded, pushing Alex far away enough to tug at the dressing gown. "Alex, did she burn you? Alexandra!"

Alex shook her head, salt and sick burning her mouth as she yanked down her T-shirt, water slopping against her skin.

"She didn't burn you?" Elizabeth whispered, placing her hand over Alex's sternum, but there was no warmth to its weight. How could she run that cold?

"Where did I go?" Alex asked.

Elizabeth didn't reply. She just buried her face in the crook of Alex's neck, hand still on her chest, almost silent but for the shudder in her shoulders.

Cold bit at Alex's bones.

She nestled her head against Elizabeth's shoulder. She could've just slept there, rested there, finally found peace in those arms.

"It was her earlier," Alex realised, her mind warming up at least, "during the witching hour. When you wanted me inside. Wasn't it?"

"Aye," was the one word she got in return.

"What's the time?" Alex mumbled.

"Just gone five."

"Already?" Alex asked, letting Elizabeth pull her even closer.

Blanket.

She'd brought the blanket out.

That was the weight around Alex's shoulders.

"I'd only come out for a glass of water," Elizabeth murmured. "Front door was wide open, the blanket in the hallway."

"I'm sorry."

Elizabeth pushed her away just far enough to finally look her in the eye.

"I've never really sleepwalked before," Alex said. "It's not like I just wander off into the night—"

"You were lured into The Other Side," Elizabeth said shortly as she fluffed the blanket around Alex's neck. "Not the same thing."

"The what?" Alex asked.

"The Other Side," Elizabeth said, frowning at Alex as if she was having to explain some kind of basic concept like the alphabet or gravity, "You must ... No?"

"The other side of what?"

"I just assumed ..." Elizabeth shook her head and dragged Alex up, despite mumbled protests of being too cold to move.

A tired glare was enough for Alex to decide that maybe she could move after all.

Not another word was said, not until Elizabeth had guided her up the beach, across the promenade and back into the flat, where Elizabeth locked the door and the windows, poured salt over every threshold, and finally, scraped a flannel over Alex's cheeks and asked:

"What do you know about dreaming?"

"If you're gonna start talking symbolism," Alex replied, "can it wait till—"

"The Other Side is where we wander when we're asleep," Elizabeth explained. "It's also where you were taken just then. It's the Realm of Dream and Death. When we dream, we go there. When we die, we go there, before we, apparently, move on to somewhere else."

"Apparently?"

"The point is," Elizabeth said, peeling sand out of Alex's broken nails with a heart-twinging care, "most of what's on The Other Side is just memory, illusion. It's a one-way mirror. You see them, they don't see you. You hear them, they can't hear you. You can't really touch it, it can't really touch you, unless you encounter something that shouldn't be there."

"Like that spirit?"

"Aye," Elizabeth said, her face contorting into an echo of a snarl before she clenched it away, "like that."

"I felt the Ether there," Alex decided to say, "on The Other Side. Is it all Ether?"

"There's more Ether there, aye. Only people with Power can tell."

"And Pandora was there," Alex said. "She looked Dead. She was all grey and she was choking on seaweed. Was that real?"

"She might be struggling to move on." Elizabeth sighed, pushing herself up from the chaise longue. "Want a drink?"

"Bit early in the morning, isn't it?"

"We've had a terrible shock," Elizabeth said. "How are you feeling?"

"I'm cold inside," Alex admitted, feeling like a child at how she just didn't have the words for such a strange sensation, a morbid dread seeping through her in sluggish surges that reminded her of that frigid water gripping her ankles.

Elizabeth waited and watched her with those tired eyes, the last traces of panic still there in the clench of her jaw, the press of her lips.

"It's not cold," Alex realised, "I don't feel cold. I feel ..."

Dead.

"I don't feel like I'm alive."

Finally, a feeling, or a phantom of a feeling as Alex fumbled for her own wrist, trying to find—

Cold fingers pressed against her throat.

"Definitely alive," Elizabeth said, her thumb ghosting over Alex's skin, "promise."

Alex found herself reaching up in a shuddery imitation, trembling as she tried to find a pulse under those pale scars ...

There.

The faintest throb.

It was slow and sure like the tide inching its way in and out, but just like those waves, those black waves in that chill and churning sea, it was there.

"She has that effect on people," Elizabeth said, squeezing Alex's hand. "It'll pass."

Alex tried to push away flashes of memory, of the spirit board, of their hideous, *hideous* mistake, but as she watched Elizabeth busying herself with the bottle and two heavy-bottomed glasses, she was left with the lingering feeling that Elizabeth knew the Shadow too.

They'd had a terrible shock, after all.

8
Tears Turned to Dust

And Darkness and Decay and the Red Death held illimitable dominion over all.

Thirteen words which greeted Matthew when he awoke that morning.

He knew where they were from but he had no idea why.

Why now?

But no matter, because that was an hour and twenty-six minutes ago and if anything helped him struggle through interminable day after interminable day it was the structure, the routine, and now, post-shower, he opened his diary and commenced his checking-off:

06:00: run – 10km

07:00: make coffee, shower

07:15: dress, drink coffee, smoke cigarette

Matthew consulted his wristwatch: twenty past seven. Close enough. He was dripping water onto his tiles and the scent of mint was heavy in the air, but he had been waylaid by no fewer than three acquaintances on his run, so the fact he hadn't got round to dressing himself was moot. He would commence work promptly – just the light administration: paperwork on completed cases, responding to minor enquiries, et cetera, et cetera.

Of course, that waited until he finally dried and dressed himself in his most casual suit, sleeves rolled up, jacket over the back of his chair, in the knowledge that he could be called to represent a client with no notice at all.

His second cup of coffee was placed in the top left-hand corner of his desk, the desk which faced away from the window for fear of distraction, and Matthew ensured the window was locked open, just enough to allow the sound of rolling rain and just a touch of a cold breeze to slip through.

Everyone thought Paris in the rain was romantic.

It was actually just as cold and grime-riddled as everywhere else fifty degrees north in October, which was exactly how Matthew liked it.

Nine years of speaking another language could make someone a different person if they tried hard enough and Matthew had been amazed to discover how polite and eloquent he could be in French, to his clients, to his colleagues, and especially to his assistant, an apparently attractive young woman whom he had gently been trying to dissuade in the most professional and polite manner for the better part of three years.

It was at two minutes past nine that Matthew took an impromptu break for another cigarette and another coffee and another paracetamol from the packet he had bought after his run, as the back of his head had been twinging all morning. In fact, the pain had started the night before well, the early evening, when halfway through representing a client in an interview, it felt like someone had taken a mallet to his head. One of the police officers had said something about migraines, but Matthew could hardly have told her that he had never suffered so much as a headache in his life and therefore it was highly unlikely for his brain, *Matthew Wilde's* brain, to be turning against him.

It could have been in sympathy. It could have been, but Matthew had received no phone calls to suggest that something else had happened, therefore ...

Unless something had also happened to ...

Matthew returned to his administration with trembling hands, cigarette burning down on the ashtray. They would be fine. She would be fine. People without Power could die by simply falling over awkwardly, but people with it, surely ...

What was the point of healing, otherwise? It had to be some kind of catastrophic injury, like when their mother ...

That was fifteen years ago.

Matthew was a different person back then, a child.

A child who had sat in that study, night after night, trying to work out what had gone so wrong, how that *thing* had been allowed in, and why ...

Why his mother's ghost hadn't yet come to him.

Perhaps she would have if he had dared to visit her corpse, like ...

The coffee cup shook with frustration.

Well, that was an aspect of his Power that rarely made itself known, so rarely, in fact, he'd almost forgotten he had it entirely. From David's line, they'd always assumed, seeing as neither their mother nor their uncle had ever shown anything that could be described as telekinetic. No, their mother had to resort to picking up a plate to fling it at a wall (where it would shatter into a thousand pieces, just as she had). His sister just had to look at a piece of crockery to have a cupboard's worth wrecking itself in an unnecessary cacophony.

The cup trembled again, teetering on the very edge of the table.

With his hand, Matthew pushed it away from the corner, smoothing his palm over the sharp corner of the desk.

Perhaps he should have paid her after all.

Matthew picked up the phone. She had only given him the number on the off-chance, in the absolute *unlikelihood* that he would ever need to phone her, but his headache was strengthening, it was crowding his mind, and the number was punched in before he even realised.

It rang.

And rang.

And on the third ring, Matthew was ready to put the phone down—

"Hello?"

It couldn't have been.

When she repeated herself, Matthew realised he hadn't said a word.

So, in his best French accent, he forced out:

"Uh, *bonjour*, may I speak to Mademoiselle Black?"

"I'm afraid Elizabeth's otherwise indisposed," she said. "Can I take a message for you?"

Her voice was cracked around the edges (by age, he supposed, certainly not smoking like his), but it was her voice.

It was Lexy's voice.

It was Lexy.

"*Oui*," Matthew eventually said, "Just that her friend in Paris wanted to say... *bonjour*?"

He winced.

Was that the best he could do?

"And your name?" Lexy asked.

His name? Any of the variations Matthew could use, and indeed had used in the past: Harry Wilder, David Sharpe, Sam Evans, she would see straight through.

Besides, he was pretending to be French.

It really wasn't as if Elizabeth or Matthew had even been caught up in the social whirl, and nearly everyone they knew there was now Dead, and therefore it really only could be him calling from Paris and it was almost irresistible to tell Lexy to sod off, but through gritted, extra Parisian teeth, he said:

"James *La Souris*."

"I'll let her know, Mr Luhsoree," Lexy said, and although Matthew knew he should mutter his *merci beaucoups* and have done with it, he found himself saying:

"May I ask your name, mademoiselle?"

"Oh," Lexy said, that lightly surprised tone in her voice, the one she used to use when Matthew caught her stepping absent-mindedly off the promenade into traffic, "it's Alex."

Of course it was. She wouldn't have introduced herself to a perfect stranger using his name for her, but even so, the sensation creeping through Matthew felt remarkably similar to a rusty blade being dug into his chest cavity.

He should never have entertained Elizabeth's suggestion.

"Are you still there?" Lexy – *Alex* – asked.

"Yuh – you are also a friend of Mademoiselle Black?" Matthew asked, clinging to every moment. "I just ask to see if she is settling into Coldharbour?"

The pause was long enough for Matthew to feel his pulse in his throat. Could she have realised, even after all this time, even with the *'Allo 'Allo!* accent?

"You'd have to ask her that," Alex said.

"And yet you are in her apartment alone?"

"I didn't say I was alone, monsieur," she said, polite enough, but Matthew recognised the stiffness of an

Alexandra Wilde one comment away from blowing up an item of furniture, "just that Mademoiselle Black is otherwise indisposed."

He took a breath. And another, when the first didn't reach his chest. He couldn't trip over another word. If he did, surely she would know? Although it wasn't like he was the only one: the king had one, Churchill, even Marilyn Monroe.

He took yet another breath, just to fortify himself, before he asked how Elizabeth was indisposed exactly.

"You can ask her yourself, *monsieur*, she has returned."

Matthew pressed the receiver closer to his ear, determined to catch Alex's mutterings.

"Some French bloke," he heard her say, "Luhsoree? I dunno, Elizabeth, I don't speak French. I said you were indisposed but he wouldn't take no for an answer and I could hardly say you were on the loo – that's what he said his name was, your 'friend in Paris' wishes to say *bonjour* and—"

"*Bonjour*," Elizabeth said, "Monsieur La Souris?"

"Is she still there?"

"*Évidemment*," Elizabeth said, before continuing hesitantly in her French. "But your sister doesn't speak French, right?"

"No," Matthew replied, slipping into his second language, where he was determined to remain. "I can't wait to hear you conduct this entire conversation in French. It'll be as painful for you as it is for me having to listen to you mangling your *accents graves*."

"I don't really have a choice, do I?"

"Can't you send her to the shops?"

"No, I can't," Elizabeth said, before slipping into English. "Alex, can you do me a wee favour? I left my specs in the caff."

"Now are we alone?" Matthew asked.

A pause, long enough to roll his eyes.

"Yes," Elizabeth snapped, "but make it quick. You're giving me a headache."

"Speaking of headaches," he said, "did she hurt herself last night?"

"She's fine," Elizabeth said, her voice darkening over the crackle of the line, "and she can't hear, you know, so you might as well switch back to English as well."

"I know that she's fine," Matthew said, continuing in French. "When did you meet her?"

"Yesterday afternoon."

"I said to check she was alright, not befriend her."

"Aye, well, then we got involved in a murder investigation."

"A mur ..."

Matthew sighed and pinched the bridge of his nose.

"That's not the problem," Elizabeth continued. "Probably."

Matthew groaned, his head thumping. How did normal people walk around like this?

"What kind of problem?"

"You-know-who showed up earlier."

"Voldemort?"

"Who?" Elizabeth said. "No, Eleanor. Now, no getting mad—"

"Elizabeth."

"She managed to find your sister on The Other Side," Elizabeth explained, "while she was sleeping. I don't know why, but she tried to lure her into the sea. Obviously, I got her out of it."

"And why," Matthew hissed, the sudden burst of fear making him nauseous, "would she be trying to hurt my sister?"

"I don't know," Elizabeth said. "To piss me off? That's usually the way it goes, isn't it?"

"Leave Coldharbour."

"Excuse me?"

"Do I need to make it more obvious?" Matthew said. "Leave Lexy alone, leave them all alone. I know enough about Eleanor to—"

"I warned her off; she was just playing with Alex."

"Like she plays with her fucking food, Elizabeth," Matthew said, stumbling back into English. "You're putting my sister in danger."

Elizabeth scoffed. "As if you really care."

It was Matthew's turn to spit out an indignant "Excuse me?"

"I've heard enough about you, Wilde," Elizabeth said, dropping her voice into a venomous murmur, "I've seen the look in her eyes when she says your name."

"Did she tell you?" Matthew asked, that familiarly dark, heavy weight pulling him down. "What I did?"

"Not yet," Elizabeth said, "and I'm not after asking. And *La Souris*? Why are you calling yourself after an old French film?"

"I'm not," Matthew snapped, "it was the first thing that came to mind."

"Mouse?" Elizabeth sneered, and when Matthew found his voice stuck in his throat, "Anyway, excuse me if I don't follow your advice when it comes to Alex."

"She's *my* twin, Elizabeth."

"You're twins?" Elizabeth asked, apparently surprised.

"Yes," Matthew hissed, "and?"

"You never said," Elizabeth replied. "Which one of you's the dominant – aye, thanks, darling."

"Darling?"

"I wasn't talking to you."

"Elizabeth—"

The phone clicked off.

"At least tell her to take care," Matthew muttered, as if the phone could possibly transmit the idea right into Elizabeth's mind.

Perhaps if he tried harder.

Matthew glanced at his watch. Seventeen past nine.

After a further cigarette to steady his nerves, Matthew returned to his work, almost shaking off the strange dread coursing through his body. No, not just dread: Power, stronger than he had felt in years, so strong that his skin was beginning to shimmer turquoise—

Matthew tutted and cracked his hands through the air, vanishing the Power.

No more distractions for today.

He continued perusing his notebook, turning another page where, scrawled in fresh ink, in handwriting he hadn't seen for almost fifteen years on account of its writer being long dead, were two words:

COME HOME

9
Candles are Dark

David Alexander Wilde
1945–1969

After fifteen years, Alex finally dared to return to the grave.

There were places in Coldharbour that Alex probably should've avoided: the sea, the cliffs, the house. But she didn't. Of course she didn't. Well, alright, the house for nine years and she hadn't exactly made an effort to go back there the night before …

Instead, she avoided an empty grave for a missing man, a grave she hadn't known existed until she was nine, when Sam had come back from the synagogue and told her he had stumbled upon a gravestone that shared her name.

Alex had dragged Matthew to the grave as soon as possible, where he'd stood, frowned down at it, and declared in a small, confused voice that the grave was empty.

So she dragged him *back* to the house and into the kitchen, where Carrie was rushing around as usual and Alex announced, ignoring Matthew's insistent prodding at her mind:

We found Daddy.

Carrie had stiffened, hands clenched around a wooden spoon.

So Alex started with the questions:
Why is there a grave with Daddy's name on it?
Why is the grave empty?
Where is Daddy?
Is he really in Heaven?
If Daddy is Jewish, why aren't we Jewish?
Are you Jewish, Mummy?

Carrie had slapped the spoon down, hard enough to make both the twins jump, and told them that there was no such thing as Heaven or God and if they were going to keep prodding, she would block their Power even harder: no healing, no mind-reading, nothing.

And now Alex was being told that there was such thing as The Other Side.

And now Alex was wondering what really happened on the night Carrie died, what really happened when that Shadow had erupted from the spirit board.

And now Alex was trying to remember when it had started, the keeping things from Carrie, and she was pretty sure it was here, at just nine years old: visiting the empty grave as often as she could sneak away, carefully placing another rock on the gravel, talking to a monolith in the hope it would talk back.

The rest of the stone was in Hebrew, but Alex could still recall her fifteenth birthday, kneeling at the grave with Sam. He'd taken her hand in his and traced it over every letter from right to left, revealing their secrets one by one and explaining the Hebrew names.

Their hands entwined and she'd kissed him.

It wasn't long after that ...

Anyway, she'd taken a pebble from the beach this time.

The smoothest, most silvery one she could find, her idea of "sorry".

"Bound up in the bond of life", that's what the stone said, apparently.

Alex hadn't understood it then and certainly didn't now, because how could she, when she didn't even know if David Wilde was Dead or Living?

Something could've happened to him. Like Pandora.

Pandora had been homeless, Alex didn't know her surname, and now her body was lost to the North bloody Sea.

Were there people looking for her? Wondering where she was? Wondering if she was Dead?

Oh, Lexy. Can't you see?

"It's been a while."

Alex smacked against the grave edge, knees bursting with burgundy Power as she winced. With a serial killer on the loose, she really should've heard someone creeping up on her.

She shook her head at the hand Sam was offering and as she stumbled to her feet, knees crying out, told him that she thought the service started later than that.

"You're not the only one with family in here," he said. "Granddad's round the corner, isn't he?"

"At least he's in there," Alex said, staring down at the wrongness of an empty grave. "I don't know who's put the other rocks on it though."

"Who do you think?" Sam asked, holding two gleaming stones in his right hand. "One for Granddad, one for your old man."

"Someone has to, I suppose," Alex muttered, glancing up at Sam.

But then she couldn't help herself.

She never could, not when Sam was standing there with a smile that was so unexpectedly warm that she just had to take in every line and freckle as if she were never going to see them again.

"Got more time for me today, then?" Alex asked, brushing gravel off her knees.

"I thought you were ..."

Sam sighed and shook his head. When had the grey started at his temples? When had his frown deepened?

"And then you said there'd been a murder, Al," he said. "How on earth did you manage to get yourself involved in it this time?"

"It's a long story," Alex said, rolling her eyes when Sam pulled out his notepad like the *Acting* Detective Chief Inspector he was, "like I said last night. Hang on; are you on duty or off?"

"It's Shabbat," Sam replied with a lick of his pencil, "of course I'm off."

"Well, now you've got a promotion, they might be funny about it."

"If they were funny about it," Sam said, "I wouldn't have got it. Anyway, it's temporary."

"Even so," Alex said, giving into that annoying little feeling niggling away at her, "*mazel tov.*"

"But being Acting DCI," Sam continued, "means being in charge of investigating what is now looking like a serial killing spree. How I'm meant to explain that to everyone, I do not know. Any suggestions?"

"We live in a country where unmade beds win prestigious art prizes," Alex replied. "Nothing makes sense anymore."

It really wasn't very often that Sam glared at Alex. In fact, she could probably count the occasions on one hand.

Occasion number one:

Tackling him during football (and therefore *accidentally* breaking his nose, which a nine-year-old Matthew had done a valiant job in attempting to heal, with blood streaming through his tiny glowing fingers) in Year 4.

Occasion number two:

Telling his parents that he'd been suspended (along with Alex *and* Matthew *and* Shaz) before he did – that was after a little incident involving Power, cigarettes, and the school bike shed.

Occasion number three:

At some point during the extremely short-lived custody battle, before they had both decided that they just didn't have the heart for it, with a bit of pushing from Harry.

Nearly nine years without a glare.

"Just don't get involved," Sam said. "Promise me you're not going to charge off and 'investigate' Pandora's murder."

Elizabeth's voice ricocheted around Alex's mind:

You've been missing all the fun.

"Maybe," Alex mumbled, picking at the fresh scar on her hand, "a light bit of investigating won't do anyone harm."

"I don't want to have to find your body again," Sam said.

"I've already apologised for that," Alex whispered, kicking her feet against the path. "And it wasn't my body cos I'm still alive."

"Apologised?" Sam said. "You weren't even in any fit state to say your name! Shaz had to break Christ knows how many of your ribs to bring you back!"

"Then I'll apologise now!"

"I don't want an apology," Sam said, "I don't want you to die!"

Alex wished she hadn't been looking at him. Then she wouldn't have seen that fear flash through his eyes.

"Look," she said, "I didn't plan to stumble across Pandora. Alright, I never want to use my Power again, the same thing I've been saying for nine years but ..."

She sucked in a breath and said, as if she were announcing something truly earth-shattering:

"Things are different now."

"Yeah," Sam said, "you've been in an institution."

"Not that," Alex said. "Something's in the air, and, you know, I was good, you know I was good. I was good at my job and bringing up our daughter and what happened a month ago doesn't just wipe it all out."

"It had been building up a long time before that," Sam said. "We both know that. You've got that look in your eye."

Alex scoffed.

"What look? Cos it ain't the look of love, I can tell you that."

"Like someone's put an idea in your head."

"Someone's put an idea in my head?" Alex laughed. "Cos I have some supposed *look* in my eye?"

"Like when *Matthew* would say something to you and you'd let it fester," Sam said, with the kind of gravity that suggested he was giving her a terminal diagnosis and that actually, it was all her fault. "Or before."

"Before?"

"David," Sam explained, the gavel of judgement finally falling on Alex as he pointed at the grave. "Like when you wanted to find David."

"Nice work," Alex sneered. "The only one you haven't brought up is Mum."

Sam shook his head and raised his hands in surrender. "I just—"

"No," Alex said, suppressing her shudder, which just meant the gravestones started rattling around them instead, "you've brought up the arsehole brother, the missing father, you might as well go for the dead mother. Go on. Get the hat-trick."

She nodded at his dodgy leg and told him that'd be the only way he could nowadays.

"I don't know what you want me to say." Sam sighed. "Your mam gets brought up in arguments too much as it is."

"Not my fault," Alex spat back, "I'm not the one constantly comparing me to her."

"Well, at least she got to thirty-five before topping herself."

Alex's voice failed her.

What could she say to that?

She didn't mean to?

She didn't succeed?

"She was thirty-six," she ended up whispering, "actually."

Sam tutted to himself, the regret seeping from him. At least it overwhelmed the resentment.

"Alex, I didn't mean—"

"No, it's fine," Alex said, letting out a bitter laugh. "If you've been stewing on it for the past month ..."

"Worried sick isn't the same as stewing—"

"Not that you ever called."

"I didn't think you'd want me to."

"'Sam says hi,'" Alex continued. "All that Shaz ever said. Right at the very end. She'd ask me what I was up to, which wasn't much, obviously, cos they wouldn't even let me walk round that piddly little lake on my own, and then she'd tell me about her week and she'd pass on messages from Harry and tell me what Maddie did at school and then, 'Oh, and Sam says hi.'"

"Would you have let me call?" Sam asked, blinking at her with those big, sad, brown eyes of his. "Cos I can put two and two together—"

"Don't flatter yourself," Alex warned, "I wasn't doing it cos of you."

"Then why were you doing it?" Sam said. "Cos there was no note. We looked, all of us, all around that mess of a flat of yours."

"Look," Alex said, a bit put out by her flat being described as 'that mess', "I'm fine. So if you can tell Maddie I'll be round to see her ..."

Sam swallowed. Hard enough to make his throat work.

"Our daughter does know I'm back?" Alex asked. "Yeah?"

Sam's response was to stare at David's grave, the rocks glinting in the silvery sunlight.

"That's a 'no' then," Alex muttered, not bothered enough to hide the sour disappointment leeching through her. "When's she back at yours?"

"By dark; Shaz'll pick her up—"

"By *what*?"

"She's started Duke of Edinburgh—"

"What?" Alex said, "We didn't do DofE."

"Well, I wanted to," Sam said, "and then you three made it clear I'd be on my tod. Anyway, Maddie wants to do it so she's doing her volunteering. She's having to go round keeping old folks company."

"On a Saturday?" Alex asked. "We're talking about the same Matilda Meyer? Can't even get up in time for

Live and Kicking? Old people? What's she doing with old people?"

"We read all the stuff together, I signed the permission slips—"

"Fine, whatever." Alex sighed. "I'll come round tonight. Shaz wants to make sure I'm eating anyway."

The silence sat between them like one of those old duvets in the house: a comfortable familiarity turned heavy, misshapen, awkward.

If David *were* Dead, if he *were* watching them now, those two kids now all grown up at his graveside and just as likely to kiss again as that grave was going to finally get an occupant ...

Well, at least he'd share in the absolute mortification Alex was feeling as she made herself ask:

"How's stuff going for the wedding?"

"Fine," Sam replied. "I feel like I'm at that bloody manor every day at the moment, trying canapes and looking at curtains and where does the DJ want to set up for the dance floor ..."

"Oh," Alex laughed, "you're going all out this time?"

"Mam and Dad are paying for part of it."

"Suddenly found ten grand down the back of a sofa or something?"

"Al ..."

"It's fine," Alex said, "registry office and a pub reception for your kids' mother, but her sister the doctor ..."

"Well," Sam said, "can you imagine the kvetching if they had paid for all *that*? Just for you to ... well, you and Matthew to wreck it all."

"If it wasn't for him," Alex argued, "I wouldn't have waited till we were at the altar, would I?"

Why were they even digging away at an old wound? Was it really that much better to draw blood than just stand there in silence, staring at a stone?

Something shifted between the trees at the other end of the path. By the time Alex turned, it was ...

Gone?

"Well, I'm sure Shaz won't jilt you," she said, squinting into the shadows anyway. "She is the sensible one, after all."

She had meant it when she'd told Elizabeth she was tired.

She'd been tired of it all for a very long time, but most of all, she was absolutely exhausted of pretending that she was alright with everything.

"I'm sorry for flying off the handle last night," Sam said. "I just thought, seeing you on the beach ..."

He squeezed her arm.

She shrugged him off.

"We live in a seaside town, Sammy," Alex said, "I'm gonna be on the beach occasionally."

"Knee deep in water in the middle of the night?" Sam said, frowning when Alex's face fell. "Al?"

"I'll come round later," Alex replied, drifting away from the grave before her thoughts could get hijacked by the Shadow. "So if you can tell Mads to start packing what she needs at Harry's—"

"About that—"

"There's no 'about that' to it," Alex said. "Monday afternoon to Friday morning. As usual. The same as it has been for nine years. I'm back and I'm fine."

"Well, maybe Mads isn't."

"She's our daughter," Alex replied, but her chest was tightening and the fact was ...

Alex had lied. To Sam, to herself.

When he'd declared that she had that look in her eye, like someone had put an idea in her head, and she had laughed him off.

She knew what that look was because it came with that pressure behind her eyes and, even under any anxiety agitating its way through her, a strange, serene certainty that she probably didn't deserve and absolutely couldn't explain.

It was in her again, possessing her, overwhelming the thought that this was just history repeating itself, and even if her smile was tight, even if her gaze lingered just a little too long on the grave ...

"You speak French, don't you?" Alex asked.

"It's not as good as my German and Yiddish," Sam said, "but better than my Hebrew. Definitely better than my Hungarian. Same as my Russian."

"What does *ta soeur* mean?"

"Tosser?" Sam laughed. "I think we both know what that means, Alex."

"No," Alex said, her mind snagging on Matthew, who'd knuckled down so hard in French until he was far more fluent than he'd ever been in English, his speech flowing so freely it had fascinated his twin who would just listen without understanding, "*ta. Soeur.*"

"Your on?"

"You're on?"

"No," Sam said. "Was it *sur*? Or *soeur*?"

"The second one," Alex said, but it was hard to parse a Glaswegian speaking French, "I think. Does that make more sense?"

"Your sister."

"Shaz?"

"No." Sam laughed. "*Ta. Soeur.* Your. Sister."

"*Mais ta soeur ne parle pas Français, non?*"

Alex repeated the sentence to Sam, who paused before saying:

"But your sister doesn't speak French, right?"

"Why can't a Frenchman's sister speak French?" Alex asked.

Sam shrugged and said it just sounded like one of Maddie's riddles, so Alex wished him a *shabbat shalom* before starting back down the path.

"Do you even know what that means?" Sam called.

"Something about a good weekend, yeah?" Alex yelled back, her voice echoing through the graveyard, the sensation stirring in her soul that peace was going to remain as elusive as it ever was.

10
Under the Weather

"Got a moment?"

On a different day, Alex might've noticed the not-always-subtle glances Elizabeth was shooting her between orders.

On that day, however, it took until they were locking up for Alex to wake up and feel the full weight of Elizabeth's stare prickle her skin.

More annoyed at herself than Elizabeth, not that it was any of Elizabeth's business and therefore she would not be enlightened to that particular fact, Alex shoved the broom behind the coat rack.

"Is this where you tell me my sweeping ain't up to scratch and I'm sacked?"

"The sweeping's not the problem," Elizabeth said as she gave the counter a worryingly rudimentary wipe down, "it's the daydreaming."

The rock had remained in Alex's thoughts throughout the day, even as she absent-mindedly swept the café, as her past got dredged up over and over like the waves retching up ...

Well, it seemed to retch up more bloated bodies than shining stones.

Pandora's was only a matter of time.

She'd looked so much younger on The Other Side, maybe only a handful of years older than Maddie, who apparently was now being allowed out until dark and, if Alex had been there, she'd have said something about it, but of course, she hadn't been, had she? She'd tried her hardest to not be there, to never be there again, and that was the thought that really stuck to the side of her soul, not the regrets over David or Carrie or The Shadow because they were old wounds, half-scabbed, not quite healed but picking at them didn't draw that much blood anymore. No, this was fresher, this was *well, Mads isn't.*

A month without Matilda.

This wound would weep forever if it could.

And Alex had no one to blame for it but herself.

"Poor old Joe," Elizabeth continued, "even asked me if this is a care in the community thing."

"Then I'll try and pay more attention," Alex muttered, ripping off her apron. "Apologies."

A cool hand took hers.

It had been probably aiming for the apron.

Too late.

And it had the effect it always seemed to have on Alex, which was to raise a strange warmth in her skin despite the coldness of the fingers wrapped around hers.

"I was wanting to check if you're feeling alright," Elizabeth said.

"Why wouldn't I be?" Alex scoffed, pushing the apron into Elizabeth's hands with all the aggression of someone shoving a turd through a letter box.

"Pandora?" Elizabeth suggested.

Alex resisted her instinct to run at the sea and said:

"You said it yourself. There was nothing we could do."

"It doesn't mean it doesn't hurt."

Alex found herself caught in that gaze again and finally realised what was ...

Not wrong about it, but different.

It wasn't just knowing.

It was weary.

"You've seen this kind of thing before, haven't you?" Alex realised.

"Comes with the territory."

Alex watched Elizabeth shrug that enormous black coat on and asked:

"Power?"

"Sometimes," Elizabeth said, dragging her hair over her shoulder as she wrapped her grey tartan scarf loose around her neck. "Alex, you don't have to help me."

"It's fine," Alex said, before trying out an even bigger lie, "I'm fine. I'm up for it. It's just Power."

She waited, swallowed her heartbeat, and watched the tiniest narrowing of Elizabeth's eyes.

It was just Power.

If Alex had spent the last month telling herself that seeing wasn't believing, she could try to convince herself that Power was just Power and that what they were doing was perfectly normal.

Standing on a beach on a late Saturday afternoon was normal, after all, even in October, the wind battering their cheeks and blistering their fingers.

Marking out traces of Power and blood with cutlery and salt cellars was maybe less so.

"But why hasn't the tide taken it all?" Alex asked, sticking a spoon in the sand. "I swear it was coming in when it took Pandora."

"Power's sticky," Elizabeth called across the breeze, "it lingers."

"But you couldn't see the Power in it," Alex said. "Why not?"

"Everyone's Power is different," Elizabeth said, with a shrug that was nowhere near as casual as she thought. "Anyway, Powerful blood isn't normal blood: it's more like tar or molasses. You can scrub and scrub but it's a bugger to get rid of."

"Speaking from experience?"

"Yes," Elizabeth said, with the kind of straightforwardness that just dared Alex to run or scream or, at the very least, give her a funny look.

Not so casual now.

Something about the way Elizabeth was looking at her, so close to the waves, reminded Alex of the strange familiarity between her and the Shadow of all things, a knowing antagonism that Alex almost recognised, like a song constantly played on the radio one summer years ago only to be never heard again, until a snatch of a lyric or the hook in the melody stirred up just enough ...

The Shadow had called Elizabeth "Lizzie". Maybe it was Power, maybe it was just instinct, but Alex was absolutely certain that Elizabeth liked being called Lizzie as much as Alex liked being called Lexy.

Which really wasn't much at all anymore.

"Well, like you said," Alex conceded, "comes with the territory."

It was so small, so quick, but there was a twitch of a smile at the corner of Elizabeth's mouth, Alex was sure of it. Hidden in the stretch of the scars, but it had been there, and the glint of teeth as Elizabeth bit down on her own lip suggested that she also knew she'd been caught out.

It almost felt reassuring, all things considered.

"What have you got?" Elizabeth asked.

"The rock I saw yesterday," Alex said, pointing to that faint trace of gore up the shore, "and where Pandora went in the water and where you knocked your teeth out. You?"

"Where body number two came up," Elizabeth replied, gesturing to a pepper shaker, "and some scorch marks that must've been our fella spunking out all that Power."

"Eloquent as ever."

Alex's laugh caught in her throat at the smile that shone through the salt-speckled air. Had she ever wanted to make someone smile that much?

"How would you describe it?" Elizabeth said. "He was spunking it all over the place!"

"But you weren't," Alex realised, her laugh drifting away into the wind.

"Of course I wasn't," Elizabeth said, "I know what I'm doing."

Even Alex knew what she was doing with Power.

More or less.

Sometimes less.

Usually less.

But that didn't stop her striding towards Elizabeth, thoughts rushing formed-enough out of her mouth.

"Exactly. He's sloppy. I stopped him once and then he was killing Pandora right in the middle of the beach. Plus, he's an opportunist who doesn't know how to use his Power without blasting people with it. Who does that?"

"It might be a choice," Elizabeth said, "he wants to inflict pain."

She turned just enough for her own burns to catch the fading light, the scars glistening silver.

"Or he can't help himself," Alex suggested, glancing down at the scorch marks. "There was this time, right, when we were kids and Shaz had just moved in and Matthew was just being a bit of an arsehole and my Power just sort of spurted everywhere. I threw him clean across the garden, and I mean clean, cos he went smack against the old well. But the point is, I burnt him. Accidentally, but I burnt him with Power and it never faded."

If he was still alive, he was probably still walking around with that strap-shaped scar on his shoulder.

If.

"But our man is not nine years old."

"Well, exactly," Alex replied, running away from thoughts of her brother as fast as she could. "He doesn't know what he's doing but he's trying to steal other people's Power? What's that about?"

"If our killer's Master Power really is stealing other people's Power, well," Elizabeth said, "it's as rare as rocking horse shit and ..."

That was one thing of many Alex had noticed about Elizabeth, beyond her suspicious nails and suspicious flat and how frustratingly beautiful she found her:

There was a certainty to her.

Like she knew who she was and what she was and why she was and that went for the whole world too.

It was in the way she said Alex's name and took her hand with no hesitation, how she'd flourished a hand around her own café or stuck a fork into the sand.

So to see her now, twisting a knife in her hands with an almost lethal level of distraction, stare fixed on the sand, was more than a bit disconcerting.

"Elizabeth?" Alex whispered.

Elizabeth snapped up her head, eyes full of ominous intent.

"What colour was it? The Power?"

"The killer's?" Alex asked, "Or Pandora's?"

"The killer's."

"Just dark. I couldn't make out anything in particular. Just sort of muddy. Maybe brown."

By the sinking of Elizabeth's shoulders and the terse nod, it seemed to be the correct answer. Another twist of the knife in those cold hands.

"Pandora's was purple," Alex continued.

Like lavender in full bloom.

Elizabeth asked if Pandora had told Alex what her Master Power was.

Alex shook her head.

"I thought that was a myth anyway, people having a Master Power."

"It's not a myth," Elizabeth said. "So you've at least heard of that?"

"It's like the strongest element of your Power, isn't it?" Alex replied. "Like my uncle can get in people's heads and my brother could do weird things with the Dead – not like that."

And Mum – Carrie – could fly. Until she couldn't.

"I know what you mean," Elizabeth said, "but aye, exactly. Anyone with Power has one, beyond your everyday healing and psychic stuff."

"I don't," Alex said. "Mine's just ..."

Her hands spurted out some washed-out burgundy, like blood leeching into the shallows.

"Just bleurgh."

"Well, perhaps," Elizabeth said, shooting her a significant look, "if you stopped ignoring it ..."

"Yeah yeah," Alex said. "Anyway, our killer. Can being a psycho be a Master Power?"

"Perhaps his Power's just failing him," Elizabeth suggested. "He may have just found a way, or so he thinks, to bolster it."

"He attacks people on their own, right? Vulnerable people," Alex said, pulling at each finger in turn. "Pandora, that student girl, that homeless alcoholic. He kills them, probably at night or at least when it's dark. Dumps them in the sea. And he's probably been getting away with it for a month, at the very least, yeah?"

"Aye."

"Then why was he willing to take on you and me? I'm not saying we're all that—"

"We are all that," Elizabeth sniffed, "but proceed."

"But he could've just run."

"Then he's stupid as well as slow," Elizabeth said. "Do we really need to build a psychological profile of the man?"

"That's what Sam does. He's even got a degree in it."

"The man who hasn't caught the killer," Elizabeth sneered, "great."

Alex scuffed her foot across the sand.

"So what now?" she asked. "If you don't want to Kiss the Girls it?"

"Not sure."

"You're not sure?"

"Is your Power psychometric?" Elizabeth asked.

"Is my Power what?"

"Like extra-sensory perception," Elizabeth explained. "You touch things and you see things about them. It's called psychometry."

"Isn't that everyone's Power?" Alex asked.

"Not mine."

"But you knew who I was. As soon as I walked into the caff."

"That was different," Elizabeth replied. "You're a person with a soul."

"That's the nicest thing anyone's ever said to me," Alex said, trying not to revel in her delight at Elizabeth's smirk. "Then what's your Power like?"

"Like a lot of other things. But right now, I'm interested in yours."

Alex remembered that moment with the gore on the rock the day before, scared stiff by that burning sensation.

"Well, I suppose I can," Alex mumbled, kneeling over the scorch marks, which still glistened like fresh cinders. "My brother was better at all that but he ain't here, so ..."

"Do you always compare yourself to your brother?" Elizabeth asked.

"Only when it comes to Power. Nothing to compare otherwise."

"Not alike?"

"Never used to be," Alex said, trying, *failing*, to fixate on where ash met sand.

"And now?"

Alex looked up at her interrogator, who loomed over her at the best of times, but now ...

"I have no idea," Alex confessed, "and I don't want to know."

That was another satisfactory response, judging by Elizabeth's nod at least.

"Anyway," Alex explained, tracing her finger around the biggest scorch mark, "he actually used his Power. He liked it. Too much. So what should I do? It won't hurt me if I touch it?"

Elizabeth shook her head, the wind whipping her hair.

"Just reach out with your Power," she said, "let's see if it reacts to you first."

"Hang on," Alex said, "if you don't even know if it'll react to me, how d'you know it won't hurt me?"

"That's the point of an experiment," Elizabeth said, her eyes lingering on Alex's arms. "We've already both got war wounds."

"If I end up hospitalised," Alex warned, pushing her sleeves down, "you'll have Sam and Shaz to answer to."

Something stirred at the very back of her mind, but she shook it off. It was probably just one of those "intrusive thoughts" they used to talk about at the facility: the urge to jump from a bridge and so on. The problem was, with Alex's grip on everything still being slippery at best, there was a chance that Elizabeth could tell her to jump ...

And she would.

Just to see her smile.

"I don't mind trying," Elizabeth said.

"It's fine," Alex said, feeling the shallows start to wash in around her.

The longer they went on about it, the likelier it was that everything *would* just get washed away.

"No," Elizabeth said, "fine's not good enough. You don't need to martyr yourself—"

"I'm bloody doing it!"

Alex plunged her hand into the sand.

She seized at the pain surging up her arm.

Was this what it felt like? The killer? The murder? It burned as it whipped its way up her nerves ...

Elizabeth hauled her out of the shadows and grabbed her hand.

"I can't," Alex gasped, her breath stuttering and failing.

"That wasn't your Power."

A whip-white welt throbbed thickly through Alex's hand, every queasy pulse punching pain into her wrist.

"It's a jellyfish sting." Elizabeth laughed. "You just grabbed a jellyfish."

Tentacles flailed about in the foam, spraying sand through the shallows.

"You are kidding." Alex groaned, sinking back into Elizabeth's arms with a hysterical giggle.

It wasn't her Power betraying her.

It was a bloody ...

As she laughed hysterically, Elizabeth asked if she was going to heal it or not.

"Can't feel it properly."

Alex's arm convulsed with a wild insistence like someone was pulling at its strings.

"Deep breaths."

Silver Power flowed from Elizabeth's hand and soothed the sting until the tell-tale tingle of pins and needles spread up Alex's arm, warming as she began to glow burgundy.

"God," Alex whispered, "I am really shit at this, aren't I?"

"You're just out of practice," Elizabeth said, releasing her hand. "Happens to the best of us. Some of my most dramatic scars are just from being stupid."

Flexing her fingers, Alex examined her palm, the blister fading, the skin stiff. What was it about her hand? It was healing fine, but what was she missing in the web of gleaming lines? What was she searching for when she pressed down on the unnaturally smooth pads?

"Last night," Alex said, trying to will some kind of knowledge into existence.

"We tried," Elizabeth said. "You really tried to save her, Alex."

"No, not that. We burned the killer," Alex realised, "remember?"

A surge of pure Power, deflected, or rather, reflected at the murderer, who had to continue on, one-armed. His left hand. Burnt at best, scorched off at worst.

"I know there's no way to heal it," Alex said, "but what could you do? In that circumstance? Cos as Shaz told me last night, Savlon and cling film don't exactly cut it."

"Grin and bear it," Elizabeth replied, with a grim smile that wouldn't have been out of place on a hangman with a high level of job satisfaction.

"But he's not like you."

Elizabeth snorted.

"He's certainly nothing like me."

"We know he's inexperienced, right?"

"We *think* he's inexperienced."

"Inexperienced enough to not know not to go to a hospital?" Alex asked.

"Alex ..."

"The point is," Alex laughed, nudging their shoulders together, "guess whose big sis works in A&E?"

And was picking up Matilda Meyer *by dark*.

11
Over the Edge

While Alex had been in "that place", with its antiseptic décor and rather middling view of one of Wordsworth's lesser-talked-about lakes, she'd been asked the same question, over and over and over again.

What was her goal?

What did she want to aim for?

In terms of her life. How it would look. How it should look.

What were her priorities? In other words, all those things that should've been giving her inner peace and happiness but, for a variety of reasons connected to brain chemistry and unresolved trauma, just weren't.

The same question every day.

As if there was an answer she had to find that was somehow enough.

On Day One, Alex was too shell-shocked to even understand, her nerves numbed, her memories a mess, her sense of self still sliding away from her.

By Day Nine, Alex could understand. She understood the letters and the sounds and the words, but how could they have any real meaning when Coldharbour and its chill, churning sea were so far away?

Day Seventeen gave her an answer that won nods and smiles, praise and sympathy she could almost feel. Her answer was: a proper family dinner, just like how they used to. There still wasn't much expression in her voice so it wasn't hard to keep the cynicism out and they weren't to know just how rare those dinners had become or how, when Alex had been there, she felt like she wasn't anyway.

It was Day Twenty-Three that she knew. Days Twenty-One and Twenty-Two had already been different. Maybe it was the medication winning the fight against her still-subdued Power. Maybe it was just the break from Coldharbour and the churning sea and the cliffs and an empty grave reaching out to her, but there had been a difference. She could look at herself in the mirror, she could feel her own skin, and she could say that she was Alex Wilde. She was awake again. She wasn't drowning and dreaming and drowning anymore. On Day Twenty-Three, she gave the same answer as she had every day since Day Seventeen, all those imaginary figures in her mind who should've been sitting around that table, because she imagined the kitchen table in the house, regardless of all the other kitchen tables she'd ever had or ever sat at, she imagined everyone she ever lived with or loved, from Matthew to Maddie, Sam and Shaz, Harry, her parents.

But this time, on Day Twenty-Three, she believed it.

She believed herself.

And she believed that she could smile and laugh and pretend to sleep just enough to get herself back there, in Coldharbour, with her daughter.

Her daughter.

Which apparently was easier said than done when Alex was standing in a Crossgate car park, unfolding a map of the city centre across the bonnet of Shaz's car.

"Right," Shaz announced, battling her way around her own car in a stream of scarves and sticky notes, all various gaudy colours (scarves and notes), "I could really get in trouble for this."

"It's for a good cause," Alex said.

"I think Sam would argue that he should have this information."

"And he can have it," Alex said, "after me. Code Bananarama."

"Aye," Elizabeth said, "Mr Muscle can wait."

"This is technically illegal," Shaz warned.

Elizabeth gave the kind of shrug that suggested abusing patient confidentiality would've been very far down her list of potential misdeeds.

Then she just had to bloody smirk at Alex.

"Can we just get on with it?" Alex asked, something that definitely was not Power burning her from the inside. "When's Mads due here?"

"Ten minutes," Shaz replied, "but it'll be more like twenty."

"More …"

The clocks might not have changed yet, but the sky already seemed like it had been drenched in ink, indigo seeping into steel blue.

Ten, more like twenty, when there was a killer on the loose.

Alex pinched the bridge of her nose, but as she did so, she could smell the petrichor of rain, not the petrichor of Power, and coffee, she could smell coffee that was sharper than the weak piss they were serving in the café …

A murmur of a foreign language.

"Alex?"

She stumbled into Elizabeth's arms.

The fog faded.

Shaz was staring at Alex.

Why was a Frenchman's sister not French?

Alex insisted that she was fine, that it was just a funny turn, and told her sister to talk them through the suspects. Squinting over her glasses, Shaz held up a flamingo-coloured note about an adventurous toddler and then a lurid lime one with a woman's details.

"That wasn't a woman I was fighting," Elizabeth said. "Completely different strength profile."

"So much for Girl Power," Shaz said. "That leaves three blokes."

"And they all live in Crossgate?" Alex asked.

"Aren't they still in hospital?" Elizabeth said.

"Friday night in A&E?" Shaz laughed. "We fix 'em up, ship 'em out before they can vom on us even more. And they live ..."

She peeled the sticky notes off her fingers and pressed them into different sections of the map.

Alex examined the closest:

Gideon Barrett, 78. 4, The Cottages. Crossgate.

"Cos the toddler wasn't bad enough?"

"I can rule him out too," Shaz said, but Alex slapped her hand away.

"The Cottages," she said, "is that the little row of houses between the graveyard and the cathedral? Opposite the theatre? I'll take him."

"Well, he'd be the quickest to rule out, wouldn't he?" Shaz said. "Surely I should take him so I'd be back at the car for Mads?"

Alex glanced up at Elizabeth, who was scrutinising the map with those ludicrous NHS glasses of hers, apparently unaware that the woman next to her was concocting a plan that made her feel just as queasy as potentially confronting a murderer.

"Yeah," Alex said, pointing to another sticky note, "but that one's just around the corner and if you think it is a Power burn, just, I dunno, say your pager's going off and you're on call so you have to scarper."

"And if he tries to burn me?" Shaz suggested.

"You don't have Power," Alex replied through gritted teeth and a flash of her eyes that her sister really should've recognised. "You'll be fine."

Finally, Shaz looked at Elizabeth and winced in realisation.

"I'll meet you back here in ten," Shaz said. "Have fun."

As Shaz rushed off in her whirlwind of wool, Elizabeth asked if her one was in the same direction as Alex's.

"Five minutes that way," Alex said, leading her onto cobbles that sounded with every pound of her heart.

"Sharon won't really be in trouble, will she?" Elizabeth asked.

"Nah," Alex replied, "probably not."

If Shaz really shouldn't have got the names for Alex, she would've said. Probably.

"My daughter doesn't know about Power, by the way," Alex said, "so if you could just, you know, not mention any of this when you meet her. If that's alright."

"Fine," Elizabeth said, "although if she's as bright as her mother and her family, she might work it out for herself."

"Are you including Sam in that or not?"

"A man who looks like he's just stumbled out of a Brit Pop band and accidentally found himself a detective?" Elizabeth said. "No comment."

Alex was still working up her courage when they strode towards The Cottages, a little cobbled cul-de-sac just off Crossgate High Street.

"My fella only lives round the corner," Elizabeth said, "so if you tick off your man—"

"I thought they could wait a minute," Alex said, willing her heart to not pummel her ribcage into submission.

"It's a murder investigation, Alex," Elizabeth said as she glanced down at her sticky note, "even if it's taken Meyer a wee moment to catch up. Do *Power wounds always look like burns?*"

"I just thought, seeing as it's the last performance of *Tosca* tonight," Alex said, waiting for Elizabeth's nod of understanding, "and I sort of wrecked your plans last night, I could buy you a – well, buy *us* ..."

She pointed across the square at Crossgate Theatre, one of those Art Deco buildings that was just slightly too plain to appear in an episode of *Poirot*, its geometric architecture taking more inspiration from a cardboard box than the Chrysler Building, while inside it pretended to be Victorian, with all its red carpets and burgundy curtains and its little box office gilded with "gold".

Elizabeth didn't even turn to look.

"This isn't a *quid pro quo* situation."

"No," Alex rushed out, "obviously. I ..."

Well, if it hadn't been painfully obvious before that Alex had just endured a month of speaking to almost no one but other depressives and people bouncing off the walls in not much more than small talk and non sequiturs ...

"It was just an idea," she said, "but you're right. Let's just stick to the investigation."

Elizabeth continued to stare at her as if she was trying to work her out, like she was a particularly tricky puzzle. As far as Alex was concerned, she was one of those wooden ones that got given to toddlers: all smooth edges and solvable by brute force alone that shouldn't have taken Elizabeth long at all.

"So I'll tick off the pensioner and then I'll see my little girl," Alex said, frantically glancing around the square, "and you visit—"

"I'll get the tickets."

Alex blinked up at Elizabeth with a mumbled "excuse me?"

"I'll get the tickets," Elizabeth said, the matter-of-fact tone not quite so chilling when Alex saw the warmth in her eyes. "Any preferences?"

Alex shook her head and dug out her credit card from her jeans.

"It might not work," she said. "It's an old work one, technically."

Elizabeth curled her fingers around Alex's clenched fist, plastic piercing their palms.

She was finally sort-of smiling.

"I'll pay. I don't want you committing fraud."

"I will pay you back," Alex said.

"Go and tick off your pensioner," Elizabeth said, brushing her fingers over Alex's knuckles. "See you back here?"

Alex nodded through her daze as Elizabeth slipped off towards the theatre.

They were going on a date.

Was it a date?

"One of those fancy box seats," Alex called across the square, returning Elizabeth's nod and smile.

God, it was going to be extortionate. The Scotch in the pub had been bad enough.

Alex pulled the sticky note back out of her pocket:

Gideon Barrett, 78. 4, The Cottages. Crossgate.

She crossed the street and knocked rather firmly on the green door, the paint flaking under her knuckles.

She scanned Shaz's tiny writing again. Barrett had been in for a fall a few months before. Serial killers didn't have falls, did they? People with Power definitely didn't.

The door opened and Alex rattled off her story about coming from the social, but as she glanced up into the face of a young woman, all gangly limbs and sharp bob and Juicy Tubes and brilliant blue eyes …

"Mum?"

12
Darker than Sin

Matilda Meyer had grown.

Pedal pushers that should've been down to her calves but were now up to her knees, hair cut to her chin, a year's supply of Hubba Bubba getting chewed to oblivion, and what was even worse, *towering* over her mother on the doorstep and ready to blurt out at the same time as Alex:

"What are you doing here?"

Maddie blinked at her in that way only nonchalant teenagers did.

No more Beanie Babies and Yowies for her. No more standing on the *Yellow Pages* to reach the top cupboard in the ... well, in the flat they no longer had.

"How long have you been back?" Maddie asked.

Her face was already changing, right in front of Alex. Those big blue eyes were widening, her eyebrows crinkling, and Alex hated to admit it to herself, but she recognised that furious pressing of her daughter's mouth.

She held onto her daughter's shoulder and tried not to wince at the hurt radiating up her wrist.

"Since last night, but your dad told me you were busy."

"Whatever," Maddie muttered, "Shaz is probably waiting for me. What are you even here for then?"

Even the way she stared at the wall seemed so much older, so tired, and Alex even wondered, she actually wondered, for a good second, what had happened to her.

Alex had happened to her.

Alex had abandoned her.

It had been a difficult month. Mads wasn't fine. Et cetera. Et cetera.

"It doesn't matter." Alex sighed. "I'll walk you down—"

"You're investigating something, aren't you?"

"Listen—"

"Don't tell me to listen!" Maddie hissed furiously.

"Excuse me, young lady?" Alex scoffed. She knew she was catching flies but she didn't bloody care.

"Last time I listened to you," Maddie went on, "you said you were investigating something and then I don't see you again and I'm having to live with Dad and I don't know where you've gone!"

"Listen to me," Alex whispered, stepping up into the cottage, "I'm not leaving you again. I will never leave you again."

"Then when can I move back in with you?" Maddie demanded. "Uncle Harry said we're living with him but Dad just kept saying 'we'll see' and then Shaz keeps rolling her eyes when he's not looking."

"Monday."

Alex clawed at the wall, choking on the ricochet of adolescent emotions. She'd rather have gone one-to-one with the waves again: yeah, she'd get battered, but at least she stood half a chance of fighting back.

"And Dad?"

"And Dad what, sweetheart?"

"Will he let me?" Maddie asked. "Cos I heard him say that that house ain't a house for kids."

"Isn't," Alex corrected, queasy at the thought of yet another confrontation, "and if he changes his mind, then I'll be having words."

Words. The bombs that Alex could drop ...

Maddie's nod was all wobbly lip and earnest eyes, even if she tried to shake it off with a shrug. Maybe there was still hope that Alex could ply her with a Furby. Or at least a Happy Meal.

"D'you wanna get your stuff?" Alex asked. "Have you got a bag?"

"Yeah," Maddie said, tugging Alex further into the house by her hand, "I just need to say goodbye to Gideon."

No.

Alex hadn't been tugged further into a house.

She'd been dragged into a time capsule.

From the dusky pink wallpaper to the ducks in flight on the wall, and then there was the carpet: some hideous yellow and brown argyle pattern that would've given Alex a migraine if she could've had one, although her head was twinging and her nausea was rising in her chest again, so it was clearly giving it a bloody good go.

But it was more than that.

It was much more, because under that cloying old-person smell that must've been some mix of stale piss and staler perfume or cologne and out-of-date teabags, there was the unmistakeably pungent tang of Power.

And it might have all been a coincidence, that Gideon Barrett, seventy-eight, of 4 The Cottages just had Power, because Alex had been bumping into people with Power like she was a buoy bashing against the waves and that image of those mangled up buses rose in her mind again, but just in case, *just in case* ...

Alex asked if she could meet "this Gideon".

"Oh, yeah," Maddie said. "Is that why you're here?"

"Has he got a burn on his left hand?"

"It's all bandaged up," Maddie said. "He did it on the kettle. How did you know? It's not one of your 'I just know' things again, is it?"

"Where is he now?" Alex asked, as if she couldn't sense him through the wall. And she could only sense other people with Power, couldn't she? Like only people with Power could see other people's Power? More questions for Elizabeth to do her best not to wince at.

Maddie embarked on some long explanation about how volunteering was *wicked* and just having a cuppa and making sure the old man took his tablets—

"I've got a friend waiting outside," Alex said. "D'you wanna go and say hello? Say I'm your mum and that I think I've found him?"

"Eh?"

"*Eh?*" Alex said, "You mean 'pardon'. I've got a friend—"

"Who?"

"You'll know her when you see her."

"A friend?" Maddie scoffed.

"Yes. She's about Matthew's height."

"Uncle Matthew?"

Had Alex's mind just dropped a stitch? Well, as long as it wasn't unravelling again ...

"I mean, about your dad's height," Alex said, "and she has red hair and a long black coat and I don't want you gawping at her scars."

"What scars?"

"You will know her when you see her, sweetheart," Alex said, grabbing Maddie's bag herself. "What do you need to say to her?"

"But I need to introduce you to Gideon," Maddie said, "I can't just—"

"Matilda," Alex warned.

"Alexandra," she mimicked.

Alex knew it was cruel, but she still let her face drop into the cold, blank stare that she'd inherited from her own mother and that had, of course, scared the bejesus out of all three kids. She'd never used it much on her daughter and watching her flinch made her soul lurch, but Maddie still took the bag from her.

"What's really going on?" Maddie whispered.

"Has your dad told you about the missing people?" Alex asked.

"It's why Shaz has been picking me up," Maddie said, with the contemptuous roll of her eyes that belonged on a different face that was far, far away from them both, "even from *school*. It's so embarrassing."

At least Alex had Sam to thank for something, even if he was letting their little girl scorch the ethnicity out of her hair.

"My friend's called Elizabeth, alright?" Alex said.

She kept her eye on the living room as she reached back to ease the front door open, the handle slipping in her sweaty fingers.

"I really should say goodbye to—"

"I'll say goodbye for you," Alex said. "Elizabeth'll be in the square and then I want you to go straight to Shaz."

"I'll get told off if I don't say bye properly," Maddie said, sticking her head into the living room. "Oh."

Alex shook off the dread creeping over her shoulders and slowly slid towards her daughter.

"Oh what?" she whispered, convinced that once upon a time, her daughter had known how to articulate herself in full sentences.

"He's asleep," Maddie said. "That happens, you know. I was halfway through reading the paper to Doris earlier and she nodded right off. Like, I had to check her pulse, you know."

Alex hushed her and took a look for herself.

Gideon Barrett was asleep.

Gideon Barrett was asleep and was very clearly of a pensionable age, one liver-spotted hand resting on the arm of his chair, the other bandaged in his lap.

His shirt and jumper looked far too loose from where Alex was standing and there was a waxiness to what was left of his cheeks that, if his chest wasn't softly rising and falling, would've had Alex thinking he was doing a Doris.

She didn't even have to step into the living room to feel it.

There may have been Power in that cottage, but it was now accompanied by that stringent sourness that smelt like death, like that care home Sam's Granddad Alan had been in towards the end.

"He burnt his hand on the kettle?" Alex whispered, keeping one eye on the sleeping man.

"Yeah," Maddie said. "He's had a couple of accidents recently. He had a bad fall about a month ago, but the social's being slow so the only people who see him are me or whoever else gets him on their list and some of the people that go to his church. His neighbours check in on him but not often enough."

Alex frowned down – no, up – at her daughter.

"What are you doing around old people, Mads?"

"Well, volunteering's part of DofE," Maddie said, "and I like old people."

"You don't know any."

"Grandma Edda."

"She lives in Manchester! And your dad's gran don't count, she's eighty going on forty. Don't you ..."

"What?"

"Find it a bit creepy?"

When Maddie shrugged, Alex turned back to the old man in his armchair, the paisley pattern long since faded. He didn't look like he could get up without assistance, let alone throw a grown woman against a wall or onto the beach.

But still, if he had Power, he would be the third person in twenty-four hours that Alex had met.

There were only so many horrible coincidences, surely?

"Keep an eye on him," Alex said, starting towards the stairs. "Just gonna use his loo."

"So you don't think he's about to murder me?" Maddie asked.

Alex clung onto the banister, opened her mouth, shut it again, and tried to glare at that cheeky smile.

"I didn't say that."

"Being paranoid again," Maddie teased, leaning against the wall.

"I'm being cautious," Alex said. "And now I'm back, I'll be walking you home from school."

"What?" Maddie groaned. "I have to *walk*?"

"Yes, lazybum," Alex replied, edging into the darkness, "you have to walk."

It was just a cottage, an ordinary cottage belonging to an old man shuffling his way towards death, but Alex couldn't help but feel like Little Red Riding Hood wandering into the wolf's trap – although if her worst fears were true, she'd rather have taken on a lupine cross-dresser. At the top of the stairs, in the murk that told her that this wasn't a house that saw a lot of sunlight, she glanced right at the bathroom and then left at the bedroom. It made a nice change, only having two rooms to think of.

She stepped into the bathroom first, assaulted by beige, all cracked plastic and time-spotted enamel. It made her bathroom look liveable.

Dust smeared the medicine cabinet, which made the finger-streaks easy to spot, as if it was being used. A curious thing for Alex, really, as Carrie had taken down their medicine cabinet at some point in the early Seventies. It had to have been the early Seventies, because Alex couldn't quite remember it, just the brown outline seared into the wall. After all, they didn't need it. And then Shaz had moved in, which had led to the four of them standing in the chemist's one Saturday afternoon a lot like that afternoon, with Shaz quietly instructing Carrie on what normal people might need: plasters, paracetamol, TCP. And later Shaz had insisted on a proper first aid box, just in case no one with Power was around in that death-trap of a house in the middle of an emergency – completely ignoring the fact that usually it was the people with Power causing the emergencies.

But this medicine cabinet, Gideon Barrett's medicine cabinet, was chock-a-block with boxes and bottles of tablets, most of them plastered with prescription labels. Statins, aspirin, beta-blockers ...

All prescribed to him.

Then again, Alex had a prescription because the facility had strongarmed her into it and if she had tried to explain that she'd been born with magical powers that burned up most drugs and alcohol in minutes unless she went on the lash like Gazza, well ...

Feeling like she was wasting someone else's medication would've been the least of her worries. Every bottle and every box in Barrett's cabinet was half-empty. Even if he was taking them in case someone checked, and hadn't Maddie said something about that, something wasn't quite right.

What was she missing?

Alex grunted and dug her nails into her hands.

She used to be so quick, so sharp, before ...

She turned her hand over, where the jellyfish sting had been.

If Barrett had Power and burnt his hand on a kettle, he wouldn't have needed to go to hospital.

If Barrett didn't have Power, then why there was so much of it in the house that it was choking Alex?

Whereas if he did have Power and he had burnt his hand in a way that simply couldn't heal...

Alex let her fingers drift over the edge of the mirror, wondering if it would tell her anything

Mirrors were magical. Mouse – Matthew – had said that once.

Alex should leave.

She should've left already.

She should've just turned around and walked right out of that cottage, but instead, she closed her eyes, pressed her hand against the mirror, and let her Power flow through her. If Elizabeth wanted psychometry or whatever it was called, she was going to get ...

Everything.

Screams shot through Alex's soul, scorched her breath, choking her, and the beating started and the cutting ...

Alex's blood roared in her ears as she crushed the mirror under her fist, shards of glass slicing through her hand.

How many people had he murdered?

How long?

How?

Blood gushed down her wrist. She'd known. All along. All those unexplained disappearances or mysterious deaths ...

How many were down to Gideon Barrett?

Alex unfurled her fist and peeled out the largest bit of mirror, the one that had degloved the pad under her thumb. Degloving: that was something else Matthew told her about. Probably on the same day as grave wax, which reminded her of that gruesome picture of poor Heather Abbott in the paper, and there it was, Pandora's hand slipping out of hers, that tentacle-whipped, glass-degloved hand that Alex could barely feel as she forced the skin to smooth itself over exposed muscle and she flew down the stairs with trembling legs and a bleeding hand, not caring how much it still stung or how much it still bled, because if that man had Power, then she was going to see how far that Power went. How much blood could he lose? How much of a kicking—

The armchair was empty.

Alex glanced into the hallway.

At least Maddie's bag was gone.

No, she hadn't heard the door go, but the point was she definitely hadn't heard it go *twice*. If she had to hunt down an old man in his own house, she would. Going around murdering people and then daring to drink tea with her daughter ...

Alex strode into the living room and scanned it, keeping her back against the chimney because she was not taking her eye off that door, she knew that much. Was he really just some common or garden serial killer? But the Power ... But the *dying* ...

Gideon Barrett was dying.

She sensed it.

Just like she should've sensed her own child sooner.

Because all she could see was the bag sticking out from behind the other chair, but it shouldn't have taken her that long.

Alex rushed towards the window.

Blood-streaked vomit seeped from Maddie's mouth, just like Matthew's overdose, but she didn't have Power, she couldn't get out of this by herself, so Alex slammed herself down, biting back the panic that wanted to seize her by her bones, and rolled Maddie into the recovery position, trying to remember all those things Shaz had shown her "just in case".

"Sweetheart," Alex whispered as she wiped sweaty hair from her little girl's cheek, "can you hear me?"

Maddie was pale, she was clammy, but she had a pulse and she was, she was breathing, well, wheezing, pink sick bubbling in the corner of her mouth, but ...

What the hell had Barrett done to her?

"It won't be long now."

Alex shoved the armchair into the wall with a burst of Power.

Gideon Barrett stood in the doorway, leaning on his walking stick with a shit-eating smile.

"What have you done to her?"

Alex rubbed at her daughter's back as she stared the old man down.

"Arsenic," Barrett said, like he was exchanging recipes. "In the tea, of course. I had hoped, you see, once I knew she was your daughter, that there might have been Power there, but I had to force the issue. Although ..."

He jabbed the stick at them.

"I think we can assume it's a 'no'."

"How much?" Alex demanded. "How much arsenic?"

"How much do you want to save her?"

"How much? She's my child!"

"Then give me your Power."

"Fine!" Alex screamed, burgundy flaring from her, "I don't want it! I never wanted it!"

Barrett creaked out a nod.

"We just have to wait."

"Wait for what?" Alex snarled.

Maddie's pulse was flickering wildly under Alex's fingers. Too fast. Much too fast. Her poor heart must've been straining and hadn't Shaz said that was what happened to Matthew when he overdosed, his heart had given out under the sheer strain of whatever he'd pumped into his veins and he'd said, the next morning, *that* day just before it all went wrong, that he'd known he was dying, that Death itself was sitting on his chest and he'd even thought he'd seen the Half-Faced Man.

"She'll be back," Barrett said, wisely staying the other side of the room because if he came closer, Jesus Christ, what Alex was going to do to him. "She knows."

"You're a parasite," Alex realised. "You don't have Power, do you? Not really."

"Oh," Barrett said, "I'm just the host."

Power grew from his—

Alex smashed him into the wall.

And waited, letting her own Power continue to build and thrum.

Barrett's eyes stayed closed. Blood dribbled from his ear.

Alex grabbed Maddie by her shoulders. She should've paid more attention to healing someone who didn't have

Power, she knew that all along, but all she could do was flood her daughter's body with the stuff, trying to think of nothing but purging the poison, because if Matthew had been there, he'd probably have had some proper logical solution like he was the Sherlock Holmes of healing, but as it was, all she could do was hold on and beg whatever was out there, even as clammy fingers clung to her arms ...

Clammy fingers were clinging to her arms.

Alex held back her Power, just for a moment, just to whisper her daughter's name.

She waited.

Just as she'd waited nearly fourteen years ago, sitting on the floor in the study, sweat-soaked, shuddering, waiting for that first cry.

Maddie spluttered her way onto her side, tangling herself up in Alex's arms as she groaned about her stomach hurting.

Alex gathered the girl up by all of her lanky limbs, pressed her face into her ludicrously straight hair, and just breathed in all the Skittles and Charlie Red and petrichor and that smell that was just her child and had been since that first cry nearly fourteen years ago.

"Mum?"

"In a minute, sweetheart."

Alex tried to clench her tears away. If she just focused on those Skittles and that Charlie Red—

"What's happening to Gideon?"

"I just had to knock him out. Long story."

"No," Maddie said, "he's glowing. How is he doing that?"

The Power had been pink. It had been *that* pink, which meant ...

"Oh, Lexy," Barrett said, in a voice that wasn't fully his own, "he warned me about you."

13
Fade in the Air

There was never a choice not to look. It wasn't like Alex was in the wild, faced with a bear or a leopard, where her life could've depended on very much not looking it in the eye. She knew how fast the Shadow could move.

So Alex faced both Barrett and the thing behind his eyes. No blinking.

"It's you," Alex said, dragging Maddie up behind her, "isn't it?"

She could see it clearly now: the Shadow moving inside Barrett, behind him, through him, puppeteering, possessing, but even so ...

"I do what I can," Barrett said. "It's not what you think. It's mutually beneficial."

"Murdering people and stealing their Power?"

"You can talk," Barrett said, giving the air a long, rattling sniff, "you stink of *her*."

"What?" Maddie said. "What the bloody hell's going on?"

"Language," Alex warned. "Which one of you am I talking to?"

She'd only seen a possession once before, but she knew what she should've been looking at. Shaz hadn't been in control, the Shadow was *using* her, but this ...

"Both," Barrett and the Shadow said.

"So, what is it?" Alex asked, trying to edge Maddie back towards the window. "The Shadow helps you kill people and you share the Power? That determined not to die, Gideon? Classy move."

"You're not usually this brave, Lexy," the Shadow said through Barrett, and that was definitely the Shadow.

"You just tried to murder my child."

With a squeeze of Maddie's arm, Alex eased her against the windowsill and warned her as quickly and as quietly as she could that it was really going to hurt but that Elizabeth would heal her.

"Heal— What are you talking about? What's happening to Gideon?"

"Did you think you were protecting her?" the Shadow said. "Never telling her about Power? Hoping it'd pass her by?"

Barrett's head snapped to the side and they sneered:

"Just like your mother."

"Yeah," Alex said, "and she got rid of you and all."

When Barrett – the Shadow – whoever or whatever was really in charge – tipped its head back and laughed, Alex crumbled the window into ashes with a clench of her fist and threw Maddie into the garden.

"You can't run, Lexy!"

"Do I look like I'm trying to run?" was the last thing Alex managed to get out before Barrett yanked her back and smashed her skull against the wall, but at least there was no more pain ... because there is no pain in this place, in the darkness, where the sea isn't water and the wind doesn't move.

Alex blinks.

She cradles her jaw with a careful hand.

It isn't pain.

But it is there, a dull throb that makes her feel that her teeth are about to drop out of her mouth.

She slips against the shingle ...

But then she remembers it's not really wet on The Other Side.

Shingle. In the darkness.

She must be unconscious.

She's just unconscious.

Barrett couldn't have been strong enough to ...

The thought chills her.

The Shadow, though.

But no, no, her Power must've kicked in.

It always kicks in, whether she likes it or not.

She was already using it, she's just thrown Maddie through the window.

Unless they've ...

Unless she's just bleeding out on that horrible bloody carpet and she'll never know because now she's ...

"Alex?" Pandora asks, appearing in front of her. "Where are we going?"

Back.

Alex was back.

She was peeling herself out of blood and gore, but she was back, blinking as she clawed at an ancient carpet.

But that didn't matter.

What mattered was *Elizabeth* charging at Barrett, charging at the Shadow, and rugby-tackling them into the dining table.

"Get out of him!" Elizabeth screamed.

The Shadow erupted in a roar of Power, slamming Elizabeth back into the wall.

The cottage shuddered to a halt.

Barrett collapsed.

The Shadow had vanished.

Alex called for Elizabeth as she dragged her way up the sick-soaked armchair.

"She's gone," Elizabeth groaned, waving a hand at the slumped Barrett. "It's just the auld one again."

"No," Alex said, "but he's not just an old man."

"She's cleared off," Elizabeth insisted. "Clearly didn't wanna take on both of us. She's not suicidal, trust me."

"I know," Alex hissed, "I mean he was a murderer before he was ever po—"

Alex was launched out of the window, skidding across glass and grass that burned up her back.

"Oh my – Lex!" Shaz yelled.

There was a crack and a splatter inside.

Alex warned her sister to stay there.

And her daughter.

She climbed back into the house. Barrett was on top of Elizabeth, blood streaming from her nose, throat vanishing under those dark-glowing hands.

Alex hooked her foot in Barrett's chest. His ribs crunched against her boot. But he stayed on Elizabeth, even as she shoved her chin down, even as she clawed at his face, and if she couldn't get him off ...

So Alex did it again: she kicked him, in the side, in the shoulder, driving her boot into bone and muscle until a hand spasmed with pain, jerking just long enough for Elizabeth to haul him off her and they wrestled him down onto damp carpet, grabbing at his arms as Alex screamed at him to give the last of the Power up, her own burning burgundy up her arms.

"Make me!" Barrett snarled.

"She's trying!" Elizabeth yelled and she pressed her knee into his broken ribs for good measure.

Alex gasped for breath, squeezing Barrett's bruised shoulder when he tried to snake out of her grip.

"How do we make him give it up?" she asked Elizabeth.

"Was thinking about that before," Elizabeth panted, blood gushing from her nose, her cheek blooming with bruises.

"You don't know how to stop this?"

"Was hoping he'd just burn through it," Elizabeth said. "Our Power's infinite, but his needs—"

The smack of the floor under Alex made her ribs twinge and her head ring.

"You were saying?" she slurred, cold fingers clawing at her shoulder.

"Can we save it for after?" Elizabeth mumbled. "There's another idea but I don't know if—"

It might've been the best idea ever, if Elizabeth's violent cascade of blood-spiked vomit hadn't interrupted it. But even through her ears throbbing, Alex could hear Maddie shouting and she knew, before she even managed to sit up, that her daughter was doing something as Wilde-stupid as running towards the danger, and she knew, before she could do anything else, that Barrett was up first, that he was lurching towards Maddie, and before Alex could even scream, he was launching Maddie into the air, punching her through the ceiling—

Where she stopped.

Maddie stopped.

Hanging in the air, plasterboard cascading around her, groaning in absolute agony, but stopped nonetheless, suspended in a cloud of burgundy Power.

Stomach still somewhere in her throat, Alex took a shuddering breath, letting her Power rush through her. This Power didn't burn.

It was warm. It was bright. But best of all, it was right.

"Is that you?" Shaz called from the empty window frame.

"That's me! And bloody stay outside, will you?"

As Elizabeth rugby-tackled Barrett again, Alex dared to clamber up, arms outstretched, and she took careful step after careful step closer and closer as she pulled on her Power, willing it to bring Maddie to her, just a little at a time. She warned her not to move.

"I don't have much choice!" Maddie shrieked, wobbling in the air.

Alex ignored the heat in her arms and dug her heels into the carpet, focusing on this one vital thought: of Maddie close enough to grab the armchair.

Pure Power cut between them, sending Maddie smashing into the wall.

"I've got her!" Shaz called, clambering in the house, "Al, I've got her!"

"What did I just tell you?" Alex screamed at her sister, but she didn't need an answer, because when she turned back to Barrett, Elizabeth was on the floor behind him.

Unmoving.

Elizabeth, unconscious at least.

Maddie, bruised and yelling.

Pandora, Dead and dreaming.

Later, when Alex thought back to that moment, that precise sliver of time, she would realise that she couldn't remember exactly what she was thinking or feeling, because this was instinct. It was instinct to reach out to Gideon Barrett and yank him into the air with one hand, draining him of his ill-gotten Power. It was instinct to reach out to her family with the other hand, dragging them back from the wall. It was all instinct as she rose into the air, drenched in Power and fear and rage, and breathed awareness back into Elizabeth.

And when Barrett finally screamed and begged for mercy, mercy he had never shown anyone else, writhing in a pathetic, shivering heap, she stopped.

She stopped, still suspended in space, sure, *somehow*, that she had seized all the stolen Power.

And in an exhale, Alex returned it to the Ether.

She slammed back onto the floor, carpet scorched hot under her fingers.

She'd done it.

Staggering her way upright as usual, Alex turned to Maddie, who was wrapped up in Shaz's shuddering arms.

"I'll explain everything later."

But why were they looking at her like that? Like she hadn't just saved Maddie's life? Everyone's lives?

No.

No, they weren't looking at her.

No, those faces fixed in terror were looking *past* her.

Alex twisted around, just in time to see a glint through the air. Just in time to register the shock through her shoulder.

Face-to-face with Barrett, his hand still on the handle, Alex heaved in a breath, frozen around the knife, hoping he wasn't going to pull—

A flash of agony flashed as Barrett ripped out the blade from her shoulder and raised it above their heads and there was too much Power rushing towards the wound for Alex to divert it, to stop him, and the others were too far away ...

After everything.

A stabbing.

What a rubbish way to—

A shadow threw itself onto Barrett's back.

A pale hand clawed for the knife.

Alex lunged forward and grabbed the hand, just as the blade nicked Barrett's skin.

"Not like this," she whispered, squeezing the cold hand.

Elizabeth stilled, tiny specks of crimson just starting to sparkle between her fingers. Hot gusts of blood were still pumping from Alex's shoulder when she tore her eyes from the blade to Elizabeth's flushed face. In the silence, ignoring Barrett between them, they just ...

Looked at each other.

They looked at each other and Alex knew that she could finally see Elizabeth in her entirety. The unchipped nails, unlived-in flat, unslept-in bed, all those things Alex had tried to convince herself didn't matter.

No. No, because to say they didn't matter was to disregard Elizabeth Black, Elizabeth the Unkillable or whatever else the Shadow had called her, and who she was and what she meant, because a day working with her was enough to know she didn't have the first idea about running any kind of business, but fighting a man and holding a knife to his throat ...

Alex finally got the joke.

"Just do it," Barrett snapped. "Put me out of my misery."

"Nah," she said. "No, you deserve all the misery that's coming to you."

When Alex stepped back, she made sure to take Elizabeth's hand with her left, because with her right ...

She punched Barrett, crunching his nose under her knuckles with a satisfying splatter.

"See?" Alex said, shaking Power through sore fingers. "Hurts, doesn't it?"

14
What it's like to be Damned

Tosca was beautiful.

A bit long, but Elizabeth had insisted that it was actually on the shorter side for an opera, especially considering how quickly the plot barrelled towards a conclusion in which everyone ended up dead.

Alex hadn't expected Tosca to jump to her death though.

That final aria, piercing through the darkness and then ...

Alex's fingers had convulsed on the armrest until a cold hand gripped hers and let her squeeze back.

Their eyes had met, then, in that darkness, Elizabeth's faintly glowing silver, so Alex's must've been glowing burgundy, healing those fractures in their crushed fingers.

And they just sort of stayed holding hands all the way back to the house, where, as they wandered up the drive, the fluttering in Alex's stomach lurched into waves of nausea.

She touched the front door with just the tips of the fingers of her free hand.

It opened.

Maybe it was exceptional.

Maybe Pandora was right.

Pandora with her arm crackling, before she'd be choking on seaweed ...

"Thank you," Alex said, reluctantly releasing Elizabeth's hand. "It was really ..."

"You paid for the tickets." Elizabeth laughed softly. "But aye, my pleasure."

Alex hovered in the doorway, untethered and uncertain, like she was fifteen again in front of that empty grave with that language she just couldn't understand and asked ...

"So, do you open the caff on Sundays?"

The question startled Elizabeth enough to make her flinch.

"Oh," she said, "I don't know."

"You don't know?" Alex made herself laugh, because if she hadn't, if she'd just let herself fall into that gaze, those arms ... "What kind of caff owner are you?"

Elizabeth just shook her head, heartbreakingly bashfully.

"D'you wanna come in?" Alex asked. "See that study I was telling you about? If it's still unlocked, cos ..."

"Won't we disturb your uncle?" Elizabeth replied.

"He must be out," Alex said, pointing to the empty space where his car should've been. "He's a bit of a workaholic."

"If you're sure."

Alex nodded and leant back on the front door, letting Elizabeth across the threshold, although she hadn't been expecting ...

This.

Elizabeth had been charging into, well, just about anywhere like she owned the place, but now ...

Now she was taking tentative step after tentative step down the hallway and into the study, like a child creeping into somewhere they shouldn't be.

Something Alex knew all too well.

But then the study was exactly as she'd left it *that* day in 1990.

The huge wooden ottoman under the wonky window, the cushion still faded in its vibrancy. The bookcase, covering the left wall. The table, sturdy and time-battered, in the centre of the room. The floorboards, creaking with every step.

"One of *those* houses," Elizabeth murmured.

"It does its own thing," Alex said, "did warn you. The study's alright though."

"So the study is safe, but the rest of the house?"

"I don't think the house likes me anymore," Alex confessed. "I demolished it. Nine years ago. On my wedding day. What *was* my wedding day."

"It's still standing," Elizabeth said, tapping the edge of her stiletto against a flaking floorboard.

"I resurrected it," Alex said, "with a single breath and a wave of my hand. The wood was burning with burgundy fire and the brick was crumbling into ash. And I was picking sawdust out of my ears for weeks."

"Can I ask ..."

"Someone broke my heart."

Alex was ready to let Elizabeth assume, to put two and two together and make four when it should've been five, but when there was no wisecrack about Sam not knowing what was good for him, just that heavy, solemn stare so like the one Elizabeth had given her that morning on the beach, frost-shocked awake ...

Yeah, Elizabeth knew it wasn't Sam.

"It's a lot, isn't it?" Elizabeth said, sliding deftly past the grief hanging between them. "The atmosphere."

"You can feel it?"

"Aye," Elizabeth said. "The study's welcoming us in. Or you, at least, but I don't think it's too arrogant to say it doesn't mind me."

"The others used to think I was mad," Alex said, though she wasn't sure there was much "used to" about it as she knocked her knuckles against the table. "Even ... even Matthew couldn't feel it like I do."

"Really? Not even Matthew?"

Alex might've questioned the confusion on her face but she was too busy being overtaken by something primal, something that made her surge towards Elizabeth with purpose.

"But you feel it?" Alex said. "You feel it too?"

"You feel safe in here," Elizabeth said, "don't you?"

"It's stupid really. So much has happened in here that I shouldn't, but ..."

"There's a warmth in here," Elizabeth agreed, gazing around the room. "And the books put mine to shame."

Elizabeth took Alex's hand, giving it a squeeze as she coaxed her into the middle of her own study.

"Matthew really couldn't feel this?" Elizabeth asked.

"Not properly," Alex said, "but the first time we got in, he saw a particularly gruesome ghost and then when Mum caught us, she put the fear of God in us, and then, the next time ..."

The next time.

Alex glanced around, making sure that the Half-Faced Man wasn't about to step out of a shadow, before her gaze drifted to where the spirit board had once been.

"Go on," Elizabeth said, making Alex realise that she was just staring at a bare table, the wood worn smooth.

"There was an incident with a spirit board and four kids who thought they knew better," Alex said, "so no, I don't think Matthew ever really had anything good to say about the study."

Elizabeth frowned in thought, though what she could've been thinking about, Alex had no idea.

"It's like time doesn't really exist in here," Alex tried to explain.

Her eyes drifted down to her broken watch, blood caught in the grooves of the strap. What a great impression she was making, even if it wasn't the first anymore. She tried to slip it off as discreetly as she could with sweat-slicked fingers, but then Elizabeth was wrapping her cold hand around her wrist.

"Was it sentimental?" Elizabeth asked, peeling the watch from Alex's skin with an embarrassing amount of dexterity.

"I can't remember," Alex confessed.

She held onto it for a moment, almost mournful, before she slipped it into her pocket.

"Want something more durable?" Elizabeth said, holding her arm up to the light until the gold glinted and the burgundy leather shone just right. "Matches your Power."

"You can't be giving me your watch." Alex laughed.

Her stomach lurched as Elizabeth shrugged and unhooked the watch from her wrist.

"Consider it a loan."

"You'll have to put it on me," Alex said, daring the kind of bare-faced lie that her siblings would've seen right through. "My fingers still aren't the same after decking Barrett earlier."

"Boxer's fracture," Elizabeth said with that dark gleam in her eyes as she encircled Alex's wrist with the watch. "I've had it plenty of times. Need healing?"

"Maybe a bit," Alex said, holding up her other hand just to feel that cool silver Power slide through her skin, revelling in it so much that it took her far too long to register Elizabeth's glances at the insides of her arms.

She ripped her hands away and mumbled her thanks.

"Alex," Elizabeth said, "we've all got scars."

She pointed at her face and when Alex couldn't find anything to say, Elizabeth dragged her hair right away from her cheek and shoved it into the light, the iridescence as bright as Power.

"That's different," Alex whispered.

"It's still something I'd rather forget," Elizabeth said, leaning back on the table. "And it's a wee bit difficult every time a stranger flinches at me."

"I didn't flinch."

"You stared though."

"Not …"

Alex gave up fighting the heat flooding her body and sighed:

"Not like that."

"Like what then?"

"If you haven't worked it out yet," Alex said, with as much hauteur as she could muster, which wasn't much at all once she caught herself gazing at that crooked mouth, "I'm not telling you."

Elizabeth's smirk was a wicked thing in the purest sense of the word, not in Maddie's new way of speaking: it had to have been the work of a witch, drawing out this burning want from Alex, this level of coveting that she couldn't remember ever feeling before, that *thrall* …

"Go on," Elizabeth said, "ask."

"Ask what?" Alex – well – asked.

Elizabeth let her scarred cheek hit the light again and flexed her hand, drawing Alex's gaze down her burnished arm.

"Pandora's burns didn't go as far as yours," Alex realised, letting her mind drift back towards The Other Side, "even when she was Dead."

"Which means?"

"I don't know," Alex admitted. "Why are you walking about when she's ..."

That lifeless hand slipping from hers.

"How did you survive?" Alex asked. "You said ..."

She groaned to herself and shook her head, letting out a laugh when Elizabeth smirked at her.

"Last night," Alex said, "we even said you shouldn't have survived, let alone have your Power, when you were burned."

"In fairness," Elizabeth replied, "we were then very distracted."

"So how did you?"

"I didn't."

Alex pressed her hand to Elizabeth's throat, feeling a faint pulse, just as vague as it had been that morning.

"You're alive," she said, "I *know* you're alive."

"I am," Elizabeth said. "Can you keep a secret?"

"What do you think?" Alex chuckled, but her breath caught in her throat when Elizabeth stepped even closer.

"My Master Power is resurrection," Elizabeth said. "I die and then I come back."

"How many ..."

Alex caught her breath again before it ran away from her. Did she need to count down? Five things she could see – no, all she could see was that Shadow and those grey eyes and that pink Power, so she swallowed back her sick, Riesling still fuzzing the roof of her mouth, and asked:

"How many times have you died?"

"Enough to be confident that you," Elizabeth said, tucking a curl behind Alex's ear, "don't need to worry about me."

"But is there a limit?" Alex asked. "To how many times you can resurrect yourself?"

Elizabeth shrugged. Of all the things to shrug about.

"Elizabeth, you've just told me …"

"Thank you for the concern," Elizabeth said, resting her hand on Alex's cheek, her thumb stroking the very edge of her mouth, "but I will be fine."

"I know you're deflecting," Alex said, surrendering to the coolness of Elizabeth's touch as it soothed away the heat searing through her skin, "again."

"Aye, I'm deflecting, because I still haven't told you what your Master Power is," Elizabeth replied. "Would you like to know?"

Well, there was nothing like dangling a life-altering question in front of Alex to rip her out of her reverie.

"But I don't have one."

"That's what I used to think."

"Until you died," Alex realised.

With a knowing nod, Elizabeth flexed her hand.

A book floated from the bookcase to the table.

"Neat, isn't it?" Elizabeth said, flicking off the silver clinging to her fingers.

"Is it?" Alex said. "Not being funny, but I was doing that when I was five."

"You gave me that."

"Gave you what?"

"That little quirk of Power," Elizabeth said, "your Master Power."

"I'm just telekinetic?"

There wasn't really a "just" about it, but Master Powers were meant to be supreme, the zenith, a showstopper. If it was that rubbish, no wonder she'd never got to grips with her Power. Or was it because she'd never got to ...

Alex tutted to herself, just as Elizabeth shook her head.

"That's inherited from someone," Elizabeth said, "I'm assuming the levitating is too?"

"Yeah, Mum could fly, apparently," Alex said. "I think someone said that David could freeze or move stuff. So the telekinesis is from him. I suppose."

"When you drowned last month," Elizabeth said, "did you come back by yourself or did someone help you?"

So Elizabeth did know.

All the signs were there, that sympathetic look on the beach, the wandering around the words in *The Chronicle*, how fast she'd got her out of the water twice.

The way she looked at her arms.

"I thought I didn't have to tell you anything," Alex muttered, pushing her nails into the corner of the table.

"If you believe this makes me think any less of you," Elizabeth murmured, her voice as gentle as the fingertips ghosting over Alex's nails, "after everything we've seen and done, then ..."

"Then what?" Alex asked, too tired to fight her misery.

She'd thought she'd been shaking it off, she'd thought that this was moving on.

"Then you are bonkers."

Alex flinched her way upright.

Elizabeth was staring at her so fondly ...

Was sympathy not so bad after all?

"Well," Alex said, deciding not to interrogate the tears prickling her eyes and pressing at her ears, "had I known

I'd be subjected to your terrible banter, I might've tried harder."

Elizabeth laughed, that cascade of auburn hair glowing in the lowlight, and Alex knew she was falling, she was stumbling closer to the abyss, but she couldn't care, not when she knew that laugh, that smile, all of that fire was for her.

"Shaz resuscitated me," Alex explained. "She had to do the same for Matthew when he overdosed years ago. Our Power kind of kept us just about alive long enough for her to do the job, but we were dying."

"Alex," Elizabeth said, leaning on the table, "my Master Power is that I resurrect myself."

"Yeah, I know. I can keep up. But what's that got to do with mine?"

"Just for a moment, in Barrett's cottage, you were Dead."

"And you brought me back."

"You brought yourself back cos you'd already been exposed to my Power yesterday, first when I healed your hand, then when my Power restarted when Shaz reset my knee."

"Elizabeth, I'm not following," Alex said. "What's this got to do with *my* Power?"

"Alex," Elizabeth said, "your Power is Power. I resurrect, you can now resurrect. I don't know how permanent it is or—"

"So I take everyone's Power? Is that what you're saying? Like the thing possessing Barrett?"

"You're not like that," Elizabeth snapped, a glint of that ... What was it? Fear? Hate?

Whatever it was, Elizabeth frowned her way out of it before she continued.

"You don't just take Power, you give them yours too. Telekinesis, fixing my window last night, wasn't part of my Power before I met you. You *share* Power. Your Power reflects, responds to, recreates other people's Power. I couldn't have done what you did with the Ether today."

"So is this where you say that I'm squandering it or something?"

"No," Elizabeth said, urgency in her intense glare, "but the fact is, the more you use your Power, the more you need to learn to control it, sooner rather than later. This uncertainty in the most uncertain time in a thousand years puts you at risk of …"

Elizabeth looked down at her hands, cracking her knuckles as she frowned again.

"Of what, Elizabeth?"

"Of the kind of arsehole that lures you into the sea in the middle of the night."

Grey eyes and pink Power and endless, bloodstained Ether …

"She'll be back," Alex whispered, "won't she?"

Thump.

Alex jolted into Elizabeth's arms.

"Christ," Alex gasped, "sorry."

"Old house," Elizabeth murmured, gazing up at the ceiling.

"It was probably one of my boxes falling over," Alex explained, "cos I actually have unpacking to do."

"Wanting to check?"

"No" was the answer. Obviously. But after rambling on about ghosts, where could Alex even start with why she didn't even want to go upstairs in her own house alone?

"Alright," Elizabeth said, "come back to mine."

"I can't keep imposing on you, Elizabeth," Alex whispered.

"It's not imposing if I want you there."

"And do you?"

"If you haven't worked it out yet," Elizabeth replied, "I'm not after telling you."

Elizabeth's gaze gleamed.

Storm-soaked. Alex had always thought that and now, as they leant in to each other's embrace ...

"Can I?" Elizabeth whispered, brushing together their mouths.

Dark eyes and a sneer flashed in Alex's mind.

She whipped herself away, cracking her head against the bookcase.

"Alex?"

"I'm fine," Alex mumbled, letting Power melt away the bruise before it could start, "I just ... Just try again."

She leant in, letting Elizabeth's lips ...

Did she tell you? What I did?

Alex couldn't help the jolt, Elizabeth's hands catching her this time.

Going mad. She must've been going mad, to be seeing Matthew, hearing his voice after all those ...

"I don't know." Alex laughed weakly. "It's probably a manifestation of guilt or something, isn't it? Taking the form of my brother, just to ..."

Elizabeth was staring at her.

"I don't think it's *your* guilt," Elizabeth whispered.

"Have I misread this?" Alex asked, but Elizabeth was pulling a photo from her wallet, the slide slow and painful until Alex found herself gazing at ...

At herself.

At herself and Matthew, one of the few photos of them together as adults. Twenty-first birthday. New watch gleaming on her wrist. Six months, more or less, before ...

She'd moved out by then. He would've been using by then.

Alex could see the discomfort in the way their shoulders weren't even touching. She'd been attempting a rictus grin, he hadn't even been trying at all. He was barely looking at the camera. Christ only knew how much he'd probably already drunk that evening.

"Where ... where did you get this from?"

Elizabeth gave her that same solemn, *sombre*, stare again and Alex knew.

Why couldn't a Frenchman's sister speak French?

Because the Frenchman wasn't French.

15
Fall in the Sand

Even Matthew couldn't feel it like I do.
Really? Not even Matthew?
Oh, and it was starting to make sense. Horrible coincidence after horrible coincidence. She'd known who Alex was as soon as she'd walked into the café. She'd insisted on helping her. She was there, with her, *with* her—
Matthew can't always be right.
She knew him. She'd let Alex go on about him and ...
And now Alex was alone again, curled up on the ottoman, chin to her knees as the wind battered the wonky window.
Elizabeth knew Matthew.
Knew him well enough to have a bloody photo of them in her wallet.
What if they were ...
No.
Even if Elizabeth wasn't gay, Matthew was Matthew.
God, and they'd *spoken*.
That morning.
They'd spoken.
He was putting on a stupid voice, but they'd spoken.
Paris.
Paris, that was where he'd gone.

He must've thought it was hilarious, Alex having absolutely no idea that she was speaking to him. She bet they'd been laughing behind her back, when Elizabeth sent her downstairs to get her glasses. Show Lexy a bit of attention—

The shadows in the corner of the room shifted.

"I'm really not interested, alright?" Alex said, wiping her face until the tears were just a sticky mess on her scarred wrists. "Just leave me alone."

A single finger emerged from the darkness and pointed to the floor.

The Polaroid.

Elizabeth must've dropped it.

Alex held her hand out and caught it, smoothing the photo over her knee.

She didn't even need to think of her Power now. It just did.

He'd bothered to write a caption. She hadn't noticed that before.

Me & Lex, 19th February 1990

What did he even want from her?

She had made it abundantly clear: she would kill him if he ever came back.

And now he was using someone else, someone like *Elizabeth*, to get to her.

The shadows shifted again.

"I don't wanna stay here anyway," Alex snapped, hauling herself off the ottoman with the force of someone ready to give someone else a good kicking.

Elizabeth could probably have outkicked her, but she wouldn't out-argue her.

Door upon door swung open as soon as Alex looked at them and she strode out into the night as forcefully as she could in high heels that slipped around her ankles a lot more than they had the last time she wore them.

She couldn't do it.

Alex stumbled to a stop, slid off the heels, and threw them into the bushes.

She'd never liked them anyway.

She continued down the street with a surge of adrenaline and apparently enough Power to get the streetlights flickering, but at least she wasn't ripping them out of the tarmac like she had on *that* day, because at least, as she turned onto Hangman's Hill, she knew that this betrayal was just heart-deep, not soul-deep, even if she couldn't help but remember how that cold hand holding hers had clenched around the knife at Gideon Barrett's throat and that look in that bloodshot-blue gaze, that ferocity, that fire, that fury that would've drenched Alex in a murderer's blood, a warrior's trophy just for Alex—

She fell into waiting arms.

And propelled herself back out of them just as quickly, glaring as hard as she could at an Elizabeth clenching her jaw.

"What are you doing?" Alex spat.

"Coming back to yours," Elizabeth said, her flush furious even away from the one street light that still worked. "We need to talk."

"Well, I want answers."

"And I'll give them to you," Elizabeth said, then, nodding at the Polaroid, "You can keep that."

"Don't want it," Alex replied, shoving it into Elizabeth's hand, those cool fingers brushing against her wrist. "Don't."

"Whatever you're thinking—"

"You have no idea."

"Well, you seem to think I've been seducing you on behalf of your brother."

"Half-heartedly at best," Alex spat.

"Half – cos if we'd slept together and *then* I told you that I knew Matthew, that wouldn't have gone down like cold sick?"

"Well, now we'll never know," Alex muttered.

"He felt you drown last month," Elizabeth explained. "He was scared. He just wanted to know you were alright. As soon as I told him, my favour was finished."

"Yeah," Alex said, resisting the urge to ask about her brother, "I'm fine. So why are you still here?"

"I have my own reasons."

"Yeah, and I'm asking," Alex said. "This is hardly Clinton's impeachment, Elizabeth, I just want a straight answer. He knows I'm fine, so why are you still here? Why are you taking me on dates to the bloody opera like you actually ..."

Elizabeth shook her head.

"There is no master plan," she said, "I don't know what else to say. I'm not playing games with you, Alex. And I'm sorry. Alright? I didn't imagine that this ..."

Blue light washed between them, illuminating the shimmer in Elizabeth's eyes.

And yet again, Alex was pretty sure her own eyes showed the same.

"D'you know what he did?" Alex managed to say with tears clogging her throat, and when Elizabeth shook her head again, "Yeah, well, he broke my heart."

"Alex," Elizabeth said, "he's not my friend. He's an acquaintance at best."

"I could work that one out for myself, thanks, I'm not a total thicko," Alex said, as another wave of bright blue crashed between them. "Matthew don't have friends."

Matthew didn't have anything close to friends, let alone anything else, because just like Alex, Matthew was a Wilde and Wildes had rules and they'd always said, her and Matthew, that they'd never *ever* end up like their mother: charmed, married, and heartbroken with children all in the space of a year or so.

Apart from Sam, because Sammy Meyer had always been the Wildes' strange exception with an odd place in all three of their hearts; for Alex at least, other people had been useful for passing the time. She was content with having the odd overpriced dinner or fleeting fumble with them, but there would always come the point where Alex would find a plausible enough excuse to move on.

She didn't wear these people's dressing gowns or sleep in their beds or actually want to go on dates or blush like an idiot every time they looked at her when they should've been taking an order and she should've been making sandwiches. She certainly didn't stand in the street scared that if she pushed either herself or the other person too hard, someone would break.

Wildes had rules. And Carrie had died bitter and alone. And Shaz was marrying a man used to being held at a distance by them. And Alex just went through the motions. And Matthew ...

Well, Alex assumed Matthew was still Matthew.

What a sad bunch they were.

"I mean it," Elizabeth said, "I'm not playing."

"Then what the hell do you want from me?"

Elizabeth stepped back with a wince.

"Well?" Alex said, but that blue light was washing between them again. "The lights?"

"Aye, the blue ..."

Alex swallowed her disappointment and followed Elizabeth onto the promenade.

A police car sat further down the road, its lights swirling through the darkness.

In sombre silence, Alex and Elizabeth walked with the leaden legs of a funeral procession as they neared the body on the beach.

A body with pink hair.

With seaweed.

Alex felt her legs go and started muttering an apology as Elizabeth heaved her up and told her it was no bother.

"We can't just leave her with ... with *them*," Alex whispered. "They don't know her."

"Alex," Elizabeth sighed, "neither do we."

"But ..."

Power hung in the air between them.

But it wasn't silver.

It wasn't burgundy either.

It was purple.

Like lavender in bloom.

Alex and Elizabeth lurched towards the wall, just far enough to see ...

"She ain't Dead," Alex said, stating the obvious when actually, all things considered, it really shouldn't have been obvious that someone she'd seen get washed into the waves the night before was back, living and breathing, but there the girl was.

Pandora was sitting up.

Pandora was scrabbling around on the sand.

Pandora was shouting through the seaweed slipping from her lips.

"Aye." Elizabeth laughed. "Pandora isn't Dead."

Sunday 3 October 1999

16
Running Silent and Deep

Matthew stormed towards the Seine with an intensity of purpose that had shoppers and tourists sidestepping him for fear of receiving worse than a warning glare. So much for Elizabeth not returning to Paris until the monastery business had been straightened out, until Matthew had done a lot of begging to various people on her behalf.

For all he knew she could have been shot on sight, by her former employers, by a Caretaker, or by a rightly pissed-off priest having to pick up the slack on behalf of all his Dead colleagues.

Jacques greeted him at the door of the café with a cautious smile that seemed to be trying its best to reach his eyes, but then fear was a potent emotion.

"Monsieur Wilde."

Matthew asked, in French of course, if Elizabeth were there yet, glancing around the café to take in the usual tourists, students, pensioners …

No former fixer in the vicinity.

Just that rich, biting aroma of overpriced coffee that always permeated Jacky's, embedding itself into the walls like the skulls in the Catacombs.

"No," Jacques said, "but I understand the train of Mademoiselle Black was only due in Gare du Nord thirty minutes ago and you are a little early, Monsieur."

"Barely," Matthew muttered.

He didn't check his watch.

He never needed to.

"May I get you a drink while you wait for her?" Jacques asked, his relief eye-gougingly palpable when Matthew allowed him to guide him into the usual corner, a secluded and shaded spot that gave them a view of the Seine and, more importantly, the door.

Matthew took the seat facing the view. If she wasn't going to arrive on time, he was hardly going to let her have her pick.

He asked for a sparkling water, ice and lemon, remembering at the last moment to thank Jacques, who with a warmer nod, approached the waitresses with an urgent whisper. One of the waitresses, Jacques' niece Danielle, shot Matthew a smile from behind her curtain of black hair, a smile that faded into something slightly stiffer at whatever her uncle was telling her, most likely a warning that Monsieur Wilde wasn't in the best of the moods. Danielle was the only one to ever receive those notes, but then Jacques had been trying to matchmake them for the better part of two years, even if Matthew couldn't quite understand why.

He managed a grimace back at the poor girl, which somehow emboldened her smile and when she gave him a little wave, Matthew rummaged for his cigarettes and tried to focus on taking long, careful breaths, the type that helped him when his brain was determined to trip up his mouth.

However, that was easier said than done once his mind drifted to Elizabeth.

Why the impromptu visit?

Why not a call?

How many evenings was he going to have to self-medicate a splitting migraine?

And why on earth was Alexandra in Elizabeth's flat yesterday morning? They'd sounded so familiar, as if they were friends, but that was an impossibility, a mathematical one more than anything else, and now Elizabeth was returning to a city in which she was not welcome, arranging appointments against his will.

Eventually, as Matthew stubbed out what remained of his cigarette ...

She appeared.

Even at the best of times, Elizabeth Black wouldn't have looked out of place on the Red Square at Brezhnev's funeral or one of the others, but now, as she strode along the Seine with that ludicrous combination of black coat *and* tartan scarf *and* leather gloves, she could have stepped out of *The Master and Margarita*. As one of the demons, of course. Hella, perhaps, with none of the charm.

After the usual greetings to Jacques, Danielle, and the others, Elizabeth stood behind the unoccupied chair and pointed to it with a gloved hand.

Those gloves.

As children, the Wildes had called them "murderer's gloves".

Evidently, they had been correct.

Matthew reminded her that it was her reservation.

"In English," Elizabeth tutted, "please. It has been a month."

Something had changed about Elizabeth Black. She seemed tired, which was disconcerting in itself, but that wasn't it. Matthew was forced to scrutinise her as she unwrapped herself and sank into the chair with a tight smile in Danielle's direction and a request for a Turkish coffee, sweet.

"Is she alright?" Matthew asked, reluctantly relenting to her request in a language that felt leaden on his tongue. "Alexandra."

Elizabeth half-nodded as she waved Danielle back to ask for an almond croissant, warm.

"Then why – in fact, *what on earth* was she doing in your flat yesterday?" Matthew asked, demonstrating as much patience as his sister used to on Christmas Eve, scratching at her handful of paper-wrapped boxes like a feral kitten.

"That's irrelevant, Wilde," Elizabeth said, glancing around the café with a stretch of her shoulders and that keen (keenly paranoid) eye of hers.

"I just asked you to see if she was alright," Matthew hissed, "not to become friends with her."

Elizabeth spat out a laugh, unable to crush an odd smirk in time.

"What?"

An imperceptible shake of her head was the only response Matthew received and he only just remembered to not growl at Danielle when she brought their refreshments over.

Thanking Danielle for her coffee and croissant, Elizabeth lit a cigarette before offering the box to Matthew, who declined. For now.

Elizabeth gave him an insouciant shrug, but she wouldn't meet his eyes. He'd given up trying to read her a long time ago, because how could one read someone who had been a monolith for so long? However, something had been chipped away. Chiselled, a little. Bashed around a bit? Perhaps it was the obvious exhaustion, but he knew she almost never slept, she never needed to after all, so sleep deprivation couldn't possibly have been the cause.

But it was, as Matthew had initially thought, disconcerting, because in his experience, there was only one thing in the world that could've had a chance of wearing down Elizabeth Black.

"You've told her, haven't you?" Matthew realised. "She knows about me."

Elizabeth's response was a heavy sigh and a roll of her eyes.

"You," Matthew spat, slamming his clammy hands down on cold Formica, "are meant to be the soul of discretion."

"Then you should've hired me. Or at least paid me."

"You wouldn't let me!"

"I did your wee favour," Elizabeth continued, evidently and infuriatingly unrepentant, "I made sure she was fine and I told you she's fine."

Elizabeth took a long drag of her cigarette before flicking the ash into the ashtray as she added:

"More or less."

"So how did she react," Matthew asked, unable to escape his own curiosity, "when you told her?"

Elizabeth looked at where her watch should have been and tutted. She never took that watch off. What had happened to it?

"That study of yours is interesting, isn't it?"

Elizabeth should have known better than to attempt such obvious tactics on an *avocat*, but there they were. Sitting opposite each other on a bloody freezing autumn afternoon, those bright eyes staring him down. Matthew swallowed sharply and snatched up the cigarettes.

"It's a room," he said, fumbling with the packet, "in a house."

"A room," Elizabeth replied. "A room drenched in Power that isn't yours or Alex's or Sharpe's and it's the only room your sister'll sleep in, but aye, it's just a room in a house."

"Power that isn't ours?" Matthew asked.

That was impossible. Both their mother and the Shadow had been in the room for a split second, but there was ...

That ghost.

But he was just a ghost.

He didn't have Power.

But if the study had been drenched in Power that Matthew had somehow never noticed, and the study's one permanent occupant was—

"They didn't get married, by the way," Elizabeth was saying. "Alex and Meyer."

She really hadn't gone through with it?

Matthew had always imagined that, after he'd left, they would've worked something out. That Sam would've begged her, persuaded her, convinced her with his doe eyes and his sad frown that they were meant to be together after all, because if they weren't, then what had been the point of it all?

What had been the point of Matthew abusing Alex's trust in that way? Or worse, letting his conscience intervene when she made her way down the aisle with that glazed look in her eyes? And then all that Power she didn't even know she had, pulling the bricks from the mortar like a toddler tearing apart its building blocks in a tantrum.

"Which is what you were wanting, I'm assuming?" Elizabeth continued, utterly ignorant of the nausea that Matthew was struggling to suppress with his smoking. "You seem the type to ruin your own sister's hopes and dreams."

"You know nothing about it."

"Tell me I'm wrong then."

Matthew coughed more than scoffed.

"You're wrong."

Elizabeth raised an eyebrow, as if she could possibly understand anything about it, not when her own family were long Dead and buried, mostly, at least.

"I am?"

"I was trying to make sure she *did* get married," Matthew snapped at her, furious at how pricklingly hot his face felt, "not that I think it's any of your business."

"But why?"

"And quite frankly," Matthew got out before his throat could seize, "I don't know why you couldn't have just called. Or has she banished you too?"

He may as well have slapped Elizabeth. He imagined it would have had a similar effect.

It was hard to glower at someone who was blinking back tears.

Although, if Matthew could interpret that about her, that *upset* radiating from her, a disturbance that hadn't even occurred when he'd had to pull her out last month from under dozens of corpses, then the façade commonly known as Elizabeth the Unkillable really had been cracked. Was cracking.

"Mademoiselle Black?" he asked.

She cleared her throat and stared down at her trembling hands.

"Things are changing in Coldharbour," she explained. "It's not just Eleanor, *things* are circling your sister. You know, I have not stopped since I met her. I don't know if it's me or her or just the future coming, a new Millennium and that total eclipse ..."

"Elizabeth—"

"How do you live with it?" Elizabeth asked, finally looking into Matthew's eyes. "Seeing her look at you like that?"

"By going into exile," Matthew replied, but it was even harder to maintain his hauteur when he thought of that familiar scrawl in his notebook commanding him to come home. "Have you hurt her?"

"It doesn't matter—"

"Because I told you to leave that seedy little backwater—"

"We've made some unpleasant discoveries," Elizabeth declared.

Matthew glanced at the scars creeping up Elizabeth's hand. He used to stare and she used to let him – he assumed she understood it was just his morbid curiosity about Power and the effects thereof, nothing as base as gawping at a funny-looking stranger in the street. He'd appreciated them as something truly fascinating, those strange signs of survival, patina on the monolith, immortality as art.

"Ah," he said, "regarding Eleanor?"

"Your mother was murdered, Matthew."

17
Love in the Dark

Pandora was *young*.

In the faint sunrise that dappled Elizabeth's bedroom, hours before her brother would be storming towards the Seine and startling tourists, Alex smoothed the pink hair off Pandora's forehead, noticing for the first time how freckled she was. How young she was. In fact, Alex had no idea how she'd been planning to get into The Neptune's Arms, because she was only two or three years older than Maddie, if that. The eyeliner had washed off in the sea. Just little clumps of black and salt were left, clinging to her lashes like limpets.

When Shaz had been round to check Pandora (and sedate her), she said that Pandora's arm had healed, at least in the sense of how old the scars looked, so people would probably just assume it was a childhood chip-pan fire.

Elizabeth brushed her hand over Alex's and asked if she could look at Pandora's arm again. Alex leant back as Elizabeth revealed Pandora's Power-damaged arm, almost identical to her own: silvery, scaly, iridescent under the low lights.

"So it won't hurt her no more?" Alex asked. "If it's healed?"

"Exactly," Elizabeth said. "It doesn't look pretty, but ..."

She gestured at her own arm, her face, and shrugged, leaving Alex with the overwhelming urge to grab her, to tell her—

No.

Things were different now.

All that mystery around Elizabeth that had intrigued Alex had coalesced and soured into the shape of someone she never wanted to see again. Matthew's practical jokes had always been the sickest.

"How long did Sharon say the sedation would last?" Elizabeth asked.

"Not long," Alex whispered, wondering if she should've asked her sister for the same treatment because then at least she wouldn't have to think about their brother. "Just to take the edge off. You know, the trauma of ..."

She waved her hand through the air. Weakly.

"Being murdered and waking up surrounded by pigs?" Elizabeth suggested.

Now that had been a master class of Power and pure aggression: an agitated Elizabeth Black "explaining" to the police that clearly *her little sister* had had one too many to drink and she was going to take her home.

Shockingly, or perhaps for a quiet life, the coppers had shrugged and gone along with it. Sam would've been mortified had he known.

"Do you think he'll be a problem?" Elizabeth asked. "Meyer?"

"Shaz'll keep schtum," Alex replied.

"It's not Shaz I'm worried about," Elizabeth said. "The girl was attacked—"

"We know it was Barrett," Alex said, "and Barrett's banged up."

Alex stared at Elizabeth.

Elizabeth stared at Alex.

Neither of them had said a word about Matthew for hours, not since they'd found Pandora. There were priorities. They had priorities.

And if Alex was glaring more than staring, then that was hardly her fault. Was it?

Elizabeth sighed and sat on her hands. She must've realised Alex kept clocking those twitching fingers and perfect nails. Just happening to own a café …

What was it Elizabeth had said? That she was there for a reason?

"Shaz said something about your uncle," Elizabeth said. "Harry?"

"He can sort this," Alex muttered, "he can sort anything."

Alex gently squeezed Pandora's hand. Harry could sort anything. But this …

And Sam had told her to stay out of trouble. Begged her, almost.

Alex braced herself for questions from Elizabeth, but in the end, it was just the insistent ticking of a clock disturbing the silence.

She looked up just once. Elizabeth was already watching her in unsaid understanding. They should've been holding hands. Eight hours ago, before *Matthew*, they would've been holding hands, tight, fingers slipping together, clammy clinging to cold.

That's how they should've continued their vigil.

It should never have felt that natural, holding onto that hand, onto Elizabeth's hand, when only a day and a half before they'd been imperfect strangers. But there Alex was, that country crossed. Now she was surrendering to that strange certainty that had been surging deep in her soul, slowly but surely like the tide that had somehow returned Pandora to them. And the certainty coalesced into a single, clear belief:

It would take more than Barrett or the Shadow or even Matthew to make Alex want to stay away from Elizabeth. No matter how any of them, Alex included, tried.

"What did happen to you?" Alex eventually dared to ask. "Your burns."

"One of my sisters," Elizabeth said, rubbing her hand down her face, "my twin sister. She tried to kill me."

"There's tried to, like the time I pushed Matthew out of his bedroom window when we were seven, and there's tried to ..."

Like *that* day, when Alex and Matthew, ablaze with Power, had demolished the house around themselves, screaming accusations at each other until their throats ripped apart and healed and ripped apart again, Matthew's face twisted in fury, Alex's wedding dress streaked with blood and dirt.

Harry had to use his Master Power to separate them, invading their minds with brute force, yanking on their strings like a particularly sadistic puppeteer.

And then Matthew was gone.

Elizabeth smoothed her hand over her scars, letting them shine in the dawn light.

"Your sister did that?" Alex asked.

"Not all sisters are lovely like Shaz."

"Can I ask—"

Alex stopped herself and sighed, ready to apologise, but Elizabeth was staring at her. In fact, Elizabeth even gave her a nod.

"What did she do to you?" Alex asked.

"She – *Eleanor* – tried to take my Power."

"But she was born with her own, right?" Alex said. "So she shouldn't have been as, well, as messy as Gideon Barrett."

"She chose to burn me," Elizabeth said, gazing down at Pandora's arm. "She had the idea that the pain would make my Power break away more cleanly, like meat off a bone."

Darkness flitted across Elizabeth's eyes, ageing her, wearying her with a heavy misery that pulled at the air between them.

"And she just liked me in pain."

Alex swallowed tightly. What could she even say?

"Anyway," Elizabeth continued, "it killed me. But I came back because she hadn't taken my Master Power, you know, my resurrection abilities, because I had to die first for my Master Power to come into being. So I came back, waited for the rest of my Power to regenerate, and then I destroyed her."

Alex reached for Elizabeth's arm, made herself retreat, and apologised. Elizabeth asked why.

"Because it sounds awful," Alex said. "Because she put you through that—"

"It's been a long time," Elizabeth mumbled, dragging her hand across her face again, "I'm just tired of it. Besides, she tried to put you through that too."

"What?"

The Shadow had called Elizabeth "Lizzie".

She'd known how to wind her up.

How to get right under her skin.

She was beautiful. So beautiful. Objectively beautiful, with that golden, angelic face, not the stomach-flippingly beautiful that Elizabeth was to Alex, but truly stunning.

But there had been something familiar there. Something about their smiles, their gazes, one avid, the other ravenous, that gravity they both had that compelled Alex against her instincts, that told her she wanted to be devoured.

And one of them had a Master Power as rare as rocking horse shit.

Only a twin could cause the kind of desolation Alex felt from Elizabeth.

Only a twin.

"The Shadow is your sister?"

"Yep."

"So she was tormenting you yesterday?" Alex asked. "Not necessarily me?"

"I imagine Eleanor's taking the opportunity to kill two birds with one stone," Elizabeth replied, rigid with bitter resignation.

"Right."

Alex stared down at Pandora. What else could she do?

"Trust me." Elizabeth sighed. "Aiding and abetting an elderly psychopath isn't even that high on Eleanor's rap sheet. Meyer would have a fit."

It was all beginning to make a horrific kind of sense, because there really were too many horrible coincidences: Elizabeth, Carrie, Barrett ...

What the Shadow, what *Eleanor*, had done ...

"Can ... can I show you something?" Alex whispered. "In my mind? It ... it's not very nice, but I can't ..."

How could she have put into words all that fear they'd felt?

"Of course," Elizabeth murmured, resting her hand on Alex's shoulder, "just let me in and it'll—"

Alex threw that terrible night at her like a ticking bomb. She surrendered the panic of when they couldn't get their hands free of the spirit board, the terror of that ghost with half a face appearing by their side, the hopelessness of Shaz taken over by the Shadow – *Eleanor* ...

And then, and only then, after a pint had been poured and a glass had been dropped and a ghost had been seen and without another word or her wages ...

Carrie.

Catherine Wilde, burning with golden Power for the first time in years and for the very last time in her life, bursting through a locked door like it was nothing but air.

And finally, that knock on the door in the middle of the night, the end of Alex's cassette still clicking in the tape deck.

Alex had asked Harry, back then, that night, if Carrie could've come back.

They'd both known, deep down, that Carrie never had any intention of coming back.

Her ghost had never appeared to Matthew either.

God, and those sympathetic stares from everyone in the town, as if they hadn't spent years muttering about the family behind their backs, if they hadn't known that the kids had driven her to it in the first place ...

Who could've lived with children that were summoning things from the pits of hell?

"Oh Christ," Elizabeth breathed, horror flooding her face, "she possessed your mother?"

"What?" Alex said. "No, she possessed Shaz. Mum, well, clearly didn't exorcise her like we thought but ..."

Half a lifetime of skirting around the words.

"Mum killed herself," Alex explained, letting that hollowness spread through her chest. "She threw herself off the cliffs that night."

Elizabeth squeezed Alex's hands. She shook her head. And in the softest, solemnest voice, asked her what her mother's name was.

"Carrie," Alex whispered, "Catherine Wilde."

"I don't think," Elizabeth said, her eyes beginning to redden as her hands convulsed around Alex's, "that Carrie Wilde would've ever chosen to leave her children while something like Eleanor was still around."

Alex took a deep, stinging breath through her nose and hoped that would stave off her own tears.

"She, uh, she wasn't always a well woman."

"And if you came home one night," Elizabeth asked, "to find Maddie possessed by Eleanor? Would you just attempt to exorcise her and then off yourself?"

"Of course I wouldn't," Alex said, "I'd ..."

She would stand between them and she would fight. And for all of Carrie's faults, and there had been so, so many, she would've fought.

Alex snatched her hands back to wipe sticky tears off her chin.

"It doesn't change anything," she insisted, "we summoned Eleanor. We got Mum killed."

"How the hell did you reach that conclusion?"

"Mum told us to stay away from the study," Alex said. "She told us to stay away from the spirit board. But I didn't listen. I never listened. We were looking for our father, a man who walked out on us when we weren't even a year old, and we don't even know, even now, whether he's dead or alive, went back to Ireland for all we know and she waited and waited, stuck with two kids and then three and he never wrote to her or sent her money and she did the best she could."

Even if Alex hadn't thought it at the time. Even if she'd spent so much time screaming at her own mother.

"All cos we found an empty grave," she continued, "for David Alexander Wilde, 1945 to 1969. And I just couldn't let it go. Until ..."

"You used the board."

"You know what happened next. Let's just say, it weren't David Wilde coming through."

"You know," Elizabeth said, "it sounds to me that a malevolent, vindictive spirit took advantage of a confused, grieving child."

Alex scoffed.

"I was fifteen."

"A year or two older than Matilda," Elizabeth said. "A year or two younger than Pandora, probably. Would you blame either of them for something like that?"

"She's still Dead," Alex argued, "I started off with one parent and I ended up with none."

No wonder Matthew hadn't trusted her anymore. Not with the important stuff.

Elizabeth tutted, rolled her eyes, and twisted her scarred arm until it caught the overhead lights.

"Remember," she said, "I know Eleanor. I know what she's capable of. I know what she does to people. She'd managed to kill three of our brothers and one of our sisters before she even got to me and that was back when she was mortal. She tears her way through souls, Alex. A couple of teenagers, even if they are as brave as you and as clever as Matthew, never stood a chance against someone that single-minded and vicious. Which is why I should leave."

"Leave?" Alex asked, whatever was left of her swirling stomach plummeting into oblivion.

"Coldharbour," Elizabeth said. "The chances are she'll follow me and leave you alone."

"Right," Alex breathed, staring down at Pandora again, because her voice was failing her.

How was she meant to reply?

Was she meant to beg Elizabeth to stay? Even though ...

"No, of course," Alex made herself say, "you've got nothing to stay for anymore."

She glanced up into those eyes, long enough to decide they were a very faint blue after all, because there was a dash more colour in them than Eleanor's, and waited for Elizabeth's nod.

And with it came that same soul-shocking grief Alex felt when she'd let go of Pandora's hand in those chill, churning waves.

18
Flashes of Light

"Try again," Alex mumbled into her hand, "slower."

She had planned to do it in the kitchen or even the living room, but Pandora, still wobbly on her legs like a freshly born (or reborn) calf, had taken one look at the study and imprinted on it.

As for Maddie, who had apparently got permission to come over from either Sam, who'd been called into work on some emergency, or Shaz, who had somehow managed to let slip to her about Pandora, well ...

She'd bounded straight into the study and had started prodding books with sticky fingers while slagging off the décor and asking Pandora if she was a zombie.

And now, the crumbs of the girls' *third* lunch strewn around the table, Alex was ticking off the list Elizabeth left behind:

Age: 16 (23rd July 1983)

Description of Power: purple/lilac, lukewarm, light (as in not heavy, not as in not dark)

Master Power: unknown (Alex had pencilled that in)

Other expressions of Power:

Alex had no idea how she was even meant to go about it. Elizabeth knew she knew sod all about Power and Harry was wherever he was and now ...

Matthew was in Paris.

Pandora started to glow, faintly, with the same tepidness Alex's Power had before she started to use it again.

They'd already ruled out levitation and teleportation and it didn't seem like Pandora could get into Alex's mind, which was, as Matthew had so clearly pointed out to her on *that* day, permanently wide open with a big flashing sign, like it was a car boot sale begging for a rummage.

There should've been a spotter's guide to Power, if Alex was really having to do this on her bloody own.

You've got nothing to stay for anymore.

"We could just wait for Elizabeth to come back," Maddie suggested, kicking her feet against the table leg.

"She's not coming back," Alex replied, raising the pencil into mid-air with her gaze. "And what did I just say about sitting on the table?"

"It's not even glowing," Pandora gasped. "How are you doing it like that?"

Another question Alex couldn't answer. Instead, she told Pandora to do whatever she wanted to the pencil: to throw it, to freeze it, to disintegrate it. Whatever felt natural.

"How am I meant to know?" Pandora asked, screwing her face up with an uncertainty that Alex recognised, but where from?

"Instinct. It's always instinct."

"Not being funny," Maddie said, through a mouthful of crisp sandwich, "but the Power I saw yesterday was a bit more ... You know."

Pandora frowned at the pencil, which trembled and wobbled and ...

That was it.

"To be fair," Pandora said, blinking up at her with wide, hazel eyes, "you are really strong."

"I'm not." Alex laughed, keeping the pencil in the air with a worrying lack of effort. "But thanks."

What was it that she recognised in Pandora's face? It was in her frown, wasn't it? Whatever it was, it was enough for Alex to gently ask her if she knew anything at all about her birth parents.

Pandora shook her head, but then, with a high note of hope in her voice that would've rebroken Alex if she'd given it half the chance, asked if they could be related.

"Cos you said it's only one in a thousand—"

"I doubt it," Alex tried to say as softly as possible, knowing that twinge of hope that somebody could've been out there, and how it could all go so wrong with a spirit board and *Eleanor*.

"But your dad must've been white, right?" Maddie said. "Cos if your mum was Uncle Harry's sister and Uncle Harry's black—"

"He's long gone," Alex mumbled, thinking of that hand burning pink in the darkness of the study, right next to where she was now sitting. "There's no finding him."

"He's Dead?" Pandora asked.

"This pencil isn't gonna move itself," Alex said, setting it spinning with a glance that she kept away from her daughter's curious gaze.

"I don't know what to do, Alex."

"You must've done something with your Power before," Alex snapped, and she could imagine the spirit board by her left hand and how Carrie had made it crumble into sand, "even accidentally. We all do."

"But I'm not like you," Pandora whined, "I can't just—"

At the wave of her hand, the pencil burst into lavender flames, scattering embers across the floor.

Pandora blushed a queasy-looking pink that wasn't far off her hair.

"Well," Maddie sniggered, "I'd say you can write down 'fire-starting', but she just destroyed your pencil."

Alex still thought that Power couldn't really help anyone, but it was good enough for the occasional party trick: the washing away of wrinkles, the hovering of stationery, and ...

Her Power flowed through her, calmly, obediently, as the ashes lifted off the floorboards and swirled together to form a perfectly intact pencil, its black and yellow lines shiny and smooth.

"What?" Pandora gasped. "That is insane!"

"Good enough?" Alex asked, snatching up the pencil.

It was good. It felt good.

It felt *brilliant*.

And then, just to really show off, she sat on her hands and made the pencil write in perfectly neat letters next to *Other expressions of Power*:

Spontaneous combustion

"I'll bear that in mind," Maddie said, "next time I can't find my pencil sharpener."

"Less of the lip, young lady," Alex warned, but that familiar smirk twisting her daughter's mouth reminded her of that Polaroid and that panic pierced Alex just as profoundly as it had done in Barrett's cottage, because over the years, as Alex had watched her daughter play and run and draw and laugh and cry, she would wonder ...

Was there any Power there?

Against the odds, could Maddie be harbouring something?

A little flame, the tiniest spark?

At which point, Maddie would fall over and graze her knee or she would bring back a bug from school and her mother would go through all the reassuring motion of TCP and toilet bowls, safe in the knowledge that her own body, her Power, would resist any hint of infection. Having to purge poison from her daughter's body had been significantly less soothing for Alex, but it had seemed to prove the following:

Matilda Meyer was a normal thirteen-year-old girl.

She was brash and she was boisterous and she was bouncy and Alex hoped to any higher power that might still have been listening (did the Ether count?) that life itself wouldn't knock too much of it out of her.

Not even arsenic in her tea.

She wasn't like them.

She certainly wasn't like Matthew.

"Have I got Monster Munch on my face or what?" Maddie asked, slapping her chin with the back of her hand. "So everyone's Power's a different colour? Like you're Power Rangers or something?"

No. Nothing like Matthew.

"You really wanna know about this family?" Alex asked. "And Power?"

The eager nod wasn't Matthew's either.

Matthew wouldn't have known – Matthew wouldn't know – enthusiasm if it rampaged right at him like Mr Blobby.

Alex told Maddie to go up to her room, the first on the right, the one that still had purple paisley wallpaper, Madonna and Ferris Bueller posters yellowing at the edges, sticky tape dried and curling on the corners, a shelf of dust-laden cuddly toys ...

She had told Harry he could turn it into a second study or something. Probably when she had actually moved out, so ten years ago. Even before *that* day.

And in that room, with its hastily taped-up boxes teetering against the purple paisley wallpaper, Maddie would find a thin, white photo album.

And she was off, clattering down the corridor scattering breadcrumbs in her wake.

"That'll keep her occupied for at least a couple of minutes." Alex sighed, rubbing her eyes. "I know she can be a bit overbearing, but she's just excited."

Pandora didn't reply.

But then she wasn't even looking at Alex. She was looking beyond her.

"Earth to Pandora?" Alex asked, letting the pencil clatter against wood.

She twisted round in her chair, ready to glare at the Half-Faced Man—

Nothing there.

Alex turned back, to a Pandora smiling right at her.

"Right," Alex said, "shall we try one more time before trouble gets back?"

"Actually," Pandora said, "I'm rather tired now. Can I go for a rest now?"

"Are you feeling alright?" Alex asked, pressing the back of her hand against ...

A cold forehead.

Where she'd been expecting clammy skin to flush under her touch, Alex met a chill that reminded her of Elizabeth. Maybe it was a coming back to life thing, but Alex said that she'd phone Shaz anyway.

"I really am fine." Pandora laughed.

"Better to be safe than sorry," Alex argued, easing herself out of her seat, only to catch in the wonky window a glimpse of what could've been a sneer twisting Pandora's reflection.

She watched Pandora rise from the table, the glass warping her movement into the fluidness of a serpent ready to strike ...

The Half-Faced Man flashed into being.

Alex swore and reeled away from the window, gasp after gasp ricocheting from her body.

Pandora was still sitting down.

Playing with the pencil.

Reading Alex's notes.

Just like her reflection was in the wonky window.

And as for the Half-Faced Man ...

Nowhere to be seen. Not even in the shadows.

Clearly, seeing wasn't believing.

Maddie rushed back in with the photo album in her arms, holding it out to Alex, who let herself sound like a thicko by asking how she'd managed to find it so quickly.

A shrug with both shoulders was her reply.

Her head beginning to pound, Alex told Pandora she could go for that rest if she wanted.

"What rest?" Pandora asked.

"So I really can't tell anyone about Power?" Maddie asked. "Not even Stace?"

"I know for a fact you've done the witch hunts at school," Alex said, but she couldn't take her eyes off Pandora, who was just looking at her so docilely. "Absolutely not."

"Thought you said you weren't a witch," Maddie said, with the terrifying nonchalance of a teenager who was listening but not fully absorbing.

Alex told her daughter to wait and she asked Pandora about calling Shaz.

"Why?" Pandora asked, her dismay punching right through Alex's defences. "I thought I was fine here."

"You are," Maddie said, flailing more than turning. "She is, isn't she?"

Well, if seeing wasn't believing, maybe hearing wasn't either.

Pandora asked if it was alright if she got some more water, which of course it was, but Alex didn't miss how she carefully swiped all the crumbs onto the plates, which she stacked neatly before gathering them into her arms and carrying them out of the study.

Into the darkness.

"She really is sixteen, by the way," Maddie said. "She's one of last year's Year 11s."

"Alright." Alex sighed, thumping open the photo album. "I believe you."

She might've believed her daughter, but she hadn't missed that furrow between her eyebrows when Pandora had introduced herself, something that with most people meant resistance, but in this case ...

Well, maybe Maddie was just so sick of being the only child left in the family that she was now clinging to Pandora like a limpet, desperately trying to find common ground in the things they ate or watched or wore, while Pandora, bless her, had been demonstrating the kind of patience Alex could only dream of when Maddie tried to explain the offside rule to her or why the best hot chocolate was Spanish or her ideas for entering *Robot Wars*.

"You can't send her back though," Maddie said, so earnestly, and had her eyes always been such a brilliant blue?

"Send her back where, sweetheart?"

That was one thing Maddie did have in common with her uncle: shockingly terrible liars for who they were. It was like their eyes and mouths just couldn't help but let slip surprise or sadness.

"I, for one," Alex ended up saying, "am not going to send Pandora back anywhere. She's safe with us."

Apparently pacified (according to that non-poker-face at least), Maddie slid onto the chair next to Alex and shuffled up to see the first picture more clearly.

"The only picture I have of them together," Alex said, gazing at Carrie and David, proudly showing off their best on their wedding day, matching in blue, Carrie looking conspicuously pregnant even with the feather boa draped across her stomach, "my parents. And Harry, obviously."

"You look just like them."

There was an avid gleam in Maddie's eyes at discovering all of these connections, these people, that made Alex's heart twinge.

"D'you think so?"

"In the face," Maddie said. "You have David's nose. So was he Irish? Like Oscar Wilde? Are we related to Oscar Wilde?"

"No." Alex laughed. "He was Irish-Jewish. That's pretty much all I know."

She'd - no, Matthew had once managed to catch Carrie in a *good* drunk mood, tipsy but not bumping into the table, misty-eyed but not belligerent. "Cork" and "pogroms". He'd had the patience to coax that much out of her. Two words that he returned to Alex in her room like he'd trekked across a desert to bring her a drop from an oasis. She hadn't even known the word "pogrom" until Matthew reminded her of *Fiddler on the Roof*.

"Jewish?" Maddie asked. "Like Dad?"

"Apparently," Alex said, "he's got a grave in the synagogue cemetery."

"Why didn't you say?"

"I don't know, sweetheart," would've been Alex's response, but she did know. She knew from the tightness in her chest when she just considered digging out the album to bring here, from the pull of utter yearning every time she looked at a face she thought she would never see in the flesh again, barely able to say their names in case she lost just a little bit more of them in the whisper, so determined was she to keep those little remnants in her soul, forever in the warm and the dark.

"Why has your dad got missing fingers?" Maddie asked.

Alex glanced down at the page, where David was giving his thumbs-up, waving with the other hand where the signet ring gleamed on just one of two fingers on his left hand: the middle, index, and thumb gone.

"No idea," Alex said, wondering if she'd ever been told the story, if Matthew had managed to retrieve another little treasure of a fact from their mother. "Shall we look at another page?"

"So they had Power like you have?"

"It's inherited," Alex said, turning the page, "but both your parents have to have it."

"So I don't have it?"

"That's a good thing, trust me. You shouldn't see too many strange things around here, for a start."

Except Maddie could see Power, couldn't she? She knew it was different colours. Although Sam could see it too. Maybe it was Shaz who was the odd one out.

"What happened to them?" Maddie asked. "You just said he was long gone."

"Uh," Alex said, turning the pages, with speed, without thought, "they died, sweetheart."

Which was half true, at least.

"When did they die?"

"Him, I don't know," Alex replied. "Maybe when I was a baby. Her, when I was fifteen."

"And their parents?"

Alex shook her head.

"I don't know, sweetheart. Mum and Uncle Harry's parents came over from the West Indies at some point. That's it."

"So if it's inherited," Maddie continued, "does Uncle Harry have Power?"

"Yes," Alex said, but that catch in her throat wouldn't clear and that throb in her temple was lingering. "Yeah, yeah, he does."

"And what can he do?" Maddie asked, blissfully unaware of the discomfort crawling through her mother. "Can he throw people through the air?"

"I doubt it," Alex said, wiping her hands against her jumper. "He'd probably make you throw yourself through the air and make you think it was all your own clever idea."

Alex turned over several more pages, to be sure she had got past Carrie, only to be faced with—

"Uncle Matthew."

The sullen little boy forced to sit next to his equally unimpressed sister.

"You do remember him?"

Maddie frowned and nodded.

"You had a funny name for him."

That memory of hers ...

"Mouse," Alex whispered, "I used to call him Mouse."

"I loved him," Maddie said, as if it could ever have been that simple to love someone like Matthew.

"He loved you too," Alex said, running her hand over her daughter's smooth hair. "He adored you. Couldn't say that about many people when it came to Matthew."

Nine years of doing her best not to even think about him and now ...

Now Alex was having to push her bitten nails into the palms of her free hand.

Two days she'd been thinking she was going mad, when really it was all Elizabeth's fault and that Polaroid ...

Me and Lex.

"You and Matthew were twins, weren't you?"

Alex nodded, staring down at the boy who had been the other side of her soul for so long, from before they had even been born.

"Where did he go?"

"Away," Alex said, but she could taste the bitter crunch of coffee, which she never drank, and cigarettes, which she never smoked, burning the roof of her mouth.

And the smell of almonds. And the sound of chatter in a language she didn't—

She closed the photo album before she could dwell on it.

"But how does it work?" Maddie asked. "Power."

Alex sighed. How could she even begin to explain it? And yet, that stale coffee still on her tongue, she said:

"It's as natural as breathing. If we hurt ourselves, we heal, unless it's something immediately fatal, obviously. If we get shot through the heart, it's game over."

Or plummet off a cliff.

"Our levels of instinct and empathy are stronger than most people's," Alex continued, "and we usually can feel other people's Power. But then everyone's Power has certain ways it shows itself. Usually, it's a few inherited things and then your Master Power, which is the strongest expression of your Power. Some people talk to the Dead. Some people can move things with their minds. Some people can fly, for instance."

"Can you fly?"

"I can levitate," Alex said. "Well, I used to be able to. Your grandmother could fly. Apparently, cos I never saw it."

Apparently, because she plummeted off a cliff.

"What can you do?" Maddie asked, "apart from levitating?"

"Is that where we're at?" Alex laughed. "Levitating is boring now?"

"You did say you don't do it very well."

"I don't know," Alex said, "I haven't used my Power enough yet to know what I'm really good at. You know, it's like when you start school, you don't instantly know what you're good at. You need time."

Otherwise you could plummet off a cliff.

"But Power's good, right?" Maddie said. "Is it why you didn't die? The day the schools went back?"

"What did your dad and Shaz tell you?" Alex said. "I'll fill in the gaps."

"Just that you had an accident and you nearly drowned and that you had to have special treatment away from home to make sure you were definitely okay."

Alex watched her daughter wring her hands – had she started biting her nails?

"Mads," she started, "there's something—"

Smash.

Then a thunder of thuds.

Alex lurched down the corridor and into the kitchen, where Pandora was fitting on the floor, slamming against the table, and then Maddie was there trying to push it back and shouting that it was just like Auntie Charlie's and it was like Charlie's, they were used to Charlie's, it'd given them a fright at Sam's twelfth birthday party to have an eight-year-old throwing herself onto the floor like that but the difference between Charlie Meyer's fits and Pandora's was …

The purple Power flaring off her in thick lashes, swiping the bowls off the draining board, punching through porcelain, whipping the cupboard doors off their hinges.

Alex told her daughter to call Uncle Harry.

"Shouldn't I call Shaz?" Maddie yelled. "It's just a seizure."

"People with Power can't have seizures."

She was ninety-nine per cent sure that people with Power couldn't have seizures. Matthew's didn't count – he'd been dying on those slimy tiles that night, the night before *that* day.

Pandora was dying too.

Alex could feel it.

She shouldn't have pushed her so far with her Power, because now Pandora was going to slip out of her grip all over again and she had no choice but to watch and—

A shadow fell over them.

Dark hands glowing green pressed into Pandora's shoulders, keeping her still, keeping her steady, and Alex let go of the breath she'd been holding so long.

19
All the Seconds

"What do we do?" Alex asked. "Harry, what do we do?"

Harry pushed Pandora further into the tiles and asked who she was and where she was from.

"Pandora," Alex said, "from the streets?"

Purple Power threw Alex against the table and Harry against the cupboards.

"Which family of Power?" Harry asked.

"She's adopted," Maddie yelled over the roar of Power. "Can't you try healing her?"

"Can't you wait in the corridor?" Alex shouted, clambering back through flames that licked up her arms but didn't burn, not quite.

"Perhaps," Harry said, "but I can't heal other people, only myself."

"You can't heal other people?" Alex asked.

"Can you?" Harry replied, with the cold stare that was meant to jolt Alex into talking first.

"Sometimes," Alex muttered, thinking of Elizabeth's broken ankle, "but not good enough, not for—"

The house rumbled.

Victorian, winter-blasted pipes groaned around them, bricks that had tumbled into ash on *that* day were now shuffling in time-weakened mortar, and every floorboard creaked precariously.

But Pandora was still.

Swathed in purple, but—

Crockery shot out of cupboards.

Alex flinched and threw it back against the wall with a smash.

The lights came free from the ceiling.

She froze them.

Not suspended, like how like she'd stopped Maddie flying through every storey of Barrett's cottage.

The lights were frozen, bulbs stuck mid-surge amidst a cascade of plaster and dust that was more like a snapshot of snowfall.

"Mads," Alex called, "go and wait outside the house. Just in case."

With one hand still pointing at the cupboards, the other aimed at her little frozen diorama, Alex stumbled her way upright and asked Harry if freezing could help Pandora.

When he didn't reply, she glanced down, only to find him staring up at her with dismay in his eyes.

"I've been using my Power," Alex admitted, "I know. I know what I said and I still don't like it, but trust me, this weekend it's been really useful."

"How did you learn how to freeze?" Harry asked, his voice so low even in the still and the quiet.

"It's just hereditary, ain't it?" she said, blinking dust out of her eyes. "But I froze someone the other night, so if I freeze Pandora—"

"Why did you freeze somebody?"

"It's a long—"

Power whipped around Alex's ankles, yanking her to the floor, and as glass and plaster rained down on them, Pandora started flaring again and Alex asked her uncle if he was sure he couldn't heal.

"But Matthew must've got it from somewhere!" she insisted.

"Not from the Sharpe side," Harry said, with teeth so clenched they could've ground up whatever was left of the cups and saucers. "All I can do is block her Power."

"Block? Like last year, when …"

"Exactly," Harry explained, as Pandora started shuddering again. "It's just temporary and the excess Power should then dissipate into the Ether."

"Or I can take it on."

"How?"

Alex shook her head and told her uncle to go ahead.

"It won't hurt her," she said, "will it?"

Purple flashed in front of her.

And her head is thumping again.

She groans as she sits up on a beach that's not real.

Well, it's the Realm of Dream and Death, but that doesn't mean it's not real. A lifetime of dreaming and Alex had never even noticed The Other Side, but the moment she learns its name, tastes the Ether …

Although, to be fair to herself (and maybe to Elizabeth if it didn't cause the bottom to drop out of her stomach that's currently in a different dimension), she's never been knocked unconscious so often before.

If she didn't have Power, she'd begin to worry about aneurysms.

Arse on shingle, feet on sand, Alex stares at unmoving waves and waits.

It was probably the Power's fault.

Maybe it just knocked her back against the wall?

Pandora wasn't trying to burn her. She wasn't even conscious.

And she's not like Eleanor.

No, Eleanor's something else.

Eleanor's smile doesn't reach her eyes, but if it did, Alex thinks that then it would just be too late.

Alex pushes a hand against a wave that sort of gives, like jelly or any other non-Newtonian fluid, except Alex has never even heard the word "non-Newtonian" before and she shouldn't know what it means, but she does, deep in her soul, like a whole other language being unlocked.

But it doesn't matter, because all Harry has to do is block Pandora's Power and then he'll bring Alex back somehow, even if he's no good at healing people other than himself. It isn't that strange, really. Alex has just got used to coming across people like Elizabeth who are natural healers, plus Matthew ...

"Are we Dead again?"

Well, at least Pandora doesn't have seaweed dripping out of her mouth this time. She's clearly *not* Dead if she's all pink hair and pink cheeks and wide eyes and bright freckles, but the more Alex looks at her, the more she's reminded of someone else ...

But who?

"Alex?"

"You're just unconscious," Alex explains. "So am I. I think."

"But I was just about to do the washing up."

Alex shakes her head and tells her it doesn't matter. She can fix all the plates and all the glasses with a couple of clicks of her fingers. She *will* fix all the plates and all the glasses. And she'll sort out the lights and she'll smooth over the ceiling.

"And I'm definitely not Dead?" Pandora asks, her hazel eyes wide and earnest, but what can Alex possibly say that could actually reassure her?

No, you're not Dead, but you're fitting on a floor that hasn't been swept in nine years so you might end up with the lurgy and that's not even starting on the waves of Power emanating from you even though it's been as weak as watered-down squash since you came back?

"Can you hear that?" Pandora asks.

"Hear what?" Alex murmurs, watching the waves.

Are they moving closer? Or are they further away?

What should she know about non-Newtonian fluids?

"Hear what, Pandora?"

She turns to—

If Alex had skin to jump out of, she would. She would jump out of it and throw it at the person standing in Pandora's place and run as far and as fast as she could back into the Land of the Living, through those weird waves—

But that was before.

Before, she would've done that, but now it's worse.

Because Alex can see it now: if she takes away Elizabeth's scars and freckles, lightens her hair and eyes, adds another couple of inches to her height ...

Yeah.

There's a resemblance there.

Like how anyone with working eyes connected to a working brain can see that Sam's sisters are sisters, just different builds and noses, but there's enough there to say Cheryl and Charlie are swimming in the same gene pool, and once Sam is added, they're practically the Jewish Corrs.

"Sorry about last night," Eleanor says. "That was more Gideon than me."

At least that's something: the way Alex's stomach flips at Elizabeth's smile is very different to how it lurches at Eleanor's.

"That's why I left him after that." Eleanor sighs. "He was useless, really. Oh well …"

She kicks at shingle that barely shifts.

Alex takes a step back anyway.

"Means to an end," Eleanor says, nostrils flaring at Alex. "I thought it was the other twin who couldn't speak. Cat got your tongue, Lexy?"

Alex was wrong. She can't run, even if she wanted to.

And she wants to.

It's an emotional response to the very intellectual thought that's in her head, some kind of Top Trumps for Power:

The woman in front of her murdered someone who is known as Unkillable.

The woman in front of her murdered someone who could fly.

And those are the murders she knows about.

"David was the same," Eleanor continues. "It was torture watching him trying to get out a sentence sometimes. But I suppose you wouldn't know that about him."

Alex wants to ask if Eleanor knows where David is, but after the spirit board and those insidious whispers, she knows she shouldn't.

Not that she can.

Eleanor starts towards her and Alex flings her hands up to freeze her.

"That doesn't work here." Eleanor laughs, staggering back. "Did you really think?"

Hands on her knees, Eleanor wheezes out a cackle.

How can Alex's heart be convulsing that hard?

"And trying it on me?" Eleanor spits. "Lexy, they really haven't taught you well, have they? And now …"

The laugh slides off her face, leaving behind that malevolence in her gaze.

"She's left you, hasn't she?" Eleanor murmurs. "All alone."

She slinks towards—

"Eleanor!" Alex blurts out. "Eleanor. I know who you are. I know your name, I know you killed my mother, I know you're Elizabeth's sister. Eleanor."

It's not a literal freezing, but it'll do, because Eleanor shrinks back as she straightens up.

"I know you killed her," Alex continues, forcing her voice through that catch in her throat, "and I know she killed you. Sounds like it served you right."

"Says the woman who'll kill her own brother," Eleanor sneers, striding towards her. "I can smell it, you know. Both of you. Your Power's growing."

Alex is about to step back when Eleanor glances over her shoulder.

"See?" Eleanor says, that horrible, ravenous smile splitting her face again. "Here he is."

"Here's who?" Alex breathes, but there's no need, because she *feels* him.

"Nine years," Eleanor says. "Aren't you going to say hello to each other?"

It could be a trick. An illusion.

That was what Elizabeth said, wasn't it? About The Other Side?

Memories and illusions, a mirror that was one-way until ...

Until you meet someone there who is just dreaming, like you are.

But Alex doesn't turn, just as she knows that Matthew won't look up either, like a pair of rabbits locked in the sights of their prey, knowing that as soon as they move ...

Grandmother's footsteps.

They used to be the best.

The quietest, the quickest.

They were good at What's the time, Mr Wolf? too.

"Well?" Eleanor laughs.

Alex swallows spit from a mouth that can't really be that dry.

Holding her nerve. If there is one thing that she can do, one thing that her brother can do, in most circumstances at least ...

They can hold their nerve, even if it is close to dinnertime.

Another thing Alex can hold is her glare on Eleanor and she hopes that Matthew can just about feel what she's trying to convey to him – the kitchen, the seizure, the Power – but then Eleanor's starting towards them again and Alex flings her arms out to shield—

She opened her eyes.

Dust tickled her cheeks.

Shoulders throbbing and legs stiff, somehow, Alex had ended up crumpled between the sink and the table, contorted this way and that.

Pandora stared back at her, shivering in her own little corner of the kitchen.

Alex asked her where Harry was.

"Outside," Pandora whispered, "getting Maddie. Do you ..."

Alex nodded, assuming the word was "remember" and asked, with a mouth that *was* dry, if Harry had blocked her Power.

"For the rest of the day," Pandora said. "I'll pay for any damage. Somehow."

"What did I say to you on The Other Side?" Alex asked, clambering up the table. "It doesn't matter."

"But—"

Alex tutted and raised her arms, even as she cringed at her elbow cracking back into place, gathering up shards of porcelain and glass like she was just …

Your Power's growing.

Letting her Power rush through her, Alex flexed her fingers and formed cup after cup, plate after plate, bulbs and saucers, ornaments and glasses in mid-air, pouring particles into their rightful place with sparks of burgundy.

And turquoise.

That wasn't just the light.

That was turquoise.

"How do you do it?" Pandora gasped.

"It's just telekinesis," Alex explained, opening cupboard doors with just the thought. "Just really, really advanced telekinesis."

As neat stacks of kitchenware slid home, Alex glanced up at the ceiling, which smoothed itself over just like she'd decided on The Other Side.

The bulbs were still on the blink, though.

"See?" she said. "No harm done."

Dream after dream about Matthew and she'd known it was never him, but then, behind her …

That had been him, hadn't it?

"But d'you think it's about me coming back to life?" Pandora asked. "Or d'you think it's about Barrett?"

"Why d'you think it's got anything to do with Barrett?" Alex asked. "I took all his Power."

"Cos he's Dead," Pandora said, "isn't he?"

20
Memories Still Alive

Alex had found all of Harry's little notes. They'd even had a tenner under them, just like when she was sixteen.

And she kept them, just like she used to:

Under the old money box that sat in the corner of the kitchen. Harry hadn't even cleared out the nine-year-old notes, so Alex had just added them on top.

Friday 1st – 6.45 am

You'll find all your boxes in your room (which, no, I did <u>not</u> turn into another study so you will have to deal with that wallpaper yourself)

Regards,

Uncle Harry

Then the one Alex did feel a bit guilty about:

Saturday 2nd – 10 am

According to your sister (aka the niece who bothers to contact me), you are alive and well. May be busy at work today – an unexpected development with a client.

Regards,

Uncle Harry

And finally:

Sunday 3rd – just past midnight

I do not know how I've managed to miss you again, but judging by the opera programme on the kitchen table and the shoes I've just rescued from your mother's favourite plant, you are having a good time. Will be coming and going today – blame your daughter's father. Must have dinner together tomorrow.

Regards,

Uncle Harry

Alex had called his office once, yesterday, after stopping Barrett (who Pandora apparently thought was *Dead*), when his new secretary had insisted that she knew Mr Sharpe's niece and that Alex did not sound like her.

When she'd told Shaz that, she'd laughed and said that if Matthew came back, that would've really thrown the old bag.

By the time Alex had stopped her glare, Shaz's laugh had failed on her anyway.

But now ...

Alex knew.

Alex knew where Matthew was and they'd ended up in the same sliver of reality on The Other Side and at some point, she was going to have to tell Shaz or Sam or Harry because, as it was ...

Maddie had decided to claim his room.

Pandora had taken Shaz's and there was no way Alex was even unlocking Carrie's, which meant ...

Which meant Alex was now standing in her brother's abandoned room with the sensation that he was still only six feet away, knowing that she was there but not looking.

He had never let her in.

Never.

Those nights when they'd shared a bed out of fear, or later grief, or a little later just in case the baby stopped breathing in the night and Matthew pretended that it was so he wouldn't have to put up with Alex thumping about in the dark and Alex pretended that it was so she could get hot chocolate on command, it had always been Alex's bed in Alex's room, no matter how much Matthew complained about the mattress and the wallpaper.

If Alex had thought her room at the facility or Elizabeth's unlived-in flat were bare, this was ...

The walls were a cracked magnolia (and whether the cracks were paint or plaster, she couldn't tell), the bed was made with sheets that had ensnared dust for nine years like a Venus flytrap, and the desk looked like it belonged in a mid-range hotel: a lamp, a pad of paper, a pen, a coaster. Completely impersonal.

Hardly the representation of twenty-one years of a brilliant mind.

Alex set the photo album down on the desk and tried the drawer, which was, of course, locked.

She didn't really care what was in it, not really, but she wasn't going to let her daughter move into a room that was a shrine to *Trainspotting*, because Shaz had told her what Harry had found in Matthew's cabinet at work: all the stuff to shoot up smack with, little rattle jars of prescription pills and tiny bags of not-so-prescription pills, as well as enough coke to be done for possession with intent to supply several times over. Oh, and that wasn't counting the three bottles of spirits, one completely drained, the other two well on the way there.

Christ, how much had he been taking to actually overdose?

Had he actually been trying to top himself?

Or had he just been making a half-arsed attempt, like Alex?

Because even then, his Power did absolutely nothing to help when he thought that Death was sitting on his chest and that somehow the bloody Half-Faced Man had somehow escaped the study to hang around a grotty nightclub loo that stank of Lynx Africa and Impulse Temptation as much as it reeked of piss and sambuca.

Because even then, his Power was still slow, sluggish, the next morning because his grip on Alex's mind was already slipping, because Alex had had the jitters, hadn't she? The cold feet? Before she'd even got down the aisle, before she'd looked into her brother's eyes, and the spell just snapped right in half.

"You're thinking very loudly."

Alex flinched. It was just Harry, loosening his tie in the doorway, and knowing him, he'd probably been watching her gorm away at a closed drawer.

"Then you shouldn't be snooping in my mind," Alex replied.

"Wouldn't dare," Harry said, outstretching his arms.

"Really?"

Harry nodded, his shaven head gleaming dark in the half-light.

"I thought you might need a hug," he said. "Didn't have time with all the chaos."

"Just a quick one," Alex said, hiding her almost-smile in his chest.

She let herself inhale those fading notes of Brut that had always been Harry to her and almost relaxed into his strong arms. Steady. That was Harry. Steady against anything that could buffet the house, the man who hadn't even blinked at taking on a bunch of orphaned teenagers.

Alex eased herself away before she could outstay her welcome and asked how Pandora was.

"Resting," Harry said. "Matilda is insisting that she sit on the end of her bed until she wakes up, like that little demon in *The Nightmare*, but ..."

He shrugged and stuffed his hands into his pockets.

"But people with Power don't have seizures," Alex said.

"Just an overload of Power," he said, wandering around Matthew's room as if he'd never been in it either. "Often happens to teenagers. As soon as I blocked her Power ... Anyway. Welcome home."

"Your house, not mine."

"Think of me as its humble caretaker," Harry replied. "I saw the study's open."

"I think caretakers have to do a bit of painting and decorating sometimes," Alex said, trying to muster some kind of teasing because then she didn't have to think of the study and that reflection and the ghost ...

And the kitchen and the seizure ...

And Eleanor.

And Matthew.

And Elizabeth.

"It was thoughtful, by the way."

"What?" Alex asked, already getting lost in a conversation that Harry hadn't even made that labyrinthine yet. She was bumping into the walls, tripping up over the string, choking on breadcrumbs, but maybe that was inevitable after hearing the same dozen sentences for four weeks. They were off-script, just like *Elizabeth* and all her questions, except Alex knew why now, what she was hiding—

"Your face," Harry explained, taking the photo album from her, "Is that where you've started with the unpacking?"

"I don't want to start at all."

"So," Harry said, settling on Matthew's bed with a casual cross of his legs before Alex could warn him about the dust, "how exactly did you meet Pandora?"

"She was on the streets," Alex rushed out, rattling the handle to the desk drawer again, "and she was attacked on Friday night. I kind of saved her and then I kind of didn't and I hurt myself—"

Harry's eyes bulged at her.

"You *hurt* yourself?"

"I'm fine, it was just an accident." Alex sighed, deciding not to mention the other *non*-accidents. "But there was someone else with Power in Coldharbour and she …"

She'd slipped past Alex's defences like they were nothing but air, armed with unsaid promises that had just left Alex wanting.

"Is there a key to this or what?"

"And who was *she*?" Harry asked, hands slowing on the pages of the photo album.

"It doesn't matter," Alex said, feeling as if she had gone too far, that she'd let something slip and float away, just like Pandora's hand in the sea, "it's over. She's gone."

"Alexandra, you've been back *two days*," he said, training his careful frown on her so hard, she wondered if he was nudging at her mind after all.

"I know," Alex said, letting go of the drawer, "but—"

"Alexandra," Harry said, glancing down at the wedding photo, "I will say this only once: do not neglect the Living by searching for the Dead."

"Well, you've made me move back into a house with actual ghosts."

"Whom you can't see."

"I can't see *most* of them," Alex asked. "What is it anyway? The scarier they are, the easier it is to see them?"

Harry shrugged in confusion.

"The ghost in the study?" Alex said. "The really gory one?"

"There aren't any particular ghosts in the study," Harry said, and if Alex didn't know for sure that Matthew had also seen the Half-Faced Man, his frown really would've had her thinking that seeing wasn't believing. "Anyway, you hadn't paid the rent for four months. I'd hardly say I *made* you."

"Well, I don't remember that, do I?" Alex whispered, breaking her nails between her fingers. "A bit more notice at least would've been nice."

"It was all above board," Harry said, "though I did try to explain to her the circumstances—"

"Tried to persuade her?"

Harry wasn't a flincher, but he did rap his knuckles against the edge of Matthew's bed.

"I thought you didn't approve of that," he said, "my big, bad Power."

"Just don't use it on me," Alex muttered.

"I wouldn't dare." Harry laughed.

And he wouldn't have. Would he?

After everything that Matthew had done, surely Harry couldn't even entertain the idea of just barging into her mind. Not that he'd probably get much from it, having a solid rummage through a brain that was already struggling to reorder itself into something vaguely functional.

"Alexandra?"

Alex apologised and said something about dealing with her landlady that might've made sense as a sentence.

"I have been unusually busy this month," Harry said, "a particularly demanding client."

Alex wondered what he'd been doing in the house all those years. Had he just been coming home to an empty house night after night? Turning round as if to say something to Alex or Matthew? He'd never been a cook and judging by the state of the kitchen, he hadn't started, and Alex was pretty sure he'd lived on a rotation of takeaways, client dinners, and whatever Alex would've been cooking whenever he appeared on her doorstep with a new present for Maddie (more or less monthly). Had he sat at that abandoned kitchen table wishing it was the study? Wishing any of them were there with him?

"Not that he'll be a problem anymore." Harry sighed. "He dropped dead in his cell a few hours ago. Not that it wasn't his time either."

"Gideon Barrett?"

Harry stared up at her.

"Know him?"

"I could ask the same thing," Alex said. "Pandora said he's Dead. Did you tell her that?"

Harry shook his head and explained that Barrett had had a massive heart attack in the middle of the night.

"What kind of time?" Alex asked, and when Harry said he didn't know exactly, "well, midnight or three o'clock or what?"

Harry scoffed, like there was anything amusing about this.

"You do know what he did, right?" Alex said, feeling her heart stutter just like it had on The Other Side. "He was a murderer."

"I was duty solicitor last night." Harry laughed. "On a Saturday night. You don't have much choice on a Saturday night and as for the paperwork …"

"What paperwork?" Alex asked.

"Well, his funeral's tomorrow."

"Tomorrow?" Alex said.

"He is – or rather, was – a Catholic," Harry explained, but that careful evenness just clashed against the adrenaline driving Alex's heart faster and faster, "therefore it has to be sooner rather than later."

"But do they even know how he died? For sure? Harry, Pandora just happened to know that he was Dead and he was—"

"The police have to hold their own inquiry, seeing as it was a death in custody," Harry replied, "but it was simply a massive heart attack. No more, no less."

"But Barrett had been possessed."

Alex tried to stop herself from shuddering under Harry's frustrated gaze.

Five things she could see—

"He's Dead, Alexandra. End of story."

Cracked walls. Thick dust. Photo album. Locked drawer. Power at her fingertips.

Alex took a breath, sucked in another, and then managed to say:

"Well, it's not, is it? Cos he had Power that he shouldn't have had and I wanna know how he got that Power in the first place."

"What did I just say about the Dead?"

"This is different."

"What exactly have you been up to?" Harry said. "Shoes in a bush? The *opera*?"

"Pandora died, right in front of me, and then she came back to life and ..."

Alex's temple twinged. She sighed and shook her head. She pressed her fingertips to her forehead and pushed through the pain. It wasn't real. It couldn't be real.

"You saw a body?" Harry asked, giving her one of those stiff stares full of significance. "After your mother?"

"It has been fifteen years," Alex said, snatching back the photo album.

Nearly fifteen years.

The funeral people had done their best with what was left, stitching together with wires, pasting stage make-up over bruises, pumping veins full of preservatives until the corpse in the coffin did look more or less like Catherine Wilde:

Carefully laid edges, violet eyeshadow, crucifix gleaming under the low lights.

A faint, fusty note of white musk under all the formaldehyde.

But when Alex, all of fifteen years old, dared to take its hand, she felt nothing.

There was nothing there.

Whatever it was, it wasn't her mother anymore.

That frustration, that sadness, that had hung about her like a funk ...

Gone.

Like that was all her soul amounted to: that thwarted life, trapped in a dying seaside town.

"You're dwelling again," Harry warned.

"Are they even sure it's Barrett who's Dead?" Alex asked. "Have you seen his body? Has Sam?"

Harry sighed and shook his head at her.

"Would it satisfy you if I said yes?"

"Only if it's the truth," Alex said, "cos he murdered Pandora, Harry. Right in front of me. And he was possessed by something that's really bad."

Harry still rose an unconvinced eyebrow.

"*Really bad?*"

That dark, ravenous smile. That malevolent gleam in those cold, grey eyes. That taunt about David.

"And people come back to life," Alex said, before she could freeze up again, "Pandora came back to life."

"A fluke," Harry replied, "an inexplicable fluke, yes, but—"

"So does Elizabeth," Alex blurted out, "all the time."

Harry's gaze fell on her, hard, which Alex expected, but also ...

What was that? Surprise? Fear?

That dismay again when he saw that Alex could freeze like her father?

"Your *she*?"

"It doesn't matter," Alex muttered, "she's gone."

"And she has you using your Power again?" Harry asked. "For the first time in years?"

Heaven forfend someone came along who was a bigger Power expert than him.

Because she would've known, Elizabeth would've known what to do about Pandora and about Barrett. She would've been the first one to charge down to the morgue and demand to see Barrett's body. She probably would've stuck her knife into him to make sure.

Because it wasn't right. Pandora coming back to life, Barrett dying.

What had Alex done when she'd taken the Power off him?

What did Eleanor want with Pandora?

And why, when Alex thought that she could get away with lying to Uncle Harry's face by telling him she'd left something at Elizabeth's, was she chased out of the room by the smell of the sea and formaldehyde and the faintest note of white musk?

21
Surf's Up

"Barrett's Dead," Alex announced.

"Yeah," Shaz said, wiping her hands on her sick-splattered scrubs, "I know."

Behind them, A&E roared with chaos.

Kids chattering, crying, or launching plastic toys at other kids while the grown-ups gushed a variety of body fluids, some of which probably would've been better inside their bodies, others probably better out than in, and of course, what Alex imagined was the usual line-up on a Sunday afternoon:

The belligerent arsehole demanding to know why he hadn't been seen yet, the old biddy that had somehow lost whoever she'd come in with, and, like in Ferris Bueller, that one nurse calling out the same name over ...

And over ...

And over ...

All under those awful strip lights that made Alex's head thump.

"You know?" she hissed.

The pain wasn't real. It couldn't have been real.

When Shaz nodded, Alex asked if the whole town knew before she did.

"And more to the point," she added, "why didn't you bloody phone me and tell me?"

"They didn't call me in here for a chat and a nice cup of tea!" Shaz said, flinging her arm over her shoulder. "There was a pile-up on the A120, I've been up to my neck in the walking wounded! My fingers are crooked from the amount of suturing I've been doing, sis!"

"I'm sorry," Alex said, brushing her Power over her sister's fingers.

Shaz snatched her hand back with a yelp.

"What the hell was that?" she gasped.

"I was just trying to heal you!"

"You've made it worse!" Shaz groaned, flinching when Alex reached out for her hand, but she still caught it, along with a touch of green Power that seemed to be deepening a bruise across Shaz's knuckles.

Their uncle hadn't been hiding his light under a bushel, not that any bushel of any size or variety would survive a head-on encounter with Harry Sharpe and his many self-acknowledged skills and talents.

His Power really couldn't heal.

"Is Elizabeth with you?" Shaz asked. "I'll get her to fix it."

"It's fine," Alex muttered, "just ..."

This was asking too much of her Power, to make it bend to her will with any kind of precision, to ignore any of Harry's Power it had picked up, to prioritise a woman's who had held her hand over and over and looked at her like that and had just ...

"Just give me a sec," Alex sighed, tiptoeing towards the pain that was prickling inside her chest as she thought of overcast eyes and cold hands and ...

There.

A touch of silver that flowed through burgundy. It didn't sit awkwardly and heavily on Alex's Power like

Harry's did: it danced with hers, it sang with it, like it was happy to be there and do her bidding as it swirled around Shaz's fingers.

"You do realise," Shaz whispered, "I can't see any of this."

"So?" Alex snapped, because why did those embers of Elizabeth's Power have to feel so right?

And why wasn't her head throbbing anymore?

"So you just look like you're staring really intently at our hands."

"Does it feel better or what?" Alex asked, as Shaz stretched out her fingers. "Anyway, Barrett's Dead. Apparently."

"Apparently?"

"Well, Pandora was Dead," Alex reminded her, "and now she's not. She's having seizures."

"She's *what*?"

"Harry's got it under control, but the point is, she also knew about Barrett and I just wanna make sure that he is. *Dead* Dead."

"Like seeing his body?" Shaz asked. "Sis, you're hardly next of kin—"

"Yeah, well, we were pretty close by the end, weren't we?" Alex replied. "I just need to know where the morgue is, Shaz, just on a map or something."

There really had been only so many times Alex could go up and down the same corridors, wondering why the morgue was the only place not on any maps or signposts. If she saw one more sign for phlebotomy, she was going to draw blood herself.

"You can't just – I can't just," Shaz whispered furiously, "I don't even know the codes to get down there! It's illegal—"

"It's just trespass," Alex said, scowling at the belligerent arsehole and his thick, sickly beer breath as he turned away from the desk, "unless I'm planning to squat in the mortuary or obstruct anyone in their lawful duties, it's a civil matter."

Shaz gawped at her, in a not entirely different way to how Harry had stared at her in utter dismay when she'd frozen half the kitchen, bits of ceiling caught mid-cascade.

"But how do you know that?" Shaz asked.

"I dunno," Alex said, "maybe I got it from Harry. Point is, it's probably less illegal than you giving me those names and addresses yesterday."

"The bollocking Sam gave me for that," Shaz hissed, her cheeks flushing blood-red, "I had the silent treatment over dinner and when Mads went to her room, Jesus ... Cos he's right, you know, I could've lost my job over this. I could still lose my job over this and now you're wanting to go downstairs and prod corpses while I turn a blind eye!"

"Just blame me for it all," Alex said. "Even better, blame Elizabeth."

Shaz spat out a laugh and shook her head.

"No, go on," Alex said. "What?"

"Doesn't matter. Does Uncle Harry even know you're here, by the way?"

"It clearly does matter, Shazza."

"I just think this is a bad idea," Shaz said, her foot tapping the tiles so loudly, it spelled out the "even for you" for her. "Barrett's Dead, Pandora's back. End of story, isn't it? You and Elizabeth exorcised whatever that thing was—"

"We didn't exorcise it. It escaped. And it's the same thing we summoned in '84, Shaz, and by the way, 'it' is a 'she' and she is called Eleanor. And she's coming for me."

"What d'you mean?" Shaz breathed. "Coming for you?"

"Wants my blood?" Alex laughed. "Wants my Power? I think she just likes winding me up, to be honest. Cos everything's collapsing in around me and anyone that could help ain't here anymore—"

"There's Harry," Shaz suggested softly.

"Nope," Alex said, "God, I don't even know who'd win between them. Harry versus Eleanor."

"Harry, surely?"

As far as Alex was concerned, there was nothing sure about it, not with her little Top Trumps collection she was building in her mind.

Carrie versus Eleanor had ended up with Eleanor's decisive victory, apparently.

Elizabeth versus Eleanor was a one-all draw, Alex supposed.

Alex versus an Eleanor-possessed Barrett probably also went to Eleanor, if it hadn't been for Elizabeth's Power bringing Alex back so quickly.

And as for all of Barrett's Power-related victims ...

"But you said," Shaz said, "there's hardly anyone in Coldharbour with Power, but Barrett and Eleanor didn't dare try it with Uncle Harry."

"Yeah, cos he's not homeless or mentally ill," Alex replied.

"But even so, Uncle Harry would—"

"Not necessarily, alright?" Alex snapped, but as soon as her sister's face fell, any thought of telling her the whole truth, that Carrie had died for *them*, sank back down into the pit of her stomach with all that sick swirling around. "I just need to make sure Barrett's Dead before he gets buried, alright? I just wanna tick things off one at a time. If there's the slightest chance that Eleanor can repossess him and I dunno if zombies exist, but I just ..."

"Sis," Shaz murmured, "what else is going on?"

"Nothing," Alex said, directing her lie to the wall. "If you're not gonna tell me where this bloody morgue is, I'm just gonna dowse for it."

Shaz's foot had started tapping.

Good.

"I am really busy," Shaz insisted, but then she was pulling a small notepad from her pocket, "and they're saying winter's gonna be rough ..."

"I can just go and find it myself, Shaz." Alex sighed. "Get back to work."

"If we're gonna get in trouble for looking at a dead body we shouldn't be," Shaz said, "we might as well look at the rest."

"The rest?"

It was a sick twist of fate that actually had a lot to do with local authority procedures and a bunch of red tape that Shaz tried admirably to untangle for Alex, who was more concerned with overloading keypads to doors with just enough Power to make them unlock and not so much that they'd set off alarms or sprinklers ...

But all three of Barrett's known, and still Dead, victims were also still in the morgue, chilled in cramped refrigerated cabinets to suspend the rot that pure Power and saltwater had riddled their flesh with.

Actually, Alex was fairly interested in the story – well, one particular aspect, which was how Doctor Sharon Evans of the Accident and Emergency Department, stitcher-up of small children and Friday night drunks, knew so much about the corpses downstairs.

"Sam and I didn't just argue, you know," Shaz explained, leading them into yet another gloom-soaked stairwell. "Obviously, we didn't know that Barrett was possessed by the Shadow, well, Eleanor, but it's clear that stuff is going on in Coldharbour and neither of us can investigate it on the record so …"

She shrugged and pointed down the next corridor.

"We exchanged notes and theories, that's all."

"Some pillow talk," Alex said, painfully aware that she wasn't much better. "You were supposed to leave it to Elizabeth."

"And then I saw bits of your skull all over Barrett's carpet," Shaz said. "You're right, we can't just wait around for what happens next, if Mum couldn't exorcise this thing …"

They were now deep in the bowels of the hospital, where the strip lights flickered precariously and there was always a faint rustle of something in a store cupboard.

And there, at the end of the corridor, was the morgue.

Cleaning chemicals already lacerating her nostrils, Alex shook her head when Shaz asked her if she wanted to back out.

"It's not like I've never done this before," Alex laughed, choking on her own words, "it's just another body. *Bodies.*"

Alex shivered from the inside out. It wasn't just the lights clinging on for dear life or that smell stinging her throat. It felt like the house, heavy with haunting.

"But fifteen years ago was different," Shaz said. "It's alright—"

"This should be even easier then, shouldn't it?"

Shaz should've known by then that just looking away did nothing to hide her frown.

"I'm just thinking," she said, "shouldn't we update Elizabeth if we're not telling Uncle Harry about this yet?"

"We can update Sam," Alex said, shoving the morgue doors open. "One step at a time, Shaz."

Shaz started checking the labels on the drawer doors, pointing out Heather Abbott's first.

"But what is she still doing here?" Alex asked, unlocking the drawer with a clonk. "She's been identified."

"Parents are insisting the post-mortem's wrong," Shaz explained. "It becomes a whole legal process, but then if the parents have Power, I have no idea how they're gonna explain that away."

"Could've been adopted, like Pandora," Alex muttered, that weight in her stomach that had started at the mention of Elizabeth's name getting heavier and heavier at the thought of 1984 and Mum – Carrie – and ...

She peeled the sheet back, just enough to see Heather's burnt shoulder shining in the strange low lights of the morgue like a winter twilight deep in a dark forest.

Fingers just tracing the edges, she waited to feel—

A hot hand over her mouth, fingers scorching as they pressed into her jaw, a pulse of pain searing through her shoulder, not a clean rip like the knife but a bubbling, blistering—

Alex snatched back her hand.

"Sis?"

"Yeah," Alex gasped, wiping her hand against her jeans, "they killed her."

"But she is ..."

"Yeah, she's moved on."

But as Alex replaced the sheet over Heather, she caught the date of birth on the label:

15th June 1981.

Just a kid, just like Pandora, just starting a new stage of her life and *Barrett* and *Eleanor* thought they had the right ...

The drawer rattled.

Apologising to no one in particular, Alex softly shut it and locked the door.

"I've found Jane Doe," Shaz said, reading from her notes, "but good luck, cos Sam said she's been so nibbled at by fish, all they can say is that she was a woman, at least thirty years old, never had children as there was no evidence of parturition scars, and who probably had all her limbs pre-mortem."

As Shaz pulled out the drawer, Alex asked where her burn had been.

"What's left of her chest," her sister replied. "It went down to the sternum."

"The *bone*?"

Alex inched the cloth back with a squeamish reluctance, trying to focus on Shaz's explanation of fourth-degree burns and how the victim must've been Dead before she was thrown in the water, but it was hard when she was forcing her hand through a cat's cradle of muscle and tendon.

Alex's fingers sparked, but she reeled back before the memory of the murder could shudder its way up her arm.

"Same as before?" Shaz asked, pulling out another drawer.

"Same as before," Alex muttered, staring at her fingers. How had she really felt nothing when she touched Carrie's corpse?

"Well," Shaz said, "it's him."

And it was.

Gideon Barrett, looking as waxy and as withered as he had in his lumpy old armchair drenched in stale, stolen Power.

"He looks at peace," Shaz suggested, but that wasn't right.

It was a lie, as well, when they said a corpse was sleeping, because Alex knew there was just nothing there, that she could tell, just looking at a body with no burns or gruesome injuries, that the soul just was not there, that the final thread anchoring it from not drifting too far into The Other Side had frayed away to nothing.

And there was no soul in Gideon Barrett's body.

Not his own, nor Eleanor's.

"There's the burn," Shaz murmured, holding up his hand with an ungainly wave, "and you can see the blue tinge to his fingertips and his lips and yep, the paperwork says heart attack. They found loads of stuff, obviously, but the calcified arteries are a giveaway. Jesus, and the metastases make him sound like Swiss cheese. Yeah, you punching him wouldn't have made the blindest bit of difference. What do you think?"

"*Dead* Dead," Alex said. "Have you found the last victim?"

Shaz faffed around with the drawers and started banging on about "the homeless geezer" and how Sam should ask Pandora if she knew him because no one knew his real name.

"But," Shaz said, pulling out the drawer, "he was fiftyish, had always been on the streets as far as anyone who knew him was concerned. Nice. They said he was nice. But nice doesn't pay for a burial, so he's in the morgue another couple of weeks till the council stick him in some unloved plot somewhere."

An unclaimed body.

And there was an unclaimed grave outside Coldharbour Synagogue.

"Fiftyish?" Alex asked. "Are you sure?"

"As sure as we can be with organs as pickled as his," Shaz said. "Why?"

"What did he look like?"

"Much better than the Jane Doe," Shaz explained. "Only in the sea for a couple of days, but he's missing fingers."

In Alex's mind, 1945 – 1969 warped into 1945 – 1999.

"Which fingers?"

"Soon find out," Shaz said, still staring obliviously at her notes as she read out that the unnamed man was of slight build, about five foot eight, mid-length black hair turning grey, black beard also turning grey, blue eyes, and an accent that was variously described as Geordie, Scottish, Welsh, Scouse, and Irish, in only the way people living in the Home Counties of England can do.

"And great at card games, apparently," Shaz said. "And, as we now know, had Power. That probably helped. That's all according to what Sam's lot reported back to him."

Only one in a thousand.

Elizabeth had said that.

People with Power were one in a thousand.

And there was her and Alex and Harry and Pandora, and previously Matthew and Carrie and David, plus Heather Abbott and the other two victims of Barrett's that they knew about. That was ten people with Power she could count on her shaky fingers. It didn't matter that some of them were Dead, because Alex could always just add Elizabeth and Eleanor to the list.

"Sis?"

Alex yanked the sheet away from the corpse.

There was that grave wax Matthew told her about.

Alex stepped closer to the body, refusing to entertain any queasiness about how stiff it looked, how grey it looked, how greasy, because she had to know, she had to touch that blackened burn that stretched from the dead man's throat all the way down to his missing fingers.

"Post or pre-mortem?" Alex asked. "The fingers."

"Hang on," Shaz replied, rushing to a clipboard, "that could just be burn damage or you know, fish nibbling away."

"Fish don't just go for fingers," Alex insisted, but when she lifted that sticky, heavy hand ...

They were all missing.

Even the thumb.

And on the other side of the body, Shaz was lifting up the other fingerless hand, although at least she stopped short of making this one wave.

"We get this a lot with bodies in water," she explained. "Animals go for the extremities. So, no, I won't be able to check if the body's circumcised."

She must've finally understood the look in Alex's eyes, because then she was blurting out something about how it couldn't have been, it couldn't possibly have been David.

Alex had to look at the face.

It was easy enough to not think of the body as human when she was focusing on the burn or the hand, but now, her own fingers curling around a clammy palm that couldn't squeeze back, she shuffled around to face ...

Not much of a face.

The ear she could see was ...

Well, she couldn't see it, and a lump of cheek had gone, exposing a wet mesh of muscle fibres and teeth. But if she imagined him not grey and not pummelled and not swollen, without a beard, could it be? It was hard to tell with the tip of the nose gone, but maybe, if she leant her head that way or moved his that—

Something snapped under her fingertips.

Then a squelch.

"Careful, sis," Shaz warned, "it's a decomposing corpse."

"I just wanna see his eyes," Alex said. "They're blue. They're like Maddie's. When I see his eyes, I'll know for sure."

Shaz rushed up the tray, but Alex was already peeling back the eyelids of the corpse to reveal—

Nothing.

Nothing where the eyes should've been but then the dead hand seized hers and she sees a stranger in a strange land and there are guns and bombs and marches and grey skies and barricades and *we only have to be lucky once* and *you are now entering Free Derry*—

The hand let Alex go.

"It's not him," Alex whispered, staggering back from the drawer, "it's definitely not David."

"Alright," Shaz said, "let's go now. Come on."

All Alex could do was nod because she wasn't just choking on her own words anymore. She was choking on her own thoughts and Shaz was saying something but it was too late, her breath was being ripped through her chest, over and over, her skin was lifting from her bones, fuzzy and grey and vague—

Anchored.

Arms around her back.

Hands on her shoulder.

Chest pressing against chest.

Lungs pressing against lungs.

Alex's breath stuttered as it tried to keep time with Shaz's slower, measured inhales ...

And exhales ...

A hand slipped to Alex's neck, just pressing ever so lightly. Holding.

She closed her eyes and let go of the cry roiling in her chest, a scream as much as a sob.

22
Where are all the Gods

COME HOME.

Matthew knew his own mother's handwriting.

The curl of the C, the sharp Ms, the Greek Es.

Matthew knew it was a demand.

Wrenching open his lounge window, he rummaged in his pocket for his box of cigarettes ...

He'd left them at Jacky's.

Matthew had never left anything by accident anywhere, but he supposed he could have been forgiven, given the circumstances.

Who just *says* to someone, over a coffee, that their mother was apparently murdered?

But then, who, as the first thing with which they respond, asks if their sister believes it?

Because it had been Matthew, not Alexandra, who had spent minute after minute, hour after hour, between the séance and their mother's funeral, stalking around the study table, drawing his fingers through the ashes of the spirit board, trying to understand where it had all gone so wrong. He had said the incantation correctly, their Power hadn't been flaring or doing something strange, Sam had been there to ground them both.

All Matthew could conclude, as he ignored the Half-Faced Man always standing far too close to him, as yet another person tried to cajole him out of the study to do something as banal as sit or eat or drink or even *talk*, was that they had done everything to the letter.

If their father was Dead, he should have come through. If he wasn't, then nothing should have happened.

It shouldn't have been the Shadow.

Eleanor.

Matthew had never put the two together: after all, why would he have? A thing that terrified him as a teenager being his acquaintance's disembodied sister?

And now, Elizabeth had left Coldharbour.

She had left, to all intents and purposes, Alexandra defenceless.

How the hell had Alexandra almost *drowned* in the first place? He knew Elizabeth was never the most forthcoming of individuals, but he would have appreciated a little more than a shrug.

Alexandra didn't know the first thing about Power, let alone protecting herself with it, even if a snide little voice in Matthew's mind reminded him that she had been accomplished enough to very nearly throttle the life out of him in the ruins of their own house.

His watch beeped:

15.00.

Matthew launched himself at his desk and pulled out papers until he found a fresh notepad and one of those cheap biros he had a tendency of cracking in half between both hands. In each corner, he wrote a name:

Eleanor
Pandora
Carrie

Elizabeth

He ripped the paper from the pad and proceeded onto the next:

1999
1984
1923

Was there another significant year to choose?

Perhaps one ...

He pulled out the Polaroid from his pocket and smoothed it against the table. He'd never liked it: it had never done his sister justice as far as he was concerned, but he'd happened to have it in his pocket on *that* day and aside from what he had already packed in his running away bag (although, as he had learnt later, compulsively packing and repacking running away bags on every birthday was a ritual apparently unique to himself and his twin).

Matthew hadn't touched his for nine years and, as he pulled it out from under his bed, he wondered if Alexandra still had hers or not.

He found his old passport, still in that battered holder he'd found languishing in a corner of the house: so old, it was navy and not burgundy, with gold letters embellishing the cover:

DAW

Inside the holder, just as when Matthew had found it, was the strip of passport photos – well, to be absolutely correct, photographs taken in a passport booth but absolutely not suitable for use on a travel document.

It was a strip of colour that was so lurid, his mother's blouse was the orange of a Namibian desert, his father's eyes were a sea-deep blue, and as for the girl who appeared with them in the very last one, a teenager with the same eyes as David, her flushed cheeks glowed with the red of the roses at the end of the garden in Coldharbour.

Or was it their Power? It was impossible to tell.

However, he did know that the colours shouldn't have been that bright, because all three of them had been wearing identical clothes in that *other* photograph, the one that had stunned Matthew so violently when it had fallen out of the *Encyclopaedia Daemonica*'s pages, he had just shoved it back into the book, shoved the book back into the bookcase, and shoved himself into his bedroom until Shaz coaxed him back out.

It had been too soon, far too soon after the séance to have seen ...

Matthew still wrote "1990" into the final corner, but he did put another two years into the very centre of the page:

1968/1969

He tutted to himself. If Alexandra had been doing this, based on gut feeling, *instinct*, he would've laughed in her face, once upon a time.

Perhaps it wasn't his instinct anyway, because if he concentrated, hard enough to resurrect his headache, he could lift that biro right into the air—

Power throws him onto cold sand.

Matthew blinks and sits up, but where he expects a burn across his arms, there is none.

Just the certainty that he is on The Other Side and ...

"Your Power's growing," a voice says down the beach, but she isn't talking to Matthew. "See? Here he is."

"Here's who?"

Alexandra.

Alex.

His sister and whoever she's talking to are mere metres away, but Matthew stares at the sand, just as he knows Alex hasn't turned, just stiffened, in the very corner of his eye.

"Nine years," the voice says, and it must be the shock that has rendered Matthew so dense as to have not have realised instantly who it must be. "Aren't you going to say hello to each other?"

Matthew keeps his eyes on the sand.

Alex keeps hers on Eleanor, presumably, because she still doesn't turn either.

"Well?" Eleanor laughs.

Words would be too much and not enough, but Matthew thinks that if anyone else in existence understands that, it would be his twin, because they also both understand that a coincidence is never a coincidence and therefore something must be happening in Coldharbour—

A perfect image appears in Matthew's mind: a body on cracked kitchen tiles he recognises, purple Power flaring—

A seizure?

People with Power can't have seizures.

He tries to throw "1968" and "1969" into her mind but then shingle shifts, Eleanor's too close to Alex, he scrambles up—

And falls, face-first, onto floorboards.

Floorboards Matthew knows.

He slips as he tries to sit up in what feels like ...

What smells like ...

It smells like the monastery.

It smells like he's waist-deep in corpses again, pulling them out of a pile until he finds one alive, even if it's just Elizabeth and not ...

But it's not the monastery, it's not even the mountain of bodies transplanted into the study, because he knows the Ether can twist and turn The Other Side into anything it wants.

It's just blood.

A thick pool of blood over the table and across the floor, coalescing into clumps as if it's trying and failing to dry, and Matthew knows this is enough blood lost to be fatal.

But when is this?

Is it now? Is it 1999?

Is it even real?

The Ether does deal in metaphors, usually in the same way as a Year 9 being told to pad out their essay with something "interesting", but the blood is shoving its stench down his throat as if it is real and there, just at the edge, towards the wonky window, the boundary isn't perfect. It's smudged and smeared, as if something's been dragged through it.

As if someone's been dragged through it.

Matthew tries to tell the Ether that he needs to get back to Alex, but then he can no longer feel her anywhere nearby, nor Eleanor, so he tries something he never has before and he tries to hope for the best as he crawls along the edge of the floor towards—

The hand shoots out of the shadows.

Matthew lets out a cry—

And is slammed against his desk, elbows cringing.

There was no blood on his hands.

No study to be seen.

No Half-Faced Man looming out of the darkness.

Matthew Wilde was no longer twelve, nor fifteen, nor twenty-one years of age.

Matthew did not make mistakes like that anymore.

But as he clenched his hands into knuckle-bulging fists, he thought of the back of Alex's head and the feel of Eleanor's eyes on his skin and when the hell he'd been.

When had he been?

His watch beeped.

It had only just gone three ...

19.00.

A more mediocre mind would have decided that his watch needed a new battery after all, but Matthew's mind, even with the resumption of the headache, could tell, what with the longer shadows his pen holder and mug were casting into warmer, fainter light ...

The sun was setting around him.

"What does it mean?" he yelled out to the Ether, in English for once. "What am I meant to do with that? What am I meant to know?"

Silence greeted him.

Of course it did.

The Ether hadn't helped when the séance went wrong, it hadn't helped with anything that came after, it had turned its back on them like they were no longer worth it and Matthew spat out a litany of curses, pounding his fist against cheap wood over and over and over until his skin split and his bones burned and his blood burst because what if Alex was still *there*, with *that*, and—

Too slow.

Too dense.

Matthew had noticed the sunlight fading, but he hadn't spared a second thought to the papers strewn all over his desk, the papers he had crumpled, the papers on which he was spraying his blood.

Every single piece of paper, large or small, was covered in the same writing, in the same three words, over and over and over:

COME HOME MOUSE

His hand healed turquoise.

And burgundy.

But worst of all, his blood remained sticky, just like the blood in the study, the blood which, if he ignored the prospect of a ghost that had haunted his nightmares for eighteen years, glowed.

With Power.

Powerful blood had been shed in that house, in that study.

But when?

23

Dreaming up a Storm

When had it got so dark?

When had the thunder started rumbling?

When had this dread coalesced and curdled deep in Alex's chest?

When, when, and when again whirled around Alex's mind as she went through the motions, or rather the motions wrangled her into action, wrenching her body into the right positions and making her mouth say all the right words while she oversaw the teenagers' takeaway, half-trying not to think of Elizabeth or Matthew or Eleanor or Barrett, half-keeping an eye on Maddie and Pandora and if they were both eating enough, because she certainly wasn't, which hadn't gone unnoticed by Harry, who had then announced that he had to return to work to clear up what he called "the local constabulary's sheer incompetence".

She'd only heard snatches of his phone conversation with Sam, but she could imagine the twinkle in Harry's eyes, because there were only so many times Alex could tell Sam not to rise to it, that Harry was just one of those people who fed on – no, *feasted* on – conquering his opponent, even if his opponent had only really made the mistake of falling in love with various members of Harry's family.

Sam must've pointed out that he was an Acting DCI, because Harry had said that he'd seen better acting in nativity plays and as for after that ...

Well, apparently Pandora could stay.

End of story, for Harry at least.

But for all he'd said earlier, and she had said, Alex might as well have been fifteen again and absolutely not ready to be responsible for a child, let alone two, because now she was back on the ottoman in the wonky window, curled up around the photo album, staring down at that one picture of her parents and Harry.

Had they ever really been happy?

Did it even matter anymore?

Was it right that Alex was left chasing corpses in the sick hope that she would find her father after all?

On the far corner of the table, a glisten.

Something dark, black even, under the pale dusk.

How had Alex not noticed that before?

Sliding off the ottoman, she crept across her own floorboards, which creaked and creaked and—

The glisten was dripping.

Gushing.

It was gushing down the table leg and onto the floorboards.

If one of the girls had spilled something, they would've—

Alex sniffed and gagged and, pressing the back of her hand against her mouth, tried to swallow the sickly, metallic, unmistakeable smell of blood.

It was blood slicking the table, it was blood slipping down in thick ...

No.

No, it wasn't just blood, because blood glooped together and it didn't have pieces in it, it didn't contain smooth shards and soft slivers of what had to have been bone and brain, because Alex had seen that for herself, her own blood and bone and brain all over Barrett's living room and here it was again, gleaming as she dipped her fingertips into what was there and real and—

Her hand slipped in the cold splatter with a shudder. Swallowing around the sick in her throat, though she couldn't throw off her shudder, Alex brought her hand into the light ...

Not a drop of blood.

Not a shard of bone.

Not a sliver of brain.

Alex pulled her other hand.

Just in case.

Her hands were clean.

The table was clean.

She tried to chase the smell, but there was no trace.

"Knock knock."

Alex glanced up at Shaz. And Sam.

They really were fifteen again, hovering on the threshold just in case something jumped out at them.

"We've dropped round Maddie's stuff," Shaz explained. "More boxes than we thought so we've just put them in the hallway."

"They'll need to be moved," Alex said, "Harry'll have a fit."

"Only if you tell him I was the one who put 'em there," Sam said. "Anyway—"

A floorboard groaned above them and Sam flinched.

"It's just the girls exploring," Alex said. "Ghosts don't creak."

"If you say so."

Alex did say so. Sort of.

"This house always makes me think of Edda's stories, you know," Sam said, screwing up his nose at the ceiling. "Stories from the old country, you know, about dybbuks and golems and deep, dark forests."

"The garden ain't my priority, Sammy," Alex said. "Call *Ground Force* if you're that worried about it, but ripping out the well and putting a water feature in isn't even on my list."

"Let's start with *Changing Rooms* first," Sam muttered.

"What's a golem when it's at home?" Shaz asked.

"It's a dybbuk you wanna watch out for," Sam said. "Vengeful spirits possessing young girls."

"And you believe that?" Alex laughed, conceding a sigh at Sam's outraged splutter.

Shaz peered back into the shadows that seeped through the hallway and asked where their uncle was anyway.

"Gone back to work," Alex said, "I think. You know what this place is like. Hard to keep track of anyone."

Sam snorted.

"Living or Dead?"

"Well, I can't see the Dead, can I? Wrong twin."

Alex used to find Sam's reaction to any mention of Matthew since *that* day reassuring: it was sharp and sour, suggestive of the skin-gouging kind of vengeance that she had always had in mind. It was like he understood what that betrayal had truly meant and that, unlike Shaz, he would've been there right behind Alex if Matthew had ever dared to come back. So why wasn't it having the same effect on her now? It was still the same curl of his mouth, the same flash of something worse than just pain in his eyes, and yet …

All Alex could feel was a strange, profound sadness for something she wasn't ready to name, let alone face.

"That was Mouse's territory," she said, compelled to continue, to push and pull and prod Sam until she found whatever it was she wanted, just like—

"You're glowing," Sam said.

Alex muttered an apology and brushed burgundy off her arms, but when she looked up, it wasn't Sam staring at her with wide eyes.

It was Shaz.

"Sis?"

"Nothing," Shaz said, but no matter how hard she shook her head, she couldn't quite steal Alex's attention away from her twitchy foot.

"Have I got chow mein in my hair or something?"

"No! No, it looks great," Shaz replied. "Have you washed it again?"

Alex pulled at a curl and cringed at how dry it felt, but when she was getting covered in blood and vomit and mud and seawater three or four times a day, scrubbing her hair clean was becoming a bit of a necessity. She really had to track down that fancy conditioner Shaz had got her that Christmas, ages ago, but it was hard to really care what box Harry had put her haircare in when her sister was standing there looking like she was trying to negotiate a dangerous fart.

Alex raised her eyes above them, fixed them on the bookcase, and took as deep a breath as she could manage before she snapped out a "what?"

Now the right side of Alex's face was throbbing. Brilliant.

Alex massaged her jaw this way and that, cringing at the weak creak it made.

At least it didn't crack like the corpse's had.

"Anyway," Sam said, "I'd also like a word about Pandora. I'd like a word *with* Pandora."

"Harry said he squared it," Alex said, enough panic flooding her body to push her upright. "Can't you just blame any loose ends on the millennium bug?"

Sam could've been saying anything, because it didn't matter.

Because it was back.

The glisten.

The table leg was glistening again.

It was blood, wasn't it?

There was a tang of iron in the air that Alex could just taste if she licked her lips, it was there and it was growing and it was overwhelming that wisp of white musk still hanging in the—

"Alright," Sam said, "we're worried about you. Shaz told me about your little hospital visit earlier."

"Samuel," Alex said, trying to crane her head to – no, she couldn't see it properly from that angle, not with the moon caught in the clouds, "there's nothing to be worried about."

"You were just staring into space. Like before."

"This isn't a relapse," Alex said, turning to her sister. "Shaz, tell him this isn't a relapse."

"Don't do the Wilde thing," Sam said.

"It's not the Wilde thing—"

"I know you used to call it Code Bananarama—"

"Only works with three people, not two," Alex lied. "Sharon is a doctor—"

"In A&E—"

"Alright, Mr Psychology Degree," Alex said, creeping towards the table and its dark glisten, "what symptoms am I currently exhibiting?"

"Well," Sam replied, "what diagnosis did they decide on in the end?"

"See? You don't even know," Alex said, but Shaz was giving her that awful look again like Alex was drowning a kitten in front of her or something and shadows shifted in the corner. "I am fine."

The grandfather clock bonged outside.

It must've been a new hour.

"Maybe we should wait," Shaz said, with that combination of the gentle voice and those terrified eyes really clawing away at whatever part of Alex's mind set off the alarms, "until Elizabeth gets here. Cos if we're gonna talk about how you're feeling—"

"I'm fine."

"Alright," Shaz said, "but I'd really like to hear Elizabeth's thoughts on everything that's been happening, because if this Shadow—"

"Eleanor," Alex said.

"That *thing*," Sam said, "is called Eleanor?"

"Anyway," Shaz said, "you said you thought Elizabeth recognised her—"

"Trust me," Alex laughed bitterly, "she recognised her."

"Alright," Shaz said, "I'd like to hear it. Whatever's going on. Cos I saw an old man fracture your skull, yesterday, sis. And I don't wanna see it again. And I'm sure Elizabeth doesn't either."

Shaz almost believed what she was saying. Alex had no idea how she knew that, but she knew, as much as she knew her own name, that her sister almost, but not quite, believed what was coming out of her own mouth.

Almost.

"Great," Sam sighed.

"She has helped Alex," Shaz said. "You weren't inside that cottage yesterday."

"And we don't know the first thing about her."

Alex really didn't know the first thing about her, that was for sure.

"Fine," Shaz said, "then we need to ask Uncle Harry. This is well beyond anything we know about Power or ghosts or whatever else there is."

"Yeah," Alex said, "right. 'Uncle Harry, there's something we've never told you about the night your sister died and it involves a Ouija board and a demonic entity. Don't worry, Mum destroyed the Ouija board but the demonic entity's back and is doing a Pied Piper on me in the middle of the bloody night and is an accomplice to several murders.'"

"Al," Shaz said, "we were only kids."

"And she murdered Mum," Alex continued. "El – the Shadow – murdered Mum."

"But Mum wasn't murdered, sis," Shaz was saying, with the kind of eggshell-gentleness Alex could imagine her using on recalcitrant children who didn't want their wounds wiped clean. "She took her own life—"

"Nope. She was possessed by the thing that possessed you. Only found out this morning, in between finding Pandora and ..."

And letting Elizabeth go.

"Alex," Sam said, "are you being serious?"

"No, Sammy," Alex snapped, "I just think it's *hilarious* that my mother went careering off a cliff in the middle of the night."

"But she exorcised it," Shaz whispered. "She – she took it from me and she burnt the board—"

"She took it on herself," Alex explained. "She didn't jump, Shaz. Or if she did, it was only to stop her Power being stolen."

"We have to tell Harry," Shaz said. "If this thing could kill *Mum* of all people—"

Alex gave her head a shake so hard it yanked at her neck, torturing the muscles. She couldn't tell them. Not yet. Not about the scream she now imagined that Carrie had made when she'd plummeted, unwillingly, to her untimely death.

"Christ," Alex said, all sorts of anxieties swirling in her stomach, "he'd want to know why. He'd want to know what the hell we were doing and when I bring up David of all people ..."

"I'm sure he'd understand there's bigger things at stake here," Sam argued. "He can be an awkward old bugger—"

"Don't let him hear you say that," Shaz said, "he's still two years off fifty, as he keeps reminding anyone that'll listen."

"Then he's got enough marbles to get that there's been a bloody serial killer possessed by a demon that murdered your mam," Sam replied. "Three victims that we know of, and that's not including Lex or Pandora."

"But Al said Elizabeth knew this Shadow – this Eleanor. I think we ask her first."

The bickering must've continued because Alex surely would've been jolted out of her reverie by the sound of her name, but nothing came.

Nothing came so Alex had no choice but to watch the ghost with half a face slide out of the shadows.

24
Giving off Sparks

The Half-Faced Man stared at her with that one brilliant blue eye, unblinking, unflinching.

Every last inch of her skin prickled with cold and she would've sworn on David Wilde's empty grave that the ghost was less than five feet away from her, the broken side of his skull only just obscured, and Alex knew what that felt like and now she was wondering if ghosts could still feel pain but what did he want because he wasn't moving any closer and he wasn't going away he was just looking at her watching her like he's reaching out but he's not reaching out and Alex's head is pounding and she knows that if she tips her head forward teeth will cascade out but it won't all be teeth it'll be bone too bone and teeth and bone and blood but what does he want from her just bone and brain and her blood he wants her blood he wants blood her blood her own blood her fresh blood her own flesh and her own blood flesh and blood fresh and—

"Alex."

Seeing wasn't believing.

The ghost had gone.

And ghosts didn't go that quickly.

So he probably hadn't been there in the first place.

That wasn't how ghosts behaved anyway.

Just her own mind playing tricks on her.

Alex ripped her gaze away from the corner and wiped her hands against her jumper.

"Elizabeth's not here," she said, shoving out two chairs with a twitch of her hand, "so let's just get this over with."

The windows rattled as Sam and Shaz took their chairs with far more reluctance than they should have for two people insistent on getting everything out of Alex.

"So, what do you know?" Sam asked, pulling out his bloody notepad, "about this Eleanor?"

"It all starts a while ago really." Alex sighed. "With Elizabeth, actually. She's a twin too, but her twin was ..."

Was there even a word to describe Eleanor?

A phrase? A speech?

How could Alex put into words that shark's smile and wolf's voracity and that sense of humour that to anyone else would've been straight-up sadism?

How she could claw her way through the Ether and make a mockery of Life and Death?

And how hot she burned ...

"Her twin sister's Power was different," Alex explained, shoving aside that hungry smile and its hungrier eyes. "Everyone's Power is unique, but Eleanor, Elizabeth's sister, she could steal Power—"

"Hang on," Shaz said, "she's her sister?"

"It's always twins," Sam muttered.

"Anyway," Alex continued, "the problem is that it's hard to steal Power without killing someone and she really enjoyed the killing aspect of it. Long story short ..."

And a little bending of the truth.

She pulled on that small ugly part of her soul that had somehow made her such a good liar all those years ago, much better than Matthew at least, so good even Carrie never saw through her, so good that, in the dead of all those nights she couldn't sleep, she wondered where on Earth she'd got it from.

"She tried to kill Elizabeth but it went wrong. It killed Eleanor. Well, it destroyed her body and expelled her soul to The Other Side."

"Elizabeth's scars?" Shaz asked. "But I've seen how far they spread. How did she survive?"

"It's complicated," Alex said, sure that when her sister went away and actually thought about it, she would've put it all together in a fairly accurate order, "but ..."

The bookcase was trembling.

How could a bookcase tremble?

"But it backfired on this Eleanor?" Shaz asked. "Is that what you're saying?"

"Yeah," Alex breathed, watching the bookcase shudder, the shelves bristling with ...

Power.

She couldn't see it, but she could bloody well feel it.

It couldn't be.

A single book was sliding out of its hiding place—

Alex smacked it back where it belonged with a flick of a finger.

"Sorry," she said, when Sam and Shaz turned to the bookcase, "I thought a book was about to fall."

"So," Sam said, scribbling his notes, "the Power backfired on Eleanor and killed her?"

Alex nodded, but she could feel the rumble of the—

"God, this thunder," Shaz murmured at the wonky window.

"It's not thunder," Alex muttered, trying to steal a glance at the bookcase.

"And when was this?" Sam asked.

"What?"

"Eleanor's death?"

"I don't know," Alex said. "It has to be at some point before 1984. Obviously. And, uh—"

The bookcase.

Half of the books were now overhanging their homes.

"Uh?" Sam said.

This was getting ridiculous. All she wanted to do was have a simple conversation and she was, what, having to play tug of war with a poltergeist?

"One sec."

She did a rough count of the books. Some shelves were untouched, the others a haphazard selection of half out, half in. How the hell was she meant to manage something that annoyingly intricate?

"Is that you?" Sam asked.

He'd turned round again.

"No, of course not!"

With a wave of her hand, Alex managed to push half of the half back in.

So a quarter, really.

The word higgledy-piggledy came to mind again.

Another wave, another few books back in their rightful place.

With a litany of blasphemies caught in her throat, she clenched her fist and poured all of her Power into that one thought, one clear image of a beautifully organised …

There.

Nice and neat.

Alex huffed out a sigh of relief and shot the bookcase the dirtiest look she could muster before she continued.

"It has to be before 1984. I get the feeling from Elizabeth that they were adults though and assuming she's fortyish—"

Sam snorted, pencil poised over his pad.

"Forty-five at best."

"Fine," Alex said, "forty-five maximum—"

"Nearly old enough to be your mother."

"You're only saying that cos you knocked me up so young," Alex said, stretching out a sickly smirk, and Sam had the good grace to blush. "So anyway, if she's Harry's age, I'd put the event, if you wanna call it that, between '70 and '84. The point is, Eleanor's body was destroyed, but not her soul and because she never passed over properly—"

"So she's a ghost?" Shaz said.

How had Alex ever thought that the Half-Faced Man had gone?

That brilliant blue was glaring at her through the gloam.

"No," Alex said, forcing herself to ignore him, because he probably, really probably wasn't there anyway, "she's sort of more like a demonic spirit sort of thing. That's how she came through the spirit board that Halloween. In – in '84."

The books bolted from their shelves.

"Christ," Sam gasped, "I know you're stressed but—"

"It's not me," Alex said, deciding that if the Half-Faced Man could glare at her, she could glare right back at him. "Can you put them back please?"

The clock bonged again.

"Who are you talking to?" Shaz asked.

"That ghost with half a face. The one that freaked us out that night. And Mouse before that."

Alex shoved her chair out and stood her ground.

"Put the books back," she said. "It ain't funny."

The ghost stared back.

Unmoving. Immoveable. Without movement or motion.

It was worse than talking to a statue, because at least Alex could've been sure the statue was really there. A statue could be seen and touched and verified. A statue could be believed.

"Fine," she said, sweeping her hand through the air, "I'll do it my ..."

The books shuddered.

Unmoving.

Alex pushed her Power at them again.

And again.

"Is this you?" she asked the ghost.

"Sis," Shaz said, staring into the shadows, "are you sure it's not you?"

"I know my own Power. I'm not—"

"Let's leave this for tomorrow," Sam said, slipping his notepad into his pocket. "Between Pandora and Barrett and the homeless fella, it's too much, Alex. I think Mads should come back with us tonight—"

"It's just a stupid ghost," Alex insisted, rushing around the table and slamming the books back with her own bare hands because apparently that worked, just pressing her palms into worn cloth and cardboard over and over and over again until the pads of her fingers stung because that was something a ghost couldn't do, a ghost couldn't touch or hold or feel—

"When's Elizabeth due to get here?" Shaz asked, even as Sam made noises about the storm. "It would be good to hear her side of things."

"Uh, I, uh, don't know," Alex lied, finding another book out of place and another and yet another, even as she thought she'd pushed them all back in like it was the sickest game of whack-a-mole, "she didn't say."

"Alex," Sam said, "leave them, love. They can wait."

"No," Alex said, shrugging the warm hand off her shoulder as she shoved another book in and another and another and that when and when and when again was ricocheting round her mind again and that bloody ghost was staring at her with that brilliant blue eye and all she could think of was flesh and blood, "I'm not letting him get away with this—"

"Alex, it's probably—"

"It's not my Power," she hissed, "look."

She yanked out one of the glowing books and thrust it in Sam's face.

"Blue, see? Not burgundy. Mine's burgundy like blood, Matthew's is turquoise like the sea, Harry's is green like poison, Elizabeth's is silver like steel, Pandora's is purple like lavender in full bloom. This is blue, this is the blue of my daughter's eyes."

"Fine," Sam sighed, "but if a ghost is winding you up over some bookshelves—"

"Yeah, well, once I work out how to exorcise him, he won't be—"

The bookcase exploded.

Shelves smashed into the window, books bounced off the walls, a thunder of trees crashing into the table.

Sam and Shaz were spluttering sawdust, asking if Alex was alright.

Alright?

There was no alright.

Alex screamed.

She screamed at the ghost, Power flaring as she ripped her own throat apart, the study roaring around her.

"My house!" she was hollering, flinging her finger at the unmoving, immoveable figure, "this is *my* house! My house! Mine! My house! My—"

When.

She remembered when she'd last felt like that, in a ruined wedding dress ...

She staggered to a stop.

Because just for a fleeting moment, she could see something of Matthew in that half a face and it had just clawed up all of her rage and captured it and thrown it into the wind, leaving her clutching an empty bookcase with trembling fingers.

An empty bookcase.

She'd reformed it without even realising.

It was still glowing burgundy.

"Mum?"

Alex tried to ignore the wide eyes and pasty faces as she turned to the doorway, where Maddie and Pandora were gawping at the scattered books.

"It's just a moment," she said, wiping Power and sweat from her hands, "a supernatural moment."

But Maddie was already looking at Sam and asking if it was like before.

"Yeah," Sam said, with a brusque nod that gave Alex the impression there was no arguing about it, "yeah, I think it is, love."

"Before what?" Alex asked.

"You know what your mam's like with storms," Sam said to their daughter, as if ...

"I'm fine with storms!" Alex said. "It was *my* mum who hated storms! *I'm* fine with them!"

She turned on Shaz and told her to tell him.

"I think it was Mum, yeah," Shaz whispered, "but ..."

Alex had no idea who she was aiming that apologetic shrug at, but it should've been at her. Shaz was *her* sister, Carrie was *their* mother, David, wherever he was, would've been *their* father, and if Matthew had been there, he would've eviscerated Sam—

"I don't think we need to bring him up in front of the girls," Sam said.

"I didn't say anything," Alex said, but the way Sam was shaking his head at her, *glaring* for only the fifth time in his life, and Shaz's stare—

"If we leave now," Sam said, checking his watch, "we should get back before the rain gets too heavy."

"I think I wanna phone Harry first," Shaz said.

"No one needs to go anywhere," Alex said, "this is ridiculous."

"What's ridiculous," Sam replied, "is your Power not being under control with kids in the house."

"This wasn't me! It's the Half-Faced Man!"

"That none of us can see."

"Cos you don't have Power!"

"And I'm not a kid!" Maddie added.

"I'm calling Harry," Shaz said.

"I don't need babysitting!" Alex yelled, "I'm thirty years old! I'm fine!"

"Fine?" Sam scoffed.

"I am fine *enough*," she said, pulse roaring in her ears. "The much bigger problem is the thing that possessed your fiancée fifteen years ago and left our mother no choice but to hurl herself into the North sodding Sea."

"So you accept it is a problem?" Sam said.

And Shaz had that look on her face again!

"Why do you keep looking at me like that?"

"It's the look in your eye," Shaz whispered. "It makes you look like Matthew."

"I can see him."

Pandora and her small voice stepped further into the study. Lip caught between her teeth, she pointed to the corner of the room.

"I can see the ghost, I think," she said, "he literally has half a face, right?"

"Well, anyone could've worked that out," Sam said. "Pandora, you don't have to stick up for Alex just because—"

"It's the left side of his face," Pandora continued. "He's a bit shorter than you. His right eye, well, the eye that's left, is blue, as blue as Maddie's, and he has dark hair, though I don't know if that's just the blood. I can draw him if you like?"

There was one particular sigh Sam could do which felt extra-resigned: the one where he felt like he was losing against the Wildes, which was pretty much every time he'd ever tried to go up against them.

"I think he wants to talk to Alex," Pandora suggested. "He's been trying to get her attention."

Maddie crept into the study and clung to Pandora's shoulder.

"For real?" Maddie asked. "There's a ghost over there?"

"Seriously," Pandora said, pointing dead at the Half-Faced Man, "I can see why he scares people but I don't think he's trying. To scare anyone, I mean."

"Can you talk to the Dead?" Alex asked.

Pandora shook her head.

"I don't think so. I don't think I've ever even seen a ghost before. I'm just sort of feeling this from him."

Alex ignored the image of the Dead Pandora choking on seaweed as it encroached on her mind and turned to Sam.

"So," she said, "believe me now?"

"Either way," Sam said, "is this really a suitable place for kids?"

"I'm not a kid!" Maddie protested, "I'm nearly fourteen!"

"And I'm definitely not a kid," Pandora said, though she really had to practise looking less guilty when she said that. "I have left school, I promise."

"Regardless of age," Sam began, but Alex cut him straight off.

"It never did me any harm," she said. "Look at Shaz: she's normal."

"But," Sam whispered, stepping over one, two, three books, "there is nothing normal about this. Whatever else has happened, Alex, this is our daughter now."

"It's just Power," Alex insisted.

"Power is never just Power."

"Look," Alex sighed, "just give me five minutes with this sodding ghost. Alright?"

She glanced at Shaz, who *still* had that bloody look in her eyes, but a raise of her eyebrow had her sister pulling Sam towards the door.

"Five minutes," Sam warned.

"What are you gonna do?" Maddie asked.

"I'm going to bargain with him," Alex explained.

She asked Pandora if she would help and then, of course, Maddie put on the doe eyes and asked if she could stay.

"It might not be pretty," Alex said. "It might also look really weird."

Maddie shrugged, picked up a book off the nearest chair, and sat herself down.

When, when, and when again.

25
Left in the Dark

"He hasn't blinked."

Maddie didn't stay in her chair for long.

For the first five minutes, yes, but after that, she was as close to the Half-Faced Man as Pandora was, despite Alex's warnings.

Alex had, of course, pressed herself against the skeleton of the bookcase, arms crossed tight over her chest as she tried to direct the ...

Whatever it was. A negotiation?

They had very quickly worked out that ghosts didn't understand spoken language and he didn't seem to be paying that much attention even with three people thinking right at him. Pandora had wanted to touch him, but Alex had shot that idea down while it was still slipping out of her mouth.

Maddie had asked if it was even possible to touch a ghost.

Alex told her that tonight was not the night to find out.

Maybe it would've worked.

Maybe it would've been the one single thing that could've given Alex some kind of answer, but as it was, after five minutes and another forty, the howling wind growing ever more vehement around them, Alex, Maddie, and Pandora stood in a line, hands on their hips, and frowned at their guest.

"Seriously," Maddie whispered, "I'm sure he hasn't blinked. Can ghosts blink?"

"He must've moved though," Pandora said, daring to point a subtle finger at the books.

"That was Power," Alex said.

She decided not to mention that it was exceptionally controlled Power.

But then what did she know? She was still an amateur with all her obvious hand waving. That's what Matthew would've called it.

Amateur.

Matthew would've known what to—

So would Harry.

And Harry would've done a better job anyway, so she didn't know why her mind was still on Matthew so much.

Bloody house.

She didn't know what was worse: thinking of Matthew or thinking of Elizabeth and how, after Alex had agreed she should leave, the way she'd quietly started gathering her things around Alex, which, of course, didn't amount to much at all.

"Girls," Alex said, taking a step closer to the shadows, "d'you wanna go and prove to Sam and Shaz you're still alive?"

"I wanna stay here," Maddie whined.

"Just for a couple of minutes—"

"I mean *stay* stay," Maddie said. "Not being funny, but I've had a month solid of them, Mum ..."

"I just need to sort the ghost out first, sweetheart," Alex said, trying to give Pandora a meaningful look—

Which she got, judging by the way she corralled Maddie out of the study.

Communicating with people with Power was so much easier.

Unless, Alex thought, as she turned back to her spirit of the evening, they were Dead.

"I don't know what you want from me. You can't just vandalise my home and then ... What? D'you wanna be exorcised? I ..."

She sighed and shook her head.

What if he didn't even know she was there?

Though that time with the spirit board, he'd seen them, he'd ...

He'd touched them.

His hands on Alex's.

His hands on Matthew's.

She could touch him.

Just for a moment, a single moment, with a single brush of her fingers against the part of a hand she could just about make out, she could reach out and—

The secrets of those shadows.

The whispered words still weeping from that wound in the darkness and they overwhelmed Alex, they choked her until they froze in her throat and she couldn't even scream but how can someone scream when the terror is so impossible to comprehend that the only thought she could hang onto was that he was too young to die, far too young to die and finally he moves from the shadows but when Alex turns around, she sees ...

Herself.

More or less.

Herself and Matthew and Sam and Shaz in all their growing pains glory.

"You don't have to take part," Alex – well, Lexy as she was (is?) then (now?) – says, "we only need three people in the circle."

Shaz – Shazza – backs away from the table.

"I might just let you three do it."

"Sammy?" Lexy asks.

"I'm fine with it," Sammy says, "as long as it works how it should."

"Why wouldn't it?"

"Cos we've never done this before," Sammy says, "and I think Shazza's right to have questions. You do hear stories about the Dead. Edda knows loads."

"There's nothing to be afraid of," Lexy says. "Remember, most of Mouse's best friends are Dead."

Matthew – Mouse – slams the book down.

"Found it."

"At least put it the right way up so we can all read it."

Mouse spins the book around with a smirk.

"It's in Latin?" Lexy says, screwing her nose up just like Maddie does. Alex has never noticed before.

"Guh – got a problem with that?"

"It could say anything!"

"It's the right summons."

"You don't speak Latin—"

"No one *speaks* Latin, Lexy," Mouse sneers, "it's a language of the Dead, therefore I understand it."

"I'm sure Matthew's right," Sammy says. "Could we get on with it?"

Lexy *and* Alex crane their heads around to Shazza, who's pulled her feet up onto the ottoman.

"Sure you don't wanna join in?"

Shazza shakes her head but Alex knows that even making the absolutely correct choice in that moment won't save her.

"Suit yourself," Lexy says. "Anyone in the room we need to be aware of?"

Matthew glances at the Half-Faced Man and mutters that it's just the usual.

He presses his fingers onto the planchette.

Followed by Lexy.

Finally Sammy.

It all goes wrong so quickly, even quicker than Alex can remember. Their confusion, their catching Eleanor out in her lies, Mouse refusing to let go, and then, of course, they can't let go at all.

The three of them are stuck to the planchette, screaming and tugging at their own arms as pink Power starts licking up their arms.

Two new hands land on theirs.

The Half-Faced Man pours Power into the planchette and releases the kids.

He saved them.

He scared them, yes, but he saved them, and now lightning's splitting the sky and they're—

Gone.

Just Alex and the Half-Faced Man, sheet lightning setting the study ablaze with blue and grey and mauve.

The table might've been bare but the scorch marks still glistened on it fifteen years later and all that fear and all that pain rushed back into her because she knew that either way, her mum was gone and her dad was gone and Matthew was gone and Elizabeth had left and surely Sam was going to take Maddie and probably Pandora too and she'd forgotten just how tired she was and just how hard it was to stumble towards the study door and she didn't even care anymore, she couldn't even care about the state of the house, if it was because of her or the storm or the ghost or all of them, she was just stuck defending a house she hated to a ghost who barely accepted he was …

Just as stuck as she was.

Bong.

Alex swore and shuddered and clung onto the hallway, letting the darkness drown her.

What had even been the point in coming back?

And where was everyone?

In the dark, in the thunder, how could she tell?

Was anyone else even still in the house?

Had they all gone without her?

Would they have just left her there with all those ghosts she was now having to bat away as she slid in puddle after puddle, hiccoughing up a sob and then another?

And where had those puddles come from?

What was in the house with her?

"Please," she whispered, staggering forward into yet more cold arms—

That didn't let her go.

Arms that felt like leather and smelt like expensive cigarettes and bergamot.

Lightning flooded the hallway.

Storm-soaked, blood-blue eyes gazed down at her.

Alex flung her arms around Elizabeth and squeezed as hard as she could because how could she care if she looked ridiculous or naïve or—

Elizabeth squeezed her back, one hand gripping Alex's waist and the other caressing her neck.

"How did you get in?" Alex mumbled into Elizabeth's scarf.

"Door opened for me." Elizabeth laughed. "You should've seen Meyer's face."

Alex tried to swallow her tears with a smile and dragged Elizabeth down the spiritless corridor to—

A study full of them.

A study full of spirits.

The room was absolutely chock-a-block with ghosts: the headless monk, the plague victims, the consumptive children, all faintly blurred at the edges, all the ghosts that Matthew had ever described to her.

And each of them was carefully returning books to the shelves.

Please tell me you can see them, Alex thought.

"Aye, just about," Elizabeth said. "You've got a good system here. Pay 'em for this?"

"I don't understand."

"I think," Elizabeth murmured, "they're trying to help."

"I shouldn't even be able to see them still," Alex sobbed, yanking *green* Power off the ends of her fingers, "I've felt like I was going mad all evening."

"Oi!" Elizabeth said with enough force to make Alex's bones punch through her skin. "Have yous been bothering her?"

One by one, the ghosts turned to the Half-Faced Man with raised eyebrows and not-so-subtle nods. One of the little ghosts, one of the ones who'd waved and Alex was pretty sure Matthew had called her Adelaide, even pointed at him.

Then, with only one book left on the floor, the ghosts filed past Alex and Elizabeth, slipping into thin air.

"I don't know what he wants," Alex whispered.

"I didn't think poltergeists were real," Elizabeth confessed.

"He has Power."

They edged towards the table, but the closer they got, the further the Half-Faced Man sank into the shadows.

"*The Encyclopaedia Daemonica*," Elizabeth said, flicking through the book. "Interesting ..."

A bookmark fluttered to the floor.

"Your sister in there?" Alex said, bending down to pick it up.

"Ah, there's that Wilde sense of humour," Elizabeth said, shooting her a dark smile, that fell as soon as Alex glared at her. "Looks like it was between 'dybbuk' and 'ectoplasm'. Maybe Eleanor does have an entry ... Eleanor Lennox, let's see ..."

"Lennox?" Alex asked, turning the bookmark over.

"You didn't think Black's my real name? It's as real as Pandora's."

It wasn't a bookmark.

It was a photograph.

It was that kind of faded, jaundiced colour that photos were in the Sixties or Seventies.

It was of a whole family.

A father and a mother, four children – well, young adults, by the looks of three of them.

Stepping into Elizabeth's glow, Alex turned over the photo and read the carefully inked description:

1st May 1968

James and Grace, Jimmy (25), David (23), Siobhan (17), Amy (11)

The Wildes' flat, Blantyre Street, Cork City

She flipped it back over.

She stared at that face.

That faintly familiar face.

"Has the ghost really gone?" Alex asked.

"You don't need to worry about him for now."

Alex shook her head and looked down at blue eyes that really were so much like Maddie's.

"I just wanted to say something to him."

"Say what?"

"Thank you."

There was a final bong from the grandfather clock outside and Alex finally remembered:

It had been broken all her life.

26
No Need to Talk

David (23).

And it was a young David, face stretched into a silly grin, but May 1968? Why hadn't David been in London by then?

May 1968. She tried to do the mental arithmetic. As far as she knew, she and Matthew hadn't been that premature, at least not by twin standards, so surely they would've been conceived, not that she really wanted to think about it, in May or June?

Shotgun wedding?

She shook her head.

It was hardly important.

He was their father, wasn't he?

Wasn't he?

"Shaz said that Barrett's Dead," Elizabeth said, "and his funeral's tomorrow?"

"Yeah," Alex whispered, gazing down at her father. "Massive heart attack. Went to see the body."

"You saw his body?"

Alex mumbled that yes, she had seen it, because she couldn't care. Not when she could stare at a face she thought she understood.

"Alex?"

"Do ..."

She passed the photo to Elizabeth.

"Can you see any similarities?" Alex asked. "Anything at all?"

The milk bottle specs came out.

"The little one's the spit of Maddie," Elizabeth said. "And Matthew glowers like your ..."

She peered at the writing on the back.

"Uncle Jimmy. You said they were running from something, your parents?"

"Well, that's what Mum used to say," Alex said, "cos she and Harry are from London and obviously David was from Cork. There was no real reason for them to be here."

Alex snatched the photo back, ignoring Elizabeth's tut.

How had it taken her so long to recognise the writing?

"That's my ..."

It was the calligraphic curl of each capital letter, the Greek Es, the sharpness of the Ms and Ns.

"Mum took this," Alex realised, placing the photo with even more care on the album. "She took all our photos. Always did. She took this for them."

"Alright."

"I know that might not mean much to you, but that means they were together—"

"Alex," Elizabeth said, "count the shadows."

"What?"

Elizabeth took the rather daring decision to hold Alex's hand and lead it down to the photo.

"Look at the photograph again and count everyone's shadows."

Ignoring the cold clench of the fingers around hers, Alex looked at James and his shadow, which was cast onto the wall. Then Grace, hers also on the wall, as were Jimmy's and David's and Siobhan's and Amy's and ...

And Amy's.

Again.

On the grandfather clock.

In fact, what Alex had assumed was a flaw in the film or just a natural breakdown of the ink, was, the longer she looked at it, a pinkish aura around Amy Wilde.

"You don't think ..."

Alex flipped the photo again.

Amy (11).

"She wouldn't," she said, "that's a child. Even Eleanor wouldn't ..."

By the time she looked up, Elizabeth was staring down furiously, her jaw trembling.

"I ..."

"But there must be other spirits?" Alex asked. "Or demons?"

"Aye, of course there are, but most people with Power can shake off your common or garden angry spirit like we shake off influenza or consumption. One sneeze and we're done."

"Unless the spirit has its own Power?"

Elizabeth gave a half-hearted nod.

"Someone like your mother could've dealt with your standard entity, even if her Power was rusty. Even you could deal with your standard entity."

"Thanks," Alex said, "I think?"

"Aye! You'd boot it out in five minutes just out of sheer bloody-mindedness." Elizabeth laughed, which faded when she glanced at the photo again.

"So it's Eleanor?" Alex asked. "Time and time again?"

"She likes Power and she likes picking on people," Elizabeth muttered. "Her and Barrett were a good match."

"And if she tries to possess me?"

After a weekend together, Alex should've been less astonished at Elizabeth's face, but she was transfixed by every emotion that seemed to pass through her like fleeting spirits.

Which she hardly wanted to be, given the circumstances.

"Don't," Elizabeth said, with those bloodshot, tear-glazed eyes.

"Elizabeth."

"With your Power, you'd have to invite her in," Elizabeth ended up saying, which Alex strongly suspected was the fourth or fifth thought that had actually gone through her mind, "or stumble so far deep into The Other Side that you've left your body Living but soulless. So don't. Don't leave your body unattended and certainly don't invite her in. This close to a Millennium, so much uncertainty and excitement, the Veil Between Worlds is fragile and thinning all the time. Think of it like the ozone layer. Any wrong move makes it worse."

"And my odds," Alex asked, "if she takes me over?"

"What do you think?"

Alex gazed down at the photo and swore under her breath.

"She might kill you either way," Elizabeth said. "I really shouldn't be here."

"And yet here you are," Alex said, shifting closer, "again."

"Here I am," Elizabeth sighed, "again."

"Who are you?" Alex asked, as softly as she dared. "Really? Cos I've spent the whole day thinking that I don't actually know the first thing about you. You can't slice a block of cheese properly but you can cut a man's throat open, there's more in Pandora's backpack than in your flat, and your twin sister goes round possessing people like she's Interrailing."

For all of Elizabeth's bravado, there were cracks. There always had been with Alex. Yes, she'd been witness to her hauteur when she met Sam, that dark fury directed at Barrett and Eleanor, all of that infinite strength, but thinking about it, now Alex could breathe and think, her rage from last night and her frustration from the afternoon coalescing into something still wounded but calmer, she could pay attention to the twitch of Elizabeth's fingers, the tremor of her jaw, the shallow inhales and barely audible exhales.

Where Elizabeth's hair was still rain-damp, the colour of fading embers at the ends, all Swan Vesta at the roots, it didn't quite cover her scarred cheek when she, as usual, had let it deliberately fall forward, and Alex watched the lip getting sucked in between Elizabeth's sharpest teeth, because if it was stuck there, it couldn't tremble. It couldn't say anything else stupid. It couldn't do what Alex had wanted all weekend and had barely had a taste of last night.

"I'm really not that interesting," Elizabeth told the floor.

Her face was the white of wilting ashes, her throat a precarious, pulsing pink as livid and as vivid as Power.

Alex begged to differ.

"The truth isn't always very nice," Elizabeth said.

"I don't care."

But then Elizabeth looked up at her with red-rimmed eyes and whispered a weak "sorry".

"You ain't brushing me off with *sorry*," Alex said. "You came back, didn't you? Didn't have to, did you?"

"I'd never forgive myself," Elizabeth said, "if something happened to you."

"Really?" Alex scoffed.

"You can't see me, can you?" Elizabeth said, baring her fangs like it was somehow Alex's fault. "You're looking right at me and you can't see me anymore."

"I have no idea what you're talking about."

"Aye," Elizabeth insisted, "you do. You used to look at me like you saw me and now you just see Matthew. Or Eleanor. Whatever's worse."

"Well, that's hardly my fault, is it?" Alex spat back at her.

"And you're saying you're wanting to know who I am?" Elizabeth said, shoulders shuddering with something Alex didn't want to identify. "I'm a fixer, Alex. I fix things. Business, crime, personal, supernatural, anything in between, I can fix it. I'm a fixer. And yeah, that means I've murdered people, but no one who never deserved it. But then I fucked up. I had to get out of Paris fast. That's me. That's who I am. That's all."

"That's *all*?" Alex spluttered.

"Well, if you're asking," Elizabeth continued, "I'm a hundred years old."

Alex's laugh caught in her throat as soon as she understood that doleful gaze heading her way.

"Literally?" she asked. "Like the Queen Mum?"

Elizabeth nodded.

"Born a minute after midnight, second of December 1898. My first death, the one I've got a grave for, was 1923."

Alex gawped at her.

What could she say?

What could possibly be appropriate when she found out that the age gap was significantly bigger than she could have ever imagined?

That a decade was more like a century?

Old enough to be Alex's mother? Sam would've had a stroke if he knew.

"How many times *have* you died?" Alex asked.

Elizabeth held up her whole hand and explained that although she didn't really age, every death seemed to add on a few wrinkles and silver hairs or make a few bones creak that shouldn't.

"I bet you see me now," Elizabeth sneered bitterly. "Sorry to be such a disappoint—"

Alex kissed her.

Again.

A fleeting press, before Elizabeth could pull away first.

"I see you," Alex said, choking on her own heartbeat, "Lizzie."

She absorbed Elizabeth's quiet, fluttering panic, a butterfly trapped under a kitten's paw, and let Elizabeth feel her fear and her hope and her want because Alex didn't care anymore if Wildes had rules, because Elizabeth was the one who'd waded into the waves after her, crawled into a cottage for her, and all the rest of it. And if there was the slightest chance that Elizabeth had been telling the truth when she'd said that she wasn't playing games ...

"I'm not," Elizabeth promised, "not with you."

"Then stay," Alex whispered, cradling Elizabeth's hand to her chest, "at least for tonight. I want you to stay. With me."

The smallest of smiles crept across Elizabeth's mouth, shifting her scars, lengthening her lips and then, more delicately than Alex ever thought possible, Elizabeth leant down and ghosted her lips against Alex's, who dragged her closer, their breath lost as they finally kissed properly, and Alex swallowed her heartbeat, chest fluttering as lightning danced between them, chilling and shocking as hands slipped into hair, onto shoulders, and the languid slip of their lips deepened and dirtied into the kiss of a woman who knew that she could conquer and would conquer until Alex was gasping into her mouth, lip caught on her fang, blood blooming between them, and Alex dragged Elizabeth towards her, breath pushing them chest to chest, curling her legs around Elizabeth's hips, because she had to be closer, they had to be closer, until there was no sense of separation, and when cold lips pressed against her throat, she could've cried and she almost did, because how had it never been like this before? How on Earth could she have existed without this, without their consuming each other entirely?

Monday 4 October 1999

27
Taking in the Rain

"Lord God, whose Son left us, in the Sacrament of his Body, food for the journey, mercifully grant that, strengthened by it, our brother Gideon may come to the eternal table of Christ, who lives and reigns for ever and ever."

"Amen."

All Alex could think, as she crossed herself with the rest of the sparse congregation, was that she was grateful that she didn't believe in God. The idea that Gideon Barrett, of all people, could be living it up in Paradise with the big fella would be enough to make her head spin like the little girl in *The Exorcist*.

They'd probably absolve his guilt anyway, not that he needed it. People like Gideon Barrett didn't understand guilt. Remorse wasn't the same as repentance. He probably wouldn't have even needed the Hail Marys to sleep soundly at night, that Bible at his bedside for what? He'd thought he was untouchable. He was circumventing the natural order of things, trying to survive a death sentence. He couldn't have actually still believed in a god, because what god would've allowed him to be possessed by someone like Eleanor? To murder?

God.

Alex clenched her fists together and tried to swallow her breath before it could run away from her. The side of her head was thumping again. The broken one.

She'd faced the mirror that morning, steam rising from the sink. She'd twisted her head to the left ... to the right – at which point her shoulder twinged. There was no wound or scar or even mark to suggest that a psychotic pensioner had ever driven a knife through skin and muscle and tendon, but she was convinced she could feel it. She could feel it. It was stiff in the mornings. It throbbed every time she shoved the wonky window shut or twisted the tea urn. It cringed when she had to stretch up to wash her hair.

And as for her face ...

Shaz said she looked fine.

Elizabeth said she looked fine.

Harry had looked at her, confused, and Alex remembered that she very deliberately had not told him about losing her brains over an old man's living room.

But there was a shadow. From her temple to the end of her ear, traversing where her cheekbone should have started, she was sure that there was at least an indentation. A discolouration. A darkness that hadn't been there before.

But Shaz said she looked fine and Shaz was a doctor.

Elizabeth said she looked fine and Elizabeth had been gazing gormlessly at Alex almost as much as Alex had been gazing gormlessly at her.

Harry hadn't noticed any difference and Harry noticed absolutely everything.

Seeing was not believing if she was seeing things that weren't there.

It wasn't helping. The breath. It was catching in her throat.

She forced her gaze from the lectern back to the order of service and tried to mouth the words to a hymn she simply didn't know.

She'd never been in this church before, Saint Martha's in Northmere, because why would she have? At primary school, for the usual Advent things or the harvest festival, they were always shipped off to the Methodist church in the middle of Coldharbour town centre, the one that looked more like a municipal library than a place of worship – or rather, the rest of their class would go and Carrie would keep the twins off school, because while the Methodist church looked like a municipal library and libraries represented a particularly useful day out for two kids who could be finally shut up with a whole load of books in front of them, it was still a church.

And just as Wildes had rules, they didn't do churches. Or synagogues.

They hadn't even been allowed to go on that O level history trip to Crossgate Cathedral.

So as for a Catholic church in the oldest part of the Coldharbour district, the cobbles nearly as old as the marshes they forced their way through ...

Five.

Christ on a cross in agony. Another Christ on a cross in agony. An enormous Virgin Mary in much more lurid colours than her son. The huge glinting crucifix above the altar. A third Christ on a cross in agony.

Four.

Marsh mist prickling her fingers. Shaz's scarf against her shoulder. That chill of old, cold stone. The order of service crumpling between her hands, cheap ink lifting off rough paper.

Three.

The hymn, mumbled at the back of the church, sung with weary, weak voices at the front. The dirge of the organ reverberating off ancient pillars. The clonk of the incense thing – Matthew said it was a thurible, he'd read it somewhere once.

Two.

That incense, like Christmas but cloying, and there was something else, something damp, like they'd trodden the marshes into the church—

One.

Blood.

Alex could taste blood.

She dropped the order of service and coughed into her hand.

The hymn finished.

There was nothing there.

"So much up and down," Shaz whispered as they slumped into the pew, "I'll never get used to it. Give me a Prod service any day."

Alex tried to shrug off her chill as she glanced around the church. There had been blood in her mouth. She could taste it.

"You're about to marry an observant Jew," she muttered. "Ever even been to a Shabbat service?"

"It's Reform though, innit?" Shaz said, burying her chin in her scarves and her hands in her pockets. "And it's not like we're getting married in there anyway. It would've been alright for you what with David being your old man, but I'm not faffing about with converting. I don't get it though. Catholics rush to hold a funeral and then take a year to get through the service."

It *was* quick.

Alex was convinced that even for Catholics, holding a funeral the very next day after a death was a bit hasty.

But then Harry had told her, had insisted as he waved Barrett's dead hand at her, that it was perfectly normal, perfectly natural.

A tiny old lady who reminded Alex of Sam's Grandma Edda had shuffled up to the lectern and was making a valiant attempt to peer over it as she recited something about Barrett being a valuable member of some club, the rest of which was presumably filling up the first two pews, because after that, the cavern of a church really was bare, until the final pew, in which its four occupants dragged down the average age quite considerably simply by being not pensionable. Well, Elizabeth didn't *look* pensionable.

As the woman shuffled back to her seat, the priest, who also helped bring up the average age from what Alex could see at the back, approached the lectern.

"Before we go our separate ways, let us take our leave of brother Gideon ..."

Elizabeth nudged them into standing. Pandora stumbled over a hassock.

"You're right," Alex whispered to Shaz, "there is too much up and down."

Sam had joked (or half-joked) over breakfast that there was no way that Elizabeth Black could possibly cross the threshold of a church, but as it turned out, she was the only one of them who knew what they were doing, crossing and kneeling and praying at the right moments. She had been a little affronted that it was a church service though – only because, as she explained, she had wanted to see Barrett burn.

Just to be sure.

One by one, the sparse crowd of mourners peeled off with mutters of the pub or a cuppa. Alex did hear one man mention that Barrett had apparently been arrested for something, but the woman he was with said that simply can't have been possible. Not Gideon Barrett.

Not Gideon Barrett with his arsenic and his interest in being possessed by a lunatic.

Not Gideon Barrett, who even at the age of seventy-eight and riddled with God knows how many diseases, could still knock out a trained killer and nearly stab Alex through the heart.

Alex had always thought the idea of spitting on someone's grave a bit weird, really. Not because it was ghoulish or terrible manners, but just that it was pointless.

But not now.

Now she could feel her mouth working up enough saliva to gob at the box as a final "fuck you".

"What d'you reckon?" Shaz asked. "He thinks we're Barrett's love children or his harem?"

The priest was lingering at the vestry door, apparently talking to the tiny old Edda-like lady, but he did keep throwing curious looks over at them.

"Neither," Alex snorted, "we look like we're starting a coven."

Elizabeth lit a cigarette, flicking ash very purposefully into the grave.

Pandora glanced down nervously into the grave, her throat working out a gulp.

"This isn't *Carrie*," Alex said, "he's not gonna burst out of it."

Again, if he had his own Power ...

There'd been a quiet moment the night before, one of those lulls between bursts of passion, when Elizabeth told Alex exactly how she'd died the first time. There'd been no surprises there. What had been shocking, chilling even, was how long it had taken Elizabeth to come back that first time. That they'd buried her in the Necropolis in a grave that was luckily too shallow and she'd had to bide her time, forcing her Power to return sooner than it was ready just to keep her breathing as she clawed her way through brittle wood and mercifully loose soil. That she'd laid there, gripping the grass, sucking in the smog, heaving and hacking away because at least it meant she was alive and out of her own coffin.

"People come back though," Pandora said. "I came back."

"You're an exception," Alex said. "A happy exception."

She wrapped her arm around Pandora's shoulders and shared a knowing glance with Shaz and Elizabeth over her head. Pandora gave Alex a reluctant nod, the grey light filtering through the trees giving her face an almost waxy pallor. But it wasn't the first time. She had been fine, when she had come back. Alex was sure of it. But the past day, when Alex wasn't distracted by Elizabeth or the Half-Faced Man or spectral blood, had been a drip-drip of those occasional moments. Silver hair where the pink dye was washing out. A slowness when she got up out of a chair. Interludes in which she just wasn't quite with them.

And that moment, that reflection in the wonky window, and what had it been? Five minutes after? The seizure?

But she had been through a lot. She had resurrected herself. Or Alex had resurrected her. Nobody, least of all Elizabeth or Harry, were entirely sure of the details. But the point was, she had gone to The Other Side and back, and Elizabeth had explained over and over that it was hardly a trip to the seaside, but it was in those little moments, those strange little moments, when Alex remembered those dreams of running through colour and choking on seaweed and now, with the knowledge that someone was staring at her from the other side of the graveyard, Alex turned towards—

A warm hand slapped against her shoulder and Shaz asked if she was alright.

Alex glanced back towards the church. Of course there was no one there. Even the priest had gone inside.

"Al?"

She gave her sister a nod.

Elizabeth and Pandora were already halfway down the hill back towards Coldharbour, hair glowing like match-ends in the fog.

Alex and Shaz stepped onto slick cobbles, slipping slightly even in their best boots. But at that strange sensation of being watched again, Alex slowed down to squint over her shoulder. It was hard to tell through the mist that there was someone there, but there was enough of a shadow for Alex to feel confident enough to ask Shaz if she could see it.

"Sort of," Shaz said, pushing her glasses up her nose, "but it's not moving, is it?"

"Grandmother's footsteps," Alex murmured.

"Is that what you saw at the church?"

"I don't know."

She frowned at the figure, if it even was a figure, but even with her Power strengthening, she just couldn't quite tell. But whatever it was in the fog, it wasn't moving, so Alex let out a shaky sigh and pulled Shaz back into a stroll.

"You really are away with it," Shaz said, pressing the back of her hand against Alex's forehead. "You feeling alright?"

"Don't fuss," Alex said, linking arms with her, "I'm not about to drop dead or something."

"So what happened last night anyway?" Shaz asked. "Sam said you looked deranged."

Ah.

Alex had reluctantly broken apart from Elizabeth to rush to the living room, hair half out of her ponytail, the bite on her neck already throbbing, and told the girls that it must've been past their bedtime and that Sam and Shaz could find some spare blankets in the airing cupboard if the storm didn't ease.

"What did I say again?" Alex asked.

"That you and Elizabeth had a breakthrough on Eleanor and you needed some time alone in the study."

Elizabeth had even appeared at that moment, lipstick smudged a faint pink that made her look like she had a terrible disease, just to nod behind Alex and look imperious.

"So were you researching something or what?" Shaz asked.

"Not quite," Alex said. "She stayed the night."

She *stayed* stayed?" Shaz gasped. "You slept together?"

"Calm down, Shaz, we're not fifteen years old snogging behind the sports hall," Alex said, feeling herself blush like a fifteen-year-old behind the sports hall, "she... *stayed*."

Stayed until breakfast, when they had reluctantly untangled themselves from their blanket-enshrouded embrace on the ottoman, fingers trailing over gooseflesh as they redressed each other, lips lingering over love bites neither of them were quite willing to heal, their whispered promises hanging in the air as the sun slipped through the wonky window and bathed them in a silver as pure as Elizabeth's Power.

"With Elizabeth, though?" Shaz whispered.

"With who else, you loon?" Alex said. "One of the ghosts?"

She couldn't put it off much longer. There was a confession to make.

"She knows Matthew."

"Our Matthew?" Shaz asked.

"Our Matthew."

"What?" Shaz spluttered, "Elizabeth knows Matthew?"

Elizabeth was insistent that she and Matthew were acquaintances at best and Alex believed her. But if they were only acquaintances, how could Elizabeth be sure that Matthew was clean? Alex and Shaz and Sam had been seeing him practically every day, Harry had been living *and* working with him, and none of them noticed anything until it was too late.

Not that Matthew had been making any sense by the end and that was without even considering what he did. But *that* day, in the house, well, in the wreckage of the house, he had insisted that she couldn't come home, that she shouldn't come home, which was a bit rich after *metaphorically* blowing up her wedding and leaving her with nowhere else to live and a small child to look after.

To think that had been the same boy, her Mouse, who would sit up with her when Maddie wouldn't sleep, always ready with a hot chocolate for Alex and a strong coffee for himself. How he'd stood up to a grown-up like Marilyn Meyer when she'd suggested that they take on Maddie so that Alex and Sam could get on with "being teenagers". How he'd held Alex's hand for the entirety of Carrie's funeral, from the moment they left the house to when they returned, throughout the service, throughout the wake, throughout the endless cascade of shocked, sympathetic faces, always squeezing their fingers together a little tighter at particularly strong pangs of pity that he knew made her stomach turn.

But then there'd been *that* day. They weren't teenagers by then, were they?

And Shaz had stood there, *that* day, sobbing at Alex and Harry, saying that Matthew had needed professional help and that sending him away was the worst thing they could have done, and Harry, too tired to be anything but blunt, had told her that Alex had been killing Matthew right in front of him.

She didn't believe him, not until Alex said:

"*And I'll kill him if he ever comes back.*"

But from the next day, the day after *that* day, finally out of that ruined wedding dress but then in a hospital bed, an insidious little thought stirred deep in Alex's soul, asking her if she'd made a horrific mistake, and it had sat there for nine years.

It wasn't sitting there anymore.

It was skulking around like a beast in the jungle, just out of sight but making its presence known.

Had he not been making sense because Alex wasn't trying hard enough to make him make sense? She'd been beyond livid, ripping up lamp posts on her way back to the house *that* day, chasing him down, but he'd been dry.

He was dry. Withdrawing, definitely, but after his little stunt, an overdose of all things, the night before in the club toilets, Shaz hadn't let him out of her sight. His Power, battered though it might've been after forcing him to cling onto life, would've cleared everything from his system by the time …

"Al?"

"Did I make a mistake?" Alex asked, finally giving a voice to that insidious little fear. "Sending him away?"

"You know what I think about it," Shaz told the cobbles, "and I said it at the time and no one wanted to listen to me."

"And if I'm listening now?"

"Well, I'd say I want my brother back," Shaz said, giving her that big sister look again, "but I'd also point out that we're a month off to *my* wedding and Sam would have an absolute fit if Matthew suddenly appeared like the last nine years never happened."

"Elizabeth went to see him yesterday," Alex said, "in Paris."

"To bring him back?"

"To fill him in about Mum and Pandora and all the rest of it."

Shaz sort of scoff-snorted. It didn't really matter what weird hybrid of sound it was, because the intention was clear.

"He deserved to know!" Alex insisted.

"Yeah, I agree," Shaz said, "but you're telling me he won't be hoofing it back on the Eurostar?"

"But I didn't say he could come back –"

"But you *are* now seeing his friend—"

"I wouldn't call it 'seeing,'" Alex tried to tell herself, "it was just a one-time thing. You know, get it out of our systems."

"He'd be thirty now," Shaz murmured to herself.

"Er, I know," Alex said, "we're twins."

"A hundred quid," Shaz said, "a hundred quid he won't be on someone's doorstep by the end of the week."

"Shaz, you know I don't have a hundred quid."

"Not a problem if you think you'll win ..."

"He won't come back," Alex also tried to tell herself, and it was just as convincing. "He's too much of a coward. This is Mouse we're talking about."

Mouse who'd sent the most ridiculously overqualified person to see if Alex was alive.

Mouse who hadn't slept for a month after Carrie's funeral just in case he missed her ghost.

That Mouse.

"He wouldn't," Alex insisted, "he's not that stupid."

But that was the least of her worries, for as the fog unfurled around their feet, they tripped over Elizabeth.

Elizabeth on her knees.

Elizabeth's hands against Pandora's chest.

Pandora turning blue.

28

Nothing but Clouds

Alex hadn't run away.

Not really.

There was no point sitting on those crackly chairs while Pandora was being wheeled around for test after test, scan after scan, because it was alright for Shaz, that hospital was her second home.

She didn't twitch at the sight of the old or the injured or the ill or the just plain Dead.

She couldn't smell it, she couldn't feel it like Alex did.

And Elizabeth wasn't much better, though that was understandable, what with Victorian medicine being all operating theatres as literal theatres, experiments on the corpses of criminals, limbs hacked off with rusty, dirty saws …

There was no point when her other option was going down to the canteen with Sam and Maddie, with its harsh overhead lighting, wobbly Gopak tables, and that constant murmur of conversation and cutlery scraping: the worst of every state institution since the Second World War, except with just a hint of formaldehyde under the chip grease.

Alex had smelt enough formaldehyde recently.

And if low blue lights flashed through the darkness every time she closed her eyes, if she could hear Harry talking in a voice that couldn't have been his, if she could feel the spectre of a headache haunting her and someone, someone she should've recognised saying:

"*I can help ...*"

Well. Sleep deprivation was a powerful thing.

But it definitely wasn't because of how Pandora had woken up, suddenly so much older than sixteen but not in the way she had when Alex had first found her, armed with eyeliner and shielded by cardboard. She'd frowned at Alex through sunken eyes and flaking lips, and said that she didn't understand.

It definitely wasn't because Alex had to swallow her own sick as she tried to tell the truth, that she didn't understand either how someone with Power could just go into cardiac arrest ...

And at Alex's admission, Pandora had just nodded in acceptance, a nod that was so resigned, so weary, so weak, that Alex just had to reach out and take a waxy hand in hers.

Which left Alex sitting in what was meant to be a Garden of Tranquillity filled with the blare of ambulance sirens and rumbling of rickety trollies.

There was only so long she could stare down at the inky-black cover of Pandora's sketchbook, the edges frayed and encrusted with seawater. But to open it again ...

Yesterday Sam had asked a good question: Eleanor needed summoning, so who the hell had summoned her? Barrett, was the answer (well, most of the answer), but Alex did wonder ...

If she opened the book again ...

"Tests are over."

Alex blinked up at Elizabeth.

"Sorry, what?"

"Pandora's back in her room," Elizabeth replied. "Tests are done."

She looked Alex up and down and up, but even with those cloud-blue eyes crinkled in concern, Alex was still taking in the frostbitten cheeks, drops of dew clinging to her windswept hair, the day-fading of her make-up revealing the iridescence in her scars.

"Wanna walk the long way back up?" Elizabeth asked.

"I might just …"

The excuse faded in Alex's throat.

"I just need …"

"What do you need?" Elizabeth asked.

It was just a question, a question that should've been banal, but at the sight of Elizabeth's worried frown, Alex shattered into a shock of sobs and *sorrys* that had Elizabeth falling to her knees in front of her.

"I'm just so tired," Alex cried, trying to clutch Pandora's sketchpad while she wiped her neck with the back of her hands, "and I don't feel well and I know that's impossible but then Pandora's collapsing all over the place—"

Elizabeth hushed her – and gently reassured an old lady who must've crept up to them asking if "the girl" was alright – and rubbed her shoulders.

"I just feel like I haven't slept in days," Alex hiccoughed, the frosty air choking her. It was getting as bad as the Northmere mists and that sickly, insistent incense.

Her temple wasn't just throbbing.

It was thumping.

It was fixing itself, the pain, right in her brain and forcing it across her forehead, thrusting it through her skull, and she was bone tired, just like before, that creeping fatigue and then that insidious exhaustion until it pulled her under the waves—

"Oi," Elizabeth whispered, "darling. Look at me."

Alex obeyed. Of course she obeyed. Any excuse to gaze up at that face, even if it was pulled into the kind of grimace that must've been giving Elizabeth her own headache.

"I can't do this," Alex blurted out, "Sam was right, it's too much stress."

"I'll take responsibility for Pandora," Elizabeth said, "full responsibility."

"D'you even like kids?"

There was a shadow in Elizabeth's stare.

A shadow Alex thought she might understand.

Light flashed in front of her eyes and she wobbled, clutching Elizabeth's arm.

"Close your eyes and stick your head in your hands," Elizabeth said, "I think this is a migraine."

"But I can't get ..."

"Aye, that's what your brother said too, and then the paracetamol fell out his pocket."

"How many?" Alex mumbled.

"How many what?" Elizabeth asked.

"Paracetamol."

Eyes screwed shut, Alex listened to the breath halting in Elizabeth's chest.

"A normal number for a recurring headache. Nothing more."

"Cos you do know?" Alex said. "That he's ..."

"I've never seen him drink, no," Elizabeth said, "so I assumed that he can't."

Pressing her head into her hands, Alex told Elizabeth to look in Pandora's sketchbook and listened to her creaking it open and peeling out picture after picture, although for most of them, "picture" might've been a strong word, because for most of them, they were just pieces of paper saturated in one colour with one huge number scrawled across them in black:

Indigo. Nine.
Purple. Eight.
Violet. Seven.
Green. Six.
Scarlet. Five.
Gold. Four.
Blue. Three.
Silver. Two.
Pink. One.

But then there was the final picture, soaked in black and blood, a skeletal hand curling around the edge of the clock outlined in red.

"What did she tell you about them?" Elizabeth asked.

Alex sat up, creaked one eye open, and rattled off the story of sitting at Pandora's bed while Elizabeth was talking to Sam and being shown the pictures. Alex had asked her what had inspired them while trying to keep her own panic and dread and all the rest of it under control.

"Naturally," Elizabeth said, pulling her wind-whipped hair out of her face.

"And she says," Alex continued, between sick-laced shudders, "'I've been dreaming them'. I ask how long, she tells me that it was only last night. In other words, since she came back to life, since she's been in the house, but I saw her there Saturday morning, when Eleanor lured me into the water, and it was her, we know it was her, down to the seaweed in her mouth. But she told me, right, that every time she goes back to sleep, she finds herself running and running through the colours."

"And then?"

"Then I asked her what happens when she reaches the clock room."

"And?"

Pandora had shrugged. She'd just shrugged and said ...

"'I wake up,'" Alex said, "then she goes back to sleep and it starts all over again. And there's me, sitting on one of those shitty chairs, trying not to see her dead eyes and the seaweed and d'you know what I say to her?"

Elizabeth shook her head.

"'*You should keep up with the painting*'. Like I'm Hannah Gordon on bloody *Watercolour Challenge*."

Last night, between Alex and Elizabeth, could've been a one-off.

Alex was well aware that there were a lot of people that would've said it *should've* been a one-off if it had had to happen at all. But as she watched Elizabeth make a valiant attempt not to laugh, she knew it was too late. Having that night together had only cemented how she felt, fixed it as absolute fact, like a delicate little piece of pottery being fired in a kiln, burnished and strengthened and glistening with a new layer of meaning and beauty. She was doomed.

"Yeah," Alex chuckled, "I know."

"That was the best you could come up with?" Elizabeth asked.

"It was that or just have a full-blown panic attack."

"And then?"

And then Pandora had frowned, as though she was slipping deep into thought, and Alex had waited, breath held, for some memory from ...

But then the girl had looked up at her with a serene smile. She'd shaken her head. And that was that.

"So what does it mean?" Alex asked. "The pictures? The dreaming?"

"Eleanor knows she's there," Elizabeth explained, "or at least, that she keeps going there."

"But everyone goes there."

"Aye," Elizabeth said, helping Alex up, "but Pandora was there for longer cos she was Dead, long enough for someone like Eleanor, an opportunist, a scavenger, to understand what she was seeing and if she can't get hold of you or Matthew, Pandora's probably the next best thing and unlike you or Matthew, she clearly doesn't understand where she is and what to do."

Alex swore under her breath, nausea still prickling the back of her throat.

"I could deal with this on my own, you know," Elizabeth suggested.

"Come on," Alex said, tugging her towards the hospital entrance.

They continued their climb up to Pandora's floor in a silence edging towards uncomfortable, where Alex pulled on her reassuring smile in the corridor and forced down the tremor in her chest. Something she couldn't force down was the thought that Pandora's actual parents should be there, Pandora's parents should be the ones dry retching with worry in cramped hospital loos, Pandora—

Sam appeared in front of them and said:

"I know who Pandora really is."

29

Nowhere Fast

The Realm of Dream and Death may be the only place Matthew has ever truly felt at home, but it always takes him a moment to recalibrate and he almost forgets why he's even there, because he did not choose ...

"Oh for ..."

Of all the places to enter The Other Side, it's Coldharbour.

Of course.

He pushes his feet into the ersatz sand and grounds himself, trying to recall where he left his body:

He's on the Eurostar.

He should be coming into Waterloo any time now.

He should've taken that other coffee when he had the chance.

Instead, his unconsciousness has brought him home sooner than he thought.

A body smashes into Matthew and he only just catches the girl as she stumbles out of the water.

"Uncle Matthew?" the girl asks, shuffling her feet over the shingle.

No.

It can't be.

He's always imagined that Matilda would be shorter and she'd always seemed like she'd take after Sam—

The eyes are wrong.

The eyes aren't blue.

The hair is pink.

And neither Wildes nor Meyers produced children that milky white. Sharpe blood aside, Alex and Matthew have always been Ashkenazi through and through, all deep bone structure and "exotic" enough to attract offensive questions from idiots.

Most importantly, which it has somehow taken Matthew's mind far too long to bring to his attention, she's in a hospital gown.

"You must be Pandora," Matthew sighs.

Pandora Wilde. Alex had already started thinking of her as Pandora Wilde, but then she was used to that kind of mental gymnastics, after accepting her best friend as her sister and her uncle as her father, both times without very much warning at all. It was a flexible family. No. A plastic family, which changed shape and absorbed without a second thought.

So to stand there, stuck between Elizabeth and Sam, and be told that Pandora Wilde was not Pandora Wilde, rather some stranger called Daphne Rose Carter, born the 23rd of July 1983, whose adoptive parents lived on the other side of Coldharbour was ...

A stretch, when Alex was that sleep deprived with a migraine that was lingering as much as last night's storm.

Although Elizabeth's flinch at her side was ...

Probably nothing?

"And what do her – her parents say?" Alex asked. "In terms of why she would've run away?"

"Well," Sam said, "at the time, they made her out to be a typical teenage tearaway."

"The girl was coming into her full Power," Elizabeth said.

"I know, I know," Sam said, "and there were noises about the parents and their treatment of Daphne."

"Pandora," Alex said, "she calls herself Pandora."

"Alex," Sam said, "it's a made-up name—"

"All names are made up," Alex said. "Elizabeth – you know Black's not her name, right?"

Sam pursed his lips and said:

"Yeah, I worked that out myself, thanks."

"What sort of noises?" Elizabeth asked.

"Neighbours reporting altercations," Sam said, "but at the time, we—"

"We?"

"Well, not me personally, Elizabeth, I'm an Acting Detective Chief Inspector," Sam replied. "We spoke to all her teachers and her friends and while they said she sometimes seemed a little withdrawn, there were never any physical signs of anything untoward."

"Aye, because she heals on command."

"Just because—"

"People don't run away from home for no reason," Alex said, an insidious little voice reminding her that they would run away if they were threatened with certain death on their return.

But when did they come back?

"Either way," Sam said, "we are all in an invidious position."

"A what?"

"An awkward position."

"Cos we're now harbouring a fugitive?"

"Because she was fifteen when she went missing," Sam tried to explain, "but now she's sixteen, we don't have to tell anyone where she is, even though I would argue her parents do have a right to know she's safe."

"And what if she wants nothing to do with them?" Alex asked. "Sam, you said—"

"What if she does?" Sam asked, "What if she doesn't even know they've been looking for her? Al, she's not our—"

"She hasn't tried to run away from us, has she?"

Alex could feel her cheeks prickling from the inside out and she was far too tired to fight logic and reasoning, but ...

"She burnt their house down, Al," Sam said.

"They probably deserved it," Elizabeth said.

Sam glared at Alex, who glared back despite the way Elizabeth was squeezing her hand so hard, her bones were squeaking. Silver Power surged through her skin as an apology.

I'm fine, she thought at Elizabeth, who had been looking pasty since their little trip upstairs, but now, she looked downright ill, *But are you?*

Elizabeth gave Alex a sharp nod and turned back to Sam.

"Where's the proof? The arson?"

"Elizabeth," Sam sighed, "This isn't—"

"Are you arresting her? Cos I can get my lawyer here within hours."

"Let's calm things down," Alex said, pretty sure that Sam would punch Matthew on sight.

Alex rested her hand against Elizabeth's trembling chest, where a heart thumped frantically. Her skin was almost warm, radiating something near heat through her jumper. Her throat was breaking out in blotches again.

"I'm not arresting her," Sam said, "But—"

"You're gonna send her back?" Elizabeth asked, her accent strengthening. "To some arseholes who knock her about? Aye, it's alright, she's got Power, she'll heal! Doesn't matter if that wee slip of a thing's being back-handed every night!"

"With all due respect, you're not above the law, Elizabeth, whoever you really are."

"Oh yeah?" Elizabeth whispered, and had Sam not been the same height as her, she would've loomed over him. "Watch me."

With a flourish of her coat, she swept towards the door, where it ricocheted off its hinges with a burst of Power.

"Literally unhinged," Sam muttered, "literally."

"Don't," Alex warned.

"It's your choice in partners—"

"You have no idea what she's been through," Alex said, thinking of those deep grooves in Elizabeth's hip and the way Eleanor had taunted her, but there was also something else there, something Alex had tried to push down for decades because had it ever really mattered and hadn't it been her fault anyway, and outside, a trolley rattled past and someone murmured and a baby somewhere was beginning to cry.

Sam was saying something, probably nothing important, but Alex rushed after Elizabeth, finally catching her halfway up the corridor.

"Your legs," Alex panted, clutching her side, "d'you really have to stride everywhere?"

Elizabeth whirled around with a snarl, her coat grazing the wall.

"I'm not apologising to him."

"I'm not asking you to," Alex gasped, every breath still sour in her mouth, "but I would like to know what's going on."

Elizabeth shook her head. She suddenly looked so young and so old at the same time, eyes wide but jaw clenched, shoulders stiff but hands trembling.

"Elizabeth, you're acting like you've been caught short and now can't find the nearest loo."

"I'm not acting like anything."

"I know that face," Alex insisted, "and I know you, whether you or I bloody like it or not. And there ..."

She glanced into Pandora's room, past Harry, and couldn't help but watch the sleeping girl for a moment and think of how she looked even younger without any make-up masking her freckles at all and the pink almost completely washed out of her hair, just leaving auburn behind and ...

Alex stared Elizabeth out for all of seven seconds before deciding against pushing the matter. A cornered Elizabeth wasn't exactly a cooperative Elizabeth. But there was something there, in all that emotion that was radiating off her in thick, jagged waves, that felt to Alex a lot like panic.

"Elizabeth," Alex said, coaxing her back down the corridor, "is there something I need to know? About 1983?"

Elizabeth's stare could've cut wrists.

Alex edged closer anyway.

"You don't have to tell me anything. And there's stuff I still haven't told you. But I'm sure, whatever you did or why you did it—"

"She's in enough danger as it is," Elizabeth said, a snarl to her mouth that Alex hadn't seen since the night before, "and I don't think that Eleanor needs to know that there's more than one Lennox left alive."

"So," Alex said, "She *is* ..."

"The girl is a Lennox. Like me. Like Eleanor. That's all you need to know for now. You think Wildes are an endangered species," Elizabeth continued, her glare fierce and knowing and resentful, "remember, this is what Eleanor does: she latches onto someone with Power and tears her way through their entire family."

Alex dared to reach out for Elizabeth's arm and reminded her that they promised to keep Pandora safe. But Elizabeth shook her head, that exhaustion that came with every thought of Eleanor just emanating from her.

"Problem is, Alex, I've promised to keep a lot of people safe and I'm still the last one standing. I thought the girl would be safe, her father didn't have Power, I don't understand how she ..."

Elizabeth shook her head, glaring up at the ceiling wretchedly.

"Yeah, well," Alex said, with more courage than she felt as she heard someone approaching, "you didn't have me before."

"I thought last night was a one-off," Elizabeth said. "Don't—"

"And who might you be?"

Alex didn't need to turn. For one, she knew that tone of voice, the one that sounded light enough, polite enough. For another, she was transfixed at how any suggestion of softness had drained from Elizabeth, like a sword being pulled from its sheath. Back to sharp edges and cold stares.

With a dry swallow that didn't quite knock back her disappointment, Alex stood back far enough to keep both of them in full view and hoped that at least Harry's manners would hold up.

"Elizabeth," she said, "this is Harry Sharpe, my uncle. Harry, this is Elizabeth."

"Elizabeth Black," Elizabeth said, offering her free hand with all the calculation of a chess player. "Alex has been staying with me."

She kept her hand outstretched, but Alex clocked the way the tips of her fingers twitched, just as Harry finally went in for what she imagined was going to be a brisk shake.

A crack of Power had Harry snatching his hand back, confusion contorting his face.

"My mind's not open to guests," Elizabeth said to him with a firm stare.

"We can't all be perfect," Harry said, managing a smile.

Elizabeth turned away without another word, continuing her stride towards Pandora's room.

Harry asked how the funeral was.

"Seriously?" Alex hissed. "You just tried to get inside her mind?"

"I reserve the right—"

"Oh, save it for later," Alex sighed, shaking her head.

She charged back up the corridor towards Pandora's room. How dare he? How *dare* he? Endangered species be buggered, Alex wanted Elizabeth, she did want Elizabeth.

It was the blood she saw first.

Spreading across the tiles.

Soaking the bed sheets.

Surging out of Elizabeth's throat with a strength that had it swimming over her glassy stare.

30

Some of the Terrors are still Intact

"Where am I?" Pandora asks, untangling herself from Matthew with all the grace of a spasming octopus. "Where are we?"

"The Other Side." Matthew sighs. "Again."

"Oh," Pandora says. "Is it like *The Matrix*? Cos I didn't really get that."

Oh.

Elizabeth was right. There is something wrong with the girl.

Here, on the wrong side, The Other Side, there's ruddy colour in her cheeks, a freshness in her step ...

Life.

There's life in her here.

Here, she is a sixteen-year-old, the new Shaz of the family, young and well.

"Do you understand why you're here?" Matthew asks, slightly queasy about gripping the girl by her shoulders, but needs must when she's busy reeling around getting overstimulated.

"I was in my bed," Pandora rushes out, "at the hospital and Shaz wheeled in the telly trolley cos Mads said she didn't wanna miss Steve Owen's trial and *Walking with Dinosaurs—*"

"Who on earth is Steve Owen?"

"From *EastEnders*? Dushed Saskia with the ashtray?"

Matthew sighs and pinches the bridge of his nose.

"So there was some unmissable television." He sighs. "And then?"

Pandora shakes her head.

"And then I'm here."

"You might just be sleeping," Matthew replies, but he already knows he's missing something. "You're in hospital?"

"I had a heart attack," Pandora explains, "but I'm alright now."

Matthew resists the urge to swear and rattles off something about illness and The Other Side.

"Alex said you knew everything," Pandora says, with an unsettling sense of awe. "So, why aren't we wet?"

"You're not wet because it's not real water," Matthew explains feebly, wilting at her wide, curious eyes. This really isn't Matthew's area of expertise. In fact, other people aren't really his area of expertise, let alone teenage girls.

"Like the clock isn't real?" Pandora says.

"What clock?"

"Can't you hear it?" Pandora asks, spinning around. "Like a bong ... bong ..."

Matthew shakes his head, trying to remember what Elizabeth was saying about Alex's dreams.

Eleanor is here somewhere.

Watching, surely.

"Come on," Matthew mutters, wading back into the waves with Pandora ...

And wading back out, stumbling back up the shingle.

"That happens to me all the time," Pandora explains, dusting herself down, not that there's anything to dust down.

"You can't always get back?" Matthew asks.

Pandora shrugs, as if it's an entirely normal thing to not be able to wake up, as if ...

Her soul isn't even in her body.

Matthew doesn't realise how long he must've been staring into space until Pandora waves her hand in front of his face.

"We can't get back," Matthew decides, "not yet, at least."

"Why?" Pandora asks. "Is it a problem?"

"I have the disturbing feeling that it's an Eleanor Lennox-shaped problem."

"Eleanor Lennox?"

"Elizabeth's sister?"

"Oh," Pandora says, her eyes widening. "The one who ..."

She simulates what Matthew assumes are fiery limbs. Or limbs on fire. Panic is overtaking his imagination and he's hardly an expert on adolescent body language at the best of times.

"Exactly," Matthew replies. "The one who murdered Elizabeth and my mother—"

"And me."

"Yes," he mutters, glancing at the girl's arm, "and you. Therefore, we need to find another exit. As soon as we do, you return to the Land of the Living, alright?"

"And you'll be coming too," Pandora says, "right?"

He can barely remember Elizabeth's words to him in the café beyond "your mother was murdered". He recalls the sentiments, of course, the gist. He can comprehend the idea that her atrocious sister is the same thing they summoned that Halloween and he understands, on an intellectual level, that Carrie had taken her in, had presumably battled Eleanor but had lost, taking them both hurtling off the edge of a cliff half the height of Beachy Head.

The problem for Matthew is that he doesn't understand what he's meant to do with the information. Fifteen years of guilt, of shoulder-buckling responsibility, is still dragging him down, because it was still their fault, but he never expected to have to weave vengeance through it, a scorching righteousness that is reinforcing all of that pain.

Because, while Matthew can comprehend his mother's murder and he accepted Elizabeth's unusually gentle reassurances ...

While he is finally coming home because Carrie has called him there and Alex might (apparently) almost welcome him without lunging for him ...

Matthew has still spent the last few hours grappling with the desire to find some way to torture an incorporeal spirit until she begged him to tear her apart.

Whether he liked it or not, Matthew had understood, somewhere in the depths of his subconscious, that when he decided to attend his lunch appointment with Elizabeth the afternoon before, there was a certain inevitability about it all.

But whether he likes it or not, Matthew does know, in that deep down place that isn't quite as hidden in the murk as he wishes, that there's always been that inevitability there:

When he saw his mother's handwriting in his notebook.

When he called Elizabeth that same morning, only to hear Alex's voice.

When he begged Elizabeth to go to Coldharbour in the first place.

Yes.

It didn't start the day before he chose to come home.

It had started on his other sister's birthday, with that choking feeling in his bathroom, that sudden fear of the water surging into his basin, the panic attack that had made him so late for Elizabeth's job, that had made it go so wrong ...

And after it had gone so wrong, Matthew Wilde had been amazed that Elizabeth could've looked at him with empathy in her eyes, half an hour (if that) after yet another resurrection, and accepted the Polaroid and Alex's details with a nod and not a single word.

Inevitable.

So when Pandora looks at him like that, like he's someone worth trusting, because for some unknown reason Alex seems to have been going round broadcasting her faith in him like she was preaching a gospel on behalf of a false prophet, Matthew can't help but hesitate before he tells her to follow him and to look out for anyone as they trudge up the shingle.

"You mean Eleanor?" Pandora whispers. "Does she look like Elizabeth? They're twins too, aren't they? Like Mary-Kate and Ashley?"

Matthew realises that he has no idea. He's only ever seen Eleanor as a disembodied spirit, silhouetted by her potent pink Power, a fiery figure forcing her way through the fog, looming, reaching through the darkness.

But he knows how she feels.

Hotter and brighter than a supernova.

"I think you'll know her when you encounter her," Matthew says, helping Pandora over the beach wall.

"Could we dowse for an exit?" Pandora suggests, "Alex and Elizabeth dowse all the time."

Matthew sighs. It's not a bad idea but the house is a good fifteen-minute walk away by the Land of the Living's standards so they walk and talk and Pandora sings like a canary about how she's been feeling since she came back to life.

"We are working on it," Matthew says, which is technically the truth. "Power is a beautiful but strange thing."

"Like it can heal but also kill?"

Matthew gives the girl's arm a glance: her injuries aren't as extensive as Elizabeth's but then they wouldn't be, would they? His shoulder throbs in sympathy as he tries to give her another reassuring smile.

"Exactly," he says. "Anyone whose Power is mental or metaphysical can feel Power on a fundamental level. We know how to manipulate it. My sister's, for example, is more physical and hers is simply more instinctive."

"But she can share Power."

"She does what?"

"That's her Master Power," Pandora explains, "she shares Power, doesn't she? At least I thought that's what she said."

Now, that was something Elizabeth hadn't got round to mentioning to Matthew. That's Alex's …

"Anyway," Matthew says, leaving his subconscious to work it out as they stride towards the house, "depending on which way one's Power runs, it may be possible to use it to bend the Ether to our will. For example, Elizabeth can resurrect herself, therefore we can conclude that her Power uses the Ether to anchor her soul to The Other Side until it can be pulled back into the Land of the Living."

"And your family?" Pandora asks. "How does it work?"

Matthew sees no harm in giving a more detailed answer while he hunts under the plant pots for the spare key.

"My father – David – could freeze things. I imagine if he's still alive, he's found a way to freeze time itself. Carrie, our mother, could fly. Alexandra can freeze and fly, although apparently, as you say her Master Power is different. I've never really tried freezing or flying, I have better things to do, but my Power runs more like Harry's. More mental, if you like. In general, there's lots of synaesthesia and intuition in our family, which is why you'll catch my sister staring and frowning at things for no reason. She's good at finding things, I'm good at hiding them."

"And what's your Master Power? Is it sharing Power too?"

Well, this is going to put the girl off for life.

"I commune with the Dead," Matthew says, feigning extreme interest in the bottom of a pot, "principally."

Pandora's eyes widen, but not in fear. Astonishment.

"I prefer healing the living," Matthew adds.

Pandora winces, just as he uncovers the dull, slightly rusted Yale key.

"Sorry," she says, "it's that clock. It's getting louder."

"Louder?" Matthew asks, and he doesn't fully appreciate how hot the key is in his hand because now he can smell white musk and there's a whisper on the wind, even though there simply cannot be any wind here, and it's telling him to come home.

"Well, closer," Pandora says, "I suppose."

Matthew hears it then.

A clanging chime that sounds like doom.

"Can you hear it too?" Pandora asks.

"Nuh – now, yuh – yes," Matthew admits, trying to—

The garden shudders, throwing them to the ground, but when Matthew sits up, he finds himself swathed in indigo.

It's not a room. It's not a void.

All he can say, for all he can tell in this disorienting moment, is that he is trapped in indigo.

"Pandora?" he calls, staggering towards anything that could be considered an edge or a wall—

Purple.

The same effect, but in the purest purple that isn't indigo nor violet.

No, now he's in violet.

So he does it again, Matthew now runs towards—

Green.

And there's something familiar, something he can't quite put his finger on, but he does it again, calling Pandora's name as he falls through colour after colour—

And into a black room, with nothing in it but the grandfather clock from the house, the pendulum frozen in time, and above it, a stained-glass window casting shadows the colour of blood onto the floor, the walls, the only indication of the size of the place.

And Pandora, of course, staring back at him.

"'To and fro in the seven chambers there stalked, in fact, a multitude of dreams,'" Matthew murmurs. "'And Darkness and Decay and the Red Death held illimitable dominion over all.'"

"Are we really here?"

"Do you know where 'here' is?" Matthew asks, gazing at the clock. "Beyond the fact we're on The Other Side?"

"I came straight here this time," Pandora says. "Usually I have to run and run, but it's been happening more and more and ..."

She trails off and shakes her head, pacing the room.

It's exactly how Matthew has always imagined it.

"It's a construct," Matthew explains, something shifting in the corner of his eye, "just as the promenade and the house are constructs, mere facsimiles of the real things, where all of time happens at once. Or not at all."

"Are we Dead?"

Pandora's eyes have grown so wide it would be amusing.

In any other circumstance.

"No," Matthew says, "not yet."

"But we're not just dreaming anymore. Are we?"

Something moves again.

This time, Matthew turns, just in time to see long, black fingers curling around the clock.

"We can discuss metaphysics later," he says, holding out his hand, "come on."

But as he curls his fingers around Pandora's, he finally sees the shadow behind her, a skeletal hand digging into her shoulder.

"Uncle Matthew?"

"Don't you feel that?" Matthew breathes, trying to keep one eye on that hand and the other on the thing creeping around the clock.

"Feel what?" Pandora whispers.

Matthew's mind is screaming "abort", but this is part of The Other Side that he knows nothing about and there's no obvious way out, just a shadow behind Pandora and a shadow behind the clock and that bloody clock is still chiming even though it's already chimed twelve times and the hand on Pandora's shoulder tightens its grip and a bony arm slips around the clock—

And a cold hand clasps his wrist.

31

Heaven Can Wait

I could keep you company?

If you're planning on daydreaming a while longer?

Well. Elizabeth had finally got Alex into the morgue. That surely would've been what she would've said if she could speak. It had probably been hours and Alex kept expecting Elizabeth to sit up ...

Clear the blood from her throat ...

And smirk at her.

That brilliant, crooked smirk, full of gaps and fangs and chips that she was sure Elizabeth had been determined to draw attention to with all that red lipstick.

But she wasn't smirking.

There was no expression on that face, nothing Alex could read anyway.

Instead, Elizabeth was colder than she had ever been, blood darkened and congealed in the mess that had been her throat.

And it was messy.

She wouldn't have appreciated the shoddy workmanship. She may have been a pickpocket and a street fighter and all the rest of it, but she became a professional. It was in the way she'd held the blade to Barrett's throat, knowing how much pressure was not enough and how much was too much. She wouldn't have put her name to this kind of hack job.

Alex had felt the tangle of tendons and arteries when she tried to stop the blood, which pulsed and throbbed through her fingers, a sick mimic of a long-lost heartbeat.

The blood that had dried in and under her bitten fingernails, on her cheek, through her hair.

She hadn't even realised Pandora was awake at first, staring down in horror at Elizabeth …

At Elizabeth's body.

By the time Harry had heard her cries for help, it was pointless. He just got drenched too, the green glow of his hands drowned in crimson.

She knew she should've practised healing.

But then there hadn't even been any silver left.

Just burgundy sliding into red and Harry's green...

So Alex followed the body.

Through the flashes of forensic photography.

Through the trundle on a rusty old trolley.

Through the low blue lights that made her think of Amanda Burton.

To there.

To the morgue.

Alex could wait on that plastic chair forever.

Just in case.

Just in case all of those spontaneous resurrections hadn't just been some sick fluke.

She could wait.

If she'd waited all her life for someone like Elizabeth, she could wait a little longer.

And besides, Elizabeth couldn't really be Dead.

Not *Dead* Dead.

It was just logic, wasn't it?

That Elizabeth, with all her Power, would find a way to get back, if not properly, just to say ...

Without a goodbye, Alex was going nowhere.

And besides, she could be faking it. Alex wouldn't put it past her. To just sit up and peel away the congealed gore from all those torn up tendons and smile with blood-stained teeth and say: "See? You can handle a cadaver after all."

So she sat, in silence, pumping Power through her arm until it ached and it numbed and it felt just as dead as the hand she was holding and she just looked.

At the cadaver.

At the body.

At Elizabeth.

At all the little things she had never noticed. The crease in the bump of her nose where she must've broken it and probably more than once. How freckled her unscarred cheek actually was and how the freckles were pink and orange and brown and beige, like all the colours of twilight were dashed across her face. The way her lipstick had bled out of the corner of her mouth into frown lines that were deeper than Alex had imagined.

Elizabeth looked at peace, it was true. But then Alex had never managed to catch her sleeping: she had always been reading in those ridiculous specs, or up making tea, or just staring out the window, either into the garden or down at the beach, depending which home they were in. All those stupid little domestic moments they'd already stacked up over three days that for now were anaesthetised, but Alex knew that there would have to be a point at which she would feel everything all at once.

And that pain that she was managing to just push into the shadows, that hideous sharp grief she hadn't felt for nine long years, would be—

"I think we need a chat."

Harry strolled through the morgue, barely blinking at the various corpses before he settled into a chair the other side of the slab.

"Before you say," Harry said, face firm but eyes open, "I won't understand, try me. I've sat in this morgue before, hoping for a miracle, with my own flock of traumatised, *confused* children waiting for answers I couldn't give, answers I still can't give them. The only thing I learnt was that I couldn't wait forever, imagining that she was going to sit up, put her bones back together, turn to me, and laugh. That it'd all been a terrible, terrible joke. If it were just me, perhaps I would have stayed forever. But it wasn't just me and it isn't just you. Alexandra, they need you. They need their mother."

There was nothing for Alex to say.

"Pandora's results have been shunted back," Harry continued, "what with the ..."

He crossed one pinstriped leg over the other and tapped a finger against his knee.

"Investigation and surrounding circus."

Alex couldn't even get her mind to cohere a single thought, let alone a response.

"This is Matthew's old trick, you know," Harry sighed, "stare blankly until I go away."

And when even mentioning Matthew didn't goad her, Harry said:

"What happened to your watch?"

"What?"

"Pardon," Harry corrected her.

He twisted in his chair with a nod at Alex's wrist.

"What happened to *your* watch? I meant to ask last night"

"Oh," Alex muttered, clinging to Elizabeth's watch. Now the blood was drying on the wine-red strap, she could see it. The brown streaks. Could blood be washed out of real leather?

"Barrett," she sighed, "bit of fisticuffs. Sorry."

"It was a few years old," Harry conceded, "doesn't matter."

She'd forgotten, really, until she'd seen that bloody awful Polaroid, that it had been a birthday present. Their twenty-first birthday. She'd got one. So had Matthew. And then they'd posed for the picture.

"And the one you have now?" Harry asked.

"Elizabeth lent it to me," Alex whispered.

Harry nodded.

"It's a 125th anniversary Zenith," he said, almost appraisingly. "That's no normal watch."

"You know I know nothing about watches," Alex said, shielding her wrist from she didn't know what. "Is it expensive?"

"On a waitress' arm, yes."

Out of nowhere, or at least out of nowhere in the style of all good amateur magicians, Harry produced a delicate gold watch, gleaming so strongly, it must've been new.

"For you," he said, holding it out.

Alex crossed her arms over her body. It had been a while since Harry had tried to buy one of them off. It had never worked on Matthew, not until he'd "conducted further negotiations". On Shaz, however, it had worked every time. Not only was it an escape route from whatever rare and probably minor conflict they were having, she had always been a bit of a magpie.

But Alex had always been a bit ambivalent. Fifty-fifty. And with those fresh doubts in her mind about everything …

About how, with every step from the ward to the morgue, she couldn't remember making the same journey last night.

About how, waving Barrett's hand at her, Harry had given her a look that made her want to scurry into a corner.

"Elizabeth's just been murdered," Alex said. "I … This isn't the time you got us that cat."

The three of them hadn't even decided on a name before they found the kitten, a tiny, ginger scrap of a thing, with a broken neck at the bottom of the stairs one morning.

They didn't want another one after that.

It hadn't stopped Harry shelling out on a new tape deck for them.

"Anyway," Alex said, "aren't they meant to come in a fancy box?"

"The box fell apart a long time ago."

Harry kept his arm outstretched, the watch dangling from his fingers.

"My birthday was months ago," Alex said, "and it's ages till Christmas."

"Look at it," Harry said, an edge of impatience cutting into his voice.

"I did just say I don't know anything about watches." Alex sighed, but she took it anyway, feeling the gold strap cascade through her fingers as it slipped into her hand.

"Look at the back."

Alex rolled her eyes but obeyed, squinting at some inscription:

Catherine
Happy 21st
David

She'd always thought the idea of blood running cold was a total exaggeration.

No.

It wasn't nearly enough for the deluge of terror that overwhelmed Alex's soul.

She was hanging onto Elizabeth's body but it was the watch that was making her seize up?

Why?

What was she still missing?

"I thought it made sense to keep up the tradition," Harry explained, "a new watch on a twenty-first. I'm sure I'll do the same for Matilda."

"Wha – where – how did you get hold of this though?"

"She never wore it," Harry said as Alex stared down at the watch, at this impossible thing, like she was seeing a ghost for the first time without knowing they existed. "After all, he gave it to her and then abandoned her less than two months later. She threw it at me one night and told me to throw it down the well."

"But you didn't."

"Catherine wasn't one to change her mind," Harry said, "but no, I kept it in the safe."

"The safe?"

"The safe in the office," Harry said. "Some things have to be kept under lock and key, just in case. Now it's yours."

Just in case.

Alex swallowed her shock, forcing a deep breath as her throat clenched around her tears. She glanced up at Harry and managed to get out that it was a nice watch.

"It's not an anniversary Zenith," Harry said, "but yes, I suppose it is."

"It costs money to get stuff engraved," Alex said, thinking as she was speaking. "Thought, and all."

That time, Harry didn't reply, so Alex looked up at him again.

Watching him watching her.

"I just find it weird," she went on, something in her soul driving her forward, onward, "that he'd go to that much effort and then he'd just leave less than two months later."

"He was a very impulsive man."

"I'm impulsive, but I wouldn't ..."

Do anything like leave someone at an altar, would she? The thought erupted in her mind before she could sense it, let alone stop it.

That wasn't her thought.

That was not her thought.

And normally, she wouldn't have been able to tell, but ...

Silver Power surges through her skin as an apology.

What can I say? Picked up a few wee things on psychic barriers over the years.

Uncle Harry was in Alex's mind.

32
A Prayer in the Darkness

Uncle Harry was in Alex's mind.

Without focusing on anything in particular, Alex willed herself to close off, to lock away her own soul. She had no idea if she was doing it right or if she was doing it at all, but then, in the corner of her eye as she kept her gaze on Elizabeth's bloodstained fingers, she saw Harry flinch.

Had he been like that all along?

Sneaking into her mind?

She never would've known ...

"I'm going to find David," Alex blurted out.

If Matthew had been there, he would've groaned and pointed out that she wasn't exactly being subtle, but she was too tired, too sick, too desperate to play coy or chess or whatever else he would've wanted.

Harry shook his head.

"You know, David only had two fingers on this hand?"

"I've seen the photos," Alex said. "The house gave us one of them last night."

Was it surprise? Was it anger? Some sort of shadow shifted across Harry's face and now Alex's mind was closed, it was clear.

She could see Harry Sharpe in the same way she could see Elizabeth, Shaz ...

Anyone else.

"Could never stay out of trouble," Harry continued, "always using his Power for ill ends. He was lucky to have any fingers left at all. He was easily influenced too."

"I'm not—"

"This is how it started before," Harry warned, "your obsession, *fixation*, on that man."

"David," Alex said, "he has a name. Or Dad, actually. He's my dad."

Harry snapped his head at her with a furious nod.

"Ah, yes, the man who's always been there for you," he said, peering around the corner. "Just over there, is he?"

"Could you cut me a bit of slack?"

"Cutting you a bit of slack," Harry scoffed, "David's daughter. Truly."

"What does that even mean?" Alex asked, her head pulsing for the first time since she found Elizabeth bleeding out.

"Oh, he would've cut you slack," Harry said, a jarringly venomous note creeping into his voice. "He'd have given you enough to hang yourself with. He would never have said 'no' to you."

"I don't—"

"What have I done?" Harry sighed. "Or what haven't I done?"

"What d'you mean?" Alex made herself ask.

The taste in the back of her throat was so sour, it might as well have been sick.

What *had* Harry done?

"For you to be chasing a man who has had absolutely no involvement in your life," Harry said, "that the words of someone who has been here, constantly, steadfastly, since your mother died is having no effect on you whatsoever."

"It's not like that."

"Remember," Harry warned, "I know what you were all like at fifteen, I can only imagine what your poor mother had to put up with."

"This isn't about her."

"She would've sold her soul to keep you out of harm's way and here you are, determined to put yourself right back in it."

"I'm just—"

"There's no 'just' about it."

"Can I finish my sentence?" Alex asked.

Alex swallowed tightly around frustrated tears, glaring at her uncle, waiting for him to give in first, except of course he didn't because he was Harry and she could see him now, but as the seconds stretched out and Alex let out the breath she'd been trapping deep in her diaphragm—

"I would just like to remind you," Harry said, his shoulders shuddering with something that felt close to rage as far as Alex was concerned, and it took all her might not to sink back into the chair, "what happened the last time you went looking for him."

Alex's voice caught in her chest.

He knew?

He'd known all along?

"Matthew finally told me the truth," Harry explained, "just before the wedding. I have to say, Alexandra, out of the two of you, I'd have thought you would've told me, although I understand that that kind of responsibility must weigh very heavily on you."

"I ... I ..."

"How do you think," Harry said, lowering his voice as he leant over Elizabeth's body, "your mother would feel if her sacrifice were in vain?"

"I didn't – we didn't – I didn't know that she was gonna …"

"To be so distressed," Harry continued, his whisper more of a hiss slipping through the cold morgue air, "that she'd take her own life in such a horrific way. That they'd have to use the contents of her purse to even begin to identify her. That it would take two days for them to re-form her enough for her own brother to confidently say it was the woman he'd grown up with. The teeth were all smashed or scattered amongst the shingle, you see, so dental records were useless. Did you know that?"

Alex couldn't even shake her head.

"That's what you don't understand, Alexandra," Harry said, dark eyes boring into her soul. "You never just put yourself in danger. You have other people to think about. You have always had other people to think about."

Alex tried to swallow her misery, but it had already seized her deeper than her bones, sharpened and solidified by that stare of judgement on her face, that stare that told her that Harry had lied when he'd told her how proud her parents would've been.

Tears tight in her throat, Alex nodded. Harry was right. He was always right. She could feel enough of it, of his sincerity that there was danger, and of course, he was right, that it wasn't just her.

And yet, Alex had the strange feeling that a hand with not enough fingers was curling around her arm and she remembered, that grip around her mind slipping again:

"She didn't kill herself. She was possessed."

Harry blinked at her.

"Excuse me?"

"Mum was possessed," Alex said, "by the – she's called Eleanor. Don't ask me how I know that."

"I'm asking."

"It was Eleanor who killed Mum and it was Eleanor who was possessing Gideon Barrett when he was going round killing people for Power and someone told Barrett about her, people without Power don't just know about things like Eleanor, things like dybbuks, and they knew about Eleanor, Mum and David."

Harry twitched. He definitely twitched.

"Look," Alex said, "she's hurt me, she's hurt Maddie. Elizabeth knows the most about her—"

"Did she, now?"

"And now she's killed Elizabeth, *again*. I *know* it's her, trust me—"

"Alexandra." Harry sighed. "A month ago you told me I'd see you at your sister's birthday party and the next thing I know you've tried to drown yourself. How can I possibly trust you? Just remember, if David wanted to be found, he would've made himself known by now."

Alex clasped the watch in her hand and went to nod – in fact, she had just begun – when she sensed someone watching her from the doorway. Spirits came with that strange, loud silence and as usual, with this one, because Alex knew exactly who it was, it was deafening.

Harry could've been saying her name, she had no idea, because she was too busy slowly inching her eyes up until—

It was gone.

"Alexandra?"

Alex stared at the doorway and into the darkness, searching for any shift in the shadows as if she actually wanted to see it, as if she could possibly endure more than a second looking at that blood-splattered face and its crumbling skull.

But there was something in her soul.

Something that warned her.
Who knew where it came from?
Who knew why it was there?
Who knew why it felt so strong and sure and certain?

But it was, and as one of those few things Alex was confident of anymore, she seized it and clung on to it, she fought off that fog descending on her mind yet again, and with a squeeze of the watch in her hand until she could feel metal digging into her flesh to tell her she was right there and she was real, she turned to her uncle and told him she had just been daydreaming.

"I know," Alex said, sighing out the lie, "sleep deprived. It's a lovely watch. Thank you."

The palm of her hand was healing burgundy.

And silver.

Even from beyond the grave, Elizabeth really was protecting her.

"If I were you—"

"Do you mind checking on the girls?"

Harry pointed at the body.

"I just wanna be left alone for a bit," Alex insisted.

She ignored Harry's frown until he finally sauntered away and left her alone.

And then, and only then, did Alex take out the photograph of the Wildes from her pocket. She glanced at the little girl who looked like Maddie and the young man who bore more than a passing resemblance to Matthew and that bloody Shadow in the background and heard Elizabeth's voice in her head again, telling her that she could've just left her.

Impossible.

To leave her would've been impossible.

And as for Eleanor and now ...

As for Harry too?

Had that really been him slipping in and out of her mind?

Alex stood up and shoved her hand into a coat pocket that squelched, reminding herself that it was just Elizabeth's blood and she knew Elizabeth, even as she was pulling out a damp wallet and flicking through the pages until she found the business card again:

M. J. Wilde. Avocat. Paris.

She rushed over to the phone in the corner and punched in the number because, to be honest, she didn't really care about international call rates at that moment in time.

The phone rang.

And rang.

And as it continued to ring, a quiet dread settled in Alex's chest.

Would he even help?

The call rang off.

It was night-time after all.

But there was also what could've been a mobile number, so she dialled that.

That rang.

And rang.

And—

"*Bonjour?*"

Alex froze, remembering dust caught in her sweat-slicked fingers, blood dripping from her nose into her mouth, metallic and sour, the struggle of a wedding dress around her ankles.

"*Bonjour?*"

Her throat was hoarse from nine-year-old screams. But then she heard a stuttering breath and then a single word in English:

"Hello."

"It's me," Alex managed to get out, "I need your help."

"Go on," Matthew said.

Alex released her breath in a shudder and clung to the phone.

"Lexy, are you still there?"

"I'm here. Elizabeth's Dead. She's been Dead for ..."

She finally bothered to check the watch for its time rather than its damage.

"For five hours. She—"

The call clicked off.

"Hello?" Alex said, "Matthew? Matt—"

He wasn't going to help.

He'd actually ...

After everything, he wouldn't ...

Alex slammed the phone down and tried not to buckle under her disappointment, as bitter and as choking as—

"You arsehole," she hissed at the wall, "you absolute—"

"I know," a familiar voice called from the doorway, "but shall we save the really heart-warming stuff for later?"

Matthew was home.

33
Endlessly Searching

Alex falls onto shingle.

It should be slick under her hands, it should be cutting her, bruising her, but it's as though everything is underwater and ...

"Up," Matthew mutters, pulling at her arm. "We shouldn't dally."

Alex snorts and glances around at the gloam.

The beach seems almost real, but she can't work out what's *off* with it, what feels uncanny ...

"Oh no," she says, "mustn't dally on The Other Side."

"We've just left our bodies vacant."

"Not completely vacant," Alex argues, trudging behind her brother.

"Vacant enough," Matthew says over his shoulder, "with the likes of Eleanor about."

He climbs over the beach wall with the same easy heave as he used to and stands on the promenade, arms crossed over his body as he stares his sister down.

"I thought," Alex says, clambering over the wall with a lot less grace, "time works differently here."

"And then there's taking the piss," Matthew replies. "Come on and start thinking about Elizabeth."

"What d'you mean?"

"The Other Side is borderline infinite," Matthew explains, with all his usual impatience. "It'd be nice to narrow it down a bit."

"I don't consciously come here often, you know," Alex says. "Did she tell you about that and all? Waking up in the shallows?"

"All you need to do," Matthew says, "is think about her. It's like dowsing."

Alex nods and scuffs her shoes against a promenade that doesn't quite feel right. It's weird to be fully conscious of being there. It's even more unnerving.

"We just need to track her," Matthew says.

"Like we're Ray Mears' *World of Survival*?" Alex replies. "What if it doesn't work though?"

Matthew rolls his eyes in a face that Alex knows but doesn't. There are shards of silver at his temples, lines where he's just never stopped frowning, that slightly sallow look that Alex knows comes with being mixed-race but never getting quite enough sun. For all the Power in the world, they are both very obviously the wrong side of thirty and plummeting towards old age.

"It won't work," Matthew says, clapping his hands together, "if you stand here thinking of anything but Elizabeth."

"But think of what?" Alex asks. "What, specifically? Like what she looks like? What she smells like?"

"What she smells like?"

Matthew flinches, his eyes bright and confused in the grey shadows of The Other Side.

"Oh, come on," Alex says, "you must've noticed, with your sense of smell. She smells good. Really good."

"She smells like an ordinary human being," Matthew says, with the tight voice and taut face of someone about to vomit.

Alex dares to nudge her brother's calf with the very tip of her boot.

"Now we both know that's bollocks."

Back in the morgue, it had taken Matthew ten minutes to find out exactly what was wrong with Elizabeth: ten minutes of pacing around the slab, of sniffing her blood, of staring at the wound, and then ...

I'm going to ask you a question, which I assure you sickens me as much as it will you.

Alex had thought she'd never laugh again, but when Matthew stood there and asked if she'd been "intimate" with Elizabeth ...

The point was that yes, Alex had indeed had sexual relations with that woman and therefore had seen her "in a state of undress" (Matthew's words, not Alex's), and therefore ...

Therefore she knew exactly how far Elizabeth's scarring went.

Because Matthew could feel a fresh Power wound right in the centre of Elizabeth's chest.

Alex had peeled the blood-drenched jumper from Elizabeth's skin where, yes, concealed under that red smear, there was now a black burn over her heart.

Eleanor.

So when Matthew's next question was about if Harry had touched the body ...

As soon as Alex said that yes, of course he had, Matthew sank his fingers into the throat wound and pulled out thick tendrils of green Power, slopping it onto the floor.

Alex told him that she didn't understand, but deep down, she already knew that wasn't quite true.

Planning for any eventuality, Matthew had called it.

Alex had thought Harry had been trying to save Elizabeth.

Not blocking her Power just in case Eleanor had left any behind, just in case somebody tried to bring Elizabeth back ...

But even with that Power out of her throat, Elizabeth *still* wasn't coming back, which was when Matthew casually, as he did, dropped into conversation that he'd just seen Elizabeth on The Other Side with Pandora, something which he declared to be a long story that was worth telling later once Alex decided what she wanted to do.

As if there was any question about what Alex was going to do.

Before having some serious, furious words with their uncle, of course.

So by the time Matthew finishes the story of Pandora and the frozen waves and some clock bonging everywhere, they're in a strange, blurry version of Crossgate, the cottages (Barrett's included) oddly untethered like they're floating just an inch or two above the ground.

"Anything?" Matthew asks.

"I don't know," Alex admits, "it just feels like I'm retracing our steps."

She turns away from the cottages towards Northmere, where the cobbles give way to the dirt tracks that wind through the marshes.

A long walk.

The long way round.

But for once in her life, Alex understands that she has no choice but to be patient.

That if she thinks she really understands Elizabeth, that she can reach out and feel her ...

"The marshes," she decides, and with a nod from Matthew, they're off again.

A while later, when the cobbles have given way to that muddy trail between the reeds, Matthew, with such discomfort that it really must be his first ever attempt at small talk, makes the mistake of asking:

"So, how have you been?"

And all Alex can see, all she can feel, is herself screaming in the wreck of the house.

"How have *you* been?" she makes herself ask.

"Fine."

"I got the impression from Elizabeth that there's no one. Friends and that," Alex says, and she has no idea why. "It's just you."

"Which has always been the way I liked it," Matthew says. "No annoying sisters or coppers or uncles or kids."

His smile is tight. He's lying, but Alex isn't quite sure about which part.

"Also got the impression you're sober."

"Three thousand, three hundred and forty three days," Matthew says, pushing his hand into his pocket. "Although …"

He pulls out a pack of cigarettes and a box of matches.

"Can you smoke on The Other Side?" Alex asks.

Matthew sighs and shoves them back in his pocket.

"Probably not."

A moment later, Matthew offers, without any prompting at all:

"I run my own legal practice in Paris. I have an assistant and many grateful clients."

"Including Elizabeth," Alex adds.

"I don't know what she sees in you."

"Charming."

"But then I don't know what you see in her."

"Well, considering you don't see anything in anyone, Matthew, you're not going to see much, are you?"

"So," Matthew says, pausing at the crossroads, the sign telling them that Northmere is onwards, Crossgate is backwards, Coldharbour is to the left, and, slightly ambitiously Alex has always thought, considering how it's absolutely not walking distance at all, Colchester is to the right, "how have you been?"

The answer in Alex's head goes as follows:

Did she crumble with the slamming of the door (or rather, the remains of the door)? Has she wasted her time wondering where he is, if he's even alive? Yes, she has wasted her time wondering where he was and if he was even alive.

Instead, she says:

"I survived."

"And you've ended up with Elizabeth Black, Power Incarnate."

"Yep."

"I suppose there's no one quite like her."

Even though Matthew's mocking her, Alex does agree. Because there is probably no one else alive or dead who'd run along a promenade with her hand in hand, collapse in a blood-drenched cottage laughing up their lungs, wake up to her watching them in those NHS specs, and finds with every one of those moments that desire to keep her close and that sister fear that she'd—

The world lurches.

It greys around Alex, spinning so fast that she falls to the ground with the kind of smack that would make her bones cringe if she was still in The Land of the Living, but here ...

She coughs, instinctively more than anything, at the smoke billowing around her and she calls out for Matthew.

Is it smoke? Smog? Mist?

Matthew doesn't call back.

Dragging herself from her elbows onto her hands, Alex tries to bat away the mist, only beginning to realise that under her other hand is ...

Flagstones.

Flagstones she knows that aren't quite as worn as they should be.

Flagstones she's run across and played across and ...

And if she concentrates, she can smell white musk.

Once Alex is standing, she feels her way along the hallway and she approaches the study, for no other reason than she feels she has to, with hands that can't sweat, but they do tremble as the door opens before she can even touch it and ...

David looks up at her.

He's young, whole, with eyes that seem both keen and kind.

"There you are," he says, with a half-smile that is jolting in its familiarity.

His side teeth are crooked, just like Matthew's. Just like Alex's. It's what pulls at their smiles – well, at Alex's smile.

Before she can reply, before her mind can make her mouth move, someone else is slipping past her.

"Catherine said you wanted me."

A teenage Harry.

A teenage Harry Sharpe, where the warmth is subdued and there's a haunted look in those wide eyes and it provokes something in Alex, something she half understands, but she knows now that she's seeing the past and she knows it's far too late.

Harry's not quite at his full height yet, but all that means is that he draws level with David as he approaches the table with his hands clasped in front of him.

David turns a page in one of those books, his other hand stuffed into his pocket, and asks how college was in a way that feels light enough, but what is Alex almost recognising there?

"Fine," Harry replies, with a strange impatience Alex is also now trying to make sense of, "I have been set a lot of work for over the weekend, so—"

"We missed you, you know," David continues, gazing down at the book, "at dinner."

"I thought you might like me out from under your feet."

David laughs and nods, pushing his hair back out of his eyes.

"And I imagine that catching up with your classmates is more fun than a Friday night with two babies. It's fair enough, I'd have done the same once upon a time."

"Is that all?" Harry asks. "It's just that I've got a ton of work, Dave, and—"

"Nuh – no." David laughs again.

Alex steps towards him, choosing, just for a moment, to ignore the danger in the room to examine the man in front of her. The things she can tell Matthew, of how much they've inherited, of how David's a little shorter than Matthew but not quite as slight, of how alive he seems despite, or perhaps because of, how bone-tired he seems, of their father's voice, a voice which would never have the chance to fully deepen, a voice lilting in the strangest places, a voice that slows and hesitates over what Alex knows from what Matthew's said are difficult words when you're walking around with a just-about-manageable speech impediment, of that nose, that brilliant, all bump-and-bridge, because that's the horrible truth, isn't it?

That if Harry's capable of keeping Elizabeth Dead, that maybe if he even knows about Eleanor, that when he says that David Wilde is Dead ...

"My advice?" Harry asks, with enough sharpness to yank Alex out of her reverie.

"A guh – an excellent chance for a catch up too, I think," David says, "but my point is, your Power is much more interesting than mine and I'm sh – sure you know half the books in this place like the back of your hand."

Oh no.

David's trying flattery.

Flattery doesn't work on a man who can read minds like Harry Sharpe, even if he's barely old enough to drink.

Fear starts to coalesce in Alex's non-existent stomach. Her soul, then.

"I think," David says, beckoning Harry closer towards the book, "that I've found how to properly destroy the dybbuk."

"The dybbuk?" Harry asks, feigning interest in the book.

He is feigning it.

It's in the way his gaze barely moves over the page, the clench of his jaw that reminds Alex of Matthew when he's one question away from trying to scratch someone's face off. David is frowning at Harry and that Alex understands. She's felt that frown on her own face, when she's been so close to working out something, just like she is now.

"*The* dybbuk," David says slowly, "the dybbuk which killed Amy. The one who tried to kill me and your sister, twice. You were there. Well, you were there the second time. Do you meet so many dybbuks they all blur into one?"

Eleanor.

He's talking about Eleanor.

It's always Eleanor.

Harry gives him an adolescent shrug of his shoulders. Alex is beginning to get it now, to understand. Without that cultivated charm, without him constantly at the edge of her mind, this is the real Harry Sharpe, but what exactly is the real Harry Sharpe capable of?

"I didn't know the word," Harry says, "but we already destroyed her."

David shakes his head.

"We banished her twice."

"Isn't that enough?"

Harry snaps out the words, which takes them all by surprise.

Frustration threatens to overwhelm Alex. She knows she's missing something, some kind of a vital clue, but she's sure, she's certain to her bones that David is making a terrible, hideous misstep as he pulls the spirit board from under the book, prodding the planchette with one of the two fingers on his left hand.

"Like I said," David's saying, "I know your Power runs that way more than mine does, but I have been communing with a few friendly spirits—"

"There's no such thing as a friendly spirit. I thought Carrie would've taught you that."

"Lots in this house," David says, the edge of his hand just touching Harry's and Alex realises, that while Harry can shield his mind, she would bet serious money on David being able to just *feel*, in the way Alex and Matthew can, for example, because they must've got it from someone and that has always been Harry's downfall, just thinking, not quite feeling ...

"Met a few?" David asks.

"I *was* there when my parents were killed," Harry says, snatching his hand back.

Killed?

"With so much of your own Power, I'm just surprised that she didn't kill you too," David says, and any sense of a smile is gone, but there's still that kindness there. A steeliness, yes, but an odd compassion that Alex knows from Matthew and again, the idea of downfall is on her mind ...

Harry steps right away from David.

It's incredible, really, to see her brother split across her father and her uncle, the likeness to both of them undeniable, but she still can't quite hook onto what is wrong with the picture.

"Carrie interrupted her," Harry says.

Alex shifts, just a little bit closer to David, just enough to get a good look at Harry's eyes. They're the same brown as hers and Matthew's. She's never noticed that before. But more importantly, the real similarity is that Alex has seen that look in them before.

In Matthew's.

Standing behind Sam at the altar.

Minutes before Alex took down the house with them both still inside.

A scared little boy who thought he'd never be caught out having to deal with the fact that, yeah, he was being caught out.

Right now.

Harry is being caught out.

And David is absolutely correct.

Why on earth would Eleanor not take Harry's Power, given the opportunity?

It's weird enough she still hasn't tried to take Alex's, but Harry's ...

Some kid with that much Power before he truly knew how to use it?

"Because Catherine is sure that she's one and the same," David says, meeting Harry's panicked gaze again. "Killed your parents, killed my sister, and so on. Would you also agree that she has followed us here after all? Even after what happened in London?"

Harry seems to settle for silence, until he snaps:

"Why are you asking me?"

"You know why I'm asking," David sighs, reaching for him. "Harry, I can help—"

Harry reels away from him.

I can help.

Alex knows, as soon as she's back in her own body, she will be sick.

"Does Carrie know?" Harry asks.

"Catherine—"

"Does Carrie know?"

It's not a question.

Alex understands that now.

It's a demand.

This is where everything changes.

Alex makes herself watch in the agonising silence as David demonstrates that he has just as terrible a poker face as she and Matthew do, but it's too late, because Alex feels the pulse of Power as Harry pushes roughly into David's mind, decades before he has any real expertise but the force is there, and David grabs Harry by his shoulder and shoves him against the wall, which shudders with Power.

And there, Carrie's voice again, calling down the stairs.

Yet another mistake, as David lets go of Harry, steps back, and shouts that everything is just fine.

"She will know," David warns. "Harry, we can help—"

Harry launches himself at David.

Alex gasps.

David flinches.

Harry is frozen.

Not just suspended, more frozen in time itself, unmoving, unwatching.

Alex does get it from David.

David's glowing blue.

"Jesus, Mary, and Joseph," David mutters under his breath, frantically turning pages in the book as Carrie calls again.

David's Power is blue. The brilliant blue of his eyes. And Maddie's.

"Are you sure everything's alright?" Carrie shouts, her footsteps rushing down the stairs.

It's the blue of ...

"Yes, my love," David yells back, still throwing pages and pages and because he's so intent on something, he can't possibly notice the twitch of Harry's fingers, the flex of his neck, but even when it comes ...

The smash is sickening.

The crunch and squelch of David's skull as Harry drives it into the edge of the table again and again and again with a savage determination ...

Until he finally lets go.

And what's left of David's body slumps and then slides onto the floor.

34

Peeling out of the Dark

It's the wall keeping Alex up.

Nothing else.

Otherwise she'd be on the floor with her dead ...

With her ...

"Dave?" Carrie says, and her voice is so close. "Are—"

She's holding Matthew.

Baby Matthew, baby *Mouse*, who starts screaming at the corner of the room because David's ghost is already there in the shadows, unseen by his wife, unseen by his brother-in-law, and it's all Alex can focus on, the screaming and the shadows, as Harry rushes towards his sister with bloody fingers, saying all sorts about forgetting it all and locking the study and even though Harry's Power still feels immature and clumsy, it does the job because the hysterics melt away and Carrie's eyes glaze over and she wanders back out of the study, bouncing her crying baby, and God, as if it isn't just like when Matthew ...

Alex looks down at her dead father, blood dripping down the table leg.

She looks at her uncle, eighteen and trembling. Not trembling with fear anymore though. With Power.

Harry slips out of the room, not that Alex really notices or cares as she sinks to the floor and ghosts her hand over what's left of her poor father's face and ...

That one brilliant blue eye.

Alex looks into the shadows, at the Half-Faced Man. At her father.

Footsteps pound through the house. she has to get ready to run—

Matthew – adult Matthew – stumbles into the study, smacking straight into the table.

"It's David," Alex mumbles, half-wondering if she can be physically sick here, "it's Dad."

Before she fully understands what Matthew's doing, he has Alex on her feet and he holds onto her hand in that way they only do – did – do, when ...

"Huh – Harry?" Matthew asks, shakily.

Alex's nod is just as jerky.

"And it wasn't an accident," she whispers, as if the Dead or these reflections of the past can possibly hear them. "He murdered him. He ..."

"We ... we ..."

Matthew stops himself and shakes his head and Alex watches his eyes fall to the body and up to the shadows again and again and again like he can't stop himself either.

"He knows," Alex says. "He knows Eleanor. He's been with her all along."

Somewhere, in the middle distance, a bell.

No. A bong.

From a grandfather clock that doesn't work.

"We need to get back," Matthew says, tugging Alex towards the door, "Eleanor knows we're here."

"But Elizabeth—"

"I think we've got what we came for," Matthew explains as they rush through the house, but there's already a sense of colour seeping into their surroundings, "don't you?"

"But where's Elizabeth?"

"We'll try again."

"Promise me," Alex said, squeezing his hand so hard—

"I promise."

The Wildes break out into a run that burns with urgency as Coldharbour begins to twist and turn and tumble with kaleidoscopic colour and Matthew's telling Alex to keep up as they make it onto Hangman's Hill, but how can she when her mind is back in the house, it's back in the study, where their father's blood is dripping and dripping and his ghost is waiting—

They slam into someone.

"Pandora?"

Pandora stares back at Alex and asks:

"Where am I? Is it that place again?"

"You must be dreaming," Alex says, which would make sense because it is the middle of the night, but when she glances at Matthew, he's all narrowed eyes and tense frown.

A figure is waiting for them under the streetlight.

Eleanor.

All Alex needs to see is a glint of golden hair to know.

Matthew curses under his breath, but Alex steers him and Pandora towards the waves.

"Go on," Alex says, "I want a word with her."

"A word?" Matthew splutters. "With her?"

"Why not?" Alex says, keeping her eyes on Eleanor. "Plus ..."

She lowers her voice, just in case. This version of the beach is eerily silent, after all.

"You two can get back first without having to worry about this one chasing us."

Matthew looks bloody furious, as usual, every vein in his head and throat bulging away at Alex.

"You really wanna make it up to me?" Alex whispers to him, ignoring Pandora's curious stare. "You get her back safe. D'you understand? Keep Pandora and Matilda safe."

The veins stop bulging.

Matthew steps back with a tut.

"Careful," he warns, "no heroics."

Alex listens to the two of them trudging down the beach, but when they stop, she—

Almost turns. She must not look away from Eleanor. Grandmother's footsteps all over again.

"The girl must've returned," Matthew calls.

"Great," Alex says, shuffling back up the beach, "then I just have to worry about you."

"Alexandra," Matthew whines, "do you really need to do this?"

"Go on. I'll see you there."

Alex listens to her brother's footsteps receding into nothing before she climbs over the wall and faces Eleanor, who's being surprisingly patient.

"Lexy."

"Haven't you heard?" Alex says. "It's just Alex now. Even Matthew gets it right."

"Am I about to get a telling off?" Eleanor asks, that thin-lipped smile of hers not as restrained as it should be.

Not with that ravenous gleam in her eyes.

"It was you. Who killed Elizabeth. Again."

"I had to wait for her to die, of course, to take her Master Power," Eleanor says, "but ..."

Her smile widens, revealing those perfect teeth. But even as her skin stretches, Alex can tell it's smoother, as if it's stronger, more solid.

As if *she's* stronger.

"But you're still Dead," Alex says and why can't she think of a single question?

"Well done," Eleanor mutters with a glance at the promenade that's just a bit too reminiscent of her sister, the type of reminiscence that makes Alex's soul ache.

If she thought she missed Elizabeth yesterday ...

"Where is she?"

Eleanor shrugs.

"Beyond?" She sighs. "I dunno."

"So you don't know where she is," Alex replies, "and you've taken all her Power and yet you're still stuck here?"

Eleanor stares so long at her that Alex finally realises what's wrong.

She *never* blinks.

"Then why?" Alex asks, starting towards her. "Why can't you leave her alone?"

Eleanor recoils from Alex, mouth curling in confusion, as if Alex is the aggressor in all this.

"What's it got to do with you?"

"Judging by what I've seen tonight," Alex says, "what you've *done* to my entire family and Elizabeth, it's got a lot to do with me."

"Call it serendipity," Eleanor replies. "I didn't really have much interest in you anymore and then you go and make moon eyes at my sister ..."

She scoffs more than laughs.

"What d'you mean, anymore?" Alex asks.

"You're not all that." Eleanor sniffs.

Rage flares in Alex, burning burgundy as she squares right up to Eleanor.

"You thought that about Elizabeth before you murdered her the first time," Alex hisses, "and then she came back and she put you in your place, didn't she? Dug her way out of that grave and she spread you across those four walls, didn't she?"

"Oh, Lexy," Eleanor laughs, "Uncle Harry would be proud!"

"I'm nothing like him."

"No," Eleanor says, "that temper's all your mother's, isn't it?"

Now she's stepping up to Alex.

"She struggled," she says, "on the cliffs. She fought and she fought and she begged—"

"Where's Elizabeth?"

"Dunno," Eleanor says, gazing around the promenade. "Haven't seen her. Like I said."

"One more thing."

Eleanor shrugs and flourishes a hand before slipping it back into the other, clasped in front of her.

"What do you want?" Alex asks.

Eleanor laughs.

"What do I want?"

"Yes," Alex says, "what do you really want?"

"What I really, *really* want?"

"You're hardly a good representative for Girl Power, Eleanor. Just get on with it."

Eleanor's face twists into something darker, something more truthful, and she sneers a single, predictable word:

"Power."

"Really? Just Power?"

"Yes," Eleanor says, a terrifying kind of boredom slipping into her eyes, "I want Power and I want a life."

"That's two things—"

"Life is wasted on the Living. I don't know if you've noticed yet."

"I dunno," Alex says, "my dad was doing an alright job at it. So was Mum."

Eleanor just sighs as if Alex is somehow disappointing her, that she's somehow not entertaining enough, and *that*, that more than any other injustice that can be thrown Alex's way infuriates her.

"You can't just keep accumulating Power," Alex insists, "that won't give you a body. If you've been doing this shit for the best part of a century, you must know that by now!"

"Oh," Eleanor whispers, ghosting her lips over Alex's cheek, "but I've already found one."

"A body? You already have a body?" Alex asks, stepping—

Alex lurched forward against the slab, hip cringing in the way it only could in the Land of the Living.

Matthew released her arm with a burst of Power and snapped at her to steady on.

"Really?" Alex snapped. "Did you have to do that?"

"I wasn't leaving you there."

"She has a body," Alex said, "she says she has a body. Eleanor Lennox claims she has a human body and we still don't know where Elizabeth is—"

"And she was telling the truth?" Matthew asked. "She wasn't just scaring you?"

"Eleanor doesn't scare me."

"Want to tell Mum that?" Matthew sneered. "You lunatic."

"She could've got my Power on Saturday, *twice*, but she didn't," Alex argued. "And just then, she could've grabbed me—"

"If I hadn't got you out?" Matthew suggested with an unnecessarily sarcastic tilt of his head.

"Fine. But *Harry*, Matthew."

"I know," Matthew said. "Do you think ..."

Alex caught her twin's eye and she knew they were both seeing the same room, the same body, the same crushed skull ...

"How many times did you see David in that study?" Alex asked. "And you never once recognised him."

"He's a ghost."

"You made friends with the ghosts," Alex said. "You talked to all of them, Matthew, but you never talked to him."

"He's missing half his face, Lexy."

"There's a fucking headless monk roaming round the house! One I've now seen for myself! And you were fine with *him*!"

"You know, it's none of your business why I stayed away from him."

Alex glared at Matthew.

Matthew glared at Alex.

Alex continued glaring at Matthew.

Matthew continued glaring at Alex.

The morgue was even colder than before. The formaldehyde in the air had grown stale. There was no white musk this time. Just that sickly, sour blood between them.

"You won't like the answer," Matthew eventually said.

"Yeah, well, you also told me that you never saw Mum's ghost and now she's calling on us to come home."

"I never saw her," Matthew said, "I swear."

"Whatever."

Alex knew it was the truth, but that wasn't the point.

"Fine." Matthew sighed. "All the other ghosts, Adelaide, Maria, Cedric, and so on, they felt different."

"In what way?"

"They understood that they were Dead, Lexy," Matthew explained as if she were a child. "They weren't at peace but they accepted it. All I felt from *him* was agitation, which now, makes perfect sense, but when you're a twelve-year-old breaking into a locked room, it's pretty fucking unnerving. It was alright for you—"

"Alright for me?" Alex scoffed. "In what way was anything alright for me?"

"You," Matthew snarled, starting towards her, "haven't had to put up with all those voices and feelings in your head your entire life."

"Oh," Alex laughed, "is this where you start making excuses for getting off your face? And there was me thinking at some point tonight, I was gonna get an apology! It's only been nine years, after all!"

"You'd never accept it!"

"I want you to at least try!" Alex roared, the words ripping their way through her with a rage she hadn't felt since—

"Oh, *now* you do?" Matthew spat. "*Now* you'll listen?"

"Listen?" Alex shouted. "I have never met anyone as insecure and defensive and relentlessly fucking hostile as you—"

"Fine!" Matthew yelled, "I'm not sorry! I'm not sorry for trying to make sure you actually got married! I'm not sorry for stopping you returning to that house! I'm not sorry for actually being able to tell there was something wrong with Harry and trying to protect you!"

"It didn't stop me!" Alex screamed. "It didn't stop me though! It did nothing! I lost everything because of you!"

"You lost everything?" Matthew laughed. "You made me leave the only home I ever knew!"

"I lost my fiancé—"

"You never wanted him!" Matthew sneered, looming over her. "You only had him so no one else could, so you could turn round to me and Shaz and say, 'look what I've got'! But I could feel it, for years and years, months and months, your hesitation, letting your cold feet burrow under my skin until you practically asked me into your mind! In fact, I'd call it begging."

"You unrepentant little—"

"I'm sure you've been Mother of the Year—"

"You have no idea what the last nine years have been like for me!" Alex screamed. "You have no idea what you left behind! You have no idea what you did!"

Matthew blinked at her.

"You ruined everything!" Alex sobbed, spraying tear-laced saliva over the morgue. "We were meant to be on the same side! You were my twin and you never even liked me! You never even liked me. And you don't come home cos I asked you, oh no, you came home because *she* asked you. A Dead woman."

"Our mother," Matthew whispered.

"And what a great mother she was," Alex said, the cold air making her chest groan, "cos you can say what you like about Harry, but he never laid a finger on me."

"That hardly ever happened."

"Still happened though, didn't it?" Alex said, her own history turning and twisting in her mind as all those pieces she'd kept hidden like a broken glass gathered up in a tissue and shoved into the back of a drawer. "Still scared you so hard after the study that you had to go back to speech therapy. You started pissing the bed, d'you remember?"

"I deserved that," Matthew muttered. "We deserved it."

"We were twelve."

"She wasn't well—"

"We're not well," Alex said, "but we would never, ever do what she did or what Harry's done—"

"Well, I'm not taking after our idiot father," Matthew sneered. "He got his head caved in."

"Can't you at least try?"

Alex struggled in a breath as Matthew shook his head, his confusion at least softening his snarl.

"You might think I'm stupid," Alex said, clinging to Elizabeth's body, "or childish, or just mad like everyone else does, and yeah, it might sound ridiculous that I'd do almost anything to bring back a woman I've known for three days, but I can't lose again. I am so, so tired."

Matthew didn't respond. They just stood there, in the silence, Alex staring down at the slab, tears slipping onto Elizabeth's coat, catching in all the cracks and crevices.

And then, her brother opened his mouth and managed to say the two words that people have always sold their souls for …

"Almost anything?"

Tuesday 5 October 1999

35
All Coming Back

"Mouse?"

Alex peeled her eyes open, blinking away sticky residue of something, which was probably the same something crumbling under her broken nails ...

Which glowed violet and then, for the first time in months ...

Cracked keratin thickened, raw flesh paled, rough skin shone.

How different this Power felt.

She was so used to her own Power running warm like August sunshine and she had just remembered how fresh Matthew's felt, like those first waves on a frosty morning, the lemon in a strong gin and tonic, the bite of just-cut grass.

But *this*, *their* Power, eternally united, had a clarity, a strength, a terror to it.

It had to, otherwise how would they have bent the Ether to their will, reached between worlds, smashed down the barriers between Time and Space like they were nothing more than air?

With a cough and a splutter, waving her glowing arm through claggy gusts of dust, Alex called again for her brother.

"I feel like I've been hit by a bus," Matthew groaned from somewhere the other side of the cloud.

"And Elizabeth?" Alex asked. "Elizabeth?"

The dust and the ash faded into the air, leaving behind a broken slab where Elizabeth's body should've been.

"I don't understand," Alex breathed, crawling over the rubble. "What did we do?"

"We brought her back," Matthew insisted, "I felt it."

"Well, she isn't here, is she?" Alex yelled, throwing a lump of shrapnel at him. "What have we done? Mouse, what the bloody hell have we done?"

"Just shut up," Matthew hissed, staring down at the broken table, its jagged halves looming out of the dust like icebergs in the night. "I need to think. There might've been something I didn't foresee, something we missed, something we need to complete—"

"You're psychic!"

"Not that psychic!" Matthew spat, but his panic was pulsing out in thick waves of violet Power. "There can be consequences to anything like this, sacrifices which must be made—"

"What d'you mean, sacrifices?" Alex asked. "Matthew?"

"Things have to be perfectly balanced in the Ether," Matthew rattled off. "There's an equilibrium, you know, all the time Elizabeth couldn't die properly, Eleanor was still tethered to this world—"

"And you didn't mention this before *because*?"

"Why do you think, Lexy? You were begging me to bring her back to life!"

Almost anything?

Wasn't that a sacrifice enough? Splitting her own soul open to welcome in her twin?

"Either way," Alex said, hoping her adrenaline would just surge into her Power and not plunge her into a panic attack, "we need to fix this. If something's gone wrong, we need to …"

Matthew was staring at his watch.

"Am I keeping you?" Alex spluttered.

"Your watch," Matthew muttered. "What time is it? What does it say?"

Elizabeth's watch told Alex that it was apparently six o'clock in the morning.

What the hell had they done?

"Mine too," Matthew said. "I don't know if we've moved in time or we've just been unconscious that long."

"Six hours?" Alex said. "I thought you knew what we were doing!"

"No one's ever joined their Power like this before, it's theoretically impossible!"

"Oh, that's great to know." Alex laughed, with the desperation of a woman right on the edge of a cliff, running out of choices, wondering if she could still fly, and that tape deck was whirring in her mind. "Never been done before."

"I'm not taking this from the woman who tried to summon our Dead father on a Halloween of all nights!"

A sob echoed down the corridor.

One would've been enough to make Alex freeze in that same skin-slicing fear that had stolen away her nerve in the study, but when it continued …

She knew that cry.

She'd known that cry since the first time she'd ever heard it, on the floor of that study, the best part of fourteen years ago.

But it was Shaz who appeared first, blood dripping down her temple.

"Shazza," Matthew said with a nod to their sister.

"Matt—"

"Where is she?" Alex demanded.

Maddie stumbled into the morgue, cradling her arm. Her burnt arm.

It sparked and it sizzled and it shone with radiant Power – indigo, cobalt, electric – like it belonged to Maddie, like it was right, like ...

Alex shoved down the sick in her stomach as she guided her daughter, trembling and hiccoughing tears, towards Matthew, who put a galling amount of venom into his *observation* that he hadn't been told that Matilda had Power.

"I didn't know she had Power!" Alex yelled.

"Stop shouting!" Maddie cried.

"I'm sorry, sweetheart," Alex said, stroking her hair, deep blue Power sparking under her fingertips. "Will you let Uncle Matthew take a look?"

"Alexandra," Matthew said, "it's a Power wound. Power cannot heal Power—"

"Just take a look," Alex insisted, clinging to Maddie's shoulders.

Maddie had Power.

And Eleanor knew.

Eleanor knew and Alex hadn't even clocked it in her own child, who she thought she'd been watching so closely for all the signs, and there had never been any. There had been enough tea tree oil and TCP and Tixylix for Alex to safely say that Maddie was, physically, an ordinary child.

But then Alex had pumped all that Power into her.

Twice.

And moved her into that house.

She'd been born in that house too.

She'd been born in that study.

Alex peeled Maddie's quivering fingers away from the burn and forced herself to look at the burn.

It was a handprint, warped and wrapped around her daughter's arm. The finger marks were long, spidery, the tips bone-deep.

As if Eleanor really had dug her claws into her.

The burn was throbbing.

It bubbled and boiled.

"Mouse?"

"Eleanor's left something behind," Matthew explained. "A trace of her own Power."

The wriggling.

Alex could see it now, just under the crackling skin, through the blisters and the boils, there was something pink and pulsating.

"Can you get it out of her?"

"With care," Matthew said in a low, soothing voice Alex had never heard him use before, but when he did his best attempt at a smile on Maddie, that fear froze Alex again. "But you're going to have to be very brave."

Alex pulled Shaz to one side and insisted on an explanation.

"Long story," Shaz said, but she was already doing the bloody Riverdance across the tiles, "but this isn't like Pandora's—"

"Yeah, I can see that!" Alex snarled.

"She was in Pandora's room," Shaz said. "Sam and I heard screaming and by the time we got there, Pandora was running away and whacked into me, and Mads was stumbling out behind her like that. Sam went after Pandora and, I dunno, I couldn't find Harry anywhere so I thought I should bring Mads to you."

"Pandora was running away?" Alex asked, pointing to Shaz's head and its purpling bruise. "And did that to you?"

Alex thought of that photograph of Amy Wilde, of David standing over the book, and finally, finally, she understood.

Elizabeth had wondered why Eleanor hadn't hurt Pandora again.

And how ...

Elizabeth had died in Pandora's room.

Eleanor had a body.

Alex looked at Matthew. The look would be enough.

"I wasn't sure," Matthew said, "I only began to wonder when we saw her on The Other Side when she shouldn't have been—"

"And when the hell were you gonna say something?" Alex gasped.

"We've been a bit busy since, what with our uncle implicated in half a dozen murders!"

Alex reeled back, stumbling against the rubble. She was seizing up, like she'd been plunged into ice, and there'd only been one other time in her entire life that she'd felt like that, and that was when Harry had said something else to her, back when he was almost a stranger, telling her and Matthew and Shaz, all in their pyjamas though none of them had slept a single second, to sit down because the police had asked him to pass on some awful, awful news, that tape whirring and clicking and whirring and *Every now and then I fall apart* ...

"Uncle Harry," Matilda was sobbing, as Matthew pulled a tendril of pink Power from her burn and threw it as far away as possible.

Of course Harry would've known.

Of course.

There had been a time, of course there had been a time, when Alex believed that Harry would've done anything for her. He did do anything for her. A man who had dropped his entire life in London to look after them, the only crumbs of glamour he brought back with him being the sharp grey suits and a string of self-possessed girlfriends. He didn't have to. But like his older sister before him, Harry Sharpe stood firm. In that house, he stood firm and constant, even when the kids upped and left.

And he'd waited.

He had waited all those years for them to fall back into line, one by one, starting with Alex ...

Biding his time, like a spider on the edge of a web.

36
Empty Threats and Hollow Lies

"How much," Harry said, looking up at the twins with a tilt of his head, "do you think you know?"

Harry was still in yesterday's suit, sitting on the edge of Pandora's bed as if he'd ...

No.

No, that wasn't entirely correct and Alex knew it, and if Alex knew it, then Matthew must've known it too.

Harry was still in yesterday's suit, sitting on the edge of Pandora's bed *and* he had been waiting for them to arrive.

Alex and Matthew found themselves holding each other's hands in the kind of grip that would normally break bones.

"We've been to The Other Side," Matthew began. "We saw you murder David. We know what you did to Elizabeth."

Harry snorted softly, his gaze cold as it fell on his niece and nephew.

This wasn't the Harry who told them stupid jokes and sighed at their latest schemes.

This was the Harry who'd seized David by his hair and demolished his skull.

"I'd say it's heart-warming to see the old team back together," he said, "but what is this exactly? 'My enemy's enemy is my friend?'"

"We've buried the hatchet," Alex said.

Harry scoffed and shoved his hands into his pockets.

"You wanted to bury the hatchet in the back of Matthew's head," he said. "What's changed? Has he convinced you that nine years ago, *that* day, was all just a terrible mistake? That he didn't mean to spend a *month* manipulating your emotions so that you'd manage to make yourself marry a man miles beneath you? Beneath any of you?"

"Sammy's worth a dozen of you," Matthew spat.

"Why don't you marry him then?" Harry asked, and Alex didn't think she'd ever heard a sneer so devastatingly light and innocent. "Or was one faltering kiss at fifteen enough?"

Alex couldn't resist thinking at Matthew:

You said nothing happened.

It was 1984, Matthew snarled back in his mind, his glare fixed on Harry but that vein in his throat was throbbing, *of course I said nothing happened.*

Before or after we started going out?

It was fifteen years ago—

Before or after, Matthew?

This really isn't relevant, Alexandra.

I think it is, Alex thought, throwing a multitude of memories at him, *I thought you didn't want that sort of thing.*

I don't, Matthew thought, his mouth trembling, *not that it's ever been any of your business.*

Well, I don't know now if it was my business, if it was my boyfriend you were—

"Before, alright?" Matthew snapped, furiously snatching his hand away. "Because then you were *there*, with all that *grief*, demanding all of his love and attention like he wasn't *my* best friend and I gave him up for *you*, Alexandra!"

The tension hung between them, taut and thick like a garrotte held to a throat just before the beads of blood appeared.

"But you never even liked me," Alex whispered.

Matthew shook his head and glared up at the ceiling.

What was she meant to do with that?

"Of course he didn't," Harry said, insinuating himself closer, "did he? Breaking into your mind like that ..."

He glanced between the twins, eyes gleaming as a slow smirk spread across his face.

"He hasn't even apologised, has he? Does he even know about Jamie?"

Close your mind, Matthew warned.

It is closed!

"I suggest," Harry said, "that neither of you make any rash decisions before you hear my side of the story."

"I witnessed the murder," Alex said, "Dad's murder, you murdered him, I saw it."

"Seeing isn't always believing, is it now, Alexandra?" Harry replied. "The Other Side is a land of tricks and illusions. I'm sure *she's* told you all about that."

"I saw you!" Alex gasped, a nervous laugh ripping its way from her chest. "I saw you smash Dad's head against the table!"

"Did you see this?" Harry asked Matthew.

"I believe my sister," Matthew replied, as cold as the grave.

"What were you even doing on The Other Side?" Harry asked. "Were you looking for me?"

"What does it matter?" Alex said. "We ..."

"Let me guess," Harry said, eyes narrowing, "you were looking for Eleanor."

"And if we were?" Matthew asked, just before Alex could say they weren't.

"And," Harry said, "it sounds like you found her. Her little dybbuk secret about to come out ..."

"Are you implying she possessed you?" Matthew asked.

"No," Alex said, shaking her head at Harry, "that was you, it was definitely you. I know when someone's possessed—"

"Am I the type to just snap like that?" Harry asked. "Smash someone's skull in?"

"It was you," Alex hissed, turning to Matthew, "it was definitely him, I did not sense Eleanor there, I'd have known – I know a possession when I see it!"

"Except," Harry said, "Eleanor's been treating your foster daughter like a hop-on, hop-off bus for the past forty-eight hours and you didn't notice a thing, did you?"

"But not all the time?" Matthew asked. "If it's a hop-on, hop-off situation ..."

"Even a person with Power can't be possessed indefinitely. Not," Harry said, turning to Alex, "that you've noticed."

"I've ... I've been busy," Alex said. "It's been a million and one things since Friday—"

"Does Matthew know what you did?" Harry asked, dropping his voice into an almost seductive gentleness. "Does he know it was deliberate?"

"That has nothing to do with this."

"Does he know how you'd been struggling?" Harry continued, rising from the bed. "Does he know how far you fell behind on your rent? On your work? Does he know how you were forgetting to eat? To sleep?"

"It's not the same—"

"And Matilda? Poor Matilda, watching over you while you did sleep? Just in case?"

"What?" Alex breathed, shaking her head so hard, her stabbed shoulder shuddered. "That isn't true. That's not true."

"That poor child—"

"Don't you dare—"

"They would've sectioned you if I hadn't stepped in," Harry said, "attempting to take your own life like that—"

"I'm not mad!" Alex screamed, but Harry was going on and on about her odd behaviour and how concerning it had been and now Power was rising from her skin and—

She was enveloped by warm arms that gripped her own.

"Leave her alone," Matthew warned, his thumbs rubbing her scars.

"I'm afraid," Harry said, as if Alex hadn't screamed, as if he hadn't been saying the things he'd been saying, "she's brought you back here on a wild goose chase."

"And if I don't believe you?" Matthew asked. "What's next? You remind me of how much of a disappointment I've always been to you?"

"Such a disappointment," Harry sighed, "but not for the reasons you think."

Alex shuddered as she tried to catch her breath, clinging onto her brother's firm embrace.

"I bet you gave her a little push, didn't you?" Matthew continued, far more willing to ignore Harry's comment than Alex, but then maybe he understood the game better. "Just like you did to me? Cos I knew how much I was taking, exactly how much, and I shouldn't have overdosed that night."

"I never intended to hurt any of you," Harry said, with the kind of slow blink that seemed almost honest, almost sincere.

"You've done all of it," Alex said, "haven't you?"

"Do you know," Harry said, pacing behind the bed, "the joke about the two campers?"

Alex shook her head. So did Matthew.

"Two campers," Harry said, "come across a bear. One of them drops his backpack and starts putting on his running shoes. His friend, of course, asks him what he's doing because he can't possibly outrun a bear."

Alex looked up at Matthew who said:

"All he has to do is outrun his friend."

"I was outrunning a particularly relentless, ravenous bear. Single-minded. Thirty-odd years, throwing her scraps. Innocents, victims. Anyone with Power or half a decent soul. But when I found out she'd taken your mother without my permission ..."

Harry shrugged.

"I had to put a little more effort into placating her," he said, rubbing the bridge of his nose, "and you have no idea how difficult it's been to keep her off you. You haven't the faintest idea. What I've given her ..."

He shook his head and let out a heavy, shuddering sigh that didn't move the air like it should've.

"Things could be different," Alex pleaded, "things can change. We can stop her. Somehow."

"I know."

As if it were really that simple.

A shocked silence shook the room.

Then, there was only the sound of Alex's own breathing stuttering in her chest, her blood roaring in her ears, as Matthew squeezed her shoulders.

"There is a way?" Matthew asked.

"Of course there's a way," Harry said, "there's a way to do anything."

"Then why haven't you done it before?" Alex said.

"Why should I?"

"Because she's killed half our family!" Alex cried. "She's a psycho who'll stop at nothing to get what she wants!"

Harry stared at them, blankly, impassively.

"Not my problem."

"It's your problem now," Matthew warned. "How do we end her?"

Harry didn't reply. He didn't even move.

"Did you care about Mum?" Alex asked.

"Of course I did," Harry said, "she was my sister."

"And yet you still let Eleanor kill her."

Harry looked away. For the first time in Alex's life, he wouldn't – or couldn't – look her in the eye.

"You might've put up with it," Alex rushed out, "I get it, you can't get rid of Eleanor on your own, but right now, we have a chance and we might be Wildes and I know Mum hated that and I know you hate that but if there is any chance that you care for us at all as the man we thought we knew, cos you have been there for me, you were there the night I went into labour, and after the wedding, and what happened last year, I couldn't have done it without you. You didn't just do all those things just because."

Harry shrugged.

Again.

Was there anything there?

Was there anything inside this man that was still human?

Or was he just as bad as Eleanor?

David had told him that he could help.

And he repaid him by ...

"It's complicated."

Harry had spoken.

"What's complicated?" Matthew asked. "Eleanor?"

"You need at least three people with the right sorts of Power," Harry said. "Even the last time your parents faced her, it wasn't quite the right combination. But then ..."

He huffed out a rueful smirk.

"I wasn't really trying."

"Well," Matthew said, "imagine we've got enough people and one of them isn't a double agent. What do we need?"

"You won't manage it," Harry said. "Just let her take the girl's body. She'll leave you alone now. At least you're rid of that freak of a *girlfriend* of yours."

Alex ripped her hand from her brother's and stalked up to the bed, slamming her hands down so hard on the rail, Harry flinched.

"We're not letting her get away with it," she hissed. "What Power?"

"You know, Alexandra," Harry said, "I'd always hoped you'd be the one to escape the bear—"

"Reach out," Alex said, forcing violet through her fists, "feel my Power. It's changed."

"You need more than brute force against someone like Eleanor."

"So what do we need? What did you do before?"

"You need one person to disable her," Harry began, his blink the only sign of his surprise, "for example, rendering her unconscious—"

"Or freezing her?" Alex asked.

"Exactly," Harry said, "one person to remove her Power, but as I'm sure you've learnt, there are very few people in the history of the world who can interfere with another person's Power in that way, and finally, someone with necromantic or exorcist skills. For instance, your mother and I had the necromancy, your father could freeze, but your aunt was a clairvoyant. What use was that?"

"Aunt?"

Harry's smile was serpentine in its self-satisfaction.

"A story that would've been for another day," he said. "The point is, you, Alexandra, can freeze and Matthew is able to exorcise her, but if her Power remains with her soul, she is simply banished to The Other Side and it begins all over again."

"Hang on," Alex said, "what do you think my Master Power is?"

"A blunt instrument like your father's, I expect," Harry said, with the kind of dismissiveness of a man who thought he knew it all but probably didn't know enough. "They all were in that family. Blunt instruments or insomniac fortune tellers."

He scoffed and tapped his knuckles soundlessly against the bed, eyes gleaming with undeserved triumph.

"You want to know about the Wildes," he said. He didn't ask, because no question was just a question when it came to Harry Sharpe, Alex had finally understood that. "The father would glass you as soon as look at you, the mother was a witch, the brother was a Provo, and as for the sisters, one was Dead and the other a basket case who'd put her hand in a flame if she thought it might make her feel something."

"And if it's not?" Alex asked, seizing hold of the secret and storing it safe with the others. "My Master Power, I mean?"

"With no offence meant at all," Harry said, "together, you and Matthew are special, but alone, Alexandra, you are mediocre at best."

"If I can get close enough to Eleanor," Alex insisted, "I can remove her Power. All she needs to do is touch me. She touches me, tries to take my Power, I can then take hers."

"So mediocre," Harry sighed. "You still haven't even observed the obvious."

That actually wasn't fair. Alex was observant. Maybe even too observant. But so deprived of sleep, so thrown around geographically and emotionally, still trying to absorb shock after shock, it had taken her that long to even begin to put it together what was …

Well, obvious.

Because Matthew hadn't said a single word since Alex had let go of his hand.

Because there was ozone in the air, even though the window was wide open.

Because even though the window was wide open, there was that barbecue tang.

Because a mile away, a grandfather clock that couldn't chime was going bong …

Bong …

"Before you ask," Harry said, sidling towards her, "no, you shouldn't be able to see me, and, yes, I am being pulled to move on. Call it force of will."

But Alex was only half-listening, because she'd glanced back at Matthew, who was staring beyond the bed—

He grabbed her hand and pulled her past Harry—

No, *through* Harry.

Because behind the bed …

There was a hand.

A charred hand still sizzling with cinders of green Power, curled rictus-rigid like the mummies in Pompeii.

"Perhaps," Harry was saying as he stood by his own body, "I should've just given you up."

"Why didn't you?" Alex breathed, not daring to take another step, to see more of ...

"Just because."

By the time Alex looked up, Harry's ghost was gone.

37
As Long as the Stars are Burning

Uncle Harry was Dead.

Irretrievably, irreversibly, irrevocably Dead.

Leaving everything unsaid, everything unanswered, because ...

What?

Eleanor had been bored?

"Come on," Matthew said, trying to drag Alex out of the room, "Alexandra."

Alex stared down at what was left of Harold Winston Sharpe, pools of ash where his eyes should've been, a lump of coal that used to be his tongue.

No, that wasn't Eleanor bored.

That was Eleanor vengeful.

And Alex could look, because it didn't look anything like her uncle. It wasn't like what they'd done to her mother, making her look almost like she was sleeping as long as no one looked too closely at the cracks in the foundation, the stitches keeping her skin together.

How rigid that hand had been when Alex had been trying to feel something, anything, from it.

"Alex," Matthew hissed, yanking her towards the door, "we don't have time for this again."

"And what are we meant to do now?" Alex asked, her own voice sounding hollow, foreign. "She's got Pandora, we've lost Harry, Maddie's got Power, Sam's run off, and Christ knows what's happened to Elizabeth's body. She's won. She's got what she wants. A body, Power. Elizabeth's Dead. Eleanor's won."

"No, she hasn't."

"Look at it," Alex said, pointing to the body, "she did that to Harry."

"He was just one man—"

"He was stronger than either of us—"

Matthew spun Alex around by her arms, fingers pressing into her flesh.

"He gave us the answer," he said. "Three people with Power. One to disable her, one to take her Power, one to banish her to The Other Side once and for all."

"There's two of us," Alex argued, but Matthew's face was always going to give him away, just like it had at the altar, "no."

"I can banish her," Matthew said, "you can take her Power, Matilda can freeze her. If she hasn't inherited it, we can share it with her."

"She's a child," Alex snarled, "my child, Matthew, the only child I have left as you may have noticed—"

"I noticed," Matthew muttered.

"Go on," Alex said, "ask me what happened after you left."

She threw her Power behind her shove, sending her brother skidding across ash-strewn tiles.

"Go on."

"Not right now," Matthew warned.

"Why not?" Alex cried. "Everyone else is Dead around us, *Uncle Matthew*!"

"If you don't come with me," Matthew hissed, "I'll go on my own."

Alex spluttered out a laugh that felt as hysterical as it sounded.

"Cos you're such a hero!"

"No," Matthew said, "because the stronger Eleanor gets in Pandora's body, the more likely she'll be strong enough to come after the rest of us. Time is not on our side, Alexandra, it's becoming riskier and riskier to exorcise Eleanor—"

"Why?"

"Only going to find out if you follow me," Matthew said, starting down the corridor like he was Linford Christie.

"I have little legs!" Alex yelled, but she still chased her brother down with the weary fury of a woman who hadn't bloody slept in three days.

"Pandora's spent too much time outside her own body," Matthew explained, breaking into a jog for him, a sprint for Alex, "too much time on The Other Side, she's already died once and as far as the Ether's concerned, she belongs there, if not Beyond, where souls go and can never come back, we exorcise her body now, there's no guarantee that her soul will know to come back home. We had to guide her back, remember? Twice. And that was last night. Who knows what's happened in the past six hours?"

"So, what," Alex said, clutching her side as muscles clawed at her ribs and ribs groaned around her heart, "she'd just be left an empty husk?"

"I know Matilda's your daughter—"

"No, Matthew," Alex said, squeaking to a stop.

Matthew turned back with the kind of intent stare that made Alex think, just for a moment, that Elizabeth could've been possessing him.

What a weird thing to wish for, but then Alex had been kicking the realm of impossibilities to pieces with her own bare feet for days.

"And if it's the only way?" Matthew asked.

"Then Eleanor wins," Alex said, swallowing around the ash that used to be her uncle still scraping the roof of her mouth, "then we run away, as far as we can, as fast as we can, because you cannot put a child who has just discovered that she has Power against something that obliterated someone as strong as Harry and has killed someone known as Unkillable twice."

"She'll find us," Matthew said. "She will always find us."

"Fine," Alex said, slapping her hand against her aching chest with those sore ribs and burning muscles and that heart pounding and pushing and pressing, "*we'll* go up against her, but I'm having Shaz take Mads somewhere safe."

As soon as Matthew rolled his eyes, Alex stumbled back into a run down a corridor that just seemed to deepen and darken with every thud of her tired feet.

"Has she really never tried to burn you?" Matthew asked, and when Alex shook her head, "Me neither. But why?"

"I dunno," Alex said, willing her Power into her prickling legs, "cos it's more fun to wind us up first?"

"She took Mum's Power," Matthew replied, glancing up at the ward signs, "and Harry's, so she's not averse to Sharpe Power—"

"And David's little sister," Alex said, "she would've been a Wilde."

"So there's nothing wrong with our Power," Matthew decided, "there's nothing inherently repulsive about it."

"Maybe we're too strong for her."

Matthew scoffed in the direction of Pandora's ward, back at what had been Harry.

"I don't know, then," Alex said, slamming her hand against a fire exit, "but it can't be anything hereditary cos she had no problem going after my daughter!"

"Unless she knows you're a Power-sharer," Matthew said, "She may have always known. It's too risky, even for her, to try to take yours, hence our planning for you to take her Power."

"Doesn't explain why she's never touched you," Alex said. "Not made a deal like Harry, have you?"

Matthew's mouth curled into a sneer, but he just about kept it out of his voice as he supposed that if he were Eleanor ...

"I'd perhaps avoid both twins, just in case. Our Power was unusually entwined, even before ..."

He waved a hand between them, spraying sparks in the faint cloud of green Power still lurking in the air around their knees. It was following them, skulking.

"David said they faced Eleanor twice," Alex said, starting away from those spectral sparks, "while Mum was pregnant with us. D'you think that did something? To us, I mean?"

"I don't know," Matthew admitted.

"I froze something the other day. Harry was surprised. Like I shouldn't have been that good at it."

"All things considered," Matthew said, "I don't think he was David's biggest fan."

"But what if our Power is different?" Alex asked. "What if we don't need three, just two?"

Matthew scoffed, just as Alex pulled him towards a different staircase that'd be quicker.

"Are we really going to risk it?" Matthew asked.

"But you just said, even before we joined—"

"You're a Power-sharer, I'm just ..."

"So you've never been able to throw anything through the air?" Alex asked, taking the stairs three at a time while her knees would put up with it. "Never been able to freeze anything or levitate?"

"It's hereditary, Alex—"

"You know what I mean," Alex said, the start of a washed-out sunrise casting shadows through the narrow windows of the stairwell. "Sunday afternoon. Were you drinking coffee and smoking cigarettes?"

"I'm always drinking coffee and smoking cigarettes."

"Elizabeth said you were having headaches," Alex realised, pointing to the side of her head that Barrett had decided to crush, "here?"

"Further back, actually."

Bashing her head against the wall ...

Throwing up in the alley ...

"Friday night," Alex said, tapping the back of her skull, before tracing her fingers down her temple, "Saturday afternoon."

He felt you drown last month.

"Shaz's birthday," Alex said, yanking her brother into an even dimmer corridor, "felt like your lungs were filling up? Choking?"

Why did Matthew look so furious that Alex had worked something out for herself for once?

"And?" he spat at her.

"And I don't know why you're being weird about this of all things, we've always been ..."

Alex threw her hands up in the air, because what had they always been? Where could she even start? He stole her Barbies, she threw him out a window. He wanted Sam, she took Sam. He made her hot chocolate in the dead of night, she called him back from across the sea.

"Your Power's weird!" Matthew said. "It's bizarre."

"Says the man who talks more to the Dead than he does the Living," Alex laughed. "What the hell is your problem?"

"You don't even know what to do with it properly!"

"You're right!" Alex said. "I don't! And neither does Maddie!"

Wind whipped through the corridor, but it wasn't coming from any windows. No, it was coming from within, like something was snatching the air straight out of their lungs, but it was more than that, because there was Ether in the air again, but not charred this time, no, this time it was like freshly fallen rain, gathering thicker and brighter with a glow of indigo until, like a ghost stepping out of the Veil, she appeared between them.

Maddie Meyer, not such an ordinary child after all.

Well, Matthew thought at Alex, *no surprises what her Master Power is.*

"One sec," Maddie mumbled, heaving up a splatter of Power-laced vomit.

Alex rubbed her back and asked how she did that.

"The 'how' doesn't matter," Matthew said, "I want to know when she learnt it."

"I just kept thinking of here," Maddie said, wiping her mouth with the back of her sleeve like her mother hadn't taught her better, "and here I am."

"And you've probably given Shaz a heart attack." Alex sighed.

Maddie shook her head.

"Dad called her," she said, "she's gone after him."

"What d'you mean, your dad called her?" Alex asked.

Maddie heaved in another breath and clung to the wall as she explained that Shaz had said that Sam had said that he'd tracked down the dybbuk on the beach, that he needed help, and that Shaz shouldn't tell Alex or Matthew because Eleanor wanted their Power and it was clearly a trap.

Alex let the cold creep through her as she caught Matthew's eye. He looked just as grim as she felt. It was the whirring and clicking of the tape deck, the shudder of the wonky window, the scorch of the spirit board on the table.

And every now and then they fell apart.

"And she went?" Matthew asked.

"Yeah," Maddie said, "but she told me to tell you, cos it's a trap."

"It's a trap, alright," Matthew groaned, "just not the trap she thinks it is."

"But Eleanor couldn't make Sam say anything he didn't want to," Alex said. "This is Sammy we're talking about."

"And they don't have Power," Maddie said, spinning round between them. "She wouldn't hurt them—"

"She'd snap your father's neck for fun," Matthew said, ignoring Alex's warning scowl, "and she can imitate, impersonate. We know that, Alex."

"That was different," Alex said, "David was already Dead and we had no idea what he should've sounded like. This is Shaz and Sam, a boy we've all known since primary school."

"Now *this*," Matthew said, "is Eleanor. Luring us in, like she's fishing for mackerel."

"Keeping us just close enough," Alex realised.

"And we're just standing here because?" Maddie asked.

"Because we need to stop and think for once," Alex replied.

Tell her, Matthew said, *tell her about the Power*.

"Tell me what about the Power?" Maddie asked.

For someone who claimed his mind was an impenetrable fortress, Matthew shouldn't have looked so bloody smug at a teenager accidentally trespassing into it.

"We need three people with Power," he said, "to stop Eleanor—"

"Don't you dare," Alex warned.

"And there's three of us with Power," Maddie said, "us three –"

"Uncle Matthew don't know what he's talking about," Alex snarled.

"But we can stop her, we can save Dad and Shaz—"

"And you're a child—"

"I'm fourteen—"

"Nearly," Alex said. "You're still thirteen."

"You were fifteen when you summoned Eleanor—"

"And it got our mother killed and landed us in this mess!"

"You were sixteen when you had me—"

"And I promised to keep you safe! We all did!"

"But if I help, could it save them?" Maddie asked. "Could it save Pandora?"

"It doesn't matter—"

"Uncle Matthew?"

"Don't," Alex warned her brother again before snapping back to her daughter, "I just said it doesn't matter."

"Yes, it does!"

"You've known her two days, Matilda!" Alex yelled. "Why the bloody hell would I let you put yourself in danger for someone you barely know?"

"But we can help," Maddie whispered.

Tears slid down her daughter's face.

Those brilliant blue eyes.

Harry, I can help.

How hadn't she seen it before?

And she knew that even if she might not have been able to see him, she could feel that her father was watching his granddaughter with utterly deserved pride, and seeing might not have been the same as believing, but Alex finally understood that she was looking at a Wilde as much as she was looking at a Meyer.

"Elizabeth would want us to help," Maddie pleaded.

"Elizabeth's ...."

Alex groaned and sank back down against the wall with her head in her hands.

"I'm too tired," she whispered.

Her mother, letting Eleanor possess her.

Her father, holding on for a crisis of conscience that would never hit Harry.

Her brother, coming back to a town that could kill him.

Too tired.

Too old.

Too Wilde for her own good.

"Mum?"

Alex looked up at Matthew and told him in no uncertain terms that if anything happened to her daughter, he'd wish that Alex had killed him on sight.

Matthew snorted.

"I wouldn't expect anything less."

38
A Roll of the Dice

The beach was quiet.

As it always was.

And before a sunrise, the hushed wash of the waves was eerie rather than soothing, which Alex already knew, thanks to her little Saturday morning wake-up call.

The only way Eleanor could've been more obvious was taking them to the cliffs.

Alex had said that she would've known Eleanor when she saw her and she did, because while it might've been Pandora's eyes on her, the weight of the stare, directed at the side of Alex's face, the flattened temple, the crushed cheek, wasn't wide-eyed enough to be Pandora's. It was substantial and expectant and knowing.

The other giveaway was the fact that Eleanor/Pandora – the dybbuk – was holding up a very bloody Sam by his hair and a very bruised Shaz by her scarf.

"Everyone happy with the plan?" Alex asked through sand-blasted but still gritted teeth.

Apparently, simple plans were the best, but then seeing wasn't believing and nearly everything in existence was easier said than done.

Technically speaking, all Alex had to do was freeze Eleanor and take her Power.

Technically speaking, all Matthew had to do was expel her from Pandora's body.

Technically speaking, all Maddie had to do was phase into The Other Side and drag Pandora's soul out at exactly the right moment.

The twins were even sharing (temporarily) their Power with Maddie, a deep purple dancing between their violet and her indigo.

That was all they had to do.

Technically speaking.

Alex, Matthew, and Maddie.

Ten feet away from the dybbuk, Sam, and Shaz.

The surf curled around their shoes, bubbles bursting with every step. Alex knew she was crushing Maddie's hand, but there was enough Power between them pumping through their skin.

"Don't listen to her!" Sam called. "Whatever she says, Lex! Don't do it!"

"You would've made a sweet couple," the dybbuk said, giving Sam a kick to his knee to top off the compliment. "Whatever happened?"

Alex said that it was complicated.

The dybbuk tightened Shaz's scarf around her throat and told her she could simplify it.

"Break my sister's neck," Matthew warned, as a whole new wave of nausea washed over Alex, "there won't be any simplifying."

The dybbuk smiled and released Shaz, who clutched at her neck with broken fingers as her hair got yanked instead.

"Choose," the dybbuk said. "Choose between wee Sammy Meyer, the boy with those big sad brown eyes, or the abandoned bookworm you call your sister."

"Alex," Shaz tried to shout through her damaged throat, "don't fall for it!"

"I want you all to choose," the dybbuk said, "together."

"And what happens when we choose?" Matthew asked.

That is not an option, Alex hissed into his mind.

"Well," the dybbuk said, "you know how you're such a good healer?"

"Yes."

"Did you know *Uncle Harry* was an anti-healer?"

That green Power left in Elizabeth's neck …

How Alex had made Shaz's aching hand worse …

How Harry had insisted he couldn't heal Pandora …

It wasn't just blocking Power.

"So," the dybbuk continued, "you choose Shazza and I break apart wee Sammy's leg all over again, with the bone sticking out and the screaming, or you choose the boy and I show Shazza what I was really gonna do to her when I possessed her."

"I can handle the leg," Sam said, choking on his own blood, "choose Shaz."

"I might make sure that artery gets severed this time though," the dybbuk said. "How fast can you heal him?"

"He's Maddie's father," Shaz spluttered. "Choose Sam."

Alex dug her teeth into her ash-dry mouth, that barbecue tang of what was left of Harry still lingering. She was still too far away and there was no way Eleanor would let her get much closer and there was no guarantee her Power was still obeying her after everything she'd made it do …

She cringed when the dybbuk wrenched Shaz's arm behind her back, a dull snap and a weary cry echoing through the dawn.

It might happen anyway. Surely Eleanor didn't keep to her word? Surely she'd get Alex to answer and she'd just kill both of them anyway and then she'd kill Maddie and Matthew just to make whatever point she thought she was making, which were always the most terrifying points of all?

"Mum?" Maddie hissed. "What do we do? Are we still doing the plan?"

"The longer you take to make a choice," the dybbuk called in a sickly sing-song voice, "the more bones I break ..."

"I choose Sharon!" Matthew called.

"Matthew!" Alex gasped, whacking his arm.

"I just bought us another minute," Matthew snarled.

Sam got a boot to the stomach.

"I – I choose Dad!" Maddie yelled.

I need to get close to her to take her Power, Alex thought furiously at them. *How am I meant to manage that now?*

"Ohhh," the dybbuk laughed, "the deciding vote's actually finding this difficult! Maybe you were right, Samuel. Maybe she really did never love you. That would make more sense than this thing with the runt of my family and 'runt' is being generous, believe you me. At least I've put her out of her misery now. I've put her down. Gave up your vigil, didn't you, Lexy? Left her cold in the morgue? Too many things unfinished, was it?"

And then ...

And then.

Alex knew.

She'd always assumed it was the way Eleanor looked at her so voraciously that turned her stomach, but through Pandora's eyes, as a dybbuk, it didn't have quite the same effect.

Because Alex could see it now. She understood that warning nausea because almost every day of her school life, she'd had to be ready.

Had to be ready to come face-to-face with a bully.

The problem with bullies was that they came in too many shapes and sizes, too many faces and forms.

But the good thing about them was ...

They never knew what to do when someone stood up to them.

"You see," the dybbuk said to her hostages, "if I'd just had an invite to your wee wedding, I might not have had to do this."

"And if I don't choose?" Alex asked.

The dybbuk flinched, dragging Shaz and Sam with it. "If you *what*?"

"If I don't choose either of them. What happens then?"

"Uh, that's not the game, Lexy," the dybbuk said, with a curl of Pandora's mouth that was all Eleanor. "You have to choose which one you love more."

"Uh, I don't care," Alex said. "You probably want my Power more than you want to be playing a stupid game with me like we're, what, in the playground? Did they even have school when you come from?"

"If you don't choose," the dybbuk snarled, "I'll kill both of them."

"Fine," Alex said. "Anti-heal away."

The dybbuk gawped at her.

"I don't think mind games work on her," Sam warned, blood streaming from his ear.

"This isn't a mind game," Alex scoffed, stalking towards the dybbuk. "Do you really think I've got anything left to lose? Call me 'little Lexy' all you want, but don't you forget: I'm Carrie Wilde's daughter."

"Then I'll just snap both their necks," the dybbuk said, but even with a threat like that, the wind hadn't just been knocked clean out of its sails, Alex had banished it into another dimension.

"Go ahead."

And Alex stared the dybbuk down.

"I will do it," the dybbuk warned.

"The Eleanor Lennox I know doesn't say the same threat twice—"

There.

That was the moment.

By the end of Alex's breath, the dybbuk had made the decision to break its hostages' necks and pink Power had even begun to surge in its hands, but that was exactly where it was going to stay.

Because Alex froze her.

Alex froze her and dragged Sam and Shaz free with a burst of her own Power.

"What?" Alex said, squeezing a sick-stained Shaz. "I'm David's daughter too."

"And Sharpe's niece," Sam spluttered. "Your poker-face is terrifying."

"It's not the first time you've seen it, Sammy."

"Yeah," Sam said, "I'm well aware of that and all."

The dybbuk jolted towards them.

Alex looked at it.

It stopped again, but pink Power was flaring from it like a frozen waterfall.

If it had been anyone else, Alex would've thought it was beautiful, but there was no time, not when Matthew was running towards them chanting something in some language of the Dead Alex didn't recognise.

"Get ready to get Pandora," Alex told Maddie, who was already surging indigo, "yeah?"

She turned to Shaz and Sam and told them to get inside Elizabeth's flat.

Shaz's scream punctured the cold air.

Her arm, being wrenched from the socket—

And Sam, his leg buckling—

Maddie smashing against the shingle, blood gushing from her nose but she was still conscious—

The dybbuk was pushing through the freeze.

"Help, Matthew?" Alex screamed, but he was backing up the beach and glowing a queasy turquoise-violet.

He wasn't abandoning them, was he?

He was still chanting but it had twisted, it had changed, she felt in her soul that it was something different, another intention behind it, but Alex had worse things to worry about, because she couldn't *not* heal Sam and Shaz, not when blood was spraying all over her hand and Sam's scream was even sicker than it had been at sixteen, but the flames weren't stopping and Maddie was trying to fix Shaz's arm and then ...

Alex's arms split open.

All those old slashes tearing through her skin, far deeper than she'd ever cut, breaking her to the bone and she knew.

She knew what Eleanor wanted.

She wanted to deglove her.

She was going to flay the skin from Alex and plunge her hand into her heart because she knew Alex would never give up now, she was Carrie Wilde's daughter, so—

So Alex did.

She gave up.

She ripped her Power from the dybbuk and slammed herself down into the sand, grabbing Sam's broken leg.

"Don't start," she said to Sam's filthy, furious glare, "I'm not gonna do it as well as Matthew would but he's playing silly buggers and you'll get what you're—"

Shingle scorched Alex's side as she skidded across the rocks.

"You think," the dybbuk hissed, stalking towards her with bared teeth and wild eyes, "that you can best me? Come on then, Lexy. Power versus Power. What are you really made of?"

Alex scrambled to her feet, threw a warning hand at Sam and Shaz and Maddie to stay down.

Matthew had stopped chanting.

He was just watching.

Why the hell had he stopped chanting?

His thoughts pushed at Alex's mind and she fought the urge to throw him out.

What does she smell like?

"What?" Alex breathed, tutting when her brother just rolled his eyes at her.

"Excuse me," the dybbuk demanded, "are you listening to me?"

"What does Elizabeth smell like?" Matthew called.

The dybbuk flinched.

It flinched at Elizabeth's name.

"What's the problem, Nellie?" Alex panted, trying to heal her friction burn just enough so it would stop paralysing her leg and she could focus on whatever the hell Matthew wanted. "Never wanna pick on someone your own size?"

"I've killed *her*," the dybbuk spat, "more than once."

"I thought Lizzie was just the little runt," Alex said, clutching at her hip in the hope the pain would just throb rather than scald. "Bet that gave you a shock, didn't it?

When she came back to put you right. That why you had to kill her from behind last night?"

The dybbuk had stopped coming towards her.

And, what the dybbuk probably didn't quite have the imagination to understand, is that Alex knew that face. Because that was a Lennox operating another Lennox and it might've only been four days, but Alex had spent a shitload of that time staring at another Lennox, trying to work out all those little micro-expressions, so when Alex saw that barely suppressed curl of the lip, the narrowing and the widening of the eyes, she knew that she had caught it out.

What do you see in her?

That's what Eleanor had asked her.

And it wasn't to tease.

It wasn't even out of morbid curiosity, for everything she said about moon eyes.

Because, every time Alex had shown her unshakeable faith in Elizabeth, Eleanor had thrown something back at her.

Out of fear.

Like beating down a dog in the hope it would forget it was really a wolf.

"She doesn't have Power anymore," the dybbuk snarled, but that was quite the blush roaring up her neck, "she's *Dead*."

"D'you know what, Eleanor?" Alex said. "If you learn one thing before we obliterate you, please ..."

She nodded at Matthew, who realised:

"Power isn't everything."

Power wasn't everything.

But it helped.

Because Alex and Matthew *had* bent the Ether to their will.

They *had* reached between worlds.

They *had* smashed down the barriers between Time and Space.

And if Matthew had changed what he was asking the Ether for …

If exorcising Eleanor from Pandora could wait …

If there was something more important he could call for first …

Matthew was still staring at Alex.

Think of her, he thought, wiping glowing blood from his nose, *just think and you will find.*

Five.

A flash of fire. Stormy eyes. Scarlet lips. Crooked teeth. Perfect nails.

Four.

A crackle of scars. Cold to the touch. A quiet pulse. A squeeze of her hand.

Three.

I could keep you company? We've all got scars. Here I am.

Two.

Bergamot. Leather.

One.

The faintest murmur of expensive cigarettes.

"What are you doing?" the dybbuk snarled.

"Same as me," Matthew called, glowing too, just like she was—

"And me," Maddie said.

And then …

"And me."

That was a voice Alex hadn't been expecting.

She opened her eyes and glanced at Matthew, who nodded and very, *very* almost smiled.

Turn around, he thought at her.

But Alex didn't need to.

She could feel that bright purple Power, like lavender in the fullest of blooms, brush past her as Pandora's soul marched towards the dybbuk.

"And I want," Pandora said, "my body back."

Shaz asked what was going on, but Sam just shook his head and gawped at his first ghost.

No, ghost was the wrong word.

A ghost couldn't grapple with a Living body and drag it down onto the sand.

Soul soaring, Alex caught Matthew's eye again—

"Turn," he said, "around."

Don't, she thought back at him, *if it's not true, I couldn't ...*

"Turn," Matthew insisted, "around."

There was no time, not with the fight happening in the shallows and Maddie trying to heal Shaz and Matthew resetting Sam's leg with a brutal efficiency, there was only so much Time and Space they could bend to their will, so Alex caught her breath again and turned—

Into leather-clad arms, blood-drenched and trembling.

With every whistle of breath, with every throb of a pulse much stronger than before, every touch that was warmer than they'd ever been telling Alex who was in front of her and that for once, just for once, seeing and hearing and smelling and touching and tasting was believing because when Elizabeth finally smiled, her teeth brown with dried blood, Alex knew.

"Sorry," Elizabeth croaked, letting Alex clutch at her face, that beautiful, ridiculous face, "no Power."

"Don't care," Alex said, finally giving her the kiss she'd wanted to the night before, revelling in the heat of her lips, the tang of her blood, and—

They were knocked onto the shingle, Power scorching Alex's back.

"Are you okay?" Alex asked, pulling Elizabeth up by her shoulders.

"Are *you* alright?" Elizabeth insisted, but Maddie was calling for them.

The beach had fallen silent.

Alex and Elizabeth dragged each other up and towards the others, who were staring down at the shallows, where …

Pandora stood?

"Dora?" Alex asked, trying to discreetly slide in front of Sam and Shaz. "Is that you?"

She felt Matthew shift next to her, blocking Maddie as well.

And that glint of cold against her hand was definitely Elizabeth drawing a knife.

"Nice try," the dybbuk sneered. "You've brought her back even wronger than she was before."

Elizabeth's hand flinched in Alex's.

The dybbuk – Eleanor – cackled and shook her head.

"Look at you all!" she laughed, "the four of you and the runt and a child! D'you know what this is reminding me of, Lizzie? Sixty-eight? Remember?"

Eleanor danced across the shingle and pointed at them in turn.

"Aye," she said, squinting at them. "Little Sammy could be David – both dirty Jews – Shazza could be Shiv, yous two Carrie and Harry, then Lizzie, you're still Lizzie, and Mads would be wee Rosie."

Her smirk darkened, just as Elizabeth's hand clenched in Alex's.

"Remember what happened to wee Rosie?" Eleanor said. "And now look. Yous can run, but yous can't hide."

Elizabeth stepped in front of them all, ignoring Alex's frantic, hissed pleas.

"You've got what you want," she said, "leave 'em alone."

Eleanor scoffed.

"Or what?"

Alex clenched her fist and focused on the idea of Harry and that dark, unhealing Power until her knuckles grew a queasy pea green.

Elizabeth raised the knife, Eleanor lunged towards her—

A quick swipe of Alex's hand was all it took for Elizabeth to stagger back out of harm's way, blood spraying across the sand as Matthew and Maddie and Sam and Shaz all rushed to her side to stop what Alex really hoped was superficial bleeding, just dramatic enough to buy her time.

"What are you doing?" Eleanor hissed.

"My Power's stronger." Alex laughed. "You don't need a kid."

The light in those stolen eyes ...

"Another trick."

"Maybe," Alex said, as everyone behind her was shouting and yelling, "but let's see whose instincts are stronger."

Alex plunged her hand into her own shoulder and wrenched it apart, Power-rich blood surging from the knife wound, pumping in thick waves down her chest, because this was it, wasn't it? Eleanor just couldn't help herself. Alex's Power burned through her skin as it finally surrendered to someone who actually wanted it, and Alex grabbed her.

It wasn't instinct. It had never been instinct. Her instinct had been screaming at Alex since the very beginning.

To run.

To stay well away.

To not let the waitress sit down opposite her.

To not go back for the homeless girl.

To not translate that half-remembered French.

To just accept her uncle's version of events, of all events, just like her mind wanted her to.

To forget.

This wasn't instinct. This was choice. This hurt.

And whatever came next, as Alex and Eleanor fought for each other's Power in that eternal tug of war, pink and violet Power erupting through the blood-red sunrise stirring on the sea—

39
A Chance on a Promise

Pain shooting through bones.

Heart punching through chest.

Head ...

Whatever her head's doing.

Alex groans and pushes herself—

No.

She doesn't push herself up.

She pushes, but she doesn't move. Can't move, not when she feels like she's been hit by a double-decker.

Alex forces a breath out of her lungs, her ribs aching with every catch of air, stretch of muscle.

She tells her arm to move.

Her fingertips twitch.

They feel cold.

She feels cold.

She can feel.

She can feel and she's alive and if she just tries again, she can—

Flop onto her side like a dying fish, her own breath almost choking her.

But she has moved.

She can move.

She's moving, clawing at the shingle until she's more or less sitting up, side throbbing, chest throbbing, limbs throbbing, head ...

Head clear.

For the first time in years.

Shingle.

It's dark.

It shouldn't be dark.

It's amazing how the brain, or maybe the soul, clings on in those moments before the message gets there.

How it convinced her that she's feeling things.

That she's hurting.

That she's breathing.

When, actually, when she looks up and sees that frozen wave and looks up and sees the beach wall, she finally understands that she is back on The Other Side.

She finally understands how close she is to Death.

And she knew it would happen.

That was the point of it, letting Eleanor steal just enough of her Power so it would learn from hers and pull it right back, violet burning up pink, a tug of war ripping their souls apart.

And yet Alex's soul is still hanging on.

But even more importantly, even more worthy of note, as Matthew would put it, than Alex being there ...

Is that Eleanor is too.

And even better, she looks absolutely bloody furious.

She hasn't noticed Alex yet, which is perfectly fine by her, because she can just sit there and watch her smash her fist into the frozen wave over and over again, each smash, each *scream* spiralling in anger.

Is this what satisfaction feels like?

Matthew said a word once:

Schadenfreude.

He used to say it was his favourite feeling.

Alex understands why.

She's doing it.

She's finally doing it.

Alex is doing what Carrie couldn't, what Harry should've, what David didn't even have the chance to do, and if her soul aches at the idea of what must be happening in the Land of the Living, well, then so be it.

"Oh my God," a voice calls, and there's shingle shifting behind her, "Alex!"

Pandora hauls her up.

"You shouldn't be here," Alex gasps, "you ..."

The wave isn't frozen. Not quite. The closer Pandora shuffles towards it, it gives.

Alex tells her to go back to her body, for good, before it's too late, before Eleanor notices, because Eleanor is only feet away and while her focus is failing to burn a hole in the wave where she is, the wave is bending where Pandora touches it.

"You're coming back, right?" Pandora asks. "Alex?"

"There has to be a sacrifice," Alex replies. "Go on. It's your body."

"But ..."

Alex squeezes Pandora's hands.

"They'll look after you."

Pandora nods and wipes tears away from her wobbling chin, but Alex resists the urge to hug her because there's no time, no time at all, and she pushes Pandora into the wave until she vanishes and it snaps back into place.

Frozen.

No more admissions taken.

Alex laughs.

It's a bark of a laugh that punches its way out of her chest and she's sort of aware of a nervy high note in her ears, but it's hard to care when she has no control over it and doesn't want any control over it so she just stands there, toes clutching pebbles that don't really exist, and lets it take her over, winding up and up and up even as Eleanor finally stills and spins and stalks down the beach towards her, which just makes Alex laugh harder and harder—

Black bursts in her mind.

Choking on blood that shouldn't be there, Alex scratches at Eleanor as she hauls her up.

So much for not getting hurt on The Other Side.

"Where the hell's my Power?" Eleanor hisses, dragging and dragging as Alex tries to catch her feet in the sand. "What have you done with it?"

She throws Alex onto the wet-dry-cold-warm-soft-hard sand, climbs onto her back, and drives her knees right into her spine.

It is painful.

There is some kind of pain here, but it feels more profound, more psychic than anything else and if Alex can handle any kind of pain, it's that.

"Come on, Lexy," Eleanor whispers, right against her ear, "where is my Power?"

"Dunno," Alex groans, trying in vain to turn her head, she has to—

Claws – no, nails – sink into her throat, yanking her up and onto her back with a squelch and a thud that has Alex's head thrumming.

"Where's my Power?" Eleanor screams right into Alex's face, slamming herself onto Alex's stomach, knees in her ribs so hard Alex has to turn her head just fast enough to retch up the pain and then dry, icy hands are on Alex's throat, pulling at her to look at the deranged woman snarling in her face, "Give it back to me! Give it to me!"

"I haven't got it!" Alex gasps, throat burning until she remembers it can't burn. "I haven't got anything!"

Eleanor leans over her with rage-poisoned eyes and there's something in the fury that twists Eleanor's face that Alex imagines has always been there, especially when she was a spiteful little child pinching her sister's arm and getting her into trouble.

"Then where is it?"

"Gone," Alex says. "Ether. Dunno. Don't care."

"You had no right—"

Alex splutters out a laugh.

"You can talk!" she says, trying to dig her numb nails into Eleanor's hands. "You've done nothing but take and take and ..."

"Just like your parents," Eleanor sneers. "Idiots. Savages. The lot of you. You'd rather die than just give me what I want."

Alex gasps, no, she laughs, she *laughs* when she thinks of Matthew and Maddie and Shaz and Sam and Pandora and Elizabeth and finally realises what she should've known all along.

"I just wanna live."

She just wants to live.

After all this time, Alexandra Catherine Wilde of 1, St Augustine's, Coldharbour, mother and sister and girlfriend, journalist and waitress and Power sharer, has seen enough of Death to know that she wants to live.

That's when she sees it.

The tiniest crack, the most infinitesimal chink of light slipping through the frozen wave.

Turquoise light.

Turquoise *Power*.

No.

She will live.

She is one of those miracles, because she believes in that boy who would sit up with her when Maddie wouldn't sleep, who'd stood up to the grown-ups, who'd held Alex's hand, who is somehow reaching across worlds for her.

Alex shoves Eleanor off her face-first, she clambers up with as much grace as she does in the Land of the Living, and she starts driving her fist right into that crack, paying absolutely no mind whatsoever to the part of her soul that is trying to tell her that it hurts, because it all hurts, it has always hurt, everyone and everything she's ever lost and ever found has hurt, it hurts when she thinks of the children she never had, it hurts when she thinks of the parents she should've had, it hurts when she thinks of the "just because" that means "I love you", it hurts when she thinks of her brother and her sister holding her hands, it hurts when she thinks of her daughters, both of them now, and how they hug with everything in their bones, it hurts when she thinks of that boy's smile in front of the empty grave, it hurts when she thinks of her waitress and that look in her eyes, it hurts when she thinks of that shining, made-up moment of all of them sitting at the kitchen table, it has always hurt and there's no amount of hurting herself that will ever make it better, only this, only this one thought as she slams both her arms elbows-first into the crack:

Alex Wilde lives.

40
Time until the End of Time

The sun had finally risen.

The sea was still churning away outside.

The café still had its nicotine-stained net curtains and peeling wax tablecloths and that cloying smell of grease.

Yes, that was all the same.

What wasn't the same was that Alex and Elizabeth were waiting on Shaz and Sam, Maddie and Pandora, who were sitting at the table Alex had on Friday, all comparing their war wounds with weary chuckles and too-wide eyes.

"I'll make Mads'," Alex murmured, dragging the knife through the margarine, which had all the give of a breezeblock.

They must've had enough money between them to upgrade to *I can't believe it's not butter*.

"I'm not that bad at making sandwiches," Elizabeth croaked.

"She don't like crusts, she only has marge on one slice, and if you cut the cheese too thick, she won't eat it at all."

"She's thirteen, Alex."

"And she's particular," Alex said, "like her Uncle Matthew."

Who was standing down at the shoreline, on his own.

Alex caught Elizabeth's eye, the less bruised one, and waited for the challenge as she kept buttering bread.

No.

No, Alex wasn't waiting for the challenge.

She was waiting for that smirk, growing sluggishly across Elizabeth's still too-pale face.

And then she clocked it again.

The scar across Elizabeth's throat.

Well, not scar. *Wound.*

The *wound* was still huge and red, even under the bandage. Blood, the final remnants of the Wilde Power, and what Shaz had called "serum" but Alex just knew as the stuff under blisters when Maddie hadn't broken in new shoes properly, was seeping out through the edges, muddy and (according to the girls, at least) very, very faintly glowing.

But the slash across Elizabeth's throat was the least of it really, when the burns on her arm caught the light and her hand struggled to hold onto the knife and then there was the burn, the one that wasn't like her other burns, it wasn't even like Pandora's or Maddie's or Alex's own fainter ones:

The burn that Eleanor had branded over Elizabeth's heart was a dark, angry thing, the colour of magpie wings, easily mistaken for an ink splatter or a blast of gunpowder if it weren't for the veins of Power that branched out from the blackness, spidering their way through her skin.

And such a fierce, possessive wave of protectiveness despite, or because of, the week they'd had washed through her, Alex didn't realise her hands had stilled on the counter until Elizabeth said:

"I can almost hear you thinking. Even without Power."

"Where were you?" Alex whispered. "In those in-between hours? Matthew hasn't said how he worked it out, that what we'd done was unfinished."

"I don't know," Elizabeth confessed, "I've never remembered my dreams."

"Did you know I was there though?" Alex asked. "Waiting for you?"

Elizabeth let the knife slip out of her hand onto the counter and caressed the back of Alex's fingers. She was warm. Shockingly hot. How could Elizabeth be Powerless and mortal and yet feel so alive?

Alex laced their fingers together and gave Elizabeth's hand a gentle squeeze, before bringing it up to press her lips against that warm, scarred skin.

Elizabeth's eyes betrayed her first, glazing over with tears, and then ...

The brightest, well, slightly yellowed, smile that Alex had ever seen.

Alex had assumed it was Elizabeth's Power that had made her glow under the street lights that first night, somehow less than a week ago, when Elizabeth had grinned at her with those crooked teeth and declared that Alex never took her seriously, when something small, that strange little ember had sparked and had been carefully kept warm, made strong with every shared smile, with every touch of their hands. But now, with no Power between them at all, she understood that it had actually just been Elizabeth all along.

An ember?

Who was Alex kidding?

It was more like she'd turned up to a wildfire with nothing better than a fire extinguisher and a bucket of sand.

"Even though I really am just a middle-aged waitress now?" Elizabeth asked.

"Oh," Alex laughed, "*because* you're a middle-aged waitress."

"Are we getting some grub today or what?" Sam called. "I feel like my throat's been cut."

And the spell was broken.

Shaz gave him an almighty smack on the arm, which led to a grumbled "no offence".

The way Elizabeth's good hand clenched around the knife was as close to "none taken" as Sam was going to get.

"You're allowed to help, you know," Alex replied. "We've all heard the 'I would've been the next Cantona' enough times. Kevin Keegan ain't knocking at your door, Samuel."

"I did offer," Shaz piped up, "but you told me to take a seat."

"Your arm's in a sling, sis."

"I healed that the best I could!" Maddie protested and Alex was beginning to wish she'd snuck outside with Matthew after all.

Sam's mobile phone started to ring, killing the conversation quicker than Gideon Barrett's arsenic. While he mumbled his instructions down the phone, Alex slid the slightly-less-sadder-than-usual sandwiches across the counter, telling the girls whose was whose and trying not to cringe at their docile nods.

They'd been clingy.

The girls had been clingy.

They had been just about willing to let Alex have a shower while Elizabeth submerged herself in her bath, but Alex couldn't work out if they wouldn't let her out of their sight or if they didn't want to be let out of hers.

And *now* they were insisting that Alex sit between them on a banquette that had seen better days, sand still stuck to their sweaty skin.

Elizabeth shifted in front of the counter, every movement languid. But while she still looked halfway between death and exhaustion, her eyes were living, thriving, more alight than Alex had ever seen them before.

And then she crossed her arms tight over her body.

Some things really never changed.

Sam put the phone down and muttered an apology.

"Good news," he sighed, "they've found your old man, he's in the well in the back garden. They've got him – the skeleton – out in one piece, which means the forensics will be out of the house by lunchtime."

"And the bad news?" Alex asked, stiffening down to her bones.

"The superintendent says I've got some explaining to do," Sam replied, running his hands down his face, "about everything that's happened here since Friday."

"I'm not going back home," Pandora rushed out, "I'd rather go back on the streets, I'll run away, I'll go further—"

"You're not going anywhere," Elizabeth growled, which had the unintended effect of sending Pandora flinching back into Alex's arms.

The girl is a Lennox.

Five words. No further explanation.

Like Eleanor, like Elizabeth, Pandora was somehow a Lennox.

An endangered species.

"What she means," Alex explained, "is that you're staying with us."

"I brought that thing into your home," Pandora said, "I—"

Alex shook her head, shoulder groaning as she tried to keep her arm around her.

Pandora scoffed darkly, her hazel eyes so wide, as if the shock was the only thing keeping her alert.

That same awkwardness, *wariness*, from that first night they'd met, Pandora plastered in days-old make-up, calling her "Miss", slithered back between them.

"It's not your fault," Alex insisted. "How could it possibly be your fault? You were possessed against your will. She was killing you, she … And bloody Harry knew, didn't he? If it's anyone's fault, it's Barrett's for killing you, Eleanor's for possessing you, and it's Harry's for saying nothing. It is never your fault."

Alex glanced at Sam, hoping he could see the pleading in her eyes, because she wasn't too proud to beg. Not anymore.

But all he did was stare back as he stood up and slipped his suit jacket on.

Shame the dry cleaners wasn't a drive-thru, seeing as the super probably wasn't going to be impressed at the sight of blood and sand smeared in Sam's pinstripes.

"Told you so," Maddie said to Pandora. "You're so staying with us."

"In an ideal world, yeah," Shaz said, as painfully gently as always, "but look at what's on your dad's plate: David, Barrett, Harry, Elizabeth's not-murder …"

"Not to mention the serial killings that kicked this all off in the first place," Sam muttered.

"Well?" Elizabeth demanded, jabbing her hand at the window. "Cos this time, my lawyer's right outside."

Sam was busy pursing his lips and staring outside at Matthew like he was a spectre at the feast.

"How much to make it all go away?" Elizabeth asked. "I have funds—"

"My fiancé's not bent, thank you," Shaz said, gently but firmly.

"Sammy?" Alex asked, caution clawing its way into her and anchoring her to the seat. "Do we need to have a word in private?"

The words they could have.

The bombs she could drop.

He was still staring out.

Matthew wouldn't be able to persuade him. It was best that they never set foot in the same room at the same time ever again. And Shaz was right: Sam was not bent, which had never made him friends as it was.

Sam groaned out a sigh and shook his head.

"I can be a DCI another time," he said, "another place."

"What?"

"Had barely got my feet under the table as a DI," Sam mused, still staring out at Matthew or at nothing in particular. "Being stuck on desk duty or in the records room might do me good, take the weight off my leg."

"Sam ..."

"The super wants to see me in half an hour," Sam continued, finally looking back at them, "enough time for me to drop a couple of files in the bin and blame the millennium bug?"

"You don't have to do this," Alex whispered, fighting against the burning in her throat.

"I think I do," Sam said. "They're gonna think I'm a right schmuck, but what do I care? They never liked me anyway."

Alex had thought she'd seen the impossible enough times since she'd returned to Coldharbour, but Elizabeth offering her hand to Sam and Sam taking it with the utmost sincerity and solemnity was ...

Was up there with Matthew actually turning up in Coldharbour and resisting the urge to be a total arsehole.

Shaz stroked Sam's arm and asked if he was sure.

"Are *you* sure?" he said. "Losing the promotion means losing the pay rise."

"I'd live on baked beans if I had to," Shaz said, her sweet smile doing nothing to stop Alex's grimace.

May '82. Carrie's boss had stiffed her on her wages so they'd had a Baked Bean Bank Holiday. On the Monday evening, the kids snuck out to Sam's and smuggled back penny sweets and custard creams, unwrapping them on the street corner so their mother wouldn't hear the rustling.

"Thank you," Alex said.

Sam just shrugged and wandered out of the café with a ding of the bell.

"So if the house is open," Maddie said, "does that mean we're going back?"

"Not being funny," Pandora said, "but I think I'd rather be homeless again."

Shaz glanced at Alex and said:

"We'll work something out. You can stay with us."

"But we don't have to go back to the house?" Maddie asked.

"Never again," Alex said, "not if you don't want to. I'm sure Uncle Matthew wants to sell it as much as I do."

But did she?

Still?

The house most of them were born in? Died in?

That haunted house with its locked doors and gloomy corners that had been trying to tell her all along that it belonged to her, that it was hers to reclaim?

Could she really give it up now?

"What about the ghosts though?" Pandora asked. "Your parents?"

"I don't know," Alex admitted, "I think they would've moved on now."

It was a strange feeling, to simply not know. To lack that extra layer of awareness, though ...

Did it even matter anymore?

"D'you think your Power'll come back?" Maddie asked.

"No, sweetheart," Alex sighed, "all my Power's gone now."

"And Uncle Matthew's?" Pandora asked.

Alex hadn't dared to believe it at first when she came to on the shingle, the sun slowly rising. She couldn't believe it, not even with the sheer strength of sensation assaulting her, the sog and the stickiness, the scorch and the shiver, all salt and sweat and sick, but when she had managed to creak open dry eyes in a head that felt like it had been smashed apart all over again ...

The wind had been real.

The sound of seagulls had been real.

Those pebbles as hard and slick as glass that crunched as they should've done under her hands and knees.

And with a leaden arm, she'd reached out for her brother who mumbled something about thinking he'd shat himself. She'd pointed out that she was the one who'd undergone an exorcism and couldn't he just magic it away or something?

"*With what Power?*"

Three muttered words.

Matthew hadn't needed to elaborate, not really. Not with that mournful look in his eyes. Whatever had happened while Alex was fighting for her soul meant that Matthew had also lost his Power.

And now, Alex was trudging down the shingle, the wind snatching her breath as she asked her brother:

"Still here?"

"Despite some people's best efforts," Matthew said, revealing his blood-encrusted nose, "evidently."

Alex had always known that the first thing Sam was going to do when he saw Matthew was break his nose.

It was as certain as the waves washing up the Dead.

"I am sorry," Alex said, the wind whipping her hair, "about your Power."

"This *again*?" Matthew said, turning against the air to try to light a fag. "Elizabeth said you wouldn't give it up."

"Well, you were both a bit more attached to Power than me."

"I don't know," Matthew said, but his small smile gave him away just like it always had, "I think you were beginning to like it too."

"Sometimes," Alex conceded. "On The Other Side, when I was fighting off Eleanor, I really thought that was it. You know, that if you were trying the exorcism, it was failing."

"It was."

"Mouse, are you ever gonna tell me what really happened or what? I took Eleanor from Pandora and the next thing I know—"

"It's none of your business," Matthew snapped.

"Well, something happened to me and something happened to your Power and everyone else is none the wiser—"

Alex stopped herself at her brother's stare. His jaw was clenching away so hard, he was probably grinding his teeth. She had half a mind to warn him he'd have to start going to dentists and they'd both seen *Marathon Man*.

Whatever she was going to say would have to get forced through her tightening throat, so Alex settled for:

"Yeah, you're right. Doesn't matter anymore."

"You know nothing about me, you know," Matthew told the sea. "All your bloody questions."

"I know," Alex whispered.

She scuffed her feet against the shingle.

Matthew shielded his body against the sea air.

Well, hadn't Harry called it?

They might've been pretending to have no interest whatsoever in that buried hatchet, but there they were, still shattering the ground with their heels, trying to be subtle in their desperation to get to it first.

Do you always compare yourself to your brother? Elizabeth had asked when they'd been investigating the murders.

Only when it comes to Power. Nothing to compare otherwise.

Not alike?

Never used to be.

And now?

They'd even been on that stretch of the beach during that conversation. There were still flecks of ash in the sand, even if Alex couldn't see the Power glittering in the cinders.

And now?

And now.

"What was my Master Power?" Matthew asked.

"Necromancy," Alex said, "so you just brought me back from Death?"

Matthew snorted and shook his head.

"I was a Power sharer too," he explained. "It's just that I had cultivated my Power in other areas, so it wasn't as obvious."

"What?"

"Think of a neglected weed with a single flower," Matthew replied. "That's you. I'm the flourishing bush."

"That's one thing to call you," Alex muttered. "Are you sure? We were really both Power sharers?"

"Who's the dominant twin?" Matthew asked.

"You."

"See, I thought it was *you*," Matthew said, "Shaz thought it was you, Sam thought it was me, Elizabeth was the one who worked it out. Neither of us is the dominant twin. We shared everything so I gave you everything I had. Every last spark. All gone."

"How did you know it would work?" Alex asked.

"I didn't," Matthew replied, "it was a bloody lucky guess."

"We're alive," Alex laughed, "because of your bloody lucky guess?"

Matthew gave her a sheepish shrug and a rueful frown.

He always had known everything.

They stood there in their silence that was almost comforting in its discomfort. Well, not discomfort. Just different without Power between them. No sensation of shared feeling or thought.

Just a pair of twins being battered by the wind.

And if anyone saw them reach out for each other, if anyone saw them standing there hand in hand staring out at the sea relieved that the waves were washing up flotsam and jetsam with the same certainty of the Powerless blood pulsing through their wrists ...

Then in that strange little town, where the shallows swallow the shingle, the mist settles on the marshes, and the clouds can even choke the moon ...

Seeing was believing after all.

THE END

Author Profile

Laura Clarke Walker is a writer, teacher, and lover of all things Gothic.

When she's not immersed in the world of Coldharbour, she can be found drinking espressos darker than the night, listening to podcasts in other languages, and running – although not as fast or as far as Alex and Matthew Wilde!

For more about Laura and Coldharbour, visit:

@lauraclarkewalker on Instagram or lauraclarkewalker.com.

What Did You Think of Coldharbour?

A heartfelt thank you for purchasing this book and entering the world of Coldharbour. I do hope you enjoyed your time with the Wildes.

If you loved Coldharbour, please take the time to post a review on Amazon or Goodreads. It would be much appreciated.

Publisher Information  rowanvale books

Rowanvale Books provides publishing services to independent authors, writers and poets all over the globe. We deliver a personal, honest and efficient service that allows authors to see their work published, while remaining in control of the process and retaining their creativity. By making publishing services available to authors in a cost-effective and ethical way, we at Rowanvale Books hope to ensure that the local, national and international community benefits from a steady stream of good quality literature.

For more information about us, our authors or our publications, please get in touch.

www.rowanvalebooks.com
info@rowanvalebooks.com